Let There Be Dragons

Janet Post

Let There be Dragons

Printed in the United States of America

Chapter One

Jackal

"We be getting mighty close to the city, Jackal," Slag said.

I glanced at my green friend sitting astride the Belgium draft mare he'd named Bunny, even though the mare was as mean as a cornered greenie. Slag was three-quarters orc, his mother a half-breed, his father an orc who raped her when she was hunting. Most half-breeds are sterile. Slag's mother got lucky. Slag had been given to the same wet nurse taking care of me. We were raised together along with Chub, our third companion, another half-orc.

Slag's frown emphasized the pointed ivory tusks that rose at the corner of his mouth from his bottom jaw to above his upper lip and nearly to his flat nose. At seven feet of solid muscle Slag weighed in at three-hundred pounds, was two inches taller than me, and twenty-five pounds heavier. When I noticed the sun shining off the top of Slag's head I grinned. Slag kept his head shaved to show off what he thought were his best features, a broad forehead, and small, slightly pointed ears, each pierced with three golden rings.

"Aye, the city be close," I said as I glanced around us. "The big lake be over that hill. The walls of New Orleans about a league to the south of us."

"This be dangerous ground," Chub said. "It's gettin' late and I'm terrible hungry. Let's stop and cook up some of that shoat we bagged this morning."

I laughed. Chub, always hungry, was a huge half-breed who besides food, loved me, Slag and no other being in the universe, except perhaps the draft mule he rode. The mule was always hungry too. Chub shared other qualities with his mount, such as strength, tirelessness, and a foul temper. A dangerous combination. But then all of us are dangerous.

"I'm good with that," I said. "You two set up camp. I'm gonna ride up to the top of that hill and get a looksee."

I spurred Thor, a black Friesian with feathered feet and too much mane. The big horse was a gift from my mother, the elf queen, Ashera. It was the only thing besides my light skin, pointed ears, and thick brown hair she'd ever given me. That, and she'd carried me to term and not killed me at birth, which was the custom, because I was the result of an orc rape. Elves did not tolerate half-breed abominations. Instead of killing me, she sent me to the village of Wildwhisper. She'd never raise a half-orc babe herself. Elves were all racists. They believed in the purity of the elf race and any mixing of blood was swiftly dealt with.

I was glad she'd sent me to Wildwhisper. Life in the village suited me down to the ground. I'd learned to forge and use the weapons I made.

My two warrior friends and I were raised in the same small village outside the elves' mountain fortress in what used to be Arkansas. It was also near Edenvale, a hidden sanctuary populated with humans who didn't care to be serfs to the Magics or live within walls. The people of Wildwhisper maintained themselves by hunting in the forest, tanning hides, and forging weapons. They mined ore and coal in the mountains and found old steel and metal in abandoned cities to melt in forges fueled by the coal. Their swords were highly-valued, the metal folded and then sharpened to perfection and modeled after the Japanese blade, the katana. They also forged enormous axes to be used as weapons and smaller ones for cutting down trees. If it could be made of metal, it was forged in Wildwhisper. I always carried a satchel full of weapons to use in trade if we needed food or lodging, and sometimes, I sold them for the most common form of money, silver coins.

As I galloped Thor to the top of the hill, reveling in the strength and immense power of the beast beneath me, I surveyed the landscape. Below stretched the big lake and the wall built around the city of New Orleans. The city center was too far to see clearly, just the spire of a great church, and the remains of tall buildings now crumbling ruins. Inside the wall, small farms were green with summer's bounty.

I squeezed Thor's sides sending him charging into a valley and up another hill. At the top, I spotted a group of orcs camped in the bottom of the next valley inside a copse of oak saplings. Smoke from their cook fire rose between the leafy boughs. I couldn't see all of them, but the usual orc raiding party was ten or twelve. Seven were visible, tending to the huge boars they rode. The hogs grunted and snorted from their position tied to trot lines as they snuffled for acorns under the trees. I was close enough to hear the restless animals.

This was good news to me. Finding a raiding party before it found you was always good news. Then I spotted the girl. She looked about ten and was tied face down across the back of a hog. One of the orcs dragged her off the massive pig and tossed her to his fellow who laughed and ripped off her clothes.

I felt my animal nature rising. Anger at the terrible treatment of the child, for the girl was no more than that, warred with my inner voice cautioning me to take care. I wanted nothing more than to tear down the hill and fight all of them.

Although strong and a fierce fighter, I'm not stupid.

I whirled Thor around and galloped back to camp. It was almost dark. Slag and Chub would appreciate the chance to kill some orcs.

I pulled the big Friesian to a sliding stop at the edge of the camp. Slag grabbed my reins. "I see that light in yer eye." Slag grinned. "Ye found us a bit of work, didn't ye?"

"Orcs have a girl. We gotta go now. Setting up camp can wait. Mount up and let's ride."

Slag and Chub leapt on their mounts. Chub still had his long bow slung over his shoulder, a quiver full of arrows, and his axe in a holster attached to his leather body armor. Slag favored a broad sword, a crossbow with bolts tipped with rattlesnake venom, and a spear. I still had my katana and sheath hooked to the back of my armor. Armed to the teeth, we thundered down the trail, knowing the girl might soon be dead, or worse. A ten-year old was a woman to orcs. Hell, a female of any age was a woman to orcs.

We stopped at the top of the hill overlooking the orc encampment. The sun had set, and a huge moon slowly rose over the trees behind them. The ghostly-blue light illuminated the troop of orcs gathered in a raiding party. Our orc blood gave us night vision. We could see where humans would be blind. But so could the orcs.

We sat still and silent, impatient as we watched the orcs move out. When the orcs crested the far hill and headed toward the city, I dismounted, left Thor ground-tied, and slunk down the hill staying in the cover of shrubs and underbrush. Chub stayed with the horses, but Slag followed.

The fire I'd seen earlier was extinguished, but the orcs obviously planned to return to this camp. Two huge, ugly, almost black monsters squatted close to the girl. They weren't touching her, just sitting there watching. Two gigantic hogs wandered around behind them, saddled and ready to go, but eating acorns and snuffling through the leaves beneath the trees.

I waved, sending Slag off to the left, while I went right. The hogs scented us and squealed an alarm. The two orcs jumped to their feet. One held a massive hammer, the other a multi-bladed mace, crude but effective. A brace of spears leaned against one of the trees. The hogs came close to inspect me and I shooed them away. One charged, its tusks gleaming blue in the moonlight. I held my katana high over my head in a two-handed grip as I waited for the hog, then I stepped aside and sliced its head off with my razor-sharp blade. The head rolled, foam dripping from its gaping maw as blood gushed from the body. The other hog squealed and ran away. I was ever thankful to Wildwhisper for the sharpness of their steel.

Alerted, the two orcs raced around in circles searching for us. Slag stepped up behind them and put two poison bolts into the biggest one while I slashed the other diagonally across its body from neck to thigh. Its skin was so thick I barely scratched it. I whirled and hunched low as the beast turned and charged me. The one with two poisoned arrows stuck in its back turned and thundered toward Slag, screaming in its foul tongue, huge weight shaking the earth. I understood Orcish and so did Slag. "Come at me you frigging cunt," Slag snarled. "I ain't scared of you or none of your kin neither."

The one charging Jackal was so dark to appear almost black. He raised his hammer and swung it at me. I leaped aside and slashed my sword across its back. I saw green blood flow this time from the slash across its kidney. It whirled and I pressed my attack, cutting it across the throat, the area on an orc where the skin is the thinnest. I was rewarded with a gout of green blood, so I stepped in and kicked it in the cods. When it grunted and grabbed them, I whacked off its head.

I turned to see if Slag needed any help and saw him finish off the other orc by leaping on its back, carrying it to the ground, and stabbing it through its skull with his short blade. The blade exited through the orc's mouth. "Nice work," I said and Slag grinned.

Smiling, I do love a good fight, I wiped my blade on the grass to clean it. "Get the girl."

Slag moaned. "Really? Like we ain't got enough problems?"

"If we leave her here, the orcs will find her and their two dead friends, and come looking for us after they kill her."

"Happen, they'll come for us, no matter."

"Not if we catch them first."

Slag lifted one bushy eyebrow.

"We have to go after them. They're headed for the city."

"When did you become a lover of the Magics?"

"It's not the Magics I care about. The regular folk die too, and they don't deserve it."

Slag sighed. "Let's be off then. Chub's missing his dinner and that will put him in a right bad mood."

We found the girl curled into a ball under a rough blanket made of sacking. I pulled the sacking off her face. She was redheaded, with pale skin and bright blue eyes. She pounced on me, clawing at my eyes. "Whoa there, filly." I pulled her off my head. "I ain't an orc."

"You are!" she screamed. "You might not be green, but you look just like them."

"I know I ain't pretty, but it's not kind of you to remind me. I might be half orc, but I always thought I was better looking than orcs." I held her out in front of me and noticed she was younger than I'd thought, and feistier. "We just killed your captors and we plan to get the rest." She kicked and scratched at my leather wrist guards, tried to bite me, and shrieked bloody murder.

"I can always give you back, if you'd druther."

She stopped shrieking. "Put me down."

"Are you gonna run?"

"Duh."

"Where to?"

"Away from you, that's for certain."

Slag stepped forward in all his hugeness and laughed. "Jackal be your onliest chance of surviving, missy. I'd stick with him if I was you, for a kinder heart in a bigger ass you'll never find."

Chapter Two

Belle

I followed the nun through the cobbled streets of New Orleans, head down, heart filled with hatred. The nuns know me, they know all my tricks and my talents. They hate me as much as I hate them.

"Hurry up," Sister Agnes said.

"It's pretty freaking hard to hurry in shackles." They shackled me a lot. I'm dangerous. I like being dangerous. I practice. It passes the time.

The street ended and Sister Agnes pushed me toward the big white building on the other side of the square. My hands were bound just like my ankles. Sister Agnes kept pushing me to hurry so I would have no time to try a mind contact with my sister, Noemi. The nuns knew me well.

They picked me up when I was seven in a sweep of the lands surrounding the city. I was searching for my sister. We were taken by the evil man, the terrible demon who rode a black dragon and devoured babies. In my memory, he's huge, with a red mouth, white skin and long fangs. He had a baby with him. The image of him sinking his teeth in the baby's soft throat will be imprinted on my mind for eternity.

The black fog surrounding him was something else I will never forget. It reached for me. The fog was alive. It swirled around him, filled with the open mouths of silently screaming souls.

"We did our best for you, Annabelle. If you escape and run away, who knows what will happen to you in The Withers. Your sister is gone. Please accept that. If the Master and the Guild cannot control you or fear you will run away, they'll kill you. The Trials are designed to discover your true Gifts and your Gift is strong. They'll know." The elderly nun dressed like a crow all in black, sighed. "We do. And perhaps they'll find a place for you where you can be useful. Please try to behave so you can live, because if you are uncontrollable, they will destroy you, put you down like a rabid dog. Live for your sister. She'd want you to have a life. If you love her, grow strong, allow the Guild to teach you to control your Gifts so eventually you can go search for her."

I stopped and Sister Agnes tilted her head. "What?"

"That's the first thing any of you said that makes sense to me. Learn. Grow stronger. Then leave to find Noemi. That's a real goal. Something I can do. And I will do."

The sister folded her hands inside the long sleeves of her habit. She clutched the crucifix hanging off her rosary. "If we'd only known, we surely would have told you that long ago." She sucked in a breath through her teeth. It sounded like hissing. "Especially since you listen to nothing." Her last words were muttered, but I heard them.

"You don't understand," I said. "You never will. Noemi disappeared and I did not. She'd search for me if I were lost. When you love someone, there's never a reason to abandon them. Every night I lie awake and wonder where she is, what happened to her. I cry because I know in my heart, she hurts, she's in pain, and it's my fault. They should have taken me. I could have fought them. I'm the one with power. Poor Noemi has none. I would have fought them. I would survive."

When the man on the dragon took us, Noemi leaped from the back of the dragon as it took off and dragged me with her. We fell a long way. I thought we'd die, but I wasn't afraid. Anything would be better than going with him. We didn't die. We landed in a field of soft grass as the dragon screeched and circled back. We ran and ran, found an abandoned barn and hid in the hay. Noemi sheltered me beneath her body. Too afraid to breathe, we lay silent all night. In the morning, Noemi went outside to see if the coast was clear and never came back. That was the last time I saw my sister. I would find her or search for the rest of my life.

I'm eighteen now which makes Noemi twenty. Not a day passed during all those years, I didn't try to escape, but the nuns had cells, and a deep dungeon. They fought me until this very day because they're terrified to let me go. Everyone knows about the black dragons and the evil demons riding them. The nuns feared I would draw those demons to me and they're probably right. So, they hid me, they punished me, they kept me where I couldn't contact anyone, especially not Noemi. "She's gone," Sister Agnes said. "She's dead," Mother Superior said. "You'll never see Noemi again," they all said.

The nun pushed me forward. "It's too late for your sister. You must know that. She would want you to live. If she's dead, as we believe, she died to make sure you didn't. Don't waste her sacrifice."

A dark shadow passed over our heads. It blocked the hot New Orleans sun. Sister Agnes stopped and shaded her eyes to look. I didn't have to look. I felt him. "Run," I screamed.

Sister Agnes took off and I stumbled after her. You try running in shackles. The dark shadow became a dragon. It roared, folded its wings, and shot for us. At the last minute, Sister Agnes snatched me through a church door. I panted, hunched over, and watched as the dragon snared a woman carrying a child right out of the square. The poor woman shrieked as the dragon's claws pierced her. Blood dripped onto the grass as the heavy wings beat, and the tree limbs thrashed wildly. Sister Agnes held onto me as I struggled in her grasp. "Let me go. I can fight him."

"You'll only die like your sister."

I dropped to my knees and pressed my face into my black skirt. "No, no, no, don't you understand? He's going to eat the child and turn the woman into a demon like himself or kill her outright."

Sister Agnes dragged me to my feet. "There's nothing you can do now, Annabelle. The dragon is gone and so is the woman and child. Stop fighting me. You have the Trial to think of and that poor woman's fate is already sealed."

"You give up too easily. All you nuns do is pray to your dead god and cry about how helpless you are. I'm not helpless. I can fight and I will."

"That poor woman and child just died because of you." Sister Agnes's face was inches from mine. "You draw evil to you like a magnet. This is why we kept you hidden. We should have killed you. If we had, that woman and child would still be alive."

Tears ran down my face. "I don't . . . I didn't."

"Nothing you do is on purpose. You're an angel, so sweet honey drips from your lips. The problem, Annabelle, is that demon, Slygon, knows you. He felt you come out of the cloister. He's been waiting." She grabbed my arm and dragged me back into the street. "He's got prey, I doubt he'll return right now. We tried to tell you, but you don't listen. The evil is drawn to you because of your power. Now shut up and hurry before he decides to make another attempt."

Dark thoughts swirled through my mind. I would survive and find Noemi. The nuns were just a scared bunch of old ladies believing in their dead god. They didn't understand what it was like to stand in my shoes, and they cared only for themselves, their order, their precious city.

The Trial seemed stupid to me. You either had Gifts or you didn't. Why test? The square was now empty. The black dragon and its rider had scared everyone into their homes. A few soldiers policed the vacated city and marched up and down the empty streets.

The Trial was held in the old capital house on Jackson Square, the Cabildo. Before the war a museum, now, the government of the city-state of New Orleans met there, ruling the two separate populations of New Orleans with an iron fist.

"If I fail the test, they'll kill me," I said to Sister Agnes. "So, how's that gonna help me find my sister?" It was true. All applicants to St. Catherine's Academy or Archers School of War went through the Trial, and if they failed, they were killed. "If they even think about killing me, I'll get them first. You know it's true."

"Annabelle, please, try to show some respect for the process, respect for those older and greater than you."

I snorted. "What makes them greater than me? You know the power of my Gift."

"Training," Sister Agnes said. "They have training and it's what you lack along with self-discipline. Go to St. Catherine's, study, learn to control your anger so you can reach your goals."

The nun shoved me toward the building. "They have to kill those who fail. It keeps the bloodlines pure. If applicants show some sign of the Gift but not enough to pass they're erased. The idea is to build a population with strong powers and weed out the weak. I wouldn't worry if I were you. You have a lot of the Gift. We nuns know all about it." She sighed. "You were such a pretty child. Angelic face, huge violet eyes, shiny black ringlets. We were so sure you'd be adopted. Then we discovered you were the spawn of Satan."

They'd pushed me on a lot of prospective parents thinking a child as pretty as the nuns liked to say I was would be scooped up. And poor little Annabelle was taken home with three sets of parents, all of whom brought me back within an hour. It seems they frowned upon adopting a child who could blow up their carriage, read their minds, set fire to their house, or scream so loudly windows broke.

Sister Agnes sighed. "I shouldn't say that. You're really just a sad little girl with too many supernatural talents. You possess the Gift in great measure. Only some received the Gift the bomb released. Those who received the Gift were chosen by God and must be elevated above those who did not. That's why the Magics rule, and the non-Magics slave. The Governor must maintain law and order to protect the city, which means he must keep the Magics strong in order to keep the hordes at bay. That's why it's your duty to breed more Magics."

I laughed and shook my head. "Not my duty. My duty is to find Noemi. This, I will do. You can count on it."

The nun sighed again, a long deep one. "Annabelle, please realize she's gone. You'll never find her. She died long ago when she disappeared. The demon riders of the black dragons must have taken her. She's either long dead or she's been turned into a demon herself."

"No, I would know if she were dead. I just would. She's somewhere waiting for me. I'll find her if it's the last thing I ever do on this Earth."

The nun threw up her hands. "You're impossible."

My sister was all the family I had left. I had to find her. I vaguely remembered my father as a kind man with black hair mixed with silver and pointed ears. When he held me in his lap, I knew I was safe. I remembered Mother better, Selvia. I remember cold nights beside the fire drinking hot milk with Noemi and laughing as our father made shadow figures on the wall in the firelight. Mother sang happy songs, hugged both of us tightly before bed every night.

Then the terrible storm had swept our little home away. Noemi and I found shelter in a cave with frightened animals; a bear, a mountain lion and two deer. Lots of bunnies and squirrels all huddled with us in perfect harmony as the awful storm raged outside. When it was over, the animals crept out and went their separate ways while we sat silent and terrified. Noemi finally struggled to her feet and pulled me out of the cave to look for our parents.

The world was destroyed. Down branches lay everywhere. The sleepy, shallow river that flowed by our home was a raging torrent. Noemi and I called for Mother and Father until we were hoarse as we wandered through the devastation. We finally decided our mother and father must surely have died in the flood. Noemi and I had been on the other side of the river picking flowers. When we looked across the rushing river, searching for home, our cottage was gone. Then the black dragons descended. I felt the evil coming for us and screamed a warning. Noemi didn't understand. She had no power and couldn't feel it. The black fingers felt like death creeping over my soul. I was just a little girl frozen with fear.

Noemi had to drag me to get me to move. We ran and ran, but the demons caught us. Noemi fought and we broke free. I hold onto the memory of Noemi's bravery. She tried to save me. She fought for us. She was so brave in the face of all that evil. Could I be any less brave? It was my duty to find her and save her. I had all the power.

The nuns taught me to read and write, about the history of our new world. Even though I resisted them at every turn, I learned. Almost a century ago, a huge bomb sent by North Korea to destroy the U.S. nuclear arsenal at Malmstrom Air Force Base in Montana set off massive explosions. None of the warheads detonated, but their ignition systems and the non-nuclear material exploded, triggering the once dormant super volcano two-hundred miles away at Yellowstone. The bombs and the super volcano all going off at once created an enormous rift in the earth, a pit some claimed went straight to Hell.

This was the world we now lived in. Every strange, mythological creature you could imagine came out of those holes, along with the Gift. People everywhere could suddenly read minds, levitate, talk to animals, set fire to things with their minds, and control other humans. The nuns tried to teach me that God had created the Gift so humans could fight the creatures crawling out of the Pit, though it was more like the Devil had destroyed everything and God was dead. The world we had left was Hell.

My heart pounded as we arrived at the Cabildo, and my clenched palms were sweaty. Would the nuns send me here just to get rid of me? I glanced at Sister Agnes. No, they wouldn't. As much as I fought them, in my heart, I knew they cared what happened to me.

Sister Agnes ignored the guards at the arched doorway. A man in a black uniform sat at a table just inside the door reading a book. His name tag read George Gorben, Master at Arms. He put the book down when we entered. It was as silent inside the big building as the convent. Were there no other applicants? Sister Agnes spoke to the Master at Arms while I fidgeted and waited impatiently. I wanted this entire thing over. "Why is she bound?" Gorben asked Sister Agnes.

"I'm tied up because I'm dangerous," I said and shot a bolt of anger into Gorben's head.

He winced, donned a strange metal helmet, and smiled. "Try that again."

"I'm not stupid." I'd read in his mind the helmet blocked mental probes. Instead, I held out my hands and smiled. "Do I have to keep these on?"

"I think we can handle her," Gorben said to Sister Agnes.

"The shackles, too?"

Gorben leaned over the table and stared at my feet. "Seriously, she's shackled?"

The nun cleared her throat while I swallowed my laughter. It wouldn't do to be rude, well ruder than I'd already been.

"You don't know her," Sister Agnes said. "The little incident that just happened in the square, that was her fault."

"Really? I heard it was a black dragon with a demon rider. Why would that be her fault?"

"Slygon took her sister."

He shook his head. "Probably just a coincidence." Gorben picked up a wand and pointed it at my ankles. The shackles flew open and fell to the floor. Free, I laughed and danced. "Wow, that was awesome. Do I get to learn the wand thing?"

"You have to pass the Trial first, young lady, and if I were you, I'd search for a little decorum. Manners, little things like that make the world a better place to live in. When manners go astray, anarchy prevails."

He picked up a silver bell and rang it. Another man in black robes descended the staircase. "Come with me," he said.

Sister Agnes pushed me. "Go with him. Trust in yourself and in God."

"God is dead, Sister, but thanks." I steeled my shaky nerves and followed this new guy up the staircase to a long gallery illuminated by paned windows. A man and a woman sat at a table at the far end, both dressed in black robes. Their contempt for an orphan with no known lineage was apparent. It didn't take a mind reader to see the disdain for me on their faces. I smiled. I'd show them.

I stood in front of the table for a long time, as no one said anything, and I struggled to contain my anger and impatience with this entire stupid ritual. "Can we just get on with this?" I finally said.

The woman glared at me and my return stare did not waver. The woman was light brown with narrow yellow eyes inside a lined face. Her gray hair was braided and pulled into a tight knot on top of her head. She wore a wedding ring on her left hand. Getting married and bearing children was the duty of all female Magics, even scary ones.

"You're Annabelle?"

I nodded, my voice suddenly gone.

"You know the consequence of failure?" The man spoke this time, his voice monotone to suit his apparent boredom. He was fat with sagging jowls, wet lips, and tiny little eyes glaring at me out of nests of lard. He drummed sausage-like fingers on the table as he waited for me to answer.

"Yes, sir," I said in a voice I forced to be strong.

And then I felt it.

Fingers like feathers whispered across my mind. Thoughts of rats eating flesh, my flesh, filtered into my subconscious. It was the woman. I imagined her mind touch smelled like burning cedar and incense, smiled for the first time, and slammed down a mental shield. The female Magic's eyes flew open. Reading minds must be her Gift. Well join the club. I suddenly felt good. I knew this game. The nuns had tried to shut me down with one of their Magics. It hadn't ended well.

The woman changed tactics. She smiled. "My name is Marcella." She held out her hand for me to shake. Reluctant to touch Marcella but reading from both the fat man and this woman it was required, I gingerly took her hand. Immediately, the push into my mind became a hammer blow. I snatched my hand away and shot a mental arrow into Marcella's brain. The woman cried out and grabbed her head.

The fat man nodded. "I see you have a Gift." He pulled out a long black wand and snapped it at me. A tiger flew out of the end and attacked me with razor-sharp claws. When I felt for its mind, I instantly realized it was only an image. I ignored it. It couldn't hurt me. It was manufactured fakery, not real. More creatures flew out of the tip of the wand. One, a long, bloated python was real. I felt its cold, heartless, snake mind, and soothed it with thoughts of warmth and sunshine and a full belly. It wrapped around my arm, harmless as a kitten, and fell asleep.

The man surged to his feet. "Give me back my snake. Obviously, you have the Gift." He turned to Marcella. "Did she hurt you?"

Marcella rubbed her temples. "No, but she easily could."

"Restrain yourself, girl," the man snapped.

"I could hurt you, too, if I wished." I could do much more than hurt him. I knew that. I could blow him up. He was stupid and slow and left his mind open for invasion with no guards or walls. When I handed the fat man the snake, it yawned revealing sharp, barbed teeth. The snake suddenly turned on him, coiled around his fat neck and squeezed, opened its huge mouth in front of the man's face and hissed. Terrified, he clawed at the coils. When he touched the snake with his wand, it loosened and disappeared.

"You," the man's voice quivered along with the flabby jowls. "You are an evil female with no manners. You should be erased. You will be erased."

Marcella put a restraining hand on his arm as he prepared to point the wand at me. "Go for it," I snarled. "You can try to kill me if you like. The nuns don't want me back. But you won't succeed. I'm stronger than you. You have no guards. You're easy prey."

"She's very powerful, Wilfred," Marcella said. "The most powerful Magic I have ever felt pass through these Trials."

Wilfred shuddered. "But can she be trained? She's wild, Marcella. A wild animal with a powerful Gift is too dangerous to live. We must destroy her."

I backed up, created my walls, put up strong mental guards, and prepared to defend myself. The wind began blowing hard, shooting pieces of paper into the air, grabbing my hair and whipping it around my head. I felt him before he arrived. His mind touch was solid and firm. "We've been waiting for you," he spoke directly into my mind. "We've been waiting a long time."

Wilfred leaped to his feet, tripped on his chair leg and tumbled over backwards. "Master Odiferous," he whispered. "Why are you here?"

A black cloud spun in the center of the hallway. It stopped spinning and a skeletally-thin old man stepped out of the cloud. Dressed in white, with a long white beard, his skin was like paper. The only color on him was the startling-blue eyes staring into my soul.

"I'm here because I felt a disturbance in the magic, a powerful disturbance. As I meditated, I saw her." He pointed at me. "It's her. She is the one."

Chapter Three

Belle

The girls in the school hated me almost as much as the nuns had. I was treated as though I was special by the teachers, something that drove me insane and made the rest of the students green with envy. The other girls hated me for my privileges. I felt their dislike and returned it. They were all younger than me. The nuns had kept me contained fearing I would draw the great evil to me. Only now, when I was eighteen, had they felt they could release me. And, they were sick of me. I realized now I was among other girls, other children, I'd been a tiresome child. If I'd only conformed they might have treated me better and given me freedom sooner. But children are all stupid and blind and willful. I was no different.

I had my own room, my own teachers, and met often with Master Odafarus who bestowed a wand on me. "This was my first wand," he said. "It's made from the spine of a dragon and very powerful. It's an enormous responsibility. You must promise to modify your behavior, treat the teachers with respect, and do as I tell you."

"I will Master," I said with real feeling. Odafarus was old and he knew stuff no one else did. The wand alone would have guaranteed my loyalty, but there was something so pure and good and honorable about Odafarus, you wanted to obey him. I actually wanted him to like me. This was a first. Not since the nuns had taken me in had I wished to please anyone.

I sat at his feet and he in a cushioned chair beside the fire. He patted my hair. It was winter and cold in New Orleans. The weather patterns of old were unreliable. "It's the Pit, Annabelle," Odafarus said. "The heat and volcanic ash from the volcanoes changed the weather. Winter comes early and stays late. For years after the eruptions, humans starved because crops wouldn't grow. The sun hid its face from us. Green things need the sun. It was a time of great hardship. The city-states were formed as orcs emerged from the Pit and overran our world."

"When can I learn how to use the wand?"

"Sleep with it next to you. It needs to learn you, learn your mind and heart. Long has it lain useless in my rooms. It needs to wake up slowly."

I groaned. "I'm not very patient, Master."

"I know this, Belle. But you're young and will learn. Go make friends in this school. Reach out to the other children for in them you will find companionship and healing."

"I hate all of them. Well most of them anyway. They're stupid, Master. They all want to get married and have babies. Dis-gus-ting."

He closed his eyes. "There is one like you. She is alone and sad. Find her. Now I will sleep."

So, I marched back to my class on spells with my wand tucked under my blouse next to my skin, determined to make Master Odafarus happy with me. The other girls were more like witches learning spells and making potions. They had Gifts but none like mine. I'd come to realize I *was* different, not like them at all. One of the girls could call animals to her. One could lift items off the desk with her mind. Another could cry and make it rain. I was the only one who could blow up stuff, manipulate people to do my bidding without their knowledge, and, of course, set fire to things. All the Gifts the other girls had, I also possessed. Many were afraid of me.

I bent over and stared into the huge pot of boiling green liquid. Inside, items my partner had dropped into it while I was gone circled in the swirling flow. I spotted a frog's leg, a branch of herbs and a cube of what looked like gooey brown gunk. The liquid reeked. I held my nose barely able to stand the stench. When a sudden explosion rocked the old building, the floors shook, the windows rattled, and the girls screamed.

The school was inside an old Catholic church filled with small chambers, rocky hallways, and mullioned windows. From the sound of the explosion, a familiar sound, I was pretty sure one of the windows had blown.

As the girls screamed and ran for the teacher, an older woman in a brown smock, I ran out the door with my heart singing. Master was right. Someone, another girl in this school, could blow up shit. I had to find her. Blowing shit up was awesome.

As I raced down the hall, the soles of my leather shoes slapped on the rocky floor. Billowing smoke poured out of one of the rooms ahead and I jumped for joy. Two soot-covered girls coughed and hacked as they stumbled out of the classroom and into the hall. I ignored them and forged through the acrid black smoke, waved it away, and entered the classroom. The scene in front of me gladdened my heart.

"Tina Louise Desbois!" A male teacher, his three-piece blue suit covered in greasy black soot, screamed at the tiniest girl I had ever seen. She wasn't a dwarf, just short and petite, perfectly proportioned with light, almost white, blonde hair currently covered in soot. The odd clean curl fell on her shoulders. It was the color of winter wheat. The tiny girl stood up to the scolding with a stolid expression on her face. She wasn't afraid.

I eased into the teacher's mind, felt his outrage and anger, and soothed it with gentle mental strokes. He backed away as he searched for the source of the stroking, pointed his finger at me and screamed, "Stop that."

"Stop yelling at her and I will."

"Who are you?" He demanded.

"I am Annabelle."

He rolled his neck and lifted his eyes to look at the ceiling. "It but needed this to complete my day."

I basked in the glory of my fame. I was Master Odafarus's pet and rumored to be the one chosen to destroy the black dragons, the one with enough power to face the demon, Slygon. I enjoyed the special favors and the limited power being the chosen one gave me. What else had I ever had? The tiny girl stared at me with curiosity but no fear. I reached out a hand to her. "Come with me. We need to blow this joint." And then I giggled. "Oh wait, you already did."

Tina took my hand. "Are you really The Annabelle? The one who is Master Odafarus's' favorite?"

"Yep," I said. "Master told me to find you. He knows all about you."

Tina's eyes were green. She opened them wide in her perfectly oval face. "Really? He knows who I am?"

I stopped. We stood in a long hallway leading to stairs going up to dormitory rooms or down to the kitchens. "Tina, he knows everything. He knows all the students here and at Archers Academy. He knows the past and some of the future. He's amazing."

"But I'm nobody. I'm an orphan. My parents are dead. I'd be cleaning houses somewhere if I didn't know how to blow things up."

I laughed, suddenly filled with the joy of finding a friend, a kindred spirit. "It's wonderful, isn't it? Blowing up shit?"

Tina gasped. "Don't say that word ever. The teachers will punish you."

"No, they won't because they'll never hear me say it. I know better. But you don't mind, do you?"

"Of course not," Tina said.

My eyes filled and leaked rare tears. I never cried, but suddenly I was overwhelmed with emotion. I remembered Noemi. I remembered our close relationship and I felt the emptiness her leaving left behind. I covered my face with my hands and sobbed. Tina grabbed my hands and pulled them away from my face so she could look into my eyes. "Did I say something wrong?"

I shook my head and sobbed harder. My voice was wobbly. "I'm sorry. I don't mean to cry, but you remind me of my sister, and I miss her so much. It's been forever since I had someone I could talk to."

"Do I look like her?"

"No," I sobbed. "But she never cursed, and she used to yell at me when I said a bad word." I stared into Tina's green eyes. "She had green eyes like you, but she looked like our mother with yellow hair and freckles. I look like my father."

"Where are your parents?"

"I think they died. There was a terrible storm and our house got washed away."

"And, if it's not too painful, what happened to your sister?"

"I don't know. She disappeared. The nuns say she's dead, but I'd know, wouldn't I? I'd feel it in here?" I patted my chest.

Tina took my hand and led me down the hall. "Of course, you would. You'll find her someday," Tina said and stopped again. She looked up into my eyes. "I feel that in here." She patted her chest.

Tina led me up the stairs to her room in the dorm. We sat on a bottom bunk holding hands, sharing the warmth of our new friendship. "If you're so powerful, how come they were able to catch you? The nuns I mean. Everyone knows you were raised in the convent."

"I was only seven. I had some power, but I didn't know how to use it. I did fight, and I hid for two days. They got a Magic to find me and threw some kind of hood over my head. Then they bound my hands and tossed me in a cell. They did stuff like that to me the whole time I was there. When they brought me here, I had shackles on my ankles." I grinned. "They were really scared of me."

Tears filled Tina's huge eyes. "You were only seven. That's so cruel."

"You don't know me yet. The nuns do. I don't like to do what I'm told. I fight every effort to restrict my movements or behavior. Only Master Odafarus understands me. He gave me this." I pulled the wand out of my shirt.

Tina touched it with one trembling finger. "That's a dragon-spine wand. Only the most powerful Magics have them. Can you use it?"

I shook my head as I tucked it away. "Nope, but I'm gonna learn. If I tried to use it now, I'd probably blow us up or turn us into toads."

We laughed so hard at that thought we fell off the bed.

Tina and I became the best of friends. We graduated and joined the soldiers guarding the city, lived in the women's quarters of the military, walked the walls for guard duty, and went on perimeter checks of the surrounding lands. I never went anywhere without the wand Master Wizard Odafarus, gone to his ancestors only this year, had taught me to use. With it and my skills with weapons, I was the most powerful warrior on the walls and the captain of the guards knew it well. I had the respect I'd craved all my life. When I walked down the battlements, grown men stepped aside. None dared confront me.

I loved it.

Chapter Four

Belle

I slid my longbow over my shoulder, added a quiver filled with arrows, strapped on a sword and secreted ten small throwing knives inside my vest, in sheaths strapped to both my ankles, one up my wrist-guard and two in special pockets on the left side of my vest where I can snatch and throw them without thinking. I always wear as many weapons as I can stash about my person. You never know.

"Uh, I could use a little help," Tina said. She stood on her tiptoes but still couldn't reach her vest hooked on the wall of the armory.

I laughed as I snagged it and dropped it into Tina's reaching hands. "Heard the orcs are almost on the wall," I told her. "You scared?"

"Nah, remember the three we caught raiding Farmer Huggate's grain bin?" Tina answered with a grin as she strapped on her vest.

I held up my right arm. A green spotted wrist guard protected it. "Got that big spotted bugger right here so I always remember him. Tristan saw three black dragons yesterday flying to the east. I'll get those bastards one day. Their time is coming. I need to find my sister. I feel like I'm wasting my time here. Every night, I send out a call to her, but she never answers."

"She doesn't have your powers, Belle."

"I know, but I keep trying."

It was all I ever thought of. My training was complete. Somehow, I had to find the evil demon who rode the black dragons and make him tell me what he'd done with Noemi or where she was.

"You know I'm coming with you, right?"

"I would never go anywhere without you, Tiny. You saved me from myself. You showed me how to be a real person, how to focus on becoming the best warrior in this city, and how to care again. I thought my heart was dead. You brought it to life with your sweetness, your loyalty, your patience, and your love. And the biggest thing you did for me was teach me how to bend, to get along with others. I was such a bitch."

Tina wrapped her arms around me in a warm embrace. "Never to me. You made me a warrior."

"Best friends forever," I said.

We linked arms and laughed as we headed for the walls. "Forever."

Once atop the long stretch of block wall surrounding the city, I stopped and stared at the cleared areas surrounding the walls. These borderlands were kept free of any undergrowth or trees that could shelter man or orc. Tiny stopped and pointed. "See them?"

I squinted into the dark, saw nothing, and then enhanced my vision with my power. A full moon provided eerie blue light. In the distance, on the crest of a hill, bulky shapes moved into the valley at a rapid pace. The orcs were riding hogs.

"Man, your posts!" the captain screamed as he ran along the top of the great wall.

Tiny and I raced to the far end of our section. We'd practiced this every day and had it down pat. A tower rose next to us. Stairs circled inside it leading to the outside. We were assigned as guards for the stairs. There was a barred gate at the bottom, but an orc could easily break it.

I knocked an arrow in my bowstring, loosed my sword, and touched the wand. My heart raced with anticipation. This is what I was born to do, fight. It was in my blood. I knew whoever my parents had been, one of them had to have been a warrior. Adrenaline pumped through me as I double-checked our surroundings, checked to see everyone else was ready. Pots of oil hung over open fires, heating. Catapults spaced every twenty feet were loaded with balls of ammonium nitrate; an explosive material newly discovered by the scientists in New Orleans trying to make bombs. Any military explosives from before times had become earthquake-induced eruptions that opened more gigantic rifts. Nothing was left of the massive before-times armories. The city's scientists researched weaponry they no longer possessed. Any books or material pertaining to fighting, war, weapons and fighting were highly valued.

Pots of burning wood sat ready for fire arrows. High above them on a turret, the most powerful wizard in New Orleans was ready to recite incantations, erect a shield, and cast magic fireballs.

We were prepared. We'd done this before.

The orcs split into two groups. A group of four great beasts rode left while the other headed straight at Tiny and me. My heart sang with the joy of the fight as I took aim. I concentrated and sent my first arrow flying, immediately nocking a second. The arrow hit one of the orcs in the chest and fell harmlessly to the ground. The skin of an orc was just too thick. "Fuck me," I muttered.

Tiny sent three bolts flying in rapid succession. The crossbow arrows were shorter and had more power. The bolts fell harmlessly to the ground as well. The orcs closed on our position. They were huge. This group wasn't local. Their tusks were as long as those on the hogs they rode. They carried spears and ugly axes, monstrous clubs studded with nails, and maces they swung over their heads while they screamed war cries. Even the hogs made a terrible sound. It was enough to send anyone running for cover, but we stood our ground.

"Fire!" the captain yelled.

The explosive balls of ammonium nitrate were loosed. The wizard overhead guided them. The balls exploded in midair, raining fire on the group of orcs to our left. Flames covered one, but it ignored its burning flesh and kept coming. The hog's armor deflected the flames and the beast ran on. The orcs knew about the turrets and the stairs. The group on the left closed on the wall. Another round of explosives was launched into the air. One ball fell close to the wall, exploded, and sent flames racing up the wall onto the battlement. Men caught fire and ran screaming, falling off the wall where the orcs had dismounted. I saw their distress, thought rain, and waved my wand. Floods of water put out the fires, but the men were cut to pieces.

Tina pointed her finger and one of the orc's weapons exploded. "Can you blow up one of the pigs?" I screamed.

"Too big and they're moving!" Tiny yelled back. The noise of the other soldiers shouting, the explosions as they went off, the roars of the orcs and the weird noises made by the pigs was deafening. It was exciting. I lived for it. The only time I felt alive was during battle. I pointed my wand at an orc racing for our section. When it was close enough, I connected to the wand with my mind, felt the energy flow into it and through it until a lightning bolt flew out of the end and hit the orc. It exploded.

The three remaining orcs on their side of the wall were so close I couldn't see them, which was more frightening than staring down at them as they ran toward the gate. Tiny and I turned to guard the stairs, ignoring the screams and shouting. My heart felt as though it would burst from my chest, but I felt no fear, only an excited anticipation of the conflict to come, the thrill of battle. It was in me. It had me in its grip.

Loud banging announced the orcs were at the gate. A screech followed by the sound of tearing metal and a crash. The gate was gone.

Tiny nocked a bolt while I held my wand in one hand and my sword in the other.

Two city soldiers came up behind us and pushed us aside, swords drawn. "Stay back," said the tallest one I knew as Long Tom, an older soldier possessing the art of levitation. The other soldier was young, and I'd never met him. "Fuck you," I said. "I'm a warrior and probably a better one than you. I'm motherfucking Annabelle." I elbowed the new guy aside and grinned at him. "You stay out of the way where it's safe."

He opened his mouth to complain but thought better of it as stomping and roars emerged from the narrow stairwell.

"They're coming," Long Tom said in a calm voice.

"I got your back," I told him. I lifted my sword high, thought flames, and fire raced down the blade. I held my wand in the other hand. I was ready.

The staircase was narrow, so narrow only one orc at a time could come up. The first beast burst out of the arched doorway, roaring, its axe blade glinting in the light of the fires burning behind us.

Long Tom levitated and chopped at the orc's shoulder with his sword from above. The orc used the spear in his left hand to stab me, but it gutted Long Tom before I could lop his arm off at the elbow. He stared at his amputated limb, green blood spurting, and fell backward. Long Tom crawled back down the wall. A medic and the new soldier I didn't know grabbed Tom and carried him to safety. The orc behind the one with the spear shoved his wounded companion down the stairs and advanced cautiously, swinging a mace.

Tiny loosed her bolt right into the beast. It penetrated its thick hide at this range. When the creature roared in pain and anger, I whacked off its head with my fiery sword. The orc's hideous face rolled between my feet, its lips drawn into a parody of a smile. I kicked it aside as the next orc, the last one, burst through the doorway. I quickly glanced down the wall. It was just me and Tiny now.

I unleashed three small knives into the beast's hideous face. One stuck in its eye, the other its cheek, and the last one bounced off the massive creature's helmet. Sorely wounded, but still mobile, the orc grabbed Tiny and tossed her over the wall. Rage filled me. "Tiny!"

This couldn't be happening. Tiny had to be alive. She had to survive the drop from the wall. Tiny could not be dead. I could not, would not, believe it. Poor Tiny might be down there alone, fighting off more orcs. I had to get to her.

Rage consumed me. All I saw was a red haze as I attacked the wounded orc. It batted my sword away, and before I could raise my wand, it grabbed me and crammed me under its massive, stinking arm. I still carried the wand, but I couldn't use it from this position. I tried to shoot an arrow into the orc's brain and hit emptiness. Figured. I pounded my fists against the beast's thigh as I gagged from the stench of its unwashed body.

As I struggled to get free, I saw the captain pour boiling oil into a ragged hole blown in the wall by our own bombs. The orcs swarming up the broken blocks of concrete and rocks roared with pain but didn't slow down.

The orc holding me shifted and tucked me under his other arm. I shrieked with impotent rage, kicked his ugly green leg trying to break his knee. He was like a block of wood, nothing fazed him. I thought about blowing him up, but that might damage me as well. I wiggled and managed to reach my ankle knife. I slid it out of the sheath with two fingers and stabbed the beast in the soft spot under its arm. It growled, pulled the knife out, threw it away and thundered down the steps. I tried another thought arrow and got nowhere. The minds of orcs were too simple. They ate, they killed, they slept, and they fornicated. That was it.

As the orc lumbered out the broken tower gate and across the grass, I twisted and turned trying to find Tiny. Poor little thing had sailed over the parapet without making a sound. I finally spotted her, strapped to the back of one of the hogs. Seeing her on the hog gave me hope. I renewed my effort to escape, squirming, kicking, and punching the stupid orc. It smashed me in the head with its big fist. I retched as my head spun and I just hung there for a few minutes fighting the urge to puke.

The big clod tossed me face down on the front of its strange saddle. I landed hard and ate leather. I was so dizzy I barely knew what was up and what was down. My vision blurred and I gasped for air. The stinking orc tied me to his saddle then climbed aboard the massive hog, wheeled it around and raced across the open area surrounding the city for the safety of the forest.

The bouncing was awful. My head slammed up and down against the side of the saddle. When I tried to lift it to see, I got a mouthful of dirt and a face full of brambles. We hit a flat space and I spotted Tiny behind us strapped to another hog being led by an orc on a big spotted sow.

There were five orcs left. Two had sacks of whatever booty they had found on the wall, probably weapons or personal items looted from the dead soldiers. This was a raiding party. No doubt I and Tiny, if she lived, were booty as well. The horde regrouped and galloped toward the distant hill.

The weird gait of the hog jounced and bounced me with every stride. My chest and stomach hurt. They had to be badly bruised. I'd slid enough so my head hung off one side. I lifted it long enough to see we were headed up a hill. When we crested the hill, taking a worn game trail, three huge figures mounted on massive horses attacked the orcs. They rode in, taller than the beasts riding the hogs, hacked at the surprised orcs, killed three immediately and felled two of the hogs. I have never been so glad to see anyone in my entire life. These guys, whoever they were, saved me.

Chapter Five

Belle

The orcs shouted to each other, the pigs squealed in pain or made their strange war noise as the three riders disappeared into the trees and the dark. The hit and run attack had the orcs confused and disorganized. Only two survived. The pig Tiny was tied to ran off into the darkness. "Fuck!" I shrieked. How could all this be happening? The orc on my pig motioned for his remaining man to join him. They cut off the trail and headed into another valley galloping toward a stand of trees at the bottom.

I can't speak orc, so I had no idea what the orc riding behind me said to his friends. He grunted something and growled then he shoved my head down. I ate more leather as the three attackers returned. One came out of the trees in the bottom of the valley, while two attacked from the sides. The orc riding the hog I was on turned the beast and urged it into a run. The hog's faster pace forced me to stop struggling and fight to survive as the stout hog cut into thick underbrush heavy with briars.

The orc was smart. It kept the hog to the deep, thick brush and undergrowth where the bigger horses would find it difficult to follow. Blood ran into my eyes. My face must be a scratched-up mess.

The orcs reached the river, finally out of the brambles, and I lifted my head to search for Tiny. There was no sign of her. The orc jumped off and led the hog into the muddy, swirling, brown water of the Mississippi. It swam with powerful strokes leading the hog into the slow current. The water was worse than the brambles. I fought to keep my head above the water and breathe as the cuts on my face stung.

The river seemed to go on forever. I got one glance behind and saw the riders had followed, plowing their big horses into the river at a dead run, then hanging onto the reins as the giant animals swam and they floated beside them, dragged along with one hand holding the saddle.

I shouldn't have risked looking. I got dunked and came up sputtering and choking as I breathed in river water.

The horses were gaining. They swam faster than the pigs. The orc saw he was doomed if he hung onto his war hog, so he let go and was dragged downstream, diving deep to cover his escape. One of the men or creatures following caught my loose pig's reins and dragged it out of the water. His horse climbed the muddy bank and stood quietly, huge and black, with water dripping off its heaving sides.

The man, creature, or whatever he was who saved me lifted my head by the hair and laughed. He spoke in understandable English. "You alive?"

I gasped, panting as streams of water from my dripping hair blinded me. "I think I'm gonna barf."

He untied me and helped me off the pig. My legs felt like noodles. I wobbled and he wrapped a monstrously huge arm around my waist. I looked into his face. It wasn't green but it wasn't brown or human-color either. He had thick dark-brown hair and golden eyes. There was orc blood in him for sure, but he had no tusks. "What are you?"

"I thought I be your savior, my lady," he said in a gruff voice.

My head swam and I barfed brown water right on his big bare feet.

He laughed and shook first one foot them the other.

Throwing up cleared my head. "Really, what kind of creature are you?"

"None of yer business, little girl. I be saving you and that's all you need to know."

I'd heard of half-man half-orcs running The Withers. This must be one. They were all supposed to be killers just like the orcs. I wasn't afraid of him, but just in case I whipped out one of my knives and held it in front of me, underhanded, classic knife-fighter style. "Don't come any closer or I'll stick this in your freaking eye."

"Nay, lass, I'm saving your ass. Don't be pokin' holes in me hide, cause I'm thinking you can't reach me eye."

"Maybe not," I said. "But I can throw this bitch and hit your eye from a hundred feet away."

The giant creature, beast, or whatever he was, had the audacity to laugh at me again. "Slag," he yelled. "We got us a fighter here." He stepped into the water and rinsed off his feet, apparently unconcerned by my threats.

Another huge creature surged out of the river leading the pig with Tiny strapped to it. "I found another one, Jackal. This'un be hurt. Think we need to get her to a healer."

"That's my friend." I ran to the pig emerging from the water and touched Tiny's head. I felt nothing, no thoughts, no dreams, nothing. It was as though Tiny was gone. I stroked her back as I fought panic and tears. Tiny couldn't be dead. She was all I had.

"She's alive," the huge monster who saved me said. "I can feel her life force."

"Help me get her off this gross pig," I said to him. "Please, help me."

They just stood there like they were deaf. "Hello," I yelled into his face. "Can you hear me? Please help me get her off this frigging pig."

The two burst out laughing like I was giving them a fine show. "Feisty thing, ain't she?" The one who saved me said.

The other one swung off his enormous blond mare. "Fireball fer sure."

The halfling I'd barfed on swung into action, cut Tiny's bonds and lifted Tiny to a dry spot above the water line. "She's badly hurt," I said to him. "Can you take me back to the city? I need to get Tiny home so the healers can save her life."

"Nay," he said. "Can't do that, think on. Yer friend be hurt. Fording the river again might kill her. We need to find us a healer here."

I felt for Tiny's mind again, felt for signs of injury, and smiled. She was dreaming she was flying over the city looking down at the school. I felt Tiny's arms and legs. Her left leg was broken along with one of her ribs. Her head was probably concussed, but she was alive.

"All the healers are back in the city," I said to the big halfling. He bent close to examine Tiny. "She does need some healing right quick," he said, stood up and put his hands on his hips. When his concern slid out from behind the walls protecting his thoughts, I felt it. His mental barriers were strong, the strongest I'd encountered since Odifarus.

"Then we need to take her back to the city."

"Nay," he said. "Happen you know nothing about The Withers. You got a lot to learn. There's a whole world out here. Not all folk live behind walls."

"But she needs a healer, a Magic with the healing Gift."

"Not all Magics live behind the walls, neither," he said. "I won't go back. I was on my way west to Craggy Town when I ran into them orcs. We'll keep on. Should reach it before the sun's too hot to travel."

I crossed my arms over my dripping-wet chest, took a deep breath and forced myself to maintain a civil tone. I was close to freaking out. The best healers were in the city. Everyone knew that. If Tiny died because of this stubborn half-orc, I'd kill him so slowly, he'd be begging for death. "I can't go wherever it is you're going. I can't. I have to take Tiny to a healer. Can't you see? She'll die out here. Please take us back."

The big man laughed in my face. "No. You're kinda cute and your friend does need a healer, but we're going to Craggy Town cause that be where the closest healer is and it's also where I wanna go."

Chapter Six

Belle

"Hey Slag, you see Chub yet?" The half-orc who rode the black horse asked his companion, dismissing my demands as though they were nothing. I was so angry; I was afraid I'd blow a gasket.

I felt consumed by helplessness which was not something I was used to. In my world, I was important. People did what I told them to do. This gigantic half-orc was making me want to hit him in the face with my wand.

There was nothing I could do to change his mind. I felt that; his determination was strong and easy to read. There was nothing I could do for Tiny, who moaned, pitifully still lost in her dreams. I'm not the sweet and tender kind of person, but I sat next to Tiny and pushed the strands of pale hair off her white forehead as gently as I was able.

The huge, hideously-ugly orc-like man who rode the mean mare shook his head. "Chub had the wee one with him. I saw him go into the river. I'm sure he'll be here sooner than not. That mule of his can swim like a fish."

So angry, and so frustrated, without thinking I stared at the half-orc's foot and it erupted in flames. I hid my face as he yelled and stomped the fire out and an even larger man surged out of the river on the biggest mule I'd ever seen. Riding in front of him was a child, a little girl with tangled red hair, skinny, and dressed in a man's shirt ten sizes too big for her. The girl giggled as she clung to the stiff mane of the mule. "Oh, Chubby," she said to the man riding behind her. "That was so fun."

She jumped down and ran to me. I didn't know what to do or say. I'd never been this close to a child. "Did they save you, too? They saved me." Then she hugged me. I froze. The girl bent down and put her hands on Tiny. "This one's sick. We need to get her to a healer."

The child was a ball of energy just like Tiny, but even more so. She jumped up and down, ran to the big man with the burnt foot, and hugged his tall and sturdy tree-trunk legs. "Jackal, we needs to save the one on the ground."

"We will, Flossie, we will." He picked her up and tossed her onto his shoulder. The other two men closed in and they talked.

I sat in the dirt beside Tiny, ran my hands over her face and searched for thoughts. Tiny still dreamed. With nothing to do but wait, I examined the huge man. His ears were pointed, his thick brown hair pulled up on top of his head in a knot. He had the heavy brow of an orc, but his nose was not flat and had finely-sculpted nostrils. His eyes were golden with a touch of green under sharply arched black brows, kind of like his skin which was light brown with a touch of green. His jaw was determined, square and smooth with no sign of a beard. He was covered with tattoos circling his shoulders and running down his arms. A strange tribal tattoo covered most of his vast right pectoral muscle. He was enormous and a beast, but I couldn't put a name to what he was. If Tiny died because of him, I would kill him.

Jackal

I didn't much care for the way the little Magic girl glared at me. We'd risked our lives to rescue her. The least she could do was show some respect and be a little more grateful. I examined my big bare foot and chuckled. My toes were muddy with singed hair on top. She did have spirit and under the mud and the scratches, she was the most beautiful woman I'd ever seen. When Chub glanced down to see what I was staring at, he laughed. "Your foot looks burned. You step in a fire?"

I pointed at the Magic girl sitting in the mud beside her friend. "She did it."

Slag and Chub roared with laughter.

When they quit chuckling, they sorted out the gear on the war hog, left its peculiar saddle, and went to pick up the injured girl. "What are you doing with Tiny?" The Magic girl asked in a quiet voice. She'd taken out a wand and held it like she knew what to do with it.

"Listen," I said to her. "We don't want to hurt you. We saved you and your friend. We need to get moving. We can't stay on this muddy beach much longer. There might be more orcs in the area."

"Where's this Craggy Town you speak of?"

"North and a little west of here, about half a day's ride. If we get going now, we can make it before it gets too hot."

The girl suddenly deflated. She sighed and tears flowed down her cheeks. Her misery moved me in an uncomfortable way. "She's my only friend," the girl sobbed. "I'm sorry. I never cry." She brushed her tears away with her fists, took a deep breath and tucked her wand inside her shirt.

When she pulled her rough shirt out to stuff the wand inside, I peeked. She had milk-white skin that looked as soft as silk. "Can you help me carry her?" I asked.

She nodded, sniffed, and gulped. These natural actions, unhidden or covered with usual female artifice, touched him. "Okay," she said.

Together we lifted the unconscious girl. I didn't need her help. The sick one was as light as a feather. But this girl needed to do something, be a part of taking care of her friend. When my hand touched hers beneath the girl, I felt a weird connection. I had a sudden glimpse of a dark cell, nuns, an old wizard, and the sick girl they carried laughing. These must be the Magic girl's memories. They were sad. "Me name's Jackal," I said. "I'm thinkin' you heard me friends call me that. What's yours?"

Startled, she looked up and he saw her eyes were the color of violets in the spring. "Annabelle," she said. "But everyone always calls me Belle."

With Belle and her unconscious friend riding the gigantic hog, we set off for Craggy Town. The trading station was located up stream inside cliffs that hung out over the vast river. What little traffic there was up and down the Mississippi always stopped at their docks and traded. Craggy Town was easy to protect and had electricity powered by the river. Some genius human had rigged water turbines in the flow to power the small town inside the cliffs. Because everyone stopped, Craggy Town had all the best goods for barter and a vast selection.

At night, there was a beacon for the desperate, the hungry or weary travelers like us. Not that the Craggy Towners were a hospitable bunch, because they weren't. Craggy Towners were just as likely to put an arrow in you as look at you, but my men and I had been going there for three years and they knew us. I had a satchel filled with two new swords and six knives made in Wildwhisper to trade. I was looking for traveling supplies and now for the healer.

The approach to the village was down a well-worn trail through thick willows. This time of the year, the undergrowth was filled with berry bushes, deer, and wild hogs. We waded through two shallow arms of another river that joined the bigger one here, and then started to climb out of the lowlands into the higher elevations. The sun was up and starting to roast the land when we hit the trail, and as I predicted, it was midday when the first sentry, high on the rocks beside the river, spotted us.

Not many cities or towns had been in this area in before-times, so there were few ruins. The cliffs shot out of the earth beside the river, part of a massive upheaval caused by the bomb going off around a century ago. Old timers at Craggy Town said this used to be part of the delta lands.

I pulled a white square of cloth out of my saddle pocket and waved it. It was embroidered with a black Jackal. When the sentry saw the flag, he blew his horn. The sentry blew two more blasts and we rode into an open area with stables and paddocks for the animals. While we were traveling, I didn't give the two females and the child much thought. When I climbed off Thor, I glanced back at them. Belle drooped over the hog's neck. The tiny blond girl woke when they stopped and moaned in pain. Belle had cut away her leggings to reveal a leg swollen and seven different colors of purple, black and blue. The injured girl held her left side and whimpered with each breath.

"Don't worry so much. They have a good healer here," I said to her. "You'll be surprised."

Two heavily armed men clad in rough homespun tunics over leather leggings came out of a cave in the cliffs and walked over to us. When they saw the women, they grinned. "Halloo there, Jackal, you bring us women?"

"No, I did not. These be Magics from New Orleans. Saved them from some orcs. Took care to make sure them big sons-a-bitches won't be visiting you. But one of these, uh, these ladies be hurtin' real bad. Can you bring me a stretcher and take her to Granny Hawkins?"

Belle punched me in the arm. It didn't hurt but it got my attention. "I thought you said there was a real healer here. What is a Granny Hawkins?"

"Granny Hawkins is famous in these parts. Don't be judging her talents till you've seen them."

I nodded to the two Craggers. "Ran and Otis here will help you carry your friend to Granny's place. You realize nothing here be free, right? These people live off trade. Their help and Granny's aid will cost."

Belle's eyes flew open. "But we have no way to pay."

Chub gawked at her with the reins of his mule in his hand. He guffawed and punched my shoulder hard. "I can think of plenty of ways she can pay. How 'bout you, Jackal?"

"What?" I lifted one eyebrow. "Her? You joking?"

Belle straightened her back and looked away like she didn't understand the meaning of their rude jest. Suddenly, I felt guilty. She was scared and hurting and they'd just poked fun at her. "That's enough," I said to Chub. "She's got enough to worry about without you scaring the daylights out of her."

Belle shot me a look of surprise and I read her thoughts again. She was thankful. She must be a powerful sender, because I kept picking up her thoughts in a way I'd never experienced before. It was as though we had some kind of strange connection, as though fate had brought us together for a reason. A terrifying thought hit me. What if she could read my thoughts like I was reading hers?

Oh, I can if I want to. That came in loud and clear. When I glanced at her, she winked. And my skin is as soft as silk.

My face burned. She'd read that. From now on, I better mind what I was thinking.

"I'm sure we'll think of a way to work out yer debt," I said as though none of that had passed between us.

Belle actually laughed. It was a beautiful sound. "In your dreams," she said.

I winked at her. "I'm sure ye will be, darlin'."

Flossie walked up, leading Slag by his big, green hand. She barely reached the big three-quarter orc's knee. "Jackal are you flirting with this lady?" she asked with her head tilted to the side, making her look like a sparrow. A cute little bird with a crazy red topknot.

"No, poppet, we only be joking around, having a little fun."

Flossie tip-toed to Belle where she watched the two Craggers load the injured woman onto a piece of deer hide stretched between two stout poles. She stared up at Belle as though thinking whether or not she was friend material, then took her hand. "I shall accompany you to see the healer. Maybe when I grow up, I can be one, too. I'd like to help people. I surely would."

I waved to the two Craggers who were waiting for remuneration. I knew them. Manning the walls was a job and an opportunity for gilt. Little jobs like this often fell in their way, so they waited.

"I have plenty of trade goods," I told them and patted the satchel hanging off the back of Thor's saddle.

"Good on," Otis said and waved. The two men hoisted the injured woman and took off into the brush behind the stable area. A circuitous path was hidden there, leading into the cave system that made up Craggy Town.

"Should I go with her?" Belle asked.

I could feel her hesitancy as the realization hit her things were different in The Withers. Me, and big halflings like me ruled. We could fight off orcs who were only slightly bigger than us and stupid. We could take care of ourselves. Belle might be a Magic and a warrior, but she was a stranger in this land. The rules in The Withers are different.

"Yep, go with them," I told her. "Hurry or you'll lose them in the caves. We'll be following behind directly we see to these animals."

I laughed as my warning sent her scampering after the two Craggers.

Chapter Seven

Belle

I ran after the two oddly-dressed villagers bearing Tina.

The two men were gone. I felt for their minds and realized they were on a path climbing the cliffs. After a quick search, I found the hidden way into the thick underbrush, scrambled under the limbs and onto a rocky trail leading up the side of the bluff.

When I shaded my eyes, I saw the two Craggers with the little girl. My heart ached. Children were such a rare sight. The birthrate being so low in New Orleans, I never saw children, even servant children.

I had to run to catch up to them. They entered a huge cave. Tunnels led in three directions. They chose the middle and entered the cool interior. Lights strung high on the wall lit the tunnels. My boots crunched on stone floors covered with dirt, grass, and leaves drug in on the feet of residents.

The passageway abruptly ended at a harrowing drop-off. The men turned and eased along a narrow walkway hanging over the rushing river. I followed, stepping carefully down the ledge. It ended at an open area large enough to hold an entire village. Huts circled a central gathering place. People waited. They stared at us with curiosity. Visitors pulsed life blood into a trading town. They provided their entertainment, the way they got news of the world, and supplied them with the necessities of life.

A handful of men and women greeted the Craggers. Children ran around laughing and playing. I felt like an alien. A woman carrying a baby on her hip walked across the central compound to talk to me. "Where you from?"

"I'm from the city," I said.

The woman pointed to the south. "New Orleans?"

I nodded.

"We don't get too many city folks here, just us wildings, folks who live in The Withers, you know."

"My friend was injured fighting orcs," I told her. "We're both soldiers in the city. They said they're taking her to Granny Hawkins. Can you help me get there, please?"

"It's the third hut against the west wall," the woman said, pointing behind her.

Curious, I gently probed the woman's mind. Her name was Sarah and the child's name Benjy. "Thank you, Sarah," I said. Then I stroked Benjy's soft curling hair. "Benjy is adorable."

"How do you know me name?" Sarah pulled her child close.

"I just do."

The woman turned her head away and bowed slightly to show respect. "You're a Magic." Sarah turned to the other villagers. "This one's a Magic."

I smiled and hurried toward the west wall of the cliffs, relieved to escape the rush of curious villagers. It didn't hurt to garner some respect from these people. Tiny and I might have to depend on them. What if the huge half-orcs took off and left us? Then we'd be on our own and if we already had some respect, it would help.

The two Craggers who'd carried Tina on the stretcher left the hut as I entered. I slid by them and through the doorway, an actual door crafted from rough wooden slats. An older lady settled Tina on a bed in the makeshift hospital, propped her on a pillow, and covered her with a woolen blanket. A Cragger woman on another cot set against the opposite wall wailed as she gave birth. An older woman held the woman's hand and offered her a sip of something in an earthen cup. Soon after, the woman in labor's wails quieted as her birth pang abated.

The interior of the hut was part of the cave. A fire burned in the stone hearth; the smoke sucked out a natural fissure that functioned as a chimney in the rock. Water steamed in a blackened kettle hanging on a hook over the flames. A rudimentary kitchen offered a table and chairs. A dark doorway out of that room led deeper inside the cliff. Flossie sat on a short stool next to the fire watching everything, her blue eyes alive with interest.

Suddenly, a plump woman in a fluffy pink dress popped into the middle of the room. "Am I needed here?" she asked.

"Dammit all, Dandy," The old woman snapped. "Could you just once use the door like a normal person? Popping in and out like you do is gonna be the death of me."

"Who are you?" I asked as the plump woman ran her hands over Tina.

"I'm Dandelion. I'm a fairy. Most people call me Dandy." She tilted her head and a mass of fiery red hair flew everywhere. "You should, too."

"I should what? I asked.

"Call me Dandy."

"Oh, right." I looked at Tiny over Dandy's shoulder. "Can you heal her?"

"I don't know. I need to examine her."

"Sorry," I apologized. "I was hovering." As I backed away, the older woman put her hand on my arm for a split second. "You be a Magic." She pointed at Tina. "Her too?"

"Yes, we were taken by orcs. Tina was injured fighting them."

"Dandy can heal her. Be glad she flitted in." The old woman hawked and spat brown stuff into a tin cup. I said nothing but jumped when Dandy disappeared for a minute and then popped back in right in front of her.

"Fairies." The old woman made the word sound like a curse. "Never around when you need 'em. Always flitting here and there. But they do have power."

"I've never met one," I said. "I didn't even know they existed. Are there many in The Withers?"

"No," the old woman said. "There be few and most of them are unreliable. Flibberty-gibbets one and all. I'm Hilda Hawkins. Folks in Craggy Town call me Granny."

"I figured as much. They told me you're a healer. I'm Annabelle, my friends call me Belle, and Tina is my friend. I call her Tiny."

"Yes, she is a little thing, ain't she? Dandy should have her fixed up in no time as long as that evil Slygon or one of his ilk hasn't touched her or cursed her."

"Slygon?" I shivered at the sound of his name. They knew about the evil demon, even here. Odafarus told me I was the one who would kill him. Back in New Orleans it seemed like Slygon was far away and I'd never be called upon to fight with him or kill him. It was a huge task and seemed unreal. Now these people were telling me they'd seen him. They knew of him.

"He rides a black dragon," Granny said. "Vampires ride with him. They're horrible."

"He comes for the babies," Dandy said. "He needs the blood of infants to keep him in this world."

Memories of being taken with my sister flooded me. The horrible demon with black hair had sucked the life from a baby right in front of me. What if Noemi had been stolen by Slygon? What if she was still alive and his prisoner? The need to find Noemi filled me with urgency. Now that I was outside the walls of the city, I was free to hunt for her. And I would. Nothing would stop me.

As we watched Dandy work, I examined the fairy with curiosity. I had no idea they existed, not in the real world, but all manner of mythical creatures had escaped the underworld after the rift.

The fairy's hair was a mass of red curls. She wore a shimmering pink dress with a full, flowing skirt. She danced around on tiny feet encased in red velvet slippers. Dandy pulled a crystal wand out of a pocket hidden in the full skirt and passed it over Tiny's broken leg. The wand glowed. Sparkling dust-like particles streamed out of its tip on a wave of white light that penetrated Tina's leg. Tiny screamed as her leg contorted and the bones knit.

Dandy waved the wand over Tiny's rib and Tiny grabbed her chest and groaned. A moment later her eyes blinked open.

We waited expectantly until Dandy said to Tiny, "You can get up now." She put her hand under Tiny's arm and lifted her.

"Tiny? Are you okay? I was so worried I could hardly breath."

"I-I think so," Tiny said. "Where am I?"

"You're in a safe place in The Withers. I thought you died when you went over the wall."

"I went over the wall?"

"Yep, and you got picked up by an orc. So did I, then we were rescued and brought here. We're in a town outside the city walls. Tiny, there's people living out here. People with children."

As if on cue, the woman giving birth wailed one more time as Dandy helped her child enter the world. "Look, Tiny, a baby."

Tiny and I went to examine the newborn. I touched the babe's wet hair. "It's a boy."

"I've never seen a baby," Tiny said. "He's so little."

"They are," Dandy said as she swaddled the infant in a warm blanket and handed him to his waiting mother. Flossie joined them, stared solemnly at the infant, then glanced at Dandy. "I know you," Flossie said.

"No, you don't," Dandy snapped as she walked over to the fire where she stirred something cooking in a pot hung over the coals.

"I'm glad you're well," the little girl said to Tiny. "Jackal, Slag and Chubby saved you, and they saved me too. Isn't that great? We're in Craggy Town. It's really fun here, and there are lots of interesting people and animals."

Flossie threw herself at Tiny, who patted Flossie on top of her head. "Well who might you be? Yes, I'm fine. I'm glad they saved you, too."

"I'm Flossie."

"Of course, you are," Tiny said as she shot me a raised eyebrow. I grinned.

Across the room, the infant cried. Granny took the baby from his mother and brought him to me. "Would you like to hold him?" Granny asked.

For a moment I was absolutely horrified. I'd never seen an infant much less thought about holding one. I finally blurted, "yes." Granny showed me how to support his head and cradle his body. Goosebumps race up my arms and a strange feeling filled my heart. Babies were so fragile and so innocent. This was life, brand new life. The baby looked up at me out of cloudy-blue eyes and tears filled my eyes. "He's so beautiful."

Granny took the baby back and kissed his head. "New, innocent, and so very precious."

"Is your birthrate low out here?" I asked.

Granny shook her head. "Out here in The Withers, it's normal. I know about the cities. There's something wrong, something the Magics are doing that's wrong. That's what's making your birthrate so low."

"Let me see," Tiny said. She touched the fluffy down on the baby's head with a gentle finger. Her eyes glowed when she looked at me. "This is like a miracle."

"It's been an afternoon for miracles," I said. "Getting you healed is a miracle."

"Dandy did it," Flossie giggled. "She's a fairy."

"She's as good as new," the fairy confirmed. I sent feelers into the fairy's mind and came back with nothing. It was completely empty. Then she felt a shove inside her head and the fairy was in her mind, sharing the space. "You're half elf," the fairy said to me. "Lots of magical stuff inside you."

"What? How do you know that?" I was stunned because she could read that in me and also because I'd never thought of my heritage in that way. I sent another feeler at Dandy and the fairy chuckled.

"Empty," she said, tapping her head.

A sudden blast of a horn from the lookout startled all of them. That blast was followed by three more. Granny shoved the baby back into the hands of a helper and pointed to the doorway in the rear before rushing to a table and snatching up bottles. "Go, get out, help the mother. We're being attacked!" Granny's voice was filled with terror. I read her fear and it was massive. She knew what was coming and dreaded it.

51

Chapter Eight

Belle

My weapons were back with the horses. All I had left were three knives. I bolted for the door of the hut. Outside, Craggers scattered every which way.

A huge beast roared. I grabbed my head as dark, evil, vile thoughts filled my mind. Slimy and heavy, all blood and death, skulls, people dismembered and dying, diseased humans, snakes, so many snakes, and a rabid hunger for the blood of the newborn infant. I recognized the thoughts instantly. I'd had this evil creature in my head before when I was little. This was the horrible demon who'd taken me and Noemi. Sudden hope bloomed in my chest. Maybe he'd brought my sister here. Maybe Noemi was here. I threw a circle of questing thoughts out and came back empty.

Tiny touched my shoulder. "What is it? What do you see?"

"Slygon," I whispered. "The evil demon who stole my sister."

Jackal stuck his head in the door. "Get ready. We're in for a fight."

The Craggy Towners ran into the caves to hide and over Jackal's massive shoulder, I saw a black shadow.

"Jackal. Behind you."

He turned and fired an arrow from his longbow in one smooth move. It bounced off the dragon's thick hide.

"You need silver," Granny yelled. "The dragons are Slygon's creatures. This way." She grabbed Tiny's and my hands and pulled us into the hut. Jackal and his two men surged into the small room completely filling it just as the fairy vanished.

The midwife who'd delivered the child pulled the mother out of the bed and to her feet. "Into the caves," Granny said. "Hurry. You," she pointed to the woman holding the newborn. "Hide the wee one.

Slygon has come for the infant. You," she pointed to Flossie. "Go with the girl. You're still young enough to attract his interest."

The midwife grabbed the bundled baby, ran through the room in the back of the cave, and disappeared through a door leading deeper into the cliffs. Flossie spun after her, eyes wide, stunned silent, too frightened to speak. Another roar gusted smoke and fire through the front door. Tiny screamed and I grabbed her hand and followed Flossie. Behind me Jackal helped the new mother, followed by his men. A tiny pink flying thing landed on my shoulder. When I moved to brush it off, I saw it was Dandy. Her red curls bounced. *Hurry*, I heard in my head.

The door led to a long tunnel diving deep into the mountain, once again lit by a long string of strange bulbs. Granny dropped back. "Slygon can't bring the dragons in here but he has men with him. If you can call them that."

If I wanted to, I could hear Slygon. I remembered him too well. Before I blocked him, I listened. His desire for babies was awful, but I knew that. To him their blood tasted sweet and delicious, and he craved it like a seductive drug. Consuming their innocent life force amplified his power. Slygon wished to drain the infants.

His seeking thoughts felt vile inside my head, an unclean searching of phantom fingers pushing into my brain. It was so terrible I covered my mouth so I wouldn't scream. Memories of that terrible time when Noemi had been taken made me weak. I stumbled and Jackal was there to catch me.

"Are you okay?" he asked.

"I know him," I whispered. "He kidnapped me and my sister when we were little. My sister saved me by sacrificing herself." I clung to his big arm, and for a moment forgot he was a huge ugly beast. All I felt was his warmth and concern. Comfort flowed from him into me and I straightened my back. "I'm alright now."

We came to a set of narrow stairs carved into the rock. The steps led to a cavern. Inside, the Craggers prepared their defense. They'd fought Slygon before. They knew what they had to do to survive.

They racked long wooden spears, lit a fire in the center of the cavern, the smoke drawn up to a hole many feet above. I looked at the hole. Night had fallen. Stars twinkled in the scrap of visible black sky.

The women and children of Craggy Town huddled in a far passage, waiting. The Craggers able to fight gathered special bolts and passed them out to Slag, Chub, Tiny and the rest of the men holding crossbows. "Tipped with silver," Granny whispered. "The diggers mine it here in the cliffs."

A roar sounded from above. A huge body thumped on the cavern roof. One of the dragons was up there. Chub and Slag readied their crossbows. When the sky was blotted out by shining black scales, they fired. More roars, only these were of pain. Chub's bolts were always tipped with venom and Slag now used the silver tips.

Slag handed me my sword. "Here. Thought you might be needin' this. How's the other one?"

"I'm fine," Tiny said. She held up a crossbow and nocked a silver-tipped bolt.

I lifted my sword high and thought fire. Flames raced down the sword. Jackal grinned. "Nice trick."

"I'll say," Slag agreed, raising his brows.

"Hot steel penetrates orc hide better."

"Well we ain't fightin' no orcs," Chub said. "These creatures be worse."

A scream from the tunnel to Granny's hut alerted us to danger. Half stayed to guard the hole in the roof of the cave while the other half headed to the tunnel carrying the long wooden spears. "It wants the babes," Jackal whispered in horror. "I can feel their thirst fer the wee life forces."

"I know," I said. "You can feel them too?"

"Aye, I feel you as well." He tapped his head. "And, I hear you."

Surprised, gooseflesh raced up my arms and I shivered. Jackal was so much more than he seemed. The bad memories flooded me. I was shaking with terror. Facing Slygon, facing whatever would emerge from that tunnel, took everything I had. I wanted to run and hide. I thought I was fearless and now I know I'm not. But I forced myself, taking one faltering step at a time, to join the men defending the tunnel, the only way in. If I didn't stand strong with them, I was nothing and everything I thought and planned to do, was nothing.

Jackal stood beside me. "Sneck up, lass, ye'll be fine."

Sudden screams rang out farther down the tunnel and I dropped low into a fighting stance, sword flaming. Jackal might be huge and not like the men I knew, but he was a comfort to have fighting by my side. He growled and I loved the sound. It sounded like power and strength, like a wild animal. I lifted my sword and then I growled. I smelled them.

I spotted a pale, ghostly figure dressed in black armor. His sword glowed with an unearthly green fire. It slashed the throat of a man desperately fighting, grabbed him, and drank the blood flowing from his gushing wound.

Another creature pushed him aside. A woman, as pale as the male, with long, stringy, yellow hair, red lips and green eyes, bared fangs already dripping with blood. Her hideous face was familiar in an awful way. And then I knew. "Noemi!"

The hideous creature glanced up, as though for a moment, lucid thoughts entered her head. She saw me and showed her fangs in a gross imitation of a smile. "Well if it isn't Annabelle, my little sister. Come to me child. I can give you eternal life." When she reached for me, blood dripped off the tips of her long nails, and I recognized the essence in the blood. It was Benjy's, the child of the Craggy Town woman, Sarah.

I shook my head to clear it. This couldn't be my sister. It just couldn't. Noemi was good. She'd sacrificed herself to save me. There was no way this could be my sister.

But Noemi's thoughts penetrated my head. *It is me, child. Times change. People change. Life, or the lack of it, goes on.*

Jackal lifted his sword. "Well you sure ain't my sister." He struck at Noemi, cleaved her from shoulder to waist. Noemi fell, but her wound healed immediately. His strike at Noemi snapped me out of my daze. I threw myself across Noemi and held up a hand. "No, don't kill her. Please."

Noemi sniffed me then licked my face with a long, red tongue. "You taste great. Delicious little sister."

I turned around in Noemi's arms and stared into her red eyes. "Stop, Noemi." I forced my strong will into Noemi's crazed brain. It was like being caught in a dust tornado. Noemi's thoughts swirled, black and blood-red, lusting thoughts of men and sex acts I had never even imagined possible. I pushed Noemi's thoughts aside and tried to insert love, warmth, kittens, puppies, sunshine and beautiful flowers. But the blackness took over and I was ruthlessly thrown out of Noemi's thoughts.

Another vampire pushed Noemi aside and clutched at me with long claws dripping blood. Noemi turned and attacked him, tearing out his throat with her teeth. *Run!* Noemi pushed this thought into my brain as she flicked me off of her like I weighed nothing and into the passage. Then she leaped to her feet and killed the next vampire.

I was in shock, too stunned to think clearly. For a moment, I was completely helpless, overcome with emotion. "Noemi!" My scream echoed in the narrow rock passage.

When I tried to feel for my sister again Noemi blocked me with a wall too thick to penetrate. Stunned and shocked at finding Noemi, discovering her a vampire, I slumped. Then Jackal was there with his katana. He pushed me to safety behind him, shielded me with his huge body filling the passage.

I recovered and whipped around to search for Noemi as Jackal's blade cut a swathe through another vampire's body neatly decapitating it. Thick black blood spurted across Noemi, who shook it off, licking the last final drops with her long, pointed tongue. The wounded vampire felt around for its head and reattached it.

"What the hell?" Jackal snarled.

"You need wood," a Cragger said from behind me. "Or silver."

Jackal took the wooden spear from the Cragger, shoved it through the vampire killing it, and then he pointed it at Noemi. "Do it," Noemi said. "Give me the final, true death. Give me peace." She knelt on the stone floor and opened her dress revealing stark white skin as she bared it for the thrust of the spear.

A scream rose from the center of the cavern. "Snakes!"

It was what I'd seen in my vision. It had to be. Huge vipers with flared hoods wider than Chub's shoulders, their red demonic eyes hypnotic.

Jackal looked at Noemi then at me. "Please don't kill her," I begged. "She's my sister."

"She's a freaking vampire," Jackal growled then turned to snarl at Noemi. "Disappear." Noemi grabbed at his leg. "No, don't go. Kill me, please."

I dropped to my knees in front of Noemi, heart breaking in two. Her agony was clear to see, and I loved her so much. Bloody tears rolled down Noemi's mournful face and I grabbed her shoulders. I pressed my face against her blond hair. "Live," I whispered. "I'll come for you. I swear."

For a moment, two sisters parted for many years, reunited, then Noemi hissed. "He'll never let me go."

"I'll find a way. Trust me. Now go."

Noemi squeezed my hand, turned, glanced once more over her shoulder at me, then in a flash was gone. I leaped to my feet and ran back the way I'd come as Jackal covered our retreat, fighting off the remaining vampires.

I erupted into the cavern. Chub and Slag wielded their enormous war axes, hacking off cobra heads and cleaving snakes in two. The Craggers fired silver bolts into dozens of the snakes. I sliced the head off a huge, hissing monster when it struck at me. The scene was straight from Hell. The Craggers lit torches and burned the snakes. Some had spears, stabbing them.

Suddenly, all the snakes disappeared, and a woman's scream rose above the din. "My baby!"

Holding his sword high in both hands, Jackal shoved past me and Tiny to the huddled group of women. Two Craggers and Slag rushed to assist him. I turned to join him but froze when I saw who faced Jackal.

A familiar dark-haired creature with pointed ears clutched the newborn to his chest. A perverted, demon elf with blood-coated fangs and full red lips. Startling, ice-blue eyes glared out of a perfect face.

Slygon.

"Well if it isn't little sister," Slygon said. "We've been looking everywhere for you. Your sister and I have become quite close."

"Put the babe down," Jackal growled.

"I would," Slygon said with a silky smirk, "but I want him." He gestured and a huge black cobra rose up and flared its hood. It headed for Jackal. I sliced off its head with my flaming sword and it vanished.

Slygon created more snakes, I reached out with my mind, feeling for a living snake, but they were only an illusion meant to terrify. "The snakes aren't real!" I shouted over the noise and moved toward Slygon, sword flaming.

"I remember you," I said. "How could I ever forget your evil, slimy thoughts? You made my sister into a demon."

"Noemi and I tried to get to you. Those blasted nuns kept you buried. We couldn't even read a stray thought. Had to find out where you were from one of the farmers we raided."

Slygon's thoughts entered my head, mesmerizing me, hypnotizing me into a dream state. "Come to me," Slygon whispered.

"Fuck you!" Jackal's shout snapped me out of the mist filling my mind, taking over my thoughts.

Jackal lifted his sword. Slygon was alone with the baby. He only had one hand to fight with and suddenly realized he was in danger.

"There's always someone badder, faster and smarter than you, Slygon," I said. "You'll never do that to me again." I whipped my wand out of my shirt and snapped it at Slygon. The baby flew into the air. Chub caught the infant as Jackal charged Slygon, with me right behind him.

Slygon backed away rapidly. "I want you. Your sister and you will make a nice pair, a vision I can barely stand to think about."

"Not now, not ever," Jackal said. "The thought's disgusting. You're nothing but a fucking pervert.

"We'll get Noemi back," I hissed. "I'll find you and I'll take her from you."

Slygon laughed. "You, you're just a child. My power is much greater than you can even imagine." He lifted his hands. More cobras appeared and suddenly Slygon was on the roof.

"Real!" I screamed. "These are real."

One of the snakes struck at me, but Jackal was there. He swung the katana and the snake was gone. It followed Slygon through the hole in the roof. Slag fired a silver-tipped bolt, but the snake was too fast, its tail disappeared into the night.

We'll meet again, rang through my mind. *Now that I know where you are, there will be nothing to stop me. When I want something, I get it. And I want you.*

I fired a murderous thought arrow into Slygon's head and felt his immediate mental wail. I'd hurt him. He wasn't as powerful as he thought he was. I followed my arrow into his brain, but it was dark. When I hit a wall, I realized he'd blocked me.

Chapter Nine

Jackal

I stared at the hole in the roof of the cave. Above, I heard the sound of the remaining dragons roaring as they took off. "That be the most evil, revolting creature I ever had the misfortune to encounter," I said to Slag.

Slag clapped me on the shoulder. "The bigger they are, the harder they fall."

"Happen you be right about that."

As Belle sheathed her sword, I examined her out of the corner of my eye. She was brave, in spite of the tears dripping down her face, and a skilled fighter. I wanted her. I wanted her to be mine. The man who owned Annabelle would possess the finest woman on Earth. And I wanted to be that man. I shrugged off the ridiculous feelings. She'd never look twice at a creature like me. I'd likely get my head chopped off if I told her of my interest.

"Slygon turned my sister into a monster," Belle snarled. "I have to save her. And I will if it's the last thing I do."

"I can see why you'd be wantin' to save her, lass, but how can we do that? He's rumored to live in a place you can only reach by flying, which is why he has those devil black dragons."

Belle's eyes took on a far-away expression as though she were seeing her sister and visualized saving her. She turned and lowered her eyelids shadowing her brilliant violet eyes. "I don't care what it takes. If I have to learn to fly, I will. I'm going to save my sister and kill Slygon. Odafarus said I was the one. At the time, I didn't understand why or even what he was talking about. I get it now. I understand."

"That be a grand idea, lass. And it's a grand dream. But right now, I think we should help the Craggers clean up this mess."

The Craggers were gathering their people, the children, and heading back to their village. Belle grabbed my arm. "Do you know where Slygon lives?"

The intensity of her stare startled me, and I considered putting my arm around her shoulders to offer comfort but thought better of it. Now was not the time. Her hand on my arm burned. Her touch sent heat straight to my nethers. I squirmed. Sometimes being half elf was a trial. I had morals and ethics and restraints on the animal urges of my orc nature. "No," I growled. "I ain't never seen the bastard before. I heard about him a course. Everyone in The Withers has seen the dragons and heard of the demons riding them. All I know is he comes from the west and lives in a place you can only reach by flying. I be assuming it's mountains, cause dragons like mountains. Mayhap it's some valley far to the west locked away from the world."

"Does anyone know?"

Suddenly, a red-haired woman wearing a poufy pink gown popped into the cavern. "I know where he lives," she said.

"What the holy Hell are you?" I asked.

Belle brushed me aside to stand in front of the woman. "Dandy, tell me. He has my sister. Odafarus said I was the one who would kill Slygon. I didn't understand what he meant or why he said it. Now I do."

"What is that thing?" I whispered to Slag behind my hand.

"Fairy," Slag said. "She healed the Magic who was hurt."

"Fairy, eh? Heard we had 'em. Never seen one."

"The evil one lives far from here," Dandy said. "You'd never be able to get there riding horses. That's why he has those dragons."

"How far is a long way?" I asked as I examined this new creature. She had freckles and looked a bit like Flossie with the same red hair and pug nose. "And where did you come from anyway?"

"Dandy comes and goes as she damn well pleases." Granny Hawkins spat tobacco juice on the floor of the cave and cleared her throat. "She's never here when you need her, flits around the world doing whatever the hell she wants."

"I was here when you needed me today," Dandy snapped. "I have a lot of responsibilities. There's very few of us and we have to take care of the children. It's our job. With Slygon running around killing babies, the few of us who came out of the Pit have to work very hard."

"What else came out of the Pit?" Belle asked. "I'm new to this Withers place. Everything out here is new to me."

"Valkyries, elves, fairies, dwarves, leprechauns, devils and angels," Dandy said. "Every creature you ever read about or heard in an old tale came out when the Pit opened up. Vampires, shapeshifters and orcs all walk the earth." She pointed at me. "You should know."

I shrugged and suddenly felt like an ox in a glass shop, too big, and terribly awkward.

"Who or what is Slygon?" Annabelle asked. "I thought he was a vampire and then he turned into a snake."

Granny's forehead wrinkled. "I thought he was a vampire, too. He's always come for the infants. Him and his vampire crew have been here twice before. That's why we have the silver. They know we're prepared, but the lure of the innocent draws them back. They sense when a new baby is born. We should have expected him."

"Dandy," Belle asked. "Do you know?"

Flossie emerged from the passage where the Craggers hid the children. "I know," she said.

Flossie touched my heart in a special way. Maybe it was because I'd saved her. I scooped the little girl up and sat her on my shoulder. "Of course, you do, poppet."

Flossie put one hand on each side of my head and held onto my pointed ears. "No, I really do. He killed my family and carried off my baby brother. I hided in the barn with the horses. I made my thoughts like theirs, so he couldn't even feel me."

"You can do that?" Belle asked. "I never thought of it. You know, I might be able to as well. Animals like me."

Flossie nodded, sending her out-of-control hair flying. "I can do it and animals like me, too. Me and the horses could read Slygon. The horses tolded me he was a shifter and a vampire."

Tiny walked up carrying her crossbow. "That's impossible, Flossie. Either you're one or the other."

Dandy shook her head. "It's not impossible," she said, taking a step closer to Tiny. "Just extremely rare. If a shifter gets made into a vampire, then it retains the shifter ability. And there's another possibility. If an elf gets bitten by a werewolf or a shifter, the elf can fight off the change, unless later it gets turned by a vampire, then it would have both natures. It would take an elf lost to all considerations for its own life to become either thing."

"He can be killed, right?" Annabelle asked. "I have to save my sister and I'm supposed to be the one who kills Slygon. It would be good to know if it's even possible to kill him before I start. Not that it will stop me from going after Noemi one way or the other. Nothing can."

Tiny grabbed her arm. "No, Belle, your sister's a demon now. She's dead. She can't be saved. And that demon, Slygon, snake guy, we don't even know how to kill him. He'll sure as shit get you first."

Annabelle shook Tiny off. "It eats babies, Tiny, and it has my sister. There must be a way."

Tina groaned. "You're right. We can't let him totally destroy your sister. Do you think she can be saved?"

"I don't know, but I'll find out. Saving Noemi and killing Slygon is a mission of a lifetime. I know it's dangerous and we might die, but if we die, we'll die trying to do something worth dying for."

"I knew you'd say something like that," Tina replied, her tired shoulders sagging with resignation.

"Dandy, where does Slygon live?" I asked.

"He lives on the other side of the great mountain range that divides this continent. On a mountainside in a dark and rainy place with fog and wind and very few villages like this one," Dandy said.

"It sounds impossible to get to on foot or on horseback," I said. "I'm sure that's why the demon picked it." I didn't want to chase Slygon to his lair any more than I wanted to fly to the moon, but I might agree to do it just to please Belle. And I had this sinking feeling eventually she was going to ask me.

"Is there a walled city nearby?" Belle asked. "Like New Orleans?"

"Yep," Dandy answered, "and I've been there, Old Seattle."

"Where's that?" Tiny asked.

"North," Dandy said. "Miles and miles from here." Dandy pursed her lips and closed one eye. "Dragons," she said. "We have to find dragons. They can fly us there if we really want to go after Slygon." Dandy tilted her head. "Do we?"

"I have no choice," Belle said. "He's got Noemi. My sister gave up her life to save me. I'll rescue her or die trying." She grabbed Tiny's arm. "You'll go with me, won't you?"

"Of course. You have to save your sister. But where do we get dragons? I've only seen the black ones and they're monsters."

"Finding dragons is easy," Dandy said. "And the black dragons aren't monsters. They're regular dragons captured and enslaved to Slygon's evil purpose. I know where a large pride of dragons nest. The problem is getting them to communicate before they eat you."

Belle threw up her hands. "Well that settles it. We go find the dragons. Dandy knows where they live so it should be easy."

I took her hand and she let me hold it. My fingers were monstrous next to her dainty ones. I squeezed her fingers and stroked her palm as she stared into my eyes. Suddenly, I could hear her thoughts and feel the pain of losing her sister. *Belle, I can hear your thoughts.*

She jumped and snatched her hand away.

Don't matter if we be touching or not. I can still hear you.

Get out of my head.

We're connected in some way. There's no one else I've ever met I can read. Only you. "Do you want to go home to New Orleans?" I asked out loud. "Go back to guarding the walls where it's safe?"

Belle furrowed her brow and rubbed her temples. "Have you been reading my mind all along? Invading and listening to my thoughts without telling me?"

"No, Belle, it just happened for the first time this very moment. I'm as stunned as you."

"How can I trust you're telling the truth?" She grabbed her head. "Truly, this was the first time?"

I nodded and she must have read the horror in my face. She laughed. "Oh, my, God, you couldn't lie if your life depended on it."

"Yup, I be a terrible liar. My face, you know, it gives me away every time." It wasn't the truth. I could lie like anyone, but if Belle thought I couldn't maybe we could get across this heavy patch of ground lightly.

"I never want to go back to New Orleans," she said. "I finally found Noemi. It's up to me to save her, and if the wizard Odafarus was right, I'm the one who kills Slygon. But even if I hadn't found Noemi, I wouldn't go back. I like it out here in The Withers. It's a whole new world."

"Do you want to go back to the city, Tiny?" Belle asked. "You know I can't."

Tiny smiled a wistful little grin like a fond memory drifted across her mind, then she shook her head. "Hell no, I don't want to go back. Let's go save your sister."

I pointed at Slag. "Do you be in on this? Do you think it a good idea?"

Slag laughed. "I think it be a terrible idea, but what the hell else we gotta do? Go back to Wildwhisper? Kill us some more orcs, wander The Withers looking for trouble?" Slag punched my arm which I'm sure left a bruise. "Sneck up, my friend. Gather yourself. This be a mission, a noble mission, a great way to use our miserable lives. Right?"

"Chub," I poked the big man's side. "What be on your mind?"

"Food, I ain't eaten all damn day, half the night is gone and I'm friggin' starving. Since I last ate, we killed us some orcs, forded that damn river and killed us more creepy things than I can name. Food. Feed me."

I burst out laughing. "Let's go find something for this big son of a bitch to eat. Granny, you got anything in your larder to feed him?"

The old lady still held the newborn infant they'd saved from Slygon. The child's mother took the baby and Granny limped toward the exit where Craggy-towners cleaned the passageway. The old lady looked Chub up and down. "I might be able to find half a cow somewhere, cause it's gonna take one to fill that belly."

Belle grabbed my arm. I stopped and looked down at her. She squeezed the muscles of my bicep, swallowed hard, and snatched her hand back as though she'd touched a hot stove. Had she read his thoughts, because they'd been a little warm? *Did you read my thoughts just then?*

Maybe.

He groaned. *Can you do it whenever you want?*

If I try, always.

I grabbed my head. I didn't know what to think then. I was going to have to mind my wandering thoughts. "Well stop it right now."

You asked.

"You haven't decided yet," she said. "Are you going to help me find Slygon, hunt him to his lair, kill him and save Noemi? Yes or no? Because if you aren't in, Tiny and I will do it ourselves."

You know the answer, lass. Wherever you go, I will follow.

Please stop this. It's making me crazy. I feel . . . I feel naked.

Now that's a pleasant thought.

"Ugh! Please tell me, out loud, you're on this mission with me. Just so the rest of this fine group understands."

"Okay," I said with a smile. "Slag, we're going dragon hunting and then we'll be finding us Slygon's lair. You with me?"

Slag shook his head. "You be bewitched."

"That's beside the point," I said. "You in, yea or nay?"

"I'm in," Slag said. "But I only be doing this because the asshole eats babies."

I laughed and started down the passageway after Granny and Belle.

"Seriously," Slag yelled after us. "It's the baby-eating thing. Ye know it be the truth."

Chapter Ten

Belle

I was freaking out. I couldn't find Flossie and it was time to leave. We were packed and ready to head out and no Flossie. Dandy flitted up, pink gown swishing. "What's wrong? We're about ready to get out of here."

"Flossie's missing. I swear she was here a minute ago."

Dandy tripped off, tossing over her shoulder. "I'll check with Jackal. He's packing the horses."

Tiny was helping the men. My job was securing food for the journey from Granny. All this time, I'd thought Flossie was playing with the kids in the town's center. And when I got there, no Flossie.

Damn!

Suddenly terrified, I raced to Granny Hawkins' hut. The old lady was packing a bag. "Are you going somewhere?" I asked.

"I'm coming with you. You're going to need me. Jackal said I could come."

For a moment, I was stunned. I opened my mouth to say so, then closed it without uttering a word. If Jackal said it was okay, who was I to complain? "Have you seen Flossie? I swear that child is never still."

"Last time I saw her, she was headed into the caverns. She said she heard a tiny voice in trouble."

"Oh, no, I wish you'd stopped her. You know we're leaving."

Granny huffed. "I was busy getting me medicines and me potions together. Jackal said I'll be the team's doctor."

I stared at the door leading into the caverns, memories of the passage on the other side, and my sister kneeling in the dirt begging for death washing over me in such a powerful rush, I froze. When it passed, I pointed. "Flossie went in there?"

"She said she'd only be a minute."

"Except that she's a child, so she doesn't know the difference between a minute and an hour."

Granny shrugged in her grumpy old lady way and shoved a bundle of small vials into a huge leather pack. "I was busy, not paying attention. I'll go with you. She can't be far."

We trotted down the passage leading into the cavern where they'd fought Slygon. There were several side passages all leading to rooms and storage but not to the surface. I cast a mental net and found Flossie somewhere down one side passage. We turned into it and were immediately swamped with darkness. No lights this way.

Granny plucked a torch off a sconce on the tunnel wall and I lit it with my thoughts. "That's a right good trick to know," Granny cackled.

"Yes, useful."

The tunnel narrowed. I had to duck and turn sideways to slide through. Granny, being small and short, didn't. "This sucks, but she's just up ahead. I can feel her. She's found something. Flossie!" I yelled into the dark tunnel.

Flossie burst out of the darkness, her nose a miniature light. "I finded something, Belle. I finded Squeaker."

"You can light up your nose?" I said. "What a weird trick." Even I couldn't do that.

Flossie jumped up and down with excitement. She held something small out for me to see. Something an iridescent green. It moved, then it belched fire.

"What the holy hell?" I leaped out of the way.

"It's a little bitty dragon. At least it kinda looks like a dragon, except it's not, not really. It's some kind of mini dragon," Flossie said. "I named it Squeaker because it makes a squeaky noise when it's upset. It was all alone and scared. It fell off one of the big dragons and got lost. The big dragons like them and a flock of them always hangs out with them when they fly only Squeaker got lost from his friends and hided in the tunnels and I could hear him and he's here and can I keep him?" All this was said in one rapid-fire burst.

"I don't know," I said. "We're going to be traveling. Who will look after it?" I turned to Granny, who had come up behind me. "Have you ever seen or heard of one of these things?"

"Nope," Granny said. "But every damn day I see something I ain't ever seen before. We live in some weird ass times."

"Should I let her keep it?" I whispered in Granny's ear.

Granny shrugged. "How could it hurt? It's little and maybe it'll keep Flossie occupied. She's a scamp. Always got her little nose stuck into something she shouldn't."

"Yeah, the little nose that can light up." I patted the top of Flossie's head. "Hurry and get your stuff. We're ready to leave."

Granny hustled along in the rear. "Stay in my hut, little one," she said over my shoulder. "I got just the thing to carry that little feller in."

When we got back to Granny's hut, Flossie waited with me while Granny found a small leather backpack. "Used this for hunting wild herbs and healing roots," she said. "You can put your little pet in it while we're on the road."

I helped Flossie make a bed in the bottom for the tiny dragon and Flossie gently settled it. Then Granny showed her how to slide the straps over her shoulders. "You can put other things in there, too," Granny said. "You know, personal stuff and things you find."

"Are we done?" I asked. "If we don't get our shit together Jackal is going to be mad. It had taken forever to get Flossie and Granny together. But he was the one who'd said Granny could come. Why the old woman wanted to travel with them she could not imagine. Maybe the thirst for adventure never died. Maybe it survived growing old. You never knew.

Jackal had mounts for everyone. The Craggers had been grateful for the help repelling Slygon and reciprocated by sharing their meager possessions. Flossie even had a round little paint pony with a bunch of wild mane, crazy forelock, one blue eye and one brown, and an attitude. The pony snapped at Slag when the big three-quarters orc walked by. Slag chuckled and elbowed the pony in the snout. Granny rode a stout mule. Tiny had her own little brown mare and I was gifted a tall, gray gelding that looked hungry and really old. His ribs showed, and he had a sway back.

"How old is this animal?" I asked Jackal as they all swung aboard.

"I didn't ask. You know what they say about gift horses. Well he was a gift. Besides, there's always the pig. As far as I know, it's still available. We be using him as a pack animal, but he be right there. We can switch you out in a trice."

I climbed aboard the ancient gray and settled myself in a saddle that had to be as old as him. Jackal galloped to the head of their group and looked back. "All we need to complete this group is an elephant and a herd of goats." Then the tiny dragon climbed out of its pack and perched on Flossie's shoulder. "That's so funny." Flossie giggled.

Jackal eyed Squeaker with suspicion.

"It's my pet dragon, Squeaker. Belle said I can keep him. Isn't he cute?"

Jackal opened his mouth to say something when Dandy suddenly popped into view. "The road ahead is clear," she said. "What do I ride?"

I was suddenly filled with hilarity at the situation. We were a traveling circus. Poor Jackal. "I guess you ride the pig. I was told it's available."

Dandy huffed back to the rear and poufed into a tiny fairy. She sat like a queen on top of the baggage. "Let's go," she said, and waved her hand.

Jackal snorted, took one more look at Squeaker, shook his head and urged Thor forward.

Belle spurred her old gray nag to the front of the line and rode next to Jackal. "I know you think this is a fool's errand."

"Well just look at us. Is this ragtag group actually able to fight off orcs, wandering groups of centaurs and gaggers, capture and ride big dragons and then go kill Slygon?"

"Oh, we're not so bad. We have you and your friends, definitely seasoned warriors. Then Tiny and I, who have fought our share of battles. I know Granny is an asset, though one we have to protect, and little Flossie. I think we can manage quite well."

All I got as an answer was a grunt. After we passed the cliffs of Craggy Town, we hit a well-used trail along the river. "I had no idea so many people lived outside the city walls," I said.

"You got no idea bout lots of things," he said.

"Where are we headed now?"

"The fairy says the dragons live in the Smokey Mountains."

"Is that far away?"

"Thought ye went to school and all."

"I did."

"But ye got no idea where the Smokies be?"

"Tennessee? I'm just guessing. Geography of before-times wasn't covered. I learned how to eat with the right fork, how to curtsey and simper. I learned to read and write, and we were given all the books the library had to read. If we wanted to. I didn't want to read. I wanted to fight."

Jackal roared with laughter. "Surely got your wish there."

"So, where are we headed today? I probably phrased my question incorrectly."

"Today, we be riding upstream. If we be lucky, happen we'll get to the ferry north of Old Memphis in ten days. Need a ferry to get this bunch across the river. Ain't no swimming gonna happen. The ferry will get us to the other side where we can head to the Smokies. It's a long trip, Annabelle. Long and dangerous. I got Slag riding rear guard. Can't stop worrying or watching. There's bands of greenies and gaggers roaming these lands and they'll kill us all just so they can eat the horses."

"That's gross. And truthfully, the one I'm riding is so old and stringy you'd have to boil him for days."

"Like I said, there's the hog."

Chapter Eleven

Belle

It actually took twelve days to get to Old Memphis. The river was high, and we lost time going around flooded areas. It started to rain on day three and didn't stop. I had never been this drenched and miserable in my life. It wasn't cold. It was hot and steamy wet, and then there were the bugs. Hordes of biting flies that drove the horses insane during the day and as evening approached clouds of mosquitoes descended on us like a plague.

"Having fun yet?" Jackal asked. I grunted. His thick skin protected him from the flies and the mosquitoes. Tiny, Flossie, and I wrapped ourselves in layers of cloth. The only thing we didn't cover was our eyes. Bugs didn't bother Granny Hawkins. Apparently, she had some kind of spell she used to protect herself, or an herb, or it was possible she was too ornery. Her blood probably tasted bad.

Flossie's little dragon sat on her shoulder and scarfed the flies up during the day. Every time Squeaker swallowed a fly, Flossie would shout, "He got another one."

Night times were the worst. We erected tents, but the ground was so damp and muddy finding a dry spot was a Herculean task. Last night, Jackal located a cliff with dry ground under it, so we'd been mercifully dry all night. I slept like I died. It almost made me long for the city, but my heart and my mind were set on one goal, saving Noemi. Every day, I worried about Noemi. I wondered what she was doing and if she ever thought about me. The link between two sisters is strong. Surely Noemi felt it. I could never forget what I owed her and how much I loved her.

On the ninth day of this hellish journey, we climbed a ridge and Jackal halted us. Below was the river and on the other side the before-times city of Memphis, a crumbled ruin of twisted steel, crushed concrete, abandoned cars and trucks. The concrete pilings of two bridges along with the twisted metal of the bridge's arches jutted from the wide river. This far north, the impact of erupting volcanos and explosions killed millions and destroyed cities with powerful earthquakes--registering above eight on the Richter scale. Huge sink holes bloomed out of nowhere and swallowed entire cities.

"Where'd all the people go?" I asked Jackal.

"I wasn't born then, so I'm not rightly sure. Most died, some went to live in the walled cities where the destruction was less, some wandered, lost, and were killed and eaten by the creatures from the Pit. The vampires, orcs and demons that emerged were starving. They thought this land was heaven. The humans who stayed and survived established the little villages and learned how to make do."

"Are we getting close to the ferry?"

"There's something you need to know about New Memphis," Jackal said. "It ain't like Craggy Town. Not at all."

"I don't understand. How's it different?"

Tina urged her mare closer so she could hear. "What're you guys talking about?"

"Jackal says New Memphis is weird, or different."

Jackal took a deep breath. "This is how it has to be. We make camp about three miles before we get there. I know just the place. It's even dry. Then me, Slag and Chub will go into town and hunt for someone to ferry us across the river. We need to cross soon and start heading east."

"Why can't we go?" Tiny demanded. "I don't wanna wait anywhere. I don't care what the town's like as long as it's dry. If you guys leave us, we'll be without your protection. We could be killed. Just two days ago, Slag scouted a band of orcs. If not for the pouring rain, the orcs might have spotted us. We all saw the black dragons fly over at dusk and two days ago, I smelled gaggers."

"Tiny's right. It's not safe for us to be alone," I said. "We have Flossie and Granny Hawkins to care for."

A pink flutter on her shoulder alerted me to Dandy's arrival. The fairy's voice was a peep when she was small. "He doesn't want you to go into this town because it makes its money off the base desires of men," Dandy chirped.

"What?" Tiny demanded. "I missed that."

I leaned close to Tiny. "Dandy says it's a whore town. I guess Jackal's too embarrassed to tell us the truth."

Tiny's eyes flew open. "A whore town? Out here in The Withers?"

"Really, Jackal?" I said. "A whore town? How can that even exist out here?"

"New Memphis is a lot more than just a, uh, a bawdy town," he said, as his face turned the color of ripe plums. He was blushing. He closed his eyes.

"Why are you so embarrassed?"

"I, uh, I'm not embarrassed at all. I just thought you and Tiny were, you know, uh, innocent and all and, I, uh, didn't want to sully your virgin ears. There be a lot of bars, taverns where loose women be available. Every river rat, traveler, greenie and digger coming up and down the river knows this place. It has the ferry and it has entertainment of a sort. Truthfully, Belle, it's not the kind of place ye should go to. Yer too beautiful and the men down there be rough. And then there's Flossie to be considered. It just ain't safe."

"Really? Are you questioning my ability to take care of myself and Flossie?"

He groaned. "Not in most circumstances. This be different and I be needing to conduct business, so I won't have the time to give protecting you and the child my full attention."

I snorted and then felt a thought tendril poking into my mind. It was Jackal. He was trying to push me mentally, force me to do as he wished. I threw up a wall, grinned, and pointed at him. "Got you. Does this town have an inn?"

Slag rode up. "What's the problem? We stopping already?"

Jackal sighed. "I was trying to explain to Belle about New Memphis. It ain't a place for girls or women."

Slag guffawed. "That be an understatement."

"I'm not sitting under some rock while you three go into town, get drunk and have a good time," I said. "We're going. I can take care of myself and Flossie, and Tiny can take care of herself. We'll all watch out for Granny."

"We wouldn't never get drunk while you were waiting for us," Jackal said. "Well I wouldn't. Slag might, but I be on a straight and narrow path. In a way, I be spoken for." Jackal said with his hand over his heart. "I be swearing on, on . . ."

"Your mother's life?" Slag burst out laughing again.

I looked at him and then at Slag. "What? Who's his mother?"

"No less than Queen Ashera of the Greenwood Elves," Slag said.

I turned around in my saddle to look at Slag. "Jackal's a prince?"

"Not likely," Jackal snarled. "Me ma, the queen, threw me away when I was born. Gave me to a wet nurse to raise. Slag and I were raised by the same woman. Chub came later and after him we all went hungry."

Slag and Jackal both laughed at that one, but my heart was wrung. The three shared a strange bond.

"Would you like me better if I was a prince?" Jackal asked me as we rode on.

"I, uh, I like you well enough now. Why would I want to like you better?"

"I don't know, maybe because I be liking you a lot."

I was stunned. I'd felt his interest and thought little of it. Apparently, Jackal's interest had not dissipated, but grown. It forced me to think. He was half orc, but over the days I'd spent with him, his face had started to appeal to me. He was very masculine. His jaw was strong and square. His eyes a crazy golden color with green in them. His body was beautiful. Thick bands of muscles. Not an ounce of fat anywhere, broad shoulders, long legs and flat abdominal muscles with a narrow waist and slender hips. It was a body to be proud of. He was brave and warm-hearted and a true warrior. When

Slag galloped up on his big mare, I was spared the need to reply which was a huge blessing because I had no idea what to say.

"We need to get moving," Slag said. "It's almost dusk and we have to make camp."

Jackal shot his friend a look of intense gratitude and my face flamed. Slag lifted one eyebrow. "What?"

Jackal shook his head. "Nothing, just glad to see you."

"You're full of shit," Slag snorted.

"That's a fact," Jackal mumbled. "I be stupid, full of shit, and a clumsy oaf."

"I ain't gonna disagree with that," Slag said.

"You never answered my question," I said as if none of that had happened. "Are there inns in New Memphis?"

"Of a sort," Slag guffawed. "But like you been told, they cater to men looking for female company, not gently bred city women and children."

"But there are rooms to rent?" I insisted.

Jackal sighed. "If you want to risk staying the night in a flea-sack inn rather than camping outside of town, I'm willing to make a go at it," he said. "But we gotta get moving. Dark is a bad thing out here. Ye be knowing that. And around towns like this dark brings out the vampires. They prey on the drunks and loose women."

"Do you think there will be baths?" I leaned over and whispered to Tiny, "I'd kill for a hot bath. I have bug bites and sand in unmentionable places. Hot water would feel so good."

Granny trotted up on the fat mule. "Did someone mention a bath?"

"Jackal says this town serves mostly disgusting men looking for loose women," I told her. "I'm hoping they bathe. There are inns, taverns and eateries. We might even get hot food."

"I heard of this place. You'll never find a more wretched hive of scum and villainy, but you're right. There are inns and we have Jackal and Slag, so mayhap we won't be killed in our sleep. New Memphis produces their power from methane. They have the transient population to feed and the residents, so they maintain a large herd of cattle and hogs and use the manure to make the methane, so they have lights and hot water. Annabelle, you need to cover your hair and your face. Tiny as well. There are slavers in New Memphis, and they'll kidnap you for sure if they see you." She looked at Flossie on her pony. "And no one can see the child."

"She's only eight."

"There's some who say eight is too late," Granny muttered. "No one sees the little girl."

"Flossie," I called to the girl. "Come sit in front of me."

The child obeyed for once. "There's a lot of bad men up ahead," Flossie whispered as she climbed onto the gray. "I feels them in my head."

Tiny took the reins of the pony when I pulled Flossie off of it and onto the front of my saddle. For the hundredth time, I wondered who Flossie really was. The little girl had no idea that other people didn't possess her Gifts.

I unwound the long scarf I wore to keep bugs off my hair and face and covered myself and Flossie with it as we descended a hill into the town. A before-times sign hung canted sideways off two tall poles. It announced the town to have once been called Jericho.

The main street consisted of a swamp of mud and animal waste. Every step the old gelding took sucked up stench-filled bubbles. The buildings were wooden structures, some with false fronts to make them appealing. The town had power. Red lights were lit on the fronts of several of the wooden structures. A few before-times buildings had survived. There were some squat brick homes on the side streets as well as scattered wooden houses.

Walkways lined the street and rough men leaned against the buildings smoking pipes and holding mugs. No women were visible. Horses, mules and riding hogs were tied to a rail edging the walkway. I spotted a stable with an enormous yard filled with wagons and drays all loaded with barrels, crates and burlap sacks of goods they'd just brought over the river. The draft animals were kept in a set of long stalls around the yard baited with heaps of hay.

I stared in wonder. I never imagined this kind of place existed. It was different from New Orleans. As though the two places existed in different worlds. There were still no signs of any women. Jackal led them past the stable, past a stockyard filled with lowing cattle also munching mounds of hay. The sun was gone and around the town, which was lighted, a deep, thick dark settled.

When we passed the stockyard there were more buildings. Jackal stopped in front of one with a sign out front featuring a picture of what looked like a giant weasel. The Twelve Ferrets Tavern was etched into the wood above the animal, the letters painted red. Jackal swung off his horse and tied it to the hitching rail, next to Slag and Chub's mounts. Granny Hawkins practically fell off her mule.

"You better stay little," I whispered to Dandy as she fluttered near. "If we need your help you'll be there, and no one the wiser."

There were plenty of other horses tied outside the tavern. I climbed off my tall gray and armed myself. Tiny jumped off her mare and helped Flossie down, giving a little tug to the child's scarf to make sure her face was covered.

"Follow me," Jackal said. "This be the dumbest thing I ever done in me life. If we all don't die so you can see this place, it'll be a miracle."

"Why this tavern?" I asked.

"It's one of the ferry-man's favorite watering holes. He's half-orc half-digger, squat and wide as that hog of ours. They use digger barmaids in here to keep the trouble to a minimum and he likes them."

I pointed to three very expensive horses tied at the end of the rail. The horses were highly bred, the saddles chased with silver, the bridles finely woven silk with silver bits. The bags behind the saddle were leather etched with strange runes. "Who could own those?"

Jackal stared. A massive dog lay on the board walkway guarding the horses and their valuable gear. It lifted its huge head and growled. The dog was tall and covered with thick hair. "Wolfhound," Jackal said, glancing around with caution. "Elves own those mounts."

Chapter Twelve

Belle

Thick smoke and foul smells assaulted us as we entered the tavern. Me, Tiny and Flossie were swaddled from head to toe in scarves and shawls. I'd never imagined a place like this. It ran deep with shadowed corners. A host of men, diggers, half-orcs and scantily-dressed women leaned against a long wooden bar on the left.

I grabbed Tiny's arm and yanked her out of the way just in time to avoid an enraged pair of gaggers, cursing and punching each other. Blood, the color and smell of rotted seaweed, flowed down one's face. It was no wonder they were called gaggers. Jackal pushed the fighters toward the exit and growled.

Tiny gasped and covered her nose and mouth with her hand. Chub roared with amusement and Jackal pounded Chub on the back. "This be my kind of place," Chub said.

"Well, it may be," Jackal said. "But we got women folk with us so keep your wits about ye."

Slag was last into the tavern. Ever on the ball, he latched onto the filthy leather armor of the gaggers, hoisted one in each hand and heaved them out the door where they collided with a greenie. Their flight freed a table in the packed pub.

Tiny and I scrambled to claim the now-empty table while Jackal scavenged a crude chair and held if for me. His eyes were warm on me and I felt his affection. Though more beast than man, his heart was kind. As I looked around, I realized we might have been safer staying outside of town. As usual, Jackal was right.

"Flossie," I whispered. "Go sit next to Chub."

The little girl crawled under the table and climbed onto the bench next to the huge half-orc.

Slag joined them, pushed Flossie closer to Chub on the rough bench, and sat down. "You be taking up the space of three men," Slag complained, then pounded on the pitted wood table for attention.

A busty digger maid dragged a filthy wet rag across the top, snatched up the overturned mugs from the previous occupants, and rubbed her abundant charms all over Jackal's thigh, which was exactly how high her charms reached. My face burned with . . . what? And then I blushed even harder. I was jealous of Jackal. Somewhere inside, sometime during the last few days, I'd come to think of him as mine. And the sight of the barmaid rubbing herself all over him made me mad as fire.

The digger barmaid batted thick red lashes over her blue eyes and sighed. "What'll it be, big boy?" Her voice was soft and feminine, completely out of place on the dwarf. She couldn't have been more than four-feet tall.

"Bring a jug and mugs all 'round, lass," Jackal said. "A platter full of them venison sandwiches and, a, and a cup a milk." He seemed to suddenly realize Tiny and I were staring at him. He saw the flames shooting out of my eyes and lifted an eyebrow. I had no idea what to say. All of these emotions were weird, foreign and uncomfortable.

He quickly averted his gaze from the maid's partially exposed breasts. Slag guffawed, grabbed the barmaid around her thick waist and yanked a red braid. His hand was about to squeeze one of the dwarf's bouncing bosoms when Jackal punched him in the arm. "We got ladies here," Jackal growled.

Slag's hand dropped but he didn't let go. "Had to ruin my fun, didn't you?"

The barmaid smacked Slag's shoulder. "Watch your hands, big boy." But she said it with a lingering smile as she whirled on her short legs and stumped toward the bar to fill their order.

"This table stinks," I whispered to Tiny. My mind was still trying to deal with the discovery I cared about Jackal. This was terrible. How could it have happened? What about him claimed my attention?

"Don't turn around to look at them," Tiny hissed into my ear. "But there's elves in the back corner."

I shrugged off the quiver of bolts on my back. When it hit the floor, I turned to straighten it and saw them. Where the shadows grew heavier, three elves laughed and joked, playing cards at a small table. There were other tables in the shadows with greenies, gaggers and diggers all playing at dice or cards. In the furthest corner a stage sat empty. The ceilings were low, casting everything in the rear of the tavern in deep shadows. Who knew what was going on back there?

"We shouldn't have brought Flossie in here," I said. "We shouldn't be here either. This is something out of my worst nightmare."

"I tried to tell you," Granny said. She sat on the far side of the table examining the room with disdain. "We'll be lucky to get out of here with our lives."

"We couldn't very well leave her outside," Tiny said. "And she's as hungry as we are." Flossie smiled brightly from her spot squeezed between Chub and Slag on the bench. "No one can see her there, and seriously, could she be in a safer place than between those two?"

Dandy suddenly popped in. Her appearance was startling to say the least. "I haven't been to the Twelve Ferrets for at least a year," Dandy said in her tiny voice. "A filthier bug-infested tavern does not exist. It actually serves gaggers. I mean, surely you could have chosen a cleaner place. Why'd you pick it?"

"We wanted a jug of ale and a bite to eat," Chub said. "They serve a right tasty venison sandwich."

"I'm looking for someone," Jackal said. "Someone who hangs in this tavern. He's half digger. We need his ferry to get across the river and we don't need nobody blabbing about our presence."

The elves were arguing about something. I examined them by leaning close to Jackal and glancing toward the rear of the tavern. They seemed awfully clean for a place like this. Upright, brightly-colored clothes, and handsome as all elves were. They must own the three horses guarded by the hound. A sudden flicker over an elf's shoulder caught my attention. A minute, bird-like creature flitted from the head of first one and then another elf, a silver object glinting in its hands. Must be a fairy. "Dandy, is that another fairy in the back?"

Dandy flew higher and fluttered. Chub and Slag noticed, and they looked. I sighed. Great, now we were all staring at the table full of elves.

"It's a harpy," Dandy said. "Nasty, thieving, lying little creatures." Dandy shivered.

"I believe it stole something," I said.

"Heads up," Slag snorted. "Think we be in for a scrap."

"Cheater's got a pocket bitch," a half-orc giant at a nearby table shouted. The greenie swatted the harpy, whose tinkling laughter rang out as she easily dodged the huge hand. Another greenie took a swipe at the harpy, this time connecting. The tiny creature screeched, landed on the floor, then shook herself.

All the gamblers were on their feet. Chaos reigned in the back of the tavern. The greenie keeper surged from behind the bar with a club, which only added to the confusion. Jackal swore and pushed himself upright using the table. "Get ready to get out of here," he snarled.

"But our food," Chub said. "We ain't got it yet."

"We have women folk with us, you silly clunch, and a wee one. We'll find another tavern. I don't see Oakhelm here anyhoo. He'd be in the back with the gamblers."

Fascinated, I watched the harpy flap her wings in a whirlwind of fury, and dart for the greenie. She used the claws on her back feet to gouge at his eyes, but his ham-sized fists kept her at bay. He saved his eyes but got a fearful scratching. Green blood ran down his face.

The elves jumped up and overturned their table sending piles of coins and shiny objects flying just as the digger barmaid, ignoring the scuffle in the rear, appeared at their table with a huge tray. She slapped the jug, five empty mugs and the cup of milk for Flossie on the table. The platter of venison sandwiches followed.

The ruckus in the back finally drew the attention of the bouncers who'd been dicing behind the bar. Three hulking greenies threw zapper nets over the elves. The charged metallic nets sparked with magic. I felt it. The nets rendered the elves unconscious and prevented them from using their own magic to subdue their opponents.

The bouncers tossed the elves over their shoulders and shrugged their way through the crowd toward the door.

Chub grabbed a sandwich. "Better eat this while I got the chance," he said as he chomped off half the sandwich in one bite.

Dandy was still watching the back of the tavern, so I cut a sandwich in half, truly one was more than a meal for two, and handed it to Flossie. "Eat, child, before we have to run out of here to avoid being killed."

Lights suddenly blazed above the stage in the darkest corner, illuminating a tall blond female.

"Entertainment," Slag announced with enthusiasm.

Jackal punched him in the shoulder. "Don't talk with yer mouth full."

The singer crooned a Celtic ballad, about lost love, in a sweet voice. She was accompanied by a goat-like centaur on a flute, a male digger on a guitar and a buxom greenie playing a fiddle she rested on her huge breasts. The crowd didn't like her music choice and called for something livelier. She finished her ballad and rolled into a drinking song. "Lift your glass high and drink to the sky. We'll drink till we got no more feeling. Then stamp on the tables as long as we're able and take off our pants to get beat with a ladle."

Half the bar lifted their mugs and sang along with enthusiasm.

The crowd's happiness was contagious. I took a swig from my mug and coughed.

Jackal guffawed and pounded me on the back and said, "You okay?"

"No, damn you, what is that swill?"

"Yah, it be swill. Why you ask if you know?" Chub slapped his knee and sang along with the song, reached for another sandwich and ate it.

The mood in the tavern mellowed long enough for them to consume another platter of sandwiches and another pitcher of ale. When they were finished, Jackal rose. "You still want to stay in an inn here or leave town and make camp?" he asked me.

"Is the inn close, because Flossie is asleep against Chub and I'm exhausted."

Jackal sighed. "I knew you'd say that. It's two doors down."

We paid the digger barmaid who simpered her thanks when Jackal added another piece of silver. He'd received the coins at Craggy Town in exchange for the weapons he'd traded. Jackal held out another piece. "We were never here," he said.

The barmaid nodded. "Never seen any of ye."

Jackal dropped the silver into her hand. "Let's get out of here."

We left the tavern and ran slap into the three waiting elves. "You're the halfling known as Jackal," the tallest one with long, curling brown hair and watchful green eyes said to Jackal.

"Yeah," Jackal snarled. "That be me. So what?"

"We have a message for you. A message from your mother."

Chapter Thirteen

Jackal

The elf handed a rolled piece of parchment tied with a green ribbon to me. I had no desire to read anything from Ashera ever, but I took the scroll. "You delivered yer message now take yerselves off."

The elf bowed. "My Prince, I must await a reply. My name is Torros Glynfire. I am your cousin." He indicated the other two. "That is Ivansar Ravenwing and Gormar Fairfeather. We have strict orders to deliver the scroll from our queen and wait for your response."

I sucked in a deep breath. What in all the hells could my god-cursed mother want? She'd never sent me a message before, and I could have happily passed my entire lifetime without one.

"Me and my friends are gonna stroll down to the Fat Dragon Inn and get us a room. I'll read this impressive scroll when I be damn sure ready, not a moment before. So, if yer queen ordered you to wait, better get to waitin'."

Torros bowed lower this time and backed away. He and his friends untied their mounts, leaped into the saddle, and galloped out of town to the north, followed by the lanky wolfhound. I just stood there for a minute and stared after them as the scroll burned a hole in my hand. Damn Ashera. She'd never written to me before. I was positive the scroll would have some kind of message in it I never wanted to hear. And what was with the elves' low bows and servile attitude? Elves regarded humans as little more than animals and orcs and half-orcs were considered abominations. I was worse than a nobody. I was filth under every elf's boots.

"What's in the scroll?" Belle asked.

"Got no idea. She's never even visited me or spoken to me afore."

She nudged me. "Open it and read it."

I tucked the hateful thing into a pocket in my armor. "When I be good and ready like I told them three. You want a room we better get one afore they're taken. The only clean place in this town is always busy."

On the other side of the street, the Fat Dragon Inn's windows glowed with bright light. It filled one entire two-story building spreading to encompass the whole corner to the next filthy alley. We carefully crossed the muddy road, leading our mounts to the mews in the back where we handed them to the hostlers. "See you take good care of these animals," I told the kid who took Thor's bridle in one hand and gentled the big horse. I liked the way he handled Thor. I held up a silver piece.

The head hostler was a greenie who pushed the kid aside and tried to grab the silver. I shoved him away. "In the morning. After I seen how well ye took care of our animals."

I headed for the inn. My shoulders felt weighted down, my feet leaden as I lifted them one after the other through the sucking mud. The scroll burned my chest like a hot coal. What could the bitch possibly want? A dull ache formed across my forehead, thudding behind my eyes. Gods, caring for this crew was exhausting.

We entered the inn through the back door. The keeper, a digger, sat on a high stool studying his accounts in a well-worn book. He looked up and I saw the digger was really a cross between a digger and a brownie. He was thinner than a dwarf, more human-shaped, but small with pointed ears and brown skin. His blobby nose held a pair of tiny spectacles. He peered over the top at them, his slanted eyebrows raised.

"We needs, uh," I counted in my pain-dulled head. "Three rooms and a hot bath brought to one."

The innkeeper rang a silver bell and a huge female greenie dressed in a voluminous skirt and blouse covered with a starched white apron appeared. She wore a fluffy cap over her round head to cover her lack of hair. She curtsied to the keeper who reached behind him and grabbed three keys off hooks on the wall. "Sally, take this group to rooms eight, nine and eleven," he said to her. Then he turned to me with his little brown hand held out. "I expect payment up front."

I pulled the leather purse out of the pouch at my waist. It was getting light. Traveling with this mob was expensive. "How much?"

"What you paying with?"

"Silver."

"Eight pieces should cover it."

I groaned. "I was thinking more like three."

The brownie grinned. "Six."

"Make it five and I'll throw in a knife made by the smithies at Wildwhisper. And that should cover feed for our mounts, the bath and breakfast." I produced a small throwing knife from my pocket. It was well-balanced and sharp, the hilt bone. Then I dropped the five pieces into the brownie's hand. The creature grinned, showing sharp little teeth, and the silver disappeared. He took the knife and turned it over and over in his hand. "Nice piece. I'll take it. Check out is noon and the power will go off at midnight and stay off until six in the morning."

I stomped up the steps to the rooms. They were under the eaves, the ceiling low. Belle stood in the hallway as the half-orc, Sally, dragged a tub into her room. Tiny was already inside. Granny and Flossie had the other room.

"We have to share the bath," Belle said. "But I do not care at this point, so long as it's hot."

The maid bobbed another curtsey to me and took off down the stairs. In a second, she and a tall skinny human boy returned carrying huge cans of steaming water.

Belle grabbed my arm, and I stiffened to keep from grabbing her and kissing her silly. I wanted to protect her, to keep her near me, to hold her and love her. I'd never felt like this about anyone before. When I sent a mental probe into her head, I hit the wall. She smiled and lifted a finger. "You shouldn't pry."

"I wouldn't, but you're the only person I've ever been able to read. It's too tempting to resist, especially when you want to know how someone feels about you."

Belle lowered her thick black lashes to cover her eyes. Now I couldn't even read them. "Stay out of my head, Jackal. If you want to know how I feel about you, ask, don't snoop."

"But I be terrified of a set down."

"Terrified? I doubt that."

"You have no idea how scary you can be and right judgmental. Why just the other day I asked how you were feeling, and you snapped my nose off."

She laughed then. "Now you're being ridiculous. You better tell me what's in that message." She stared me straight in the eye.

"I'll think on it after I read it," I said. "Might be nothing. Probably is just some stupid elf proclamation. They be right good at proclaiming shit like they're special, which they ain't."

"Does she write you often?"

"First time."

"Then it has to be important."

"Happen I don't want to hear from her. She's got no claim on me. Threw me out when I was a day old. I'll read her damn letter when I be good and ready."

"But she's your mother, Jackal. She has to love you. Maybe it wasn't politically correct to show her feelings for a half-orc like you. You shouldn't judge her so harshly. I'd give anything to find my mother and be able to see her one more time."

Her insistent admonitions hit too close to my heart. I wanted Ashera to love me. I'd always dreamed she loved me. When I was little, I used to pretend she was coming to visit. I'd make up scenarios about what happened when she came. She would bend over, hug me close. I even imagined what she would smell like. She'd smell like roses and sweet lilacs. I knew it was never going to happen, but children dream silly things and they hope because children believe good things do happen. It's only when you grow up, you realize how terrible the world is and how full of evil and hate.

"You know nothing of what or who my mother is so butt out."

We parted in the hallway outside the door to my room. I went into the room I shared with Slag and Chub and found them already asleep on two of the beds. A third bed stood against the wall so far under the eaves I had to crawl into it. I hadn't slept in a real bed in ages. The ceiling was inches above my nose. After tossing and turning for a long time, I grabbed the blankets, made a bed on the floor across the door, and fell asleep with my katana in my hand.

A noise woke me in the middle of the night. Or maybe it wasn't a noise, just an odd premonition. Something bad was about to happen. I sent a thought to Belle to wake her up then leapt to my feet and snatched open the door as Flossie started screaming. Two greenies and a three-quarters like Slag had Granny's door open. They were after Flossie.

I ran into the hallway, katana raised. A sudden keening arose from the room and a greenie flew out with his hair on fire. The tiny dragon followed, breathing flames at the remaining two thieves.

Grannie appeared in the doorway holding a wand. The tip was lit with a small golden orb. The orb glowed brighter and brighter as the three thieves backed down the hall. The tiny dragon swooped low and spat flames at the greenies, setting the biggest one's eyebrows on fire. It screamed and smacked itself repeatedly in the face with a massive green paw. Granny mumbled something, waved the wand and the three thieves turned into hogs. Squealing and snorting, they ran down the steps. A crash below must be the front door going down under the galloping swine.

Belle's door flew open and there she was in her shift. My jaw dropped. Her form was beautiful in leather pants and armor. Revealed by a candle held in her hand, I could see much of what her daytime clothing hid, and it took my breath away.

"What's going on?" she demanded and then focused on me. "You woke me up. You sent me a warning."

I couldn't speak. My tongue felt like it was twice its normal size. When Belle turned toward me her nipples poked the front of her shift out in two points.

Granny cackled. "Them thieves thought they'd take Flossie. We showed them bastards what for, I tell you. Squeaker set one on fire and I took care of the rest." She held up her wand.

Tiny stuck her head around Belle. "Is Flossie okay?"

"I'm fine, Tiny. Squeaker saved me." Squeaker spotted Flossie and made his signature squeaking sound. He flew to her shoulder and rubbed his head against her cheek. I heard purring.

Belle suddenly seemed aware of me staring at her with my mouth hanging open. Slag pushed me aside to see what was going on. "Holy mother of God, Belle. My, you've got a fine pair of . . ."

Belle gasped and backed into the room. I turned on Slag. "Had to say something didn't ye?"

Slag chuckled. "Owed you one, think on. Remember the bar maid?"

Chub pushed Slag into the hall. "What'd I miss?"

"Just the angelic sight of Annabelle's gorgeous . . ."

I grabbed Slag by his armor. "Don't talk about her or them. Ever."

"Oh, so that's the way of it?" Slag asked.

"The way of what?" Chub demanded. "Damn, I always sleep through the good stuff."

"Go back to bed, all of ye. The show be over."

Granny cackled and pushed Flossie into the room.

Chapter Fourteen

Jackal

I went back into my room and closed the door. My armor sat on the floor beside the pallet. I flopped onto the pile of blankets and pulled the scroll out of my pocket. I was going to have to read it.

I stared at the elegant parchment, the green-silk ribbon and wanted nothing more than to throw it in the fire right now. I no more wished to read it than I did to walk barefoot over hot coals. My gut told me it wasn't something that would make me happy. I untied the green ribbon and let the scroll unroll. The writing on it was beautiful, the penmanship elegant. As flowery and ornate as the script was I had a hard time reading it, but as I continued to stare at it the words suddenly became crystal clear.

"Dear son, Erindriel, you may wonder why I am writing after all these years."

"Yeah, good guess," I muttered. So, she had given me a name, given me a place in the land of the elves where your name was everything. My name was Erindriel, and now I was a dear son. "Fuck me," I swore and read on.

"As I'm sure you know, your half-brother Fulven was my heir and Crown Prince. Fulven was younger than you and not, I'm afraid, very wise. He and his friends attacked a roving band of orcs and it is with a sad heart I must tell you, Fulven was killed. I will make this missive brief, so it can be delivered with all speed. You are not an easy man to find so I'm sending my best men to deliver this summons, for summons is what this is. Return to Greenwood immediately upon receipt of this scroll so you may take up your rightful position as Crown Prince of the Greenwood Elves. You are needed by your true people." It was signed Ashera, Queen of the Greenwood Elves.

So, my brother, a man I'd never met, was dead. Did she expect me to feel anything other than a brief flash of anger that I'd never been allowed to know him, to actually have a brother? I crumpled the offensive scroll in my fist and growled. Who did Ashera think she was? Ordering me home like I was lost on purpose? As though I'd deliberately neglected my duty. As though I wasn't a grown man with a life. I actually did feel sad to hear my brother died, but I was angrier at my mother's arrogance than grief-stricken at my unknown sibling's passing.

I threw the wadded scroll against the wall and fell back on the pallet. Sleep would not come and by morning I was grumpy and tired. Slag and Chub, who had enjoyed a long sleep in a comfortable bed, woke up early, still talking about the interruption last night.

I ignored their cheerful faces and went to see the innkeeper, drank a scalding hot cup of some kind of tea, and ordered bacon sandwiches for all of us.

Belle and Tiny exited their room into the hallway as I hefted my pack, my armor and backed out of the room. Granny Hawkins opened the door and Flossie flew out.

"Anyone seen Dandy?" Annabelle asked.

"Fairies flit in and out whenever they feel like it," Granny grumped.

Belle hugged Flossie. "Did you sleep well, poppet?" she asked.

"Yes. Squeaker looks after me. I can sleep and not worry about anything."

Granny grumped again. "Damn dragon cleans itself all night long. Slurping away at its scales and squeaking like twelve mice."

Belle grabbed my arm. I immediately felt the odd connection between us and remembered her in her shift. The memory gave me a rush of desire so powerful, I had to think of awful things to avoid serious embarrassment. I looked at her face and saw she was blissfully ignorant of my condition and sighed with relief. Then I wondered if she also felt our mental connection. When I looked into her eyes, she covered them with her heavy fringe of lashes. She did know. Goosebumps rippled up both my bare arms.

"Did you read your letter?"

"Yeah."

"Well, what'd it say?"

"Don't wanna talk about it."

"Come on, Jackal, tell us what was in your letter?" Slag laughed and punched me in the back. I was on his way down the narrow stairs and almost fell. "We won't let up, ye know. Tell us."

All of us filed into the inn's taproom which was also the breakfast room. A bar was in the corner and the smell of spilled ale filled the room along with the heady aroma of cooked bacon. I pointed to the sandwiches sitting on a table. "Eat, we need to find Oakhelm directly, and get across the river."

"Won't he be at the ferry landing?" Chub asked around a huge mouthful.

"Christ, Chub, how many times I gotta tell you not to talk with a full mouth. Look!" I pointed at crumbs sprayed across the table.

Chub smiled around the food. "Sorry," he mumbled.

"Come on, Jackal, what'd the bitch say?"

Slag wouldn't let it go. I took a deep breath and let it out slowly. Slag would never give up. "She ordered me home," I mumbled.

"What?" Slag leaned across the table. "You're joking? She dumped you with Mam just like I was dumped. She's got no love for ye, what be her reason?"

I couldn't understand why I wanted to keep this to myself. But I did. I didn't want anyone feeling sorry for me or poking their noses into my business. Maybe I felt if my friends knew they wouldn't like me anymore. Maybe they would think I had risen above them when that couldn't be further from the truth. And I had no intention of obeying the summons from a mother who had never once been my mother. "She said Fulven, you know, me half-brother, be dead."

Slag gasped. "You be Crown Prince. No wonder she wants you at home."

"Well she can tell me to come home all she wants, but she ain't getting me cuz her home ain't mine, that's fer sure," I said. "I owe her nothing. She tried to tell me my people need me. My people? You and Chub be my people."

"Us, too," Flossie piped up. "I'm your people, right?"

Squeaker bent down and torched a loose piece of bacon. Flossie laughed and handed the smoking chunk to him. The little dragon tossed it into the air and caught it on the way down.

"Yes, darlin' ye be my people."

"You're a prince?" Tiny asked. "An elf prince?"

"Don't wanna talk about it."

"Are you going to write her?" Belle asked. "You should send her a reply."

Just as she said that, the three elves walked into the taproom. Torros, my self-proclaimed cousin, led. The three elves were immaculate. They made me feel grubby, huge, awkward and ugly. How could I claim to be their prince? It was a stupid idea. Torros, a full-blood elf, was more suited and as the son of Ashera's sister, he should be prince.

Torros sat on the bench at the end of the long wooden table. "Do you have a reply for your mother?"

"Would you like a sandwich?" Slag shoved the full platter in Torros's direction.

Torros pushed it away. "Elves rarely eat meat and never swine."

"No kidding?" I said even though I knew that. I was just playing for time. "Well, I don't think the innkeeper has much more to offer for breakfast."

"We already ate," Torros said. "Do you have a reply?"

"Aye tell me mother to shove it. I ain't going back to Greenwood today, tomorrow or ever. You should be prince, not me."

Torros gasped. "I can't tell her that. She'll have me hung."

"Well that'd be right stupid, think on," I said. "Take her the message or don't. I ain't interested in being crown prince of anything."

"She'll think I never found you and I'm lying." Torros's mouth hung open, his eyes wide with horror. "Do you think you could write your message down?"

I swung my leg over the wooden bench and stood up. "Time for us to be off," I said to Slag. "Let's go check the stock, see if that hostler's got 'em ready."

Torros bounced off his bench and grabbed my elbow. I didn't like being grabbed. I turned on him and growled. Too many folks had been grabbing at me lately. "I gave you me message. Now take yerself back to Greenwood where ye belong."

I stalked out of the taproom followed by Slag and Chub. Out in the stable yard, the hostlers had our mounts saddled and ready. I flipped the head hostler the piece of silver I'd promised and started checking Thor's tack, tightening the girth, making sure the pack and saddle pockets were secure.

Belle led her gray gelding up beside Thor. "That poor elf is clearly terrified."

"So would ye be if ye met me mother."

"She's not a nice person?"

"I got no personal opinion, having never met her," I said. "Rumors say she be a real scary bitch."

"If you're Crown Prince, it's your duty to take up your position," she said.

"Yer duty was to get married and bring more Magics into the world. How's that going fer ye?"

Belle nodded. "I get it. But I'm not royalty. You are."

Chapter Fifteen

Noemi

Noemi watched Slygon pace, first one way then the other, across the circular tower floor. The huge windows were open to let in the summer breezes. This high on the side of Mt. Ranier, where the sunrise visitors center used to be, he'd built his castle. The black dragons he ensorcelled to his use flew overhead, on the hunt for food. They circled while he paced.

"You can't have her," Noemi said. "I know what you're thinking. Let her go. Forget you saw her."

Slygon lifted one perfect eyebrow. "Who are you to tell me what I can and cannot have? I will have her, and you'll be glad of it. Don't you want to see her again? Wouldn't you love to have her here by your side?"

"You don't do anything to help other people, Slygon. You only help yourself."

"I helped you."

"You made me into a monster."

"You seemed willing enough. I'm sure, once your sister gets the feel of it, she'll like being a member of the undead as well."

"Annabelle is pure and innocent. You would destroy her."

"Yes, innocence. It's been so long since I was innocent, I've forgotten its allure. If I ever felt its allure, which I strongly doubt. Somehow, I think innocence is highly over-rated, though I would love to taste your sister's, and the blood of the newborn, is surely innocence at its purest."

Noemi closed her eyes. Looking at him, so handsome and so loathsome at the same time made her dizzy. Seeing her sister had awakened emotions inside her she'd forgotten existed. It was as though she'd just awakened from a terrible dream and found herself in a place she didn't recognize.

"Be gone," Slygon snarled. "Your newly awakened sense of remorse is revolting and hypocritical. You reveled in every terrible thing we did. You washed in the blood of the newborn. You drank the blood of the innocent. Go find yourself. Meditate or visit the seer but leave me and don't return until you're my darling, my evil, Noemi. Now send Gholug to my chamber. I wish to tell him something."

"What could you possibly have to say to that wretched orc? He reeks of dead flesh and drool."

Slygon showed his fangs. "Whatever I wish to say to him is my business and none of your concern. If you choose to go against me in the matter of my obtaining your sister, you'll have to go. I won't tolerate disobedience from any of my creatures and you are one of many and so easily replaceable."

"I thought I was special. You told me so. You said we were to be married."

"I made a mistake. I can never marry you. You are defiled. If I marry, if, it will be to a pure woman, one who has never known a man. Like your sister, for example. I will make her mine, my property, my possession. She will be of the sun, while I am of the darkness. It will be a mating like no other."

"You leave my sister alone," Noemi shrieked. "Or I'll . . ."

"Or you'll what? Hurt me? You know you can't. I'm invincible. No one can harm me."

"Where there's a will there's always a way."

"Stop," Slygon snarled. "Stop right now or I'll have you destroyed. You'll wake up in the hot sun of a scorching day and turn to ash in front of my overjoyed face. Don't push me. I would never marry you, so don't even think it. You're vampire. You're dead already and can bear no children. The urge to breed has come upon me like a sudden storm. I wish an heir of my body, an innocent babe who looks like me and will inherit my wealth, my lands and my power."

"How can you breed? You're just as much vampire as I."

"I am so much more than just vampire," he said. "You do not know the half of what I am or what I can do, and you never shall."

"Who are you, really, Slygon? Where did you come from?"

Slygon laughed. "By discovering my origins, do you hope to pick up some clue so you can destroy me?" He closed his eyes and breathed deeply. "See, I breathe. I can because I'm a living creature, a man, an elf, a shifter, but also vampire. I am unique, bred in the darkness of the Underworld. Bred to rule over all creatures. It's my destiny. Now send me Gholug."

"I'll bring him."

Noemi ran through the castle at lightning speed and found the orc in his rooms in the dungeons. The smell of the rooms was offensive even to her. She banged on the thick, wooden door. Gholug opened it. Noemi pointed up. "Slygon wishes to speak to you."

Gholug followed her at his hulking hunched-over pace. She opened the door to Slygon's room for him, stood back, then followed him inside. He waited for Slygon to speak to him, shifting his mass from side to side as he rasped through a nose, ruined and pulled to one side by puckered scar tissue. Half his face looked like it belonged to a melted wax figure. He had only one eye, black as obsidian, no white. Heavy jowls hung to his chest, smothering whatever neck he might have. His ears were huge and pointed, his skin the color of pea soup. Only two of his fangs remained, more tusks than fangs. "Master?"

"Bring me the child."

"Yers, master."

"Don't do this," Noemi begged. "You must stop this terrible ritual. You can't keep drinking the blood of infants."

"Quiet," Slygon roared. "You've slurped down your share so don't be so sanctimonious. Just because you found your sister, now you're Miss Goody-Two-Shoes?" His laugh was an evil chuckle. "We'll see how long you can abstain. When your mortality fades and you can no longer walk under the sun, you'll drink just as I do."

Gholug was gone for only a few minutes. He reappeared holding a squalling baby by its feet. "This one?" he asked, raising the wiggling infant high for Slygon's inspection.

"No!" Noemi cried. "Don't, please." She tried to take the babe from Gholug, but the orc sheltered it close to his reeking body.

"If you can't control yourself, Noemi, then leave." He took the baby from Gholug. "I wanted the one we took from Craggy Town, but this one will do." He poised with his fangs inches from the tiny white neck of the squalling infant. "Drinking the child's blood will restore my humanity for as long as a month. It lasts even longer if the babe is newborn. I can breed as a man and die like a man. I will find your sister and make her my wife."

Sobs wracked Noemi. She doubled over with the pain of her past decisions and her lost innocence. What had she done? At first, she'd only wanted to save Annabelle, but after Slygon turned her vampire, she'd grown into the role and followed Slygon like the evil Pied Piper he was. She'd wanted to please him. She'd lain with him. Her virginity was gone along with her innocence and her humanity. She'd saved her sister but paid a terrible price.

Slygon took the baby, passed his hand over the small girl's face. She immediately quieted. He smiled as he looked at her perfect features, her tuft of blond hair, her pink bow mouth and her unfocused blue eyes. Noemi lunged for him as she tried to keep him from killing the child. Slygon slammed his fist into her face knocking her to the floor as he buried his fangs in the little girl's chest, tore out her beating heart, and ate it. He drank some of the child's blood, then held the dying infant over Noemi's face. The smell of the child's blood called to her. It smelled like the sweetest perfume, the most delicious fruit. Unable to stop herself, she licked up blood, savoring the last drops dripping from the gaping wound.

The infant's blood raced into her system like fire, spread to her limbs giving her the elixir of life. She closed her eyes in shame. She was so weak. Slygon laughed at her. "Look at you. One sniff and you can't resist. You're pathetic." He kicked her and she whimpered with pain and with the agony of her tortured soul.

Gholug watched, the working half of his mouth hanging open. A thin stream of drool ran down his chin. Slygon tossed the tiny corpse to Gholug who ate its head in one bite, crunching on the soft bones of its skull with half a happy smile on his hideous face

Belle

The odd group of travelers rode out of the stable yard of the Fat Dragon. The morning still young, they headed for the river. As we rode, I pondered this new side of Jackal. His gruff manner and sharp tone reflected inner turmoil that had nothing to do with his present companions. I saw him rub at this forehead again, his eyebrows plunging downward. His headache too was a result of anxiety. He may have said he had no intention of going to Greenwood, but clearly the queen's summons troubled him. He was a Crown Prince whether he liked it or not. That came with responsibilities. How would that affect his promise to help me save Noemi? I hated to be selfish, but I needed him. There was no way I could get to Slygon's castle, save Noemi and kill Slygon without him.

He could go to Greenwood at any time and pick up his duties to his mother. Noemi's situation was precarious. I had to get to her. It was a burning need inside my breast like a hot coal. His mother would wait. After all, Greenwood and the queen weren't going anywhere. He could go after we found the dragons and went after Slygon. Now that I knew where Noemi was, the desire to get her away from Slygon made all else seem unimportant.

I glanced behind us and groaned. The three elves followed with their hound trailing. I guess Torros wasn't happy with Jackal's decision and refused to accept it because the three elves were packed and ready for a long trip.

The road gradually sloped down toward the Mississippi. I didn't know what to look for when we reached the river, so I plodded along behind Chub and Jackal as they headed south.

"The river be wide here," Jackal said. "But shallow. The ferry be more a barge with a rope stretched across the river. Mules on the far side pull it across. There be teams of mules on this side to bring it back. It's quite an operation."

We rode across a flood plain, mud sucking at the horse's hooves. A group of shacks sprouted out of the mud on a high spot. Jackal headed for it. "Hope Oakhelm be there. If he ain't I got to go searchin'." Jackal spurred Thor and galloped ahead. The big horse's metal-shod hooves slung mud everywhere.

He reached the shacks, dismounted and disappeared into the biggest of the three small, rude buildings. He popped out the door moments later, grinning. "Lucky chance, Oakhelm just come over the river from the other side. He been there two days." Jackal slapped his knee. "Finally, something is going our way."

A digger emerged from the shack. He was built like a stumpy tree, square lines, thick arms and legs and a quantity of braided gray hair. His hands were the size of a regular man's and seemed huge on the squat creature. Gray eyebrows grew like bushes over light eyes. He stood with his hands on his hips examining them. "That lot going across, too?" He pointed at the three elves and their huge dog milling around, apart from our group, but with us none the less.

Jackal growled. "They can go if they want, but I ain't paying fer them."

"I have the space," Oakhelm said. He approached Torros and had a short conversation with him while Jackal led Thor toward a flat barge pulled up on the bank.

I dismounted and followed. I had to lead the gray I'd named Old Man across thick rope stretched over the mud to six stout pilings. A barn close to the shacks housed eight mules as big as Chub's draft mule. Two diggers were feeding them hay.

The smell this close to the river was fishy. The heavy mud squelched under my boots. A large ramp led onto the rectangular, flat-bottomed, craft. The three elves and their dog followed. It was crowded, the horses lined up one right beside the other. Oakhelm signaled the digger waiting on the other side and the mules dug in, hauling the barge across the river.

The entire process was interesting. Flossie, with her little dragon perched on her shoulder, hung over the edge of the barge to examine the water and I cautioned her not to fall overboard.

We'd just reached the middle of the river when I felt *him.* "Slygon is coming!" I immediately sent out a thought, searching for Noemi's familiar mind. Was she with him? I closed my eyes and concentrated. A black arrow of desire and greed shot into my open mind. I slumped against Old Man's neck in a dizzy swoon.

Jackal saw me and ran to help. "Belle. Wake up."

I opened my eyes. "He tried to take over my mind. He's very powerful."

I took out my wand and pointed it at Slygon as Tina, Chub, Jackal and Slag nocked bolts tipped with silver in their crossbows.

Dandy suddenly appeared in her frilly pink dress. "Slygon is here for you," she said to me.

"I know. I felt him."

Dandy nodded. "Your sister's not with him." She saw my wand. "Where did you get that?"

"Odafarus gave it to me."

"That's a very powerful wand. I can't believe Odafarus gave it away."

"He said it was an old one he hadn't used in a long time."

"And you believed that?" Dandy scoffed.

"I was eighteen and what do you mean did I believe him? Of course, I did."

Dandy shook her head. "Odafarus would never have given away a wand of such power. Not unless he thought it had a greater purpose somewhere else."

"You knew him?"

Dandy's eyes blurred and tears slipped down her cheeks. "He was a great wizard."

"He saved me at the Trials. They were going to kill me because they said I was dangerous, and then he popped in and said I was the one. I guess that's why he gave me the wand."

"He said you're the one?" Dandy's head snapped and she stared into my eyes. "The one what?"

"I don't know for sure, but I think he meant the one to kill Slygon."

Dandy sucked in a big breath. "Oh my."

"I know." As I squinted into the bright blue sky, vapor rose off the water and the barge as the sun heated everything. Finally, I spotted the black dragons. There were three, winging their way toward the river.

"He wants me. I can feel his evil lust." I blinked against the sun's glare as I watched the dragons wing closer. "He slept with my sister. And he can read my thoughts if I let him. But I won't."

"He believes you'll breed him a fine son," Dandy said.

I shuddered. "Breed? He's a vampire. How is that even possible?"

As the dragons grew closer, the three elves surrounded Jackal. "Get away from me, you three," he snarled. "You be giving me the creeping willies."

"We must protect you, Prince Erindriel. If there is danger, you must be kept safe."

"Oh, fer God's sake. They want Annabelle. Guard her and leave me the hell alone. I been takin' care of meself for twenty years, think on."

The dragons swooped down, heading straight for the barge. Slygon rode the lead dragon. His pale face gleamed in the bright daylight. Full-blooded orcs rode the other two dragons.

"Shields up," Jackal ordered.

All of us hid under our shields as arrows rained down. Dandy popped into little Dandy while Flossie and Granny hid under Chub's huge mule. I fired a silver-tipped bolt, guiding the arrow with my mind. It hit the second dragon in the chest. The huge creature fell toward the water, wings folded. Jackal fired and hit the orc riding the last dragon. Slygon's dragon belched fire, burning through one of the ropes connected to the barge. The ungainly craft slewed around and stopped. It was too heavy for the single team of mules to haul across the river. The weight of it dragged the struggling mules toward the water.

Oakhelm cursed as Slygon turned his dragon around and came back. The orc on the injured dragon was in the river. It was too heavy, a bad swimmer loaded down with armor. It sank beneath the swirling brown water.

On the far bank, the mules were being dragged toward the river. The digger in charge of them had no choice but to cut their harnesses away so they wouldn't drowned. Once the mules were freed, the barge turned in the current and swept downstream.

Cursing the foulest words I have ever heard, Oakhelm rounded on Jackal. "You didn't tell me the devil was after you. I'd never have consented to ferry your party." And then he added another slew of cursing.

"Didn't know, Oakhelm. Swear to God I didn't."

Slygon swooped low. "I'll be back for you," he called to me. His thoughts were easy to read. *You know you can feel me. I'll always know where you are, and I'm going to keep coming after you until I make you mine, forever. Don't you want to be with Noemi? She's waiting for you.*

I'll soon be with Noemi and you'll be dead! I flung that thought at him and shut my mind behind thick walls he couldn't penetrate.

Oakhelm pushed a pile of long poles at Slag and Jackal. "Grab a pole. Maybe it's shallow enough fer us to pole across."

All the men, even the elves, grabbed poles and stabbed them into the water. The black dragon with the silver bolt in its chest floundered close to the barge. I felt its fear and pain. It was, after all, just an animal. I had to save it. It was crying to me and I felt its agony in my own body and mind. I jumped into the water. The current was strong, but not like further downstream and I was a good swimmer. I reached the downed dragon and yanked my own bolt out of its chest. The dragon's relief was huge as it washed over me. It stuck a wing out and I clung to it as we floated downstream toward the barge.

When we bumped into the craft, Jackal tossed me a rope. I held on as the men found bottom and slowly poled our barge across the river, towing me and the dragon. When the barge hit bottom, Oakhelm, still cursing a blue streak, dropped the ramp. Slag led the horses off followed by the three elves.

Jackal stayed with me and the dragon. "Belle, let go of the creature."

"He needs help. I won't leave him. We're going hunting for dragons. Maybe he can communicate with them, so they don't eat us."

Flossie's tiny dragon flitted over and began chittering to the big black creature. Flossie hung over the side. "Squeaker says Bazit's his name and he's very grateful you saved him."

"Ask Squeaker how badly Bazit is hurt," I said.

Squeaker chattered, flitting like a green gem around the big black head. "He's feeling better now the silver is out of him," Flossie told them. "He says he can stand up."

Bazit surged out of the water while I hung onto the barge. Jackal lifted me aboard as the dragon spread his wings and launched into the air. Squeaker rejoined Flossie as we watched the huge creature swoop toward the shore and land gracefully. Jackal and I followed the rest of our group off the barge. The water was two feet deep, so Jackal paused to scoop Flossie onto his shoulder as we waded through the mud and water and clambered onto dry land in an overgrown field.

I went straight to the dragon. He was like most animals, his thoughts more pictures than words, along with emotion. I soothed him with my mind, comforted him in his sadness, his loneliness. Huge opalescent eyes contemplated me solemnly, and when Bazit dropped his massive head, I scratched behind thick eye ridges, and the dragon sighed with happiness.

"No, Belle, no," Jackal fumed when I looked at him. "We're not taking this beast with us. We got enough folks and creatures," he stared pointedly at the elves and their wolfhound which had taken a dislike to Slag, "crowded into this parade without a bloody dragon added to it."

"That makes no sense," I said. "We're on our way to get dragons, and you say we shouldn't take one along that already likes us and wants to cooperate?"

"It be damaged, and in service to the evil one."

"Servitude, not service. It had no choice. I can read its mind and it hates Slygon and his minions and never wants to return." I rubbed Bazit's head and the dragon groaned with pleasure. "See, he's very friendly and tame."

"It be hurt by silver, mayhap you recall? It be evil, like its master. Search inside its head for Slygon." Jackal walked over and gazed into the huge creature's eyes. "Do it," he insisted.

"Okay, maybe you're right." I probed the dragon's mind, searching for a vision of Slygon, or a sliver of the evil vampire's thoughts. When she found Bazit's memories of Slygon, she gasped. Slygon stood before a half-dozen large dragons, his hands raised, as he shot streams of black particles over them. The cloud of black enveloped them and slowly seeped into their bodies. The dragons, once magnificent, iridescent red, golden or green, shrieked in agony. I clearly saw them as they writhed and cried out. The dragons had been transformed into Slygon's minions. I saw the remnant of that mind-numbing domination, felt the helpless terror within Bazit's mind, shuddered, and withdrew.

"Well? Be it he would turn on us if ordered?"

I nodded, saddened by what I'd seen and wondering what could be done, if anything, to cure the dragon.

Just then, Dandy popped in. "What you doing with Slygon's beastie? Not a pet, that one. A weapon as well as a ride."

"I know," I said. "It's wounded. Is there anything we can do to save him from Slygon's curse?"

"Hmmmm," the fairy said, popping onto the dragon's shoulder. She ran her tiny hand over its glimmering black scales, then flew up a few feet, opened her hands and sprayed that golden dust she manufactured all over the creature's head.

Nothing happened. "Use your wand, Belle," Dandy said. "Think pure thoughts and whisper a cleansing spell as I sprinkle some more of this golden dust."

I pointed the wand at Bazit. It quivered, alive in my hand. I had to use both hands to hold onto it as Dandy sprinkled her fairy dust.

White, sparking light shot from the tip of the wand to the dragon's head, and down its torso until it was enveloped with a pulsing white glow as bright and pure as Slygon's magic had been dark and evil.

Bazit roared in pain and fell onto his side, the white cloud sparking and glittering around him until he was no longer visible. All of us stared, fascinated. We stepped back out of the way as we witnessed what only I had seen in the dragon's mind. But this time, its skeleton glowed and the inky darkness leeched away until only blue-white, pulsating light indicated where its skeleton should be. A brilliant flash forced me to throw up my hand to shield my eyes.

The dragon screeched once and fell silent. The light faded and shining motes of light chased each other across the surface of the once-black creature's exterior. They appeared to settle and Bazit was a glossy, shiny emerald green.

"He's back to as normal as I can make him," Dandy said. "He won't answer Slygon's call which is the most important thing." She touched my wand with reverence. "Odafarus gave you a powerful tool."

"Think we can move on now?" Jackal asked. "We're wasting time here."

"Ready when you are, Master Jackal, or should I say Prince Jackal?" Slag said, and when he laughed, the wolfhound sitting at his feet growled. Slag threw up his hands. "What? Why does your evil beastie hate me?" he asked one of the elves.

The elf was Torros, Jackal's cousin. He shrugged. "He's his own master, not a slave. Maybe he sees more orc in you than man and believes you're evil. He was trained to kill orcs."

Slag grunted. "Great. What's its name?"

"Storm," Torros said, and the dog glanced up when he heard his name.

Slag held out his hand. Storm growled. "Hey, Storm, I mean you and yer folk no harm."

Storm sniffed Slag's hand and backed a step. His gaze softened, but he kept watch. Slag laughed. "Mayhap I can befriend him."

Torros laughed. "He does like bacon."

Just then, the dragon moved. He shifted, stood and shook his wings. When he opened his eyes, I gasped in wonder. Bazit no longer had cat-like eyes, but those resembling a human, with turquois irises that gleamed with intelligence and gratitude. When I probed his mind, I smiled with relief and joy. The images of his existence were there, and the emotions too, but I was able to mind-meld with Bazit as though he were human, and he fully understood my language.

"He knows more languages than you now," Dandy said with pride, as though she had just given birth.

Bazit tossed his head like a preening peacock.

All of us laughed, and Bazit became yet another member of this growing family. A sudden dark thought hit me. I glanced at our group. On the open ground, We were vulnerable. We needed more weapons and dragons.

Chapter Sixteen

Jackal

The three elves gathered around the dragon. "That creature is an abomination," Torros said. "It should be destroyed.

I laughed and laughed, slapping my knee. "Listen, you three, we don't want or need you with us, so don't be ordering anyone around or making any stupid suggestions none of us wish to hear. You can be on yer way, for all I care, and I'd actually prefer you hustled on back to your queen and gave her my message. I ain't going to Greenwood. Not now or ever. She threw me away as a babe. I'm no longer her child to do with as she pleases, and I won't bow and scrape to her demands."

"We have to stay with you as your guard then," Ivansar Ravenwing said. "We can't take a message such as you've given us back to Queen Ashera. We'll be killed."

"She sounds like a right big bitch," Slag said.

"Yep," I said. "Don't ye remember when you was a child. Those in the village thought she was bad and happen they're right."

Oakhelm stomped up to us his face the color of a ripe tomato. "Who's gonna pay fer this disaster? I have to buy new rope, drag the barge back to me dock. I'm out of business until it's all fixed." He waved his short arms and jumped up and down and swore at them.

The elves stepped forward. Torros took a leather purse off his belt and removed five golden coins. I been all over The Withers and inside some of the walled cities, and never seen gold coins. Silver was used because gold was rare. "This should cover your trouble," Torros said.

"You can't buy me with yer gold, elf," I snarled.

"You're our Crown Prince, Erindriel. We are responsible for your safety until you return to Greenwood."

I lifted my eyes to heaven. "I guess that means yer coming with us on the hunt for dragons, as well."

"We must," Gormar Fairfeather said. "We are sworn to protect you. If you die, Queen Ashera's line will disappear forever and we can't allow that to happen. She came from the Pit. She was born in the Middle Kingdom and is getting incredibly old even by elf standards. You are her only surviving child and she can have no others."

My annoyed sigh gusted out of my mouth. "Oh, fer god's sake. Then get in line. We got a bunch of folks on this trek and we just added a dragon." I turned to Slag. "What a circus we've become."

Slag laughed. "If they can nock an arrow and wield a sword, we'll make use of them."

Satisfied with his newfound wealth, Oakhelm left them, trudging back upstream toward his ferry dock, humming a raunchy song.

Belle found her gray, Old Man, and was about to mount when she stopped. "What is it, Belle?" I asked.
"I heard Bazit's voice in my head. He wants me to ride him."

"What? Absolutely not. It's way too dangerous. You just changed him from Slygon's personal beastie and now you want to trust him to take you up there?" I pointed to the sky.

Belle smiled. "Stop worrying." She patted my cheek like I was a drooling infant. "I'll be fine."

I took the reins of her ancient gelding. "Here," she said. "Use him to pack stuff. I'm riding the dragon."

My heart pounded and sweat broke out on my forehead at the thought of her going aloft on that beast. "You'll be in so much danger. I can't fathom it. Why, you could fall off or he could turn out to be traitorous and haul you straight to Slygon."

"I'll be fine with him," Belle said. "I can read Bazit's thoughts. Remember?"

"That don't mean it's safe," I grumbled. "I'll worry the entire time you're on its back."

Belle patted his shoulder and smiled. "I'll make sure he knows how upset you are. He just told me he'll take good care of me."

I shot the dragon a dark look and stormed off to mount Thor as Dandy rode up on her pig. "She cares about you, you know."

"You're wrong. She thinks I'm a monster."

"You might discover you're wrong about that." Dandy laughed and smacked her pig's butt with a stick. The pig trotted off, Dandy bouncing up and down.

Belle

I muttered to myself as I scrambled aboard Bazit with my heart thumping. "I don't like him at all. In fact, I think I hate him." I sighed. It wasn't true. I didn't hate him. Dandy was right. I was growing to care for the huge ass and miss him when he was absent.

When I straddled Bazit's thick, scaled neck, the sudden realization flying meant going up in the air, hit me. High in the air. *You'll be fine.*

The dragon's thoughts were comforting. I quickly braided my hair. The nuns had always kept my hair cut short. When I entered St. Catherine's, I let it grow. It was long now, past my shoulders and almost to my waist, and would blow in my face and get tangled if I didn't secure it.

Jackal stalked to the dragon and glared at me. "Are you sure you're gonna be okay on that beast?"

"Bazit says he shall take good care of me," I said. "I'll scout ahead and plan the easiest route."

I know where the dragons live. I could fly you there.

I patted the dragon's shining green shoulder. "I'm sure you could, but there are many of us and they have to ride horses."

"Is he speaking into yer head again?" Jackal asked.

"He knows where the dragons live. He wants to fly me there."

Jackal grunted. "Happen betwixt him and that damned fairy, we should be able to find them." He stared at the assembled group with disfavor. "It's already past the noon hour. We better get moving. We have at least three-hundred miles to cover to get to the Smokey Mountains."

Jackal

Thoroughly disgusted with the tangled mass of followers I'd collected, I stomped to my horse, mounted, turned in the saddle, and surveyed the assembled group. "Slag, take the rear. Chub, you watch Granny and Flossie and keep yer eyes on them three." I pointed with my chin at the three elves. "I don't trust them as far as I can throw them and their horses."

Slag mounted his mare and the wolfhound followed, taking up a position in the rear behind Slag. I had no problem with this. I didn't trust the damn dog either.

We rode most of the day, stopping once to rest and eat provisions Granny had packed. When we reached the edge of a wide swampy area, we stopped for the night. I figured we'd gone maybe twenty miles. The dragon dropped Belle with us and flew off to hunt, bringing back a deer in its jaws.

Belle said it had already eaten several and thought they might need food as well. The gift of a fine meal made me feel a little better about having the beast among us. He was actually proving to be an asset. Maybe getting dragons would prove helpful. Maybe.

In the morning and for the next three days, those on foot or horseback slogged along, seeing little and running into no one. On the fourth day, Bazit landed, slewing up a dozen feet of sod which flew everywhere. Annabelle hopped off his back and ran toward them screaming. "Orcs! They're coming at us from the trees ahead."

I drew my crossbow. "Gather in a group. Granny, you and Tiny watch over Flossie."

Tiny shook her head. "I'm fighting."

"The fuck you will. Do as I damned well say. I have plenty of fighting men. Someone has to protect Granny and the child, and I choose you."

"It's because I'm the littlest, isn't it?"

"Well, yeah. And because I don't care if them three elves live or die, but you and Belle I worry about as well as Granny and the child. Where's the damn fairy anyway?"

Dandy poufed into existence beside Tiny. "I'll watch over the child. That's what most fairies do anyway. We guard children."

"Doing a right poor job of it, ain't ye?"

Dandy shrugged. "There aren't many of us."

"Okay, that frees you up," I said to Tiny. "Belle's going aloft. You hang with Slag. Stay away from them three elves."

"I kind of like the blond one," Tiny said. "Gormar is very handsome."

"Fine. Go stand beside Fairfeather if that's your choice of a man."

Tiny ignored my bad temper and ran with her crossbow to stand beside the tall blond elf. The look Fairfeather shot at Tiny was plain for anyone to read. He was not interested in the least. Well, good luck to her in trying to change the elf's natural dislike of humans. She was going to need it.

Having deployed my men, I climbed aboard Thor. I hated fighting orcs afoot. The horse made me bigger and faster than them. Even if they were riding pigs, I still had the advantage. Slag and Chub joined me as Belle went aloft. The orcs charged from behind a copse of oaks, old buildings and a water tower on its last legs. They screamed their war cries and beat on their shields with clubs and their swords. The hogs they rode shrieked hideously. The noise was supposed to terrify their enemies but didn't bother us at all. We heard it often.

Slag and I split and went around the charging orcs. Strangely, the wolfhound followed Slag into battle. The orcs looked like a typical band of a dozen, all riding war hogs. The elves dropped to a knee with Tiny in front of the gathered horses surrounding Flossie and

Granny. They drew their bows. A pink shield formed above the child and old lady which showed me Dandy was on the job.

Chub raced toward the orcs, and Slag drove in from the left with the hound at his side. I galloped hard at them from the right. We had them in a pincer. Above, Belle swooped down with the dragon. I sliced into the closest orc, cutting off part of his head. Green blood spurted everywhere as I turned to take on the orc behind me.

Suddenly, Bazit spewed flames over the orcs coming behind. The dragon fire was blue, but when it hit an orc it blazed into bright green. The orcs screamed as they burned. Three were toast. Their burning hogs ran crazy, hitting other hogs and knocking two orcs to the ground. This was kind of fun. I laughed as I attacked another orc, engaging it in a fierce fight. The orc used his mace, swinging it at Thor. I hauled Thor's head out of the way at the last minute, saving my horse's life, as I thrust my katana into the orc's gut. The orc tumbled off his hog.

The remaining orcs seemed to realize they'd messed with the wrong band of travelers. They turned and ran, urging their hogs into an awkward gallop. The wolfhound pounced on one of the retreating hogs, rode it for a second, then took down the orc riding it. I galloped by and sliced the downed orc's head off, leaving the hound to chew up the remains. We followed the fleeing orcs for a mile to make sure they were really leaving, then returned to our people.

Belle landed the dragon and hopped off. "Glad we brought Bazit now?" she asked with a grin.

"He be right helpful in a fight, "I said, aware as always of how lovely she looked with her face flushed with excitement and her hair drawn into a long braid. When she touched my shoulder and gazed into my eyes, my heart pounded in a totally different way from when I was fighting. I felt breathless and giddy as a girl. Why did I have to love her? She'd never see me as anything but an animal, a beast. Then I remembered Dandy's words and looked into her eyes as I sent a tiny feeler into her mind. I mentally whispered one word, *love*.

She sent a message back. *Stay out of my head, halfling.* But when I got her message, she smiled and squeezed my hand. I groaned. What I did not understand about women would fill an ocean.

For the next ten days, we slogged along, so tired nobody talked much. When we reached the thick forest where the mountains began, we stopped for a rest and to regroup. "We be getting close to this dome thing we're looking for," I said to Slag. "And we be starting up into them mountains. Happen we should make a base camp here, leave Granny and Flossie with Chub and them damn elves and go on with just Tiny, you, me and Belle on the dragon. I still got no idea how we're gonna trap, capture, or coerce dragons into carrying us. Seems a right stupid venture to me, but then happen I'm stupid to even be here."

Granny slipped up beside him. "Better take Dandy. They won't likely be interested in helping you without her, though Bazit will help."

Dandy popped out of nowhere, appearing full size next to Granny. "Dragons choose their own riders, so even if the leader of the pride agrees to help you, the dragons will choose, not you. Anyone you want to ride a dragon must go. Second passengers don't need to be there, but the dragons mind meld with their riders, usually for life."

"So how do fairies ride them? Big or little?" Belle asked.

"Either," Dandy said, laughing.

"Why doesn't this shit surprise me? That means Chub has to go with us, which means we all have to go."

"Afraid so," Dandy agreed.

Chapter Seventeen

Jackal

We climbed into the mountains through thick forest. The highest point flattened into a circular plain with little vegetation and few boulders. For the life of me I couldn't figure out why dragons would live here. No caves, no crags, none of the stuff dragons liked.

"There's lots of food," Belle said to him.

"You listening to my thoughts?"

She shook her head. "What you're thinking is on your face. You also think this is a fool's errand."

"Where's that damn dragon?"

She closed her eyes. "He's soaring over the top of the mountain. In before-times, someone built an observation tower and a long walkway winding to the top. He says the dragons are nesting on the walkway and the tower."

"And how far away is this thing?"

"A day's hike for all of us."

"I want my horse. What if we get surprised by orcs up here? Or centaurs or gaggers?"

Belle laughed. "I feel sure they'll be walking too."

We stopped short of our destination and camped in a clearing. Dandy popped in, glowing in a bright yellow gown. "What happened to the pink one?" I asked.

"I feel yellow," Dandy said and chuckled.

"You look like a big chicken."

"Did you say chicken?" Chub asked. "Hiking all day has me fair gut-foundered."

A whoosh of air announced Bazit's arrival. He perched on a treetop which swayed and wobbled under his weight. I looked up in time to see the dragon drop a full-grown bear on top of a rock. Chub rubbed his hands together. "Dinner."

We built a roaring-big fire and roasted hunks of the bear on spits. Annabelle set up a bed for Flossie close to the fire. Even though it was summer, it was chilly at this elevation. Dandy sat next to the little girl and pulled a flute out of thin air. Granny Hawkins rummaged in her pack and produced a stringed instrument. Torros pulled a flute out of his pack. Gormar, who was sitting next to Tiny, found a lute in his pack and they added to the music while Slag beat two sticks on a hollow log.

Maybe it was fairy magic or Granny magic, or even elf magic, but the music made me happy. I'd been minding the fire, watching the roasting meat, but the music filled me with a strange uplifting joy. I leaped to my feet and began dancing. Chub burst into song. He had a deep baritone voice. Tiny sang with Gormar and the other elf, Ivansar.

It was beautiful. Belle grabbed my hand and danced with me as Flossie jumped up, Squeaker flying around her head, and danced beside us. Granny and Dandy changed the tempo, slowing the music to a sweet ballad. The elves sang to it. I hesitated for a moment, then bowed to Belle. "May I have this dance, my lady?"

She smiled and took my hand. My heart swelled as we danced, and filled with love for this amazing woman. We twirled around the clearing to the magical strains of the singing and music. Tiny jumped up and dragged Gormar into dancing. I'd never felt like this in my life. It was magical and beautiful dancing like this with Belle under the stars. Tears rolled down my cheeks and I was too ashamed to brush them away, as we swung around and around, Belle's feet barely touched the ground. When the music stopped, all I wanted to do was tell her how much I loved her. She put her hand on my chest and looked into my eyes. "I know," she whispered.

"Meat's done," Chub announced breaking the spell. I glared at him, but the moment was gone, and I let it go. The elves had roasted potatoes in the fire. The elves ate their potatoes, while the rest of us feasted on potatoes and bear meat.

"Tomorrow, you will meet the dragons," Dandy said. "The pride is quite large. I was surprised. Twenty-two full-grown blue and green dragons and one queen, a big gold one. There are several juveniles and a clutch of eggs warming in the sun in a sandy pit. Everyone rest well because if the dragons don't sense your purity of intention when they detect your presence, they'll eat you. Nothing I can do about it."

"What the hell mean you by that?" My happy spirit withered and croaked.

"You knew the risks. Not even fairies can force the dragons to accept you against their will. Would you have me curse them like Slygon?"

"A course not."

"Think. Your intentions are pure, your mission for the salvation of thousands. Belle wants to save her sister from Slygon. The dragons will see this truth in your minds."

"And Bazit will reassure them that we are not evil and only seek their aid to destroy a corrupt monster, and free their enslaved kin," Belle added, reaching out to touch my arm. It seemed to me, she was touching me a lot more, something I found delightful. How could I deny her anything? We were on this journey at her request, me and my friends. This was not where we'd planned to go at all. We should be wandering The Withers looking for orcs, drinking homemade ale at the small villages and enjoying ourselves, not sitting on the top of a mountain getting ready to beg dragons for help. Dumbest thing I'd ever done in a life filled with stupid decisions, and all of it, including putting my friends in jeopardy, I was doing for love of this woman. I knew that and accepted it.

"We'll need to be ready for anything then," I mumbled, renewed worry and irritation making my head throb. I covered Belle's hand resting on my arm with my own hand. Hers was so small and white by comparison, despite the tan she now sported from her time in the sun. "You and Tiny will have to keep a very close watch on Flossie and Granny so we can attend to the beasties."

"If you think I'm letting you find a dragon to ride without me there, you're nuts," she snapped. "Granny Hawkins can take care of herself and of Flossie. Why, she's better equipped for this journey than you are."

"Squeaky! I can't find Squeaky! He's gone! I've looked everywhere!" Flossie smashed into my thigh, bounced off and buried her face against Belle's leg, sobbing as though her heart would break.

I felt the loss of Belle's hand when she moved it to embrace Flossie. I thought she looked good with a child. My heart thundered in my chest as I considered how lovely her children would be. I looked around and said, "Where and when is the last place anyone saw yer pet, poppet?"

"With her," said Granny, coming up place a hand on the girl's shoulder. "Squeaker never leaves her side. He's either on her shoulder or sleeping in her bag."

"Did you check the bag?" I asked, knowing that was the first place the girl would have looked. I started walking the perimeter of our campsite. The wee beastie had begun to grow on all of us, like a mini-mascot. His ability to add protection to Flossie helped win him acceptance and his comical antics and happy character earned him affection.

A sudden gust of displaced air jerked our attention to the sky. "Seek cover!" I yelled as I pushed Belle and Flossie behind me. The rest of the party scattered as the burst of wind was accompanied by the sound of flapping wings. I planted my feet and drew my sword with no idea what I was facing. If the horde of dragons was attacking, there was little any of us could do to stop them or prevent a massacre. With a loud roar, a giant golden dragon landed on the big boulder where Bazit had deposited the bear the night before.

"Here," Slag yelled, tossing me a large shield.

You've no need of that, Elf Prince.

I heard the words in my mind and answered in like. *My name be Jackal and I be no prince.*

One day you will be a great ruler, halfling, but you have many trials and tribulations to overcome first. I can see the purity of your intentions, the humble nature of your bravery. You are worthy of our help. I have decided to aid you. Come to the top of the mountain at daybreak. You are a friend to our friends. You need have no fear.

"Thank you," I said aloud, and watched with fascination as Squeaker flew from the great dragon's shoulder to Flossie's. Gleaming golden in the last rays of the setting sun, the beast leapt upward and spread her wings. She hovered a moment above them, her gigantic head as big as Thor, then she cleared the tree line, flapping massive wings as she soared out of sight. Belle gasped in surprise as we watched Bazit follow the larger female.

"Squeaker!" Flossie cried, reaching out to stroke the purring dragon nestled against her cheek. "What?" she said, pausing to listen to a private conversation within her head. "Guess what?" she exclaimed turning toward Jackal. "Squeaker saved us. Those dragons are distant relatives and Squeaker went to tell them all about us and tell them how we saved him, and how we been trying to fight the evil Slygon and all about Belle's sister. They hate Slygon because he steals and enslaves them."

When the golden dragon was gone, we returned to the fire. The elves gathered around Jackal and bowed. "You will be a great king," Torros said. "We shall stay with you. We shall fight with you. I pledge my loyalty and my sword to you." He bent his knee to me as my mind still reeled from the dragon's pronouncements.

Then Gormar and Ivansar both bent the knee to me. "Our true king, they said. All Hail King Erindriel!"

Belle walked up and stood at my elbow. "Well, that's a hell of a thing," she said. "You're a king."

"No, I ain't. I'm not even a prince. This all be a bunch of stupidity the likes of which I've never witnessed in me life."

Belle laid her hand on the side of my face, and I put my hand over it. It was such a touching gesture from a woman not known for touching gestures. "You're their prince whether you like it or not. And one day you'll be their king. You'll be a great king, Jackal. You're a wonderful man."

"I like me life the way it is," I said, but in a softer voice.

"The only thing you can count on in life is change, Jackal. One day you'll be a king. You should accept it."

"Do you like the idea of me being a king, Belle? I could tell them to shove off. I still ain't gone to Greenwood and accepted Queen Ashera's offer. And I may never."

"You'd do that for me? I mean if I didn't want you to be a king but stay with me, I mean us, forever, you'd turn it down?" She stared into my eyes so intently I could barely breathe. I wondered what she was thinking. I could sneak a peek into her thoughts if I wanted to, but she'd know, and it would ruin her trust. Instead, I pulled her up to my level and kissed her. I knew it was too soon, but I'd been wanting to kiss her for so long, I just couldn't wait any longer. For a moment, after our lips touched, she returned my kiss. I felt it. A wave of pleasure from her wrapped around me and filtered into my befogged brain. Then she pulled away. "Put me down, you big ox," she snapped. But when she said it, she smiled.

I turned away to hide my embarrassment. I'd never been good at saying flowery things or what was in my heart. I still had her shoulders in my hands and was thinking about going for kiss number two, when Slag yelled, "Centaurs. Man your weapons."

I ran for my bow and my sword as everyone scrambled. "It be the bloody full moon," I said to Chub who was pulling on his leather armor. "I shoulda known there'd be the damn half-horses up in these woods."

Granny gathered Flossie with Dandy by the fire. Dandy lifted her wand and a golden dome of protection rose above them. She added more wood to the fire and pointed the wand at the rising flames which leapt high.

Belle stood beside me, all business, sword drawn with fire racing up and down its length. "What are we facing?" She asked.

"Centaurs. They go crazy when the moon is full and kill everything in sight. They're big and strong and, uh, sexually motivated."

"You mean they're horny," she said with a grim smile.

I burst out laughing. "That's the barber. Didn't want to use that word in front of your delicate ears, but yeah, they're raging."

"On my six!" Chub yelled.

Three centaurs, easily as tall as Thor, raced into the clearing. Thor tore free of the trot line and pawed at them with big, metal-shod hooves. Chub's mule, freed when Thor ripped the line down, kicked wildly, while Bunny, the huge slut, ran off with one of the centaurs. Two more approached the fire cautiously. I yelled my war cry and charged. The three elves loosed a volley of arrows killing two of the beasts immediately.

One of them, a dark brown half horse, the man half of the beast a handsome grinning satyr with thick brown hair and high pointed ears, went for Tiny. She screamed, and he exploded. The other centaurs witnessed her power and stopped. Tiny pointed a finger at another one. It shook its head and spoke. "No, my lady, please."

"Bring back Bunny," she snarled, "or I'll blow all of you to pieces. She pointed at the flat rock where the remains of the bear lay, closed her eyes and screamed. It exploded sending rock shards and chunks of dead bear into the centaurs.

They didn't wait to see more. They thundered out of the clearing and into the woods. Soon Bunny returned, her wild blond mane a mess, her legs wobbly. Slag ran for her. He might be a gruff three-quarters orc, but he loved that mare. He grabbed her trailing lead rope. "What have you done?" Slag demanded.

I really couldn't help myself. "I told you not to ride a mare."

Slag growled at him. "She be brave as yer Thor, maybe braver."

"Happen you be right but looks like she has needs."

With the danger over Granny went to examine Bunny. She lifted the mare's tail and pursed her lips. "What happens when a centaur breeds a horse?"

Dandy popped up next to her. "That's how they make more centaurs."

Chapter Eighteen

Slygon

Slygon stalked down the circular stone stairway to the bottom level of his keep. He had designed it to mirror his home in Underworld, and had it built by minions slaving night and day. Humans he captured and kept alive, worked themselves to death for the unfulfilled promise of eternal life as a vampire. None of them were given this gift. All were consumed by the legions of vampires that followed him out of the Underworld.

At the bottom of the steps, a corridor went off to the left. Prison cells lined the hallway. At the end, he exited through an iron door into a small round room, the walls shooting high into a tower where his seer lived. The strange quarters in the tower were designed to mimic a Japanese temple.

His seer was a member of the undead, a Japanese vampire. Blind, paperwhite, Kokusan was a Shinto monk before his death and rebirth as a vampire. He had Gifts Slygon cherished. Kokusan could see into the future and view the present with a depth no one else possessed. The ancient monk sat in the lotus position beside a well, his blind eyes wrapped with a black rag, his white silk robes arranged around him. The well was in the center of the circular room, edged with a six-inch rock wall. Slygon knelt beside him and stared into the depths of the crystal-clear water as Kokusan spread his white hands across the swirling surface.

"What do you see?" he demanded. "Can you see Noemi's sister?"

"Have patience in all things, Slygon. You have no end, time is at your disposal, death is not your enemy."

Kokusan chanted in Japanese. Slygon understood it. Vampires know all languages. "Come to my heart, the visions of truth, sent by the spirits of those who've gone before."

Slygon hovered above the well, staring into its depths. He saw Noemi's sister, her black hair silky and flying around her head as she laughed and danced. He groaned with the misery of not possessing her. Then the water swirled again, and she disappeared, replaced by the ugly visage of the half-blood she traveled with. He vanished, and an old woman's face flowed through the water followed by a babe, a newborn infant. "Is the babe mine?" His voice shook with hope and longing.

"Quiet," Kokusan said in a hushed voice. "The visions are coming faster."

An elf woman appeared, lying on a huge bed, her face gray with sickness. More elves appeared, all fighting and screaming at each other. Slygon recognized many of them. They were members of the high houses of Greenwood, a place he avoided.

He stared at the sick elf woman lying in her bed while chaos reigned around her. He knew that woman. Ashera, the elf queen. He had as much claim on the crown as any of the other families in Greenwood. His blood was just as good as theirs. He leaned back. But he would not fight for his birthright. They knew nothing of him. His father, Ulva, appeared in the swirling water. He was an old elf now, his back stooped, his once black hair turning gray at the temples and above his pointed ears.

"You could take your place among them," Kokusan said. "Your father would not fight you."

"When I take my place as their king, it will be to humble all of them beneath my feet. They will grovel and fall on their faces and beg me for their miserable lives. And I will not grant their wish."

Kokusan stared more deeply into the water, rising out of the lotus position to kneel over the edge of the well.

"Do you see her?" Slygon's desire for Annabelle, Noemi's sister, was his reason for consulting the seer. He needed to know where she was. His desire for her was fueled by the fact she was Noemi's sister. The pair would be remarkable possessions. And Annabelle was pure. Her purity drew him. It wasn't just her virginity, she was special. He sensed her power. Her power, her strength, her purity, and her beauty created a unique woman. A woman so unique, so desirable, he didn't think he could continue to exist if he didn't possess her.

The seer stuck his index finger, the digit white, the nail two-inches long, sharpened and painted blood red, into the water and stirred. "Ah, I see the woman you seek. She is flying on a dragon toward Greenwood." Kokusan backed away from the well. "You should forget about her, sire. She is forbidden to you, a danger you must not face." The seer screamed and grabbed his head. "I have seen our deaths."

Jackal

"This be the dumbest thing I've ever had the misfortune to become involved in," I said as we climbed. A sentinel of steel sat at the top of the mountain shooting high above the tall conifers. The lofty tower had a circular walkway of more steel and rocky aggregate supported by tall concrete posts, stretched across the mountain, through the trees, circling to a cluster of crumbling buildings in an overgrown parking lot. Dragons perched on the edge of the walkway above the trees, watching us approach. The golden queen sat on top of the tower with her gigantic wings open to absorb the heat of the day.

"If the beasts don't devour us outright, they'll stash us under a rock and eat us later," I said to Belle.

She laughed. "I can read the golden queen. She is welcoming us, so stop worrying about being eaten."

Grumbling and groaning, Slag, who was watching the rear, came forward. "Where do we go? I mean, where is the slaughter to take place? I'd like to pick my position."

Chub had fallen further back. Huffing, he climbed a rock and emerged from the tree line right behind Granny and Flossie. Tiny, walking beside Belle had a huge smile on her face. "This is exciting," she said. "I never knew dragons were so beautiful."

Squeaker flew high above their heads. The tiny dragon was almost impossible to see as it landed on top of the queen's head and began cleaning her eye ridges.

"Where do we go?" I asked Belle as we approached the cluster of dilapidated buildings.

"We wait down here, and they will come to us," Belle said as she slowly turned in a circle to see all of the dragons. "There are so many."

"No shit, and it has me pretty worried," I said in a low voice. "Why all of us put together wouldn't be but a snack, the appetizer for the main meal." I tried counting but lost track at thirty. There were at least twenty full-grown dragons, emerald green, bronze and brown, their scales shining brightly in the midday sun. The juveniles kept moving, lifting, flying, circling and landing back on the walkway.

"They're coming," Belle whispered.

I examined our small group. Counting the three elves who wouldn't go away, there were ten of us. The fairy had flitted off somewhere but would no doubt return. We formed a half circle across the rotting asphalt parking lot. Clumps of scrubby growth sprouted in cracks and large slabs lifted and broke apart, making the surface ragged and uneven. The dragons rose as one. The juveniles stayed aloft. Hovering on spread wings, they created a storm of flying debris and dirt. I had to lift my forearm to cover my face. The rest of the group followed suit as the adult dragons slowly settled in front of us.

Granny Hawkins gasped. "Holy shit they're big."

Flossie giggled and pointed at Granny. "You said a bad word."

"Happen Granny be right," Chub said.

"You sure this be a good thing?" Slag asked me.

"We be committed, think on. Too late to run and there be no fighting this group of beasties."

The elves clustered around me, bows drawn. I rolled my eyes. "Put them bows away. Like yer arrows be piercing the hide of them things."

"We must protect you," Torros said. "You are Crown Prince."

They were never going to leave me alone. I was doomed. "You three need to attract a frigging dragon, if you can. Othergates, you'll be walking, and I'll be flying. Good luck."

The dragons landed on the rotten blacktop amidst a huge whirlwind. A green landed and roared, blasting all of them with putrid breath and a wave of super-heated air. I stood firm and stared into the green's eyes and felt nothing. Suddenly, from behind me, Chub stepped forward in a daze. "He says his name is Emerenth, and I can ride him."

Slag was chosen by a brown named Lionth. One by one the startled elves were chosen until only Tiny and Belle and I remained. The rest of the group was aloft, flying for the first time in their lives aboard dragons. The biggest bronze dropped his head and stared into my eyes. A voice grew inside my head. The voice was connected to raw emotions. I felt love, hate, hunger, desire and rage. These passed, and I was filled with the warmth of a true joining. The voice inside my head was deep and resonant. *My name is Remoth.*

"I will ride when Tiny and Belle have imprinted their dragons, and not afore." I heard a low chuckle inside my head, telling me my dedication was appreciated.

A green approached, sparkling in the sunshine, tiny compared to the other dragons, like Tina was to the humans. "She's speaking to me," Tiny said. "She says her name is Saroth." Tiny scrambled up Saroth's big foreleg and pulled herself onto the big back. "What do I hold onto?" she asked me.

"I'm guessing whatever you can grab."

Tiny wrapped her hands around two large spines and grinned.

The only ones left standing were me and Belle. Remoth waited patiently as the huge queen walked toward Annabelle. Bazit flew in beside the queen and backed away as though honoring her. "She says she wasn't going to imprint a rider but feels drawn to me. She told me all golden dragons are female, and all are called queens. I think it's sorta like queen bees. They are rare, born only in two clutches of eggs in a queen's lifetime." The smile Belle gave me warmed me to my toes. "She says I'm brave and trustworthy." Belle closed her eyes and gasped. "Jackal, I can hear all of them."

"All of what, Belle?"

"The dragons. I can hear all of their voices. Bazit wants me to ride his queen. He says as the queen's rider, I'll be able to hear all dragons." Belle put her hand on my arm, a gesture she seemed pretty comfortable with. "He says to properly lead, one of us must be able to hear all of them. He wishes to be free so he can take us to Slygon. His mission is to free the dragons held prisoner by Slygon and save them from slavery."

"With him working to save the dragons and you able to talk to all of this lot, we'll be a better working unit and we'll have more chance to succeed," I said.

The golden queen dropped her head to the broken asphalt in front of Belle. "Her name is Oranth," Belle said. "The juveniles are all her children."

"Then get on and ride," Dandy said. "I have work to take care of elsewhere."

Belle laughed and climbed aboard Oranth. When she was safely aloft, I approached the huge bronze. "Remoth, my friend, now it be just you and me."

Chapter Nineteen

Jackal

Granny and Flossie did not have dragons. Granny stood alone in the parking lot holding Flossie's hand. Squeaker hovered above the little girl's head.

Annabelle was about to mount Oranth. "Belle, there's the child and Granny to mind," I yelled to her, realizing I should probably stay and keep them protected.

A brown dragon, older from the look of him, his scales less brilliant, gray patches above his eye ridges, landed in front of Granny. The old woman cackled. "He's older than god, but he says we can ride him. His name is Jeralth."

Granny hiked up her old black gown and stood on Jeralth's wing to throw Flossie onto Jeralth's broad back. The child giggled, quivering with eagerness. "I'm gonna ride a dragon, Squeaker." She stroked the little one and kissed his head. "No, you're my special friend. You ride with me."

With everyone mounted, half of them cruising above, I waved to Belle and Remoth took off. *Oh, shit.* My stomach lurched, rolled, and I grabbed the huge spikes on the back of Remoth's neck so tightly my knuckles were white. Remoth's first wing flaps were strong. The power beneath my butt was a hundred times greater than Thor's power and the big horse was strong. The dragon used his massive hind legs to push off, then we flew.

I discovered I was holding my breath. I let it out when we were aloft. During battle, you always have to remember to breathe. I'd forgotten and was dizzy from lack of air. The big bronze flew higher and I finally got the nerve to look down. Below, Annabelle's golden queen soared toward them on powerful strokes of her wings. Annabelle wasn't frightened. She was laughing with joy.

I swallowed hard, determined not to show my fear, but the ground was very far below, the trees tiny, the huge tower a glistening spot among a carpet of green treetops. A bird flew next to me for a second. It was an eagle. Its white head turned, and the eagle surveyed me with a golden eye, then banked and soared toward a far-distant lake.

I spotted the three elves, Slag and Chub ahead of me, and told Remoth to join them. We formed a squadron, a dangerous fighting unit ready for anything. The dragons made us powerful. Now that I was flying, I saw how this could work, how just riding the dragons made us practically invincible. This is why Slygon stole them and impressed them to his will. This was real power.

Belle flew as close to Remoth as she could. "We should land and talk," her voice carried across the distance between us. "Now that we have the dragons, we can go after Slygon in his hold. I can rescue my sister. We can do this."

I nodded, my teeth clenched too tightly to squeeze out words. *Land, Remoth*, I thought. *We done seen what it was we needed to see. Can you take us back to our camp?*

The dragon banked and headed down the side of the mountain. In two minutes, the dragons covered the ground it had taken them four hours to walk. The possibilities were endless. *We work with you, not for you.* Remoth's thoughts entered my head like clearly spoken words in a sonorous baritone. *Remember that, halfling prince. We are not draft animals used for your pleasure. We work toward a common purpose. We've allowed you to be our partners because we desire nothing as much as we wish to kill Slygon. You have Annabelle with you. Odafarus told us, she is the one who can do this.*

"Will you come when we need you?"

All you have to do to summon us is have Annabelle call Oranth. She can gather our numbers to come to your aid. If you in particular need my help for any reason, I will be at your side as soon as possible.

We landed beside our camp at the base of the mountain. Thor and Bunny shied violently when the dragons landed. Chub's huge mule never moved. Its eyes were closed. *Why are they afraid? I* asked Remoth. *Horses be silly things. And very tasty.*

Happen they know that then.

Belle landed her huge queen and climbed off. Chub walked up to him and slapped his back. "Well, that was a hell of a thing. I thought I'd be terrified, but I wasn't. Flying is something else, ain't it?"

Slag wobbled up on shaky legs. He grabbed my arm, his face green, turned and ran into the bushes. In seconds, I heard him puking his guts out. Chub laughed. "Seems three-quarters-orc doesn't give you a strong stomach."

Slag wobbled out of the brush. "I held it till I got off, didn't I?"

Chub nodded. "That reminds me, we got any of that bear left?

Belle

We all slept well that night. I slept secure in the knowledge my plan was working. We could go after Slygon, save Noemi, and destroy him. Sometimes, I could feel him slithering around my mind, seeking a way in. I was always able to repel him but had a sinking feeling that because of his touch he knew exactly where I was at all times. What a terrifying thought. I knew I should tell Jackal, but I was afraid if he knew he would call off any attempt to attack the vampire in his home, and then my hope of saving my sister would evaporate.

We rose the next morning, rested for the first time since we'd started this journey, and sat around the campfire. Granny made them a hot drink and fried some leftover bear meat for our breakfast. We were done eating when the wolfhound began barking and Squeaker flew off Flossie's shoulder squeaking up a storm.

Jackal and his men, including the elves, leapt to their feet with their swords drawn. An elf fell into the clearing dripping blood from several wounds. Torros and Gormar reached him first, but it was

Ivansar who lifted the elf onto his shoulders and carried him to the fire. They laid him on a hastily-made pallet.

Granny quickly examined the elf's wounds. "Just shallow cuts," she announced as she slathered the cuts with ointment and wrapped a bandage across the elf's chest. "Where is that damned fairy when you need her?"

"This is my little brother, Tanithlil," Ivansar said. He squatted next to the injured elf and spoke to him in his own language. After a few minutes, Tanithlil groaned, and patted his vest. Ivansar gently pulled the elf's vest open and removed a scroll wrapped in the familiar green ribbon. He handed it to Torros.

I followed Torros as he bowed before Jackal and handed him the scroll. "This is urgent, sire. There is dire news from Greenwood."

Jackal took the scroll from him and held it like it was a live snake between two big fingers. He glanced at me. "Well, should I read it? I'm afeared it be bad news for all of us."

"Just read it," I told him. "It's better to face it now then worry for hours about the contents."

He laughed. "Solid advice." Jackal untied the ribbon. The message on the scroll was short. Jackal read it. "Crown Prince Erindriel, it is with great sadness that I tell you Queen Ashera lies on her death bed and is asking for your presence. You must obey this summons and kneel to your queen. She wishes to have speech with you before she passes into the great void."

Jackal walked to the fire and dropped the scroll into the flames. "It's signed Uriel Silverheart." He stared at Torros. "Who the hell is he?"

"Grand Vizier to the queen," Torros said. "He handles all the queen's business and is the right-hand of the queen."

"No," I said. "We can't put off going after Slygon. I must get to my sister. I need to. Please listen to me," I begged.

"She was never mother to me. She's mother in name only and has no rights over me. I don't wanna go. She did birth me, and I'm grateful she didn't kill me at birth as most women raped by orcs do to children conceived of that terrible crime. But I got no desire to rush to her death bed. I need to do what's best for my men and all of you first. It is to Slag and Chub I owe fealty and affection, not this woman I've never met. I owe more to you and Tiny and Granny than her." He rubbed his forehead. "I owe her nothing, yet I feel guilty for feeling this way about me own mother. Dammit. I feel I should go, but I know damn well I'm gonna regret it either way."

Chapter Twenty

Jackal

Ivansar squatted next to his injured brother. "Tan, my brother, what happened to you?"

Suddenly Dandy popped in. Everyone backed up to give her room. This time she wore a gown covered with sparkling stars and her red hair, filled with electricity, floated like an angry cloud around her head. She bent over the injured elf and opened his vest. Belle knelt beside Dandy. "What's wrong with him?"

Dandy pointed to a graze under the elf's arm. "It looks like an arrow went under his arm and through." She touched the wound. "Is that what happened?" she asked Tanithlil kindly.

"I was just leaving the village outside Greenwood, Wildwhisper. I stopped there to speak to Eliza Finegold. She was Erindriel's wet nurse and I hoped to get news of him from her. She didn't know anything, but then when I was riding out, I felt Ivansar. He is my brother, you know, and we have a connection. When I felt him, I knew where he was. I was hoping that Ivansar would be with Prince Erindriel since he was supposed to deliver Queen Ashera's message, so I followed the link I have with Ivansar. I was just heading into the forest when arrows flew out of a thick copse of fir trees. I turned and galloped away, but one arrow got me as I rode into more woods. I wandered lost for almost a whole day, then connected with my brother again and found you."

"You're very lucky, young man," Dandy said. "One inch over and you'd have been pierced through the heart." She sprinkled some of her fairy dust over his wound and it began healing.

I moved closer to the injured elf and squatted down so I could speak to him. "Who done this to you, boy? Do you be knowing? Was it orcs?"

Tanathlil shook his head. "No. It wasn't orcs. I saw the arrow before it went all the way through. It looked like one of ours."

Ivansar touched his brother's arm. "An elf shot at you?"

"Had to be more than one because there were so many arrows."

"Who would want to stop you from delivering your message?" I asked. "I thought all you elf people wanted me to come back. Mayhap, someone or a couple a someones don't like the idea of a half orc being prince."

Tanithlil's face colored. "I know there's been some talk about it. Queen Ashera is a very powerful elf, and even though she's deathly ill, she's able to control the different factions in the castle."

I closed my eyes and sighed. This whole episode was determined to intrude on my plans. The elves were a mistrustful, racist bunch of creatures. "But with her being sick, dying . . . I knew it. I been thinkin' how could all the elves be full of gladness over a half-orc prince taking over and running things."

Ivansar stood up and bowed before me, a thing I would never get used to. "It matters not what they think. Ashera is queen and you are the Crown Prince Erindriel. Only a full-scale revolution or your death would change the ascendancy."

I grabbed my hair, groaned and scratched my chin. "So, if I was to die, who would take over?"

"There would have to be a gather of the troupe and a choosing. It hasn't happened in a thousand years. Ashera's line is unbroken. You, Erindriel, are its last surviving member if Ashera dies."

"A gathering and a choosing?" I said. "If that was to take place, who would they choose? Stop evading me question. Who has a stake in this?"

Torros joined the group. "There are several high houses that have a claim to the throne. Queen Ashera wishes you to marry Rain Fairfeather, so the Fairfeathers have a solid claim. Then Uriel Silverheart, the Grand Vizier, would certainly be a choice. I heard, before I left, he was upset that Queen Ashera chose Rain instead of his daughter, Wendislas, for your bride."

"What the holy fuck?" I threw up my hands. "Nobody's planning no wedding for me. I be choosing me own bride, think on." I carefully avoided looking at Annabelle. No one needed to know the foolish direction my thoughts took on this touchy subject, but I sure as hell didn't plan to let anyone saddle me with a complete stranger, especially a noble, uppity elf maiden who would look down on me as the ugliest of beasts.

Torros shook his head. "No, Prince Erindriel, you must marry to continue the pure line of Queen Ashera. She is a Shalandale and can trace her lineage back ten thousand years in the Middle Kingdom. She has chosen well for you by picking a Fairfeather. Gorman is a Fairfeather. They trace their ancestry to the original five elf families, as does Ashera."

"Well ain't that special? None of this is enticing me to Greenwood. Got us a bit of work to do killing Slygon. Annabelle's sister is in his disgusting hands. I swore I would help her rescue her sister and I think that be more important."

Tanathlil leaned forward and touched my leg. I glared at his hand and he removed it. "Crown Prince Erindriel, you must go to Greenwood. Queen Ashera's death will plunge the elves into chaos. There's already talk of what will happen if you don't show up and it's horrible. The high families will be at each other's throats. They'll be a revolution in the court and Uriel, the Grand Vizier, will gain control and force all of us to return to the Middle Kingdom. It's his view we should never have come into this world of blue sky and green woods. He says you are an abomination, though he is willing to *sacrifice* his daughter in marriage to you, just to gain more power. He wants control and will do anything to get it."

"Anything? Even kill my brother and my mother?"

The elves' silence was all the answer he needed. I scooted closer to the fire and stared into the flames. Chub thrust a crispy haunch of bear into my hand, I tore off a chunk, and chewed thoughtfully. When I swallowed, I turned to the elves gathered around Tanithlil. "Feels like this vizier fool is daring me to come home," I said.

"We have a job to do going after Slygon," Slag said. "And you promised Annabelle we'd save her sister. But we sure ain't afraid of no elf vizier. Should be able to take care of such an insignificant problem and get back to Slygon in no time. We already got dragons to take us wherever you think we should go, and even though riding them makes me puke, I'm ready."

"What think you, Chub?" I asked.

"I'm with Slag," he said around a mouthful of bear. "We got your back, wherever you need us to be. I been looking forward to another ride. He glanced at Slag. "Unlike Slag here, I find riding dragons to be a great adventure. No casting up me accounts in the bushes like a little girl." He chewed with gusto and swallowed.

"Happen they need me and I'm no coward," I said. "I've never run from trouble before." He gestured to Slag and Chub. "Think on. Haven't we managed to stay one step ahead of trouble?"

Chub shrugged and tore a huge chunk of bear meat off the bone with his teeth. He nodded, chewing.

"And just because you go to see your mother and settle accounts doesn't mean you have to accept the crown," Belle said. "But you need to consider that the elves have political agendas and apparently, some don't want you there. They tried to kill the messenger. Is it even safe for you to visit your mother?"

"Belle," I said. "Deciding this whole thing is rightly in your hands. It's your sister under Slygon's control. This be your mission. It was your idea. You have the deciding vote. If we go to Greenwood, it has to be you who decides."

"Jackal," Annabelle said suddenly realizing something. "Your mother told you your brother died, but do you even know how?"

We both stared at Ivansar. "Well?" I prompted him. "How did Fulven die? I was told in Ashera's letter orcs did it. Be that the whole truth?"

The elf shifted uncomfortably, averting his eyes. "His whole party died. There were four of them," Ivansar said. "We noticed several odd circumstances, but there's little interest in questioning the obvious."

"Does the queen believe orcs killed her son?"

"It's being investigated," Torros said. "But as Ivansar said, there's no evidence it was anything but an orc attack, although your brother and the three with him were seasoned warriors and should have killed orcs, but no orc bodies were found. Orcs don't pick up their dead and haul them home. There should've been bodies."

"And what of my mother? You said she's dying, right? So, from what? Does she have a disease or an injury?"

Ivansar looked down and avoided meeting my eyes.

"Assassination?"

"Possibly," Ivansar said.

"The bastards are trying to kill her to gain the crown."

Torros nodded. "It's only a suspicion, but they suspect poison, my prince."

I could feel the bile dealing with corruption and evil always brought on, rising in my throat. The bear meat churned uneasily in my gut. "You expect me to believe anything you say now, knowing you couldn't even tell me the truth about what I'd be walking into if I agreed to go to Greenwood? Seems like you'd like to lead me and me friends to certain death. Happens I'm not sure whose side yer on."

"But don't you see?" Ivansar grabbed Jackal's sleeve. "We're desperate to have you take control of things. We need you, your highness. We were afraid you might not come if you knew what we suspected, but it's all the more reason for you to come now. Infighting makes us susceptible to attack by outside enemies like the very one you seek, Slygon."

"Has he attacked Greenwood?" Belle demanded.

"Not as yet," Ivansar said to her. "But he and his minions have been sighted in the area lately. They fly over Greenwood on those hideous black dragons as though scouting for weakness."

"Even so, you can't go to Greenwood," Belle said to me. She picked up my hand and held it between both of hers. She had no idea what this simple gesture did to my erratic heart. "They don't want you, Jackal. Out here in The Withers, you're already king. No one would dare challenge you now that we have the dragons. We can fly to Slygon's lair and save Noemi. We can kill him and protect the elves and everyone else by doing it. Remember, he eats infants."

I carefully removed my hand from between hers so I could think. Her mere touch scrambled what little brains I had. "We can still go after Slygon. But it seems clear those damned elves are murdering my kin. Who's to say they won't send assassins after me, rather than waiting to see if I show up? My mother be dying. If I don't see her now, I'll never get her to answer some right important questions."

"If you make it clear you have no interest in them, they'll probably just leave you alone," Belle said.

"Probably? Though I don't like the idea of looking over me shoulder the rest of me life."

Belle

He was right. I knew that. But the idea of some elf assassin ending his life just because the mother who didn't want him was a queen made me uncomfortable, nervous, and scared for him. When did I begin to care so much about what happened to him? Well, we'd been sharing a quest, he'd been helping me toward my goal of finding Noemi, so of course I cared about him like I'd care for any companion. Like I cared for Tiny. Right? We were friends, allies.

"Wouldn't you like to know what happened to your parents? I mean if you could see them after all these years, you'd want to, right?"

"They were great parents, Jackal. They loved me and Noemi. Of course, I want to see them."

I gazed into those golden eyes searching for an answer. I wanted to go after Noemi. It was all I wanted to do. But she was so far away, and Jackal's problems were right here in our face. "You already decided to go, didn't you? You know how much I want to go after Noemi. It's in my head all the time. It's all I think about, her and Slygon," I shuddered. "Together. It's so gross and disgusting it makes me feel sick. But she's been with him for years. I doubt if her situation will get any worse if I take some time to go with you to see your mother."

I touched Jackal's huge chest right where the tribal tattoo was. A sudden premonition snaked up my spine. "This is all going to turn to shit. Greenwood's filled with nothing but hatred and ugliness." I pointed at the three elves. "I can feel it on them. I can hear it in what they don't say. Their people, your people, they hate you, and they're going to hate the rest of us even more."

Chapter Twenty-One

Belle

Jackal pulled me close. I didn't fight, just looked up into his eyes. I felt him trembling.

"You're probably right," he said. "They will hate us. I'm sure they'll hate me and it probably all would turn out terrible. But I have to go. Think on, Belle. My kin be dead. Fulven was me half-brother. If he was killed, he needs avenging. I must go and see the truth of it. Mayhap I can help."

I liked the feel of his arms around me. He was so strong. I'd grown used to his face. It no longer seemed ugly. I saw strength in it and beauty of a sort. His lips were finely molded, his chin square and his golden eyes glowed with love. I knew that and I'd grown used to that, too. I was learning to enjoy the fact he cared for me. "Fine. All of us will go to Greenwood, but we're taking the dragons."

Oranth and I led nine dragons over the thick forest. We flew low. I had a vague idea of where Greenwood lay, but Oranth, the queen, could communicate with all the dragons. The elves on their dragons had given instructions to Oranth. She knew where we were going.

The big gold swooped higher. I clutched Oranth's neck spines and dug my knees into the hollows behind Oranth's wings. Wind snatched at my hair and blurred my eyes. I wished for goggles. When they went after Slygon, all of them would need eyewear. Below, clearings appeared with small cottages. Smoke billowed from forges in a village of over fifty cottages and buildings located in a clearing with roads leading out of it and up the mountain. It must be Jackal's home, Wildwhisper.

Oranth flew higher into the mountains. Crags and cliffs surrounded by thick forests passed beneath her great wings. We rounded a turn and there, hanging off a huge cliff, sat a castle straight out of a fairytale. Tall blue towers topped with peaked roofs were encircled by a granite wall two-feet thick. The entire edifice perched on the edge of the tallest peak. Guards stood sentry on a walkway running along the top of the wall. Trees grew around it and under it making it seem to sit atop the forest.

Jackal rode his bronze beside me. He glanced once at me and nodded. This was Greenwood. It was imposing, but I wasn't afraid. We were riders of dragons. It was amazing how much power the beasts gave us, along with the sense of invulnerability.

Oranth landed on one of the watchtowers with a huge rush of air beneath her span of wings. The remaining eight dragons landed on the wall, sending the guards scrambling for cover. Torros and Ivansar leapt off their dragons and ran along the parapet, chasing the fleeing guards. Below us in the open courtyard, elves gathered to stare in wonder at the nine dragons perched on their walls.

"It be now or never," Jackal said. He climbed off his dragon and followed the two elves. The third elf, Gormar, helped Tiny dismount and followed. I was suddenly assailed by fear. The elves' distain for humans hit me like a physical blow. What weirded me out even more was I couldn't read their thoughts. Their emotions screamed at me; fear, hatred, envy all worn on their sleeves easy for me to see.

The elves were awed by the dragons but disgusted by humans and especially by the half orcs. I wanted to run and tell Jackal coming here had been a huge mistake. These creatures, the elves, would never accept him. His thoughts came into my head loud and clear. He already knew.

"Tiny, wait for me," I said.

Tina stopped. "The elves hate us," I whispered. "I can feel their loathing."

"They don't like Jackal either," Tiny said. "Gormar told me they think he's an abomination."

"Imagine how they feel about Slag. He's three-quarters orc."

"Gormar said they won't want him staying in the castle. He told me Chub and the rest of us humans will be asked to move into the castle village or perhaps the south tower."

Tiny and I followed by Granny and Flossie descended into the courtyard through the tower at the end of the parapet. Dandy popped in beside me. "They hate humans," she whispered.

"No shit," I said. "They don't want Jackal here either."

"Not at all," the fairy said and poufed out.

Jackal

I took a deep breath and made my way across the courtyard. I felt crude and ugly next to the elves who were tall, lithe, and graceful. An older elf, carrying a staff, wearing a miter hat on his head, and a sky-blue robe waited for me to approach. I had the overwhelming urge to stop and make the elf walk to me. I stopped in the middle of the open courtyard. The elf had to be the Grand Vizier, Uriel Silverheart. He held his finely sculpted nose high as though he smelled something foul. His expression was easy to read. He didn't want me here almost as much as I didn't want to be here.

I dug in and waited. I might not have a lot of experience with politics, but I know battle strategy and how to demonstrate strength. Make them come to you.

Silverheart must have figured out I wasn't moving. He gestured with his staff and several guards walked over to talk to me while Silverheart remained in position. I snorted. "Thinks he's better than us," I said to Slag.

"Happen he be wrong," Slag replied.

"I be Crown Prince Erindriel, or so they keep blatting to me," I snarled. "I ain't moving."

Belle took my hand. I knew it was her without looking. I'd know her touch anywhere. "Why is he standing over there?" she asked.

"He wants me to give in and walk over there to meet him," I said. "It's nothing more than a petty power play. I'm guessing he thinks I'm stupid. Well, he can waltz his arrogant elf ass over here if he wants to meet me."

The elf guards stopped and lined up in front of us. One held out his hand. He was older. There were silver threads in his black hair and pointed goatee. "You must be Crown Prince Erindriel. I'm Felis Fairfeather." He pointed with his chin. "That's my son Gormar. I'm to take you to meet Grand Vizier Silverheart."

I shook my head. "Nice to meet you, Mr. Fairfeather. Gormar be a fine lad. But I will be standing here for the rest of me life if that's what it takes afore I'll walk the fifty feet to meet Uriel Silverheart. He be my vassal, me mother's servant so to speak, and he can walk himself over here if he wants to shake my hand."

Felis's fine white skin colored. He glanced back at Silverheart who shook his head.

"Looks like you be in a bit of a quandary." I laughed and pointed at Remoth sitting above him on the wall. Remoth belched a fireball that hit the blue wall of the tower leaving a scorch mark. "Mayhap he'll change his mind now. I could destroy this entire castle by lifting one finger. Think ye can fight off nine dragons sitting on yer walls? I came here because I was summoned. This be fine treatment for the future king, think on. Who does Silverheart think himself, anyway?"

Felis bowed before me, something I liked even less that looking at Uriel Silverheart. "My Prince, Silverheart is a strong-willed man who doesn't wish to give up the control he's had since the queen's illness." Felis's voice was soft and low. "You do well to put him in his place now."

"If he chooses to remain on his side of the courtyard like a stone statue, let him," Slag said. "You, Felis, take Jackal to his mother. There's no need to meet Silverheart. If he wishes to make an ass of himself, let him."

Felis chuckled. "Of course. This way."

I shot one last look at the Grand Vizier standing like a stock surrounded by five guards on the far side of the courtyard. He didn't look happy. Ivansar and Torros bowed to me. "We've been away from our families for many days, Prince Erindriel. If it is your pleasure, we would like to go to them."

I grinned. "Missing yer wives and all, I'm thinking. Be gone then." The two elves shot off into the stable area and were gone.

Felis led us through an arched doorway and up a flight of stairs. The inside of the castle housed mosaics picturing flowers, fountains, dancing sprites and fairies, and colorful tile and crystal ceilings lined the hallway they walked down. When we reached a grand staircase leading to the second floor, Felis stopped. Two young female elves dressed in red livery descended the stairs. "Shaera and Vairi will take the rest of your party to their quarters," Felis said. "We've made room for them in the village."

So, this was how it was going to be. They would house my people, the ones I brought with me, somewhere similar to a pigsty while I was put up in the castle. I glanced at Gormar. "I be taking my men with me. It's not that I don't trust you . . . well actually it's because I don't trust you." I laughed when I saw Felis's horrified expression. "I see I've shown me bad manners, but there you have it, I was raised in a barn. And there's no way I'm going anywhere in this castle without support. You can take the women folk to your village, but be aware, that one," I pointed at Annabelle," can summon the dragons any time she wants, and she can blow this castle to bits if she has a mind to do it."

Felis bowed. "Yes, my prince."

Annabelle grabbed my hand. "I'm not going with them. I'm staying with you until you see your mother."

I patted her arm. She thought I needed her support in this trying moment. I knew that's what she was thinking, and truth be, I'd love to have her. But it would be bad to show these elves any weakness.

Suddenly, the Grand Vizier appeared at the other end of the hallway and walked toward us. He waved his staff. "Take that rabble out of my castle," he said in a voice used to command. His eyes narrowed when he looked at me. "Allow that one," he pointed the staff at me, "to see the woman he calls his mother."

"Are you seriously doubting me lineage?"

Silverheart sneered. "How could a creature as lovely as Queen Ashera have produced a monster like you?"

"So, ye are questioning who I be?" I leaned in close to Silverheart, placing my nose inches from his. "I was summoned by Queen Ashera. If she says I'm her son, you better believe her. She placed me in Eliza Finegold's hands twenty years ago herself. It seems to me, you be questioning the queen's word, not mine. Seems to me, you want to be king, or am I reading this ugly situation all wrong?"

Slag drew his sword halfway out of its sheath and Chub pulled his crossbow off his shoulder and nocked a bolt. Annabelle pointed her finger and the crystal chandelier above Silverheart's head exploded. Tiny glass shards rained down on all of them. Tiny laughed. "Can I do one?" she asked.

Silverheart screamed and fell backward when the chandelier exploded. His guards caught him, tenderly restored him to his feet, then began brushing tiny glass shards off his robes and head. He batted them away angrily. They bowed low and moved behind him as he pointed at Annabelle. "You've assaulted my person. Guards, take her to the dungeons!"

The guards took half a step forward and Slag drew his sword all the way out of the scabbard.

The roar of the dragons sitting on the parapet was clear even through the stone walls. Silverheart's face turned white and he clutched the front of his robe over his heart.

Belle pulled her wand out of her shirt. "If my intention was to kill you, you would no longer be breathing," she said with such softly spoken sweetness the vizier took a step back and glanced around for possible danger.

I held my hand out. "Is this how you wanted our first meeting to go, Silverheart? The dragons will destroy this keep if anyone so much as approaches Annabelle. You seem to think because the queen be ill, you be in charge. Let me assure you, it's only you who be thinkin' it, because the minute we landed here with those dragons, we were in charge."

The Grand Vizier backed up two more steps. "Why you insufferable poser. You'll never be king. I'll see to that." He pointed up the stairs. "Go. See your supposed mother." He pointed to himself. "This is my world and you don't belong in it."

"I been knowing that me entire life, think on. But if slum rats like you are all there is to run this place after the queen be gone, mayhap I do belong here. Mayhap the residents of this keep might be wantin' a real male to run things and not something what crawled out of a sewer."

"At least I'm an elf. You and your, uh, your companions are a sub-species. Elves have been superior to such for thousands of years. Orcs are animals, and humans live their short, squalid lives grubbing for money and food. Elves are far removed from such low pastimes. We create art, poetry, songs. We live hundreds of years, while humans burn out like a rotten torch with little fuel. You eat the flesh of dead animals, while we consume only fruit and honey. We know how to treat such filth. There's a perfect place for them in the human village by the south tower."

Slag, who was three-quarters orc, growled.

"Too bad you're so elevated you lost sight of yer feet," I said. "Yer feet be in the muck. I bet me last grubby piece of silver yer responsible for me mother's illness and me brother's death." I took a big stride and towered over the elf. "And if I find it to be true, you've got a comeuppance of epic proportions due ye."

Silverheart gasped and stuttered. His face turned the color of a ripe apple.

"Caught ye by the short and curlies, didn't I?" I put my arm around Annabelle, and she let me. My heart soared. I pointed at Tiny. "Now, you two stop yer tricks. I can take care of meself."

Silverheart backed up three more feet. His eyebrows slanted as his eyes narrowed. "You've made a dangerous enemy, *Jackal*," he said. "There's little support for you in this castle."

"And I suppose there's lots of support for ye." I shaded my eyes as though searching and looked around, behind him, over his head. "Where might they be hiding? I want to know who killed me brother, Fulven, and I intend to find out. Happen at this moment, I'm thinking it be you or yer supporters. There's a foul smell in this castle, the smell of treason. And I plan to get to the bottom of it." I stared with hard eyes at Silverheart. "And I ain't leaving til I find out who did it."

Chapter Twenty-Two

Jackal

Silverheart whirled on his slippered feet and stormed back the way he came. He disappeared into the enclosed staircase at its end in a swirl of deep-blue velvet.

I shook my head. "Such a rude prick."

"I'm sorry, my prince," Felis said, bowing his head as though ashamed or embarrassed. "Since the queen's illness, he's taken complete control of the palace. No one has dared stand against him."

I waved to Granny. "Where be that damned fairy?"

"She poufed out when we got to the castle," Granny said.

"Just when I particularly need her, she's gone," I said. "Well, you go up with me and examine me mother. If it's poison, mayhap we can heal her. Can you call Dandy?"

Granny shrugged. "She seems to know when she's needed. I never actually call her."

Flossie tugged at my vest. "I can call her."

I scooped precious Flossie into my arms. I loved this sweet child so much. Squeaker fluttered around her head and finally settled on her shoulder. "You do that, poppet, while me and Granny go up and see how me mother be doing."

Annabelle frowned. "I want to go with you."

I shook my head. "She be expecting to meet me, not a herd of folks. Since we don't know how sick she be, I think it best for me to go alone. Granny is only coming because she's a healer and can evaluate me mother's state of health." I carefully set Flossie down. "Since you can call Dandy, do yer best and get her to come to us. I particularly wish her to attend to me mother."

The two elf maidens, who stood to the side while they watched the proceedings with Silverheart wore horrified expressions. They led

Annabelle, Tiny and Flossie off. "You two go with them," I said to Slag. "I'm thinking they might be in need of some help, if you know what I mean."

"But Jackal, shouldn't we go with you? Annabelle and Tiny can surely take care of themselves."

"Now that be the truth. But they might need some muscle or someone to keep them from setting the place afire, so Chub, you go with them. Slag, if you insist come with me. Since orcs offend their delicate sensibilities, let's offend them as much as possible. And besides, Chub, I'm thinking where they're sticking Annabelle is probably close to the kitchens and I can hear yer stomach rumbling from here. Find yerself some food."

The tension and confrontation had drained me, and I hadn't even entered Ashera's bedroom. This entire castle vibrated with hatred, envy, greed and selfishness. Every one of these elves had their own agenda and it wasn't the good of all.

We entered an antechamber. The space was small and filled with ornate chairs that looked uncomfortable to sit in, and for me and Slag, probably impossible.

"Your ass could never fit on one of them chairs," Granny said. "You'd need at least two, and then you'd probably crush them under yer vast weight."

"Too true," I said. Granny was growing on me. She had a foul mouth and a strange sense of humor I enjoyed.

The two guards standing at the doorway leading to my mother's bedchamber bowed and stepped away when I lifted a brow. No doubt Slag's hand on his sword hilt helped. We passed through the antechamber and stopped just inside the bedroom door. I wasn't surprised at the fancy gold filigree or the numerous crystal chandeliers. Of course, my mother would live in a palace like this, but I'd expected a sick room with doctors or nurses in attendance. Instead a number of elegantly dressed nobles scattered in tight, whispering clusters, filled the room. Two human maids knelt on the floor at the foot of a great bed.

"Vultures," Slag said softly.

"Exactly." I pointed at them. "Out, get out now."

Shocked, the elegantly coifed and gowned elves didn't move. I laughed at their stupidity and arrogance. They'd never met me before. It was now time for the rude awakening they all deserved. I strode across the polished floor and grabbed an older man by the arm. "Get out of here right now." I pointed at all of them and then at the door. "Get out. I'm here to meet me mother for the first time and I don't need a freaking audience."

"How dare you touch my person," the elf said.

"I'm Crown Prince Erindriel, soon to be yer king. Now get out of this room afore I throw ye out. And don't think I can't or won't." I yanked Slag forward by his leather jerkin. "Slag, see these folks out."

Slag grinned and bowed low to me which almost set me off in a fit of the giggles. "Yes, my prince, as you command." Slag drew his sword. A snarl was all he needed to break their shocked stupor. They pushed and shoved each other in their rush to exit the room.

After the colorful group, including the two maids, hustled out, Slag slammed the doors in the guards' stunned faces.

With them gone, the moment I'd been dreading was here in all its glory. I hesitated, took a deep breath, and stopped to stare at a life-size painting of the most beautiful elf maiden I'd ever seen. He had to agree with the vizier on this one thing. He couldn't imagine a big lummox like him springing from such elegant and regal beauty.

"That be your mother then? Can't say as I see the resemblance," Slag said. "Though you've her eyes, and her ears, of course."

"Apparently," Jackal said, still not believing it himself. It's one thing to hear a woman is beautiful and another to see how pitiful the word beautiful could be. There was hardness in the porcelain visage, the firm set of her jaw, the slight narrowing of her eyes as she looked down her nose at whatever had captured her attention at the time. That hardness I related to.

"You gonna stand there like a big dummy, or meet yer mam?" Granny asked.

"Spect it be time for the meet." I took another deep breath and turned around to face the huge bed.

The room was easily four times the size of the antechamber with several other closed doors, most likely leading to closets, a dressing room and bath. Granny had already crossed the room and hovered near the enormous canopy bed. "They've left her here to die with no comfort or help," I said. "There be no doctors or aid fer her. That blasted Grand Vizier must be in control of Greenwood already. He be just waiting like a spider, hoping she dies."

My mother lay still, her thin arms outside the plush ermine-trimmed comforter. She looked like the life was being sucked out of her. Her cheeks were hollow, and her eyes sunk inside black-rings. Her hair was dirty and spread across the white sheets. A strange smell hung above the bed, chemicals and death.

There was no resemblance to the beautiful queen in the portrait.

"There's a lot of work for me to do," Granny said. She pointed to Slag. "See if you can find one of them maids Jackal sent packing."

"I wouldn't treat a dog like this," Slag said. "I'll find you someone."

The queen looked asleep, but when I moved closer, her eyes opened as though she'd been awaiting my arrival and knew I was here. She turned her head slightly and gazed at me, her eyes glassy and unfocused. Slowly, the unnatural sheen faded, and a slight smile tugged at the corner of her mouth before a coughing spell doubled her over. Granny supported the queen's thin shoulders as she coughed and coughed.

I'm no nurse. I'd spent exactly zero time attending the sick, but her condition shocked me, and filled me with an overwhelming sense of helplessness and remorse. I should have come to her sooner.

Granny reached for a glass of water on the side table, slipped her hand beneath the queen's head and lifted it so she was able to drink from the glass pressed to her lips. She took a few swallows and settled back into the pillows, taking a slow breath.

"Erindriel, you came. Thank you, my son," she said so softly I barely caught the last. I was both elated and angry with myself for caring. To hear her call me her son meant something even if it was only now she lay dying.

She pointed to a small framed painting on her nightstand. It was a portrait of me, fairly recent. "It doesn't do you justice. You're so big, strong, and solidly built, every bit the mighty warrior I've been told. You will need to be strong if you are to save our people, Erindriel," she said before going into another coughing fit.

"Why is there no doctor here? Why was there a crowd in this room viewing you, but no one helping you?" I was furious at the neglect.

"It's our custom," the queen said. "Elves live a long, long time. When we reach the end of our journey, we know. My time has come. They were here as witnesses to my passing. There's no need for you to be angry. The doctors did what they could, then they left. Death is not the enemy, Erindriel, but an old friend and a doorway to another world."

"I'll need a bit of a looksee first," Granny said, "before we be giving up on life. Your son is a fighter. I can't believe his mother wouldn't be one, too."

"No time," the queen said in a raspy voice. "I must speak to the Crown Prince at once. I have so much to say and so little time left."

An explosion of pink poufed into the room next to me and I jumped. "Damn you, Dandy, you scared the life out of me."

"Sorry, I've been busy. Slygon attacked a village close to his home and drained two children. He left one alive. I was trying to keep it from turning vampire. I heard Flossie's call and came as soon as I could."

"I think ye be too late," I said. "Me mother looks mortal bad."

Granny backed out of the red-velvet bed curtains batting them out of her way impatiently. "Pull these dreadful hangings down, Jackal, and open the windows. It smells like death in here." Granny spotted Dandy. "I'm so glad you made it. I don't know if she can be saved. Jackal, where's the damn maids I asked for?"

"Slag went fer them."

Granny rubbed her nose with two fingers. "Go find him. I need hot water. Yer mum needs a bath. And beef broth. She's weak from lack of food."

"Elves don't eat meat, Granny," Dandy said. She held out her hand and a steaming cup of something hot and fragrant appeared. "Here, this tea is filled with magic and a sustaining blend of herbs and honey. Get her to drink all of it, before it's too late."

Chapter Twenty-Three

Belle

Tiny and I followed the two elf maidens through the castle, down many staircases, past the kitchens, out a door behind the cooking area and along the wall.

Where are they taking us?" I whispered to Tiny. "Back to The Withers? We must be almost on the other side of the mountain by now and a mile from Jackal."

"They don't seem to think very much of humans," Tiny said. "Those two leading us around haven't said a word."

"We're definitely second-class citizens. I shudder to think where they're housing us."

The long walk around the base of the castle led to a series of stables. The walkway opened into a stable yard filled with horses being groomed, elf warriors and maidens practicing with weapons. A tall maiden with a long blond braid stared at us as though we were cockroaches. She even had the nerve to nock an arrow and pretend to fire it at us. A maiden beside her leaned close and laughed. Both wore the garb of huntsmen, green leggings, boots, a leather vest over a close-fitting green shirt. Leather wrist guards protected their arms, and swords hung from a belt around their waists.

Their hatred and disdain only too easy to feel, the negative force of the elves' feelings toward them since they arrived made my head throb. I had trouble reading elf minds, but their emotions surrounded them like an aura, and it was easy to read what they were feeling. I'd never experienced anything like this.

The two maidens leading them passed through the stable yard and into an area where animals were kept, and peasants grew gardens. There were carefully-tended rows of fruit and nut trees, shrubs covered with an abundance of berries and hives of bees bordering the orchard. When I glanced back the way we'd come, I saw the castle was a half mile away and growing more distant with each step we took. It seemed we were to be ostracized.

Small huts began to appear, each surrounded by a garden. Flowers bloomed in profusion bordering the path. The two elf maidens finally stopped at a hut and beckoned to them. "You will stay here," the tallest one said. "You should find everything you need to sustain yourselves in this area. Do not attempt to come into the castle uninvited."

Tiny's chest swelled, and I held out my hand to restrain her. "Don't blow her up. I'll handle this. You take Flossie inside and discover what kind of comforts have been provided for our needs."

I waited until Tiny was gone then stepped in front of the tallest elf, effectively keeping her from making the quick exit she'd obviously planned. "Excuse me. I have urgent duties elsewhere," the elf maiden said.

I shot one of my mental arrows into the elf maiden's mind and she backed a step. "You have the Gift."

"I'm a city Magic," I said. "My companion, Tina wanted to blow you up, something she could easily do. You can't isolate us from our traveling companions. I'm asking you nicely, but we have the power to do as we please. I can call an entire troupe of dragons here if I want."

The elf maiden bowed. It was more of a slight tilt of her head, just the tiniest acknowledgement of the Gift along with a little fear of dragons. She held up her hands and waved them in a circle. A lighted field of energy appeared around the hut. "I too have Gifts, much greater than you humans could ever imagine. You *will* stay where you are told to stay, and you will not bother Prince Erindriel or his men. I have been instructed to place you in accommodations suited to humans. The castle is strictly for elves. We do not allow humans to sully our serenity with their mortal complaints and weaknesses. Why, humans are little more than animals, so far removed from elves as to be a different species. That there are half elves in existence is an abomination we work extremely hard to avoid."

"So, you wish to play games?" I was so angry, I was afraid of what I might do. I was within an inch of calling all the dragons here just to ignite these two elf wenches. Gritting my teeth in an effort to control my bad temper, I waved my hands and created a wall of fire between the elves and the path back to the castle.

The elf maiden blew it out with one breath and turned the ground to ice. Now I was really pissed off. I drew my sword and put the tip at the elf maiden's throat. "I don't care that you look down on me. That's your privilege, but you won't, and you can't make me stay in this hut and twiddle my thumbs while Jackal is hanging out with his mother. I want to know what's happening, I will go into the castle when I wish, and if you try to stop me, I'll fight you."

I lit my sword with my mind and watched the flames dance.

The elf maid backed a pace which brought her right up against her companion whose mouth hung open. "You dare to threaten me?"

"You push me, I push back. You seem to think we're as nothing, lower than your servants. Let me show you something."

I was beyond being sensible. I'd never been treated like this in my life. I was Odafarus's favorite. I could do anything. I felt for the connection to Oranth. The huge golden dragon was hunting nearby. *I need you.*

In less than a minute, Oranth, Remoth and Tina's dragon, Saroth arrived, stirring dirt and debris in the gusts of wind generated by their huge wings. The elf maiden, who had yet to even tell me her name thinking me too far beneath her for pleasantries or even good manners, squealed with fright and ran into the hut followed by her companion. The dragons settled on the high rock wall behind the small hut. I rubbed Oranth's big nose and stroked her face. The dragon made crooning noises.

"You can come out," I called to the elf maidens hiding inside the hut. "As long as I say, they won't hurt you."

The tallest elf maiden stuck her head out the door. Her face was the color of library paste. "Please come out," I said.

The two came out of the hut and walked to the far edge of the hut's clearing. Farther down were three more of the huts. People had come out and were staring at the dragons. I grabbed the elf's arm. "I will go where I please and do as I please. The castle is not off limits to me. I may not be an elf, but I am a rider of dragons. You will respect me."

"Yes, mistress," the elf maiden bowed low this time. "I will tell the guard to allow this. Please don't let your beast eat me."

"What's your name?"

"I'm Shaera and this is Vairi," she said pulling her friend close. They were both trembling with terror.

"Well, Shaera, we appreciate your kindness. Can you tell Prince Erindriel where we are so he can find us?"

"Yes, Mistress, certainly I will give him the message."

I waved my hands as though shooing a flock of chickens. "Go then and give him my message."

Chapter Twenty-Four

Jackal

Twenty minutes after Dandy arrived, Ashera was stronger, clean, sitting up in bed and drinking more of the magic tea. I tried to sit on a chair with disastrous results. I completely destroyed it. A loveseat was carried in, one for me and one for Slag.

"Come with me," Dandy said. She led me into a quiet corner of the room. "Your mother was poisoned in a very subtle but nasty method. She was stung by a silkworm caterpillar. Just brushing against one of these things will kill you, and for some reason, elves are very susceptible. The bugs are native to South America and I've only seen two in my life, but they spin silk so it's possible one of the elves knew about them and their poisonous nature. A tiny brush with one brings on stomach cramps, vomiting, and organ failure. Your mother was in the last stages of silk-worm poisoning. I had to taste her blood to find the poison. Not pleasant, but I think I've got her on the road to recovery."

"Who would do this?" My head ached, and I longed for a good gallop on Thor across The Withers to clear the poisonous vibrations of this awful castle.

"I can think of one in this castle for sure."

"The Grand Vizier, right?"

"Him or a member of his family. I've been listening into their conversations, and they all want Wendislas to marry you, not Rain."

"Happen, I ain't marrying either of them."

Dandy grabbed my forearm. "You have to," she said, more serious than I'd ever seen her. Then she frowned, staring at me with such intensity, I couldn't look away. "I know you think you're out of this, above it, but you're not. The elves are vital in this new world of ours. We need them to be on the side of good, and to stand against all evil such as Slygon. Creatures like Slygon are taking control all over the world. Defeating him and others like him is the only way this world and those living in it will survive. You must take your role in these events seriously if you hope to save those for whom you care."

I closed my eyes. Court politics. People, elves, they were so devious and sly, so foreign to me. Intrigue and duplicity did not suit my nature. If I couldn't beat it to death with my sword or my fist, I didn't want to deal with the problem. "It's good to see me mother improving, and I don't mind what they be thinking of me. Truth be real, I don't know them, and they don't know me, which is all the more reason the sooner she gets better, and I leave, the better we'll all be."

"I know it's strange and confusing to you, but like it or not these elves need you, need you for what's going on now and for what's coming. The vizier isn't going to just let you walk away. You're going to have to deal with him, and deal with your kingdom. And it is your kingdom whether you like it or not." Dandy shoved him toward the door. "Think about what I said. Go take a break. Find Annabelle and talk to her. She misses you."

"What?" I tripped on the edge of a thick carpet and cursed my big feet. "Belle be missing me?"

"You are the most thick-headed individual I have ever known," Dandy said. "Of course she misses you. She's starting to love you, though she has yet to realize it."

I grabbed my hair. "Don't be playing games with me, Dandy. You know I love her, and I will until I'm dead. What do I do?"

"Be yourself. Be strong. Do your duty. Help her rescue her sister as soon as you can get out of here." She turned and stared at the queen lying on her sick bed. "Every heroic deed makes her love you more. And that's who you are. You're a hero, Jackal. You just don't know it or see it, but you are. Belle is starting to understand that and eventually, she will love you for it."

"Can't you sprinkle some fairy dust on her for me? You know, make her love me with magic?"

"That would be wrong, and you know it. It's also not necessary. Just be yourself."

"I don't fit in here, Dandy. As hard as they try to make me like one of them, it just won't take. How can I be Crown Prince when I can't even sit in one of their dainty little chairs?"

"Make changes. You're allowed. Get the queen to make you Regent. Once you're in charge, you can make all the changes you want. You can round up a force and ride against Slygon and rescue Annabelle's sister." She laughed. "You can order all the chairs made bigger and stronger."

Slag pushed into the room past two elf guards. My relief at seeing his familiar face was ridiculous. "Jackal, these people don't eat real food. Chub's starving to death. We need to go hunting, kill something tasty like red meat. All they have here is chicken or eggs and cheese. Why it's likely Chub will never shit again. He's eaten two wheels of cheese in the last three hours. They've cattle a plenty, but it's all fer milk." He hawked, looked around for somewhere to spit, and ended up swallowing, then cursing.

I'd never felt so close to anyone as I felt to Slag at that moment. This was real talk. Hunting, fishing, feeding Chub. I knew and understood these things. They were clean and unsullied by avarice or backstabbing. My men were down-to-earth, real people, while these elves lived in rarified levels I'd never wanted to visit much less reside in. I doubted I'd ever be comfortable here.

I clapped Slag on the back. "Me mother be feeling some better. I think we should take the dragons back to where we left the horses and that hound of Torros's. Can't expect them to hang around in that clearing forever, but we should be able to gather yer Bunny and that mule of Chub's. The mule be too smart to leave Chub. She knows where her oats come from."

"Can we hunt on the way there?"

"We can hunt on the way back here." He made a face. "I know, I have no love fer it neither, but I have a job to do here. I'll explain some of what's going on after we round up our animals."

We found Chub sitting in the kitchens staring at a chicken leg, a hunk of bread, and a slice of cheese. When he saw us, he leapt to his feet. "Jackal, holy mother of god, man, I be about to starve to death." He pointed to his plate. "Look at this, will ye? Chicken be all well and good as a change of pace, but fer a steady diet, ugh. I'll fade into nothing." He pulled his shirt out. "Look at me. I be down three stone at least."

My laughter rang out. It felt so good to laugh. This was the first real laugh I'd had since entering the palace. "Come with us. We be going to find Belle, have her summon the dragons, and go get yer damn mule and my Thor. I miss me horse. On the way back here, we'll do a bit of hunting."

Chub nodded. "Now that's an idea I can grab hold of." He poked Slag in the gut. "You up to flying, barf bag?"

Slag scowled. "Won't be that long a ride. I'll close me eyes."

We left the kitchen, stumbled around until we found the stables where elf warriors and elf maidens practiced their skills of war. Some sparred hand to hand. Some were shooting at targets with their long bows, and some were fighting. I spotted two maids, both tall, almost look-a-likes, with long blond braids. They were dressed as hunters in identical green outfits. They were beautiful and fierce as they fought each other with wooden swords. I thought they looked like good warriors even though maids, just like my Annabelle.

Chub grabbed a servant running for the kitchens. Only a boy, he carried a basket of fruit. "Hey, you, where be the humans kept?" Chub asked. "The ones what came with us."

"They the ones can call dragons?" The boy's eyes lit with excitement.

"Yes, they be the ones we're looking for."

"Keep going past the stables and the open yard, walk through the orchards and you'll find a group of cottages. Your friends are in the first one."

Chub let the boy run off with his fruit after grabbing a ripe peach out of the basket. He munched as they passed along the edge of the practice yard. One of the maidens I noticed glanced over at them and deliberately looked away. "That be yer affianced bride," Slag said. "Someone pointed her out to me while you were sitting with yer mum."

"Which one? They're as alike as two peas in a pod."

Chub snickered. "Heard in the kitchens they be more than just friends. Don't think she'll be fancying ye. Not only is your plumbing all wrong, but yer such a lummox."

I stopped and stared at Chub. "You mean . . .?"

"Exactly. Yer bride-to-be likes the girls almost as much as Slag. Not males, and fer sure not orcs."

"Why would the elves try to marry me to a maiden who loved another, maiden or not? It makes no sense, Chub. It has to be for political purposes, and from what I've seen of these elves, that's probably true. How we supposed to make children if she fancies girls? Do they just want me to donate my royal sperm?"

Chub burst out laughing. "Could be the thing."

"Well, I don't like underhanded dealings, plotting, or manipulating people. These sons-a-bitching elves seem addicted to gossip, petty squabbles, and grasping for power. Maybe living for hundreds of years does that to you. If that be the case, I'd rather not take part in any of it."

We arrived at Annabelle's cottage to find Flossie outside picking flowers. "Jackal!" Her sweet voice filled my heart with happiness. I needed something pure after the dirty dealings of the castle.

Flossie threw herself into my arms. Flowers went everywhere. The tiny dragon squeaked and fluttered around the girl's head as I kissed her cheek. "Where's Annabelle and Tina?"

Flossie pointed. "Inside cleaning." She made a face. "Tiny said they had real pigs living in there, and there were bugs all over. Fleas too, they ate me alive." To illustrate her comment, she scratched a red welt on her arm.

I ducked as a bench flew out the door and landed in the overgrown yard. It was followed by a woven mat, a wool blanket and a cloud of dust. Belle appeared in the doorway wearing an apron over her leather riding pants and boots, swinging a straw broom. She saw me and scowled. "They've housed us in a pigsty," she said. "I made jokes about them doing just that, and here we are. Pigs. If we have to sleep here, we'll be eaten by fleas."

Chub pushed past me and into the hut. "Got anything to eat in there? You know, like meat?"

Tiny pushed Belle out of the doorway. She carried a small chest made of wood mostly rotted and eaten by termites. She toted it to the edge of the castle, where the walls of the south tower jutted high, dropped it, and slapped her hands on her hips. "Nice of you three to show up. We've been ostracized out here in the sticks with the peasants and the bugs while you three were yucking it up in luxury."

"Happen we weren't yucking it up," Chub snarled. "All I've eaten for two days is cheese and a bite, a mere morsel, of chicken."

Tiny bent over laughing. "Oh my god, I'm so sorry. Poor Chub. You must be wasting away."

I grabbed Annabelle's arm. "I need a word with you." I glanced into the hut and added, "and whoever thought this a fit place for you."

"Let me get rid of this apron and broom."

They walked into the orchard, found a bench under a peach tree and sat down. "What's happened?" she asked.

"Me mother were poisoned. Dandy said it were a very slick method. Someone used a caterpillar, a right poisonous one."

Belle nodded. "I felt as much. Her illness didn't feel right. Not that I was allowed into her room or anywhere in the castle for that matter."

"One thing good about yer being out here. The air be fresh and not tainted by backstabbing, court intrigue, and people out fer yer blood."

"Was Dandy able to save her?"

"Oh, yeah, she be getting better now, but she needs to be under constant watch and guard until I can figure out who did it."

"So, who's guarding her?"

"Dandy and Granny and a bunch of elf guards. None from that one family, the Silverhearts. I ain't trusting none of the Grand Vizier's folks."

"That's smart. Who are you trusting?"

I rubbed his eyes. "None of them. Thinking about the entire thing be giving me a right terrible headache. Why can't people be honest and true? Just being in the castle for a day has me feeling dirty and sullied."

She laughed and patted my arm. I must have imagined her hand lingered for just a moment feeling the muscles. I must have. "I bet. It's completely opposite your nature."

"Can you call the dragons? We be needing to fetch the horses and the mule. We also want to hunt, get some meat fit fer Chub before he wastes away to nothing."

"Done," Belle said, smiling. "It will be good to get away from here, if only for a while. How much longer do you think we'll have to stay here, Jackal?"

I knew she was working hard to make her voice casual, but the hopeful look on her face, the look that said, please, we've helped you, now what about your promise to help me find my sister, filled me with guilt. She was here, all of them were here because of me, and look how they were being treated. I'm supposed to be Crown Prince and my friends were tossed into a pigsty as though they were garbage. Any one of them was worth a hundred elves. God she was so beautiful. Even with her cheeks smudged with dirt, and though I could never tell her, she fairly reeked of pig shit. She was the most beautiful woman I'd ever set eyes on. I loved the simplicity of her, the humanity. Elves were so frigging perfect.

"Don't know, Belle. I want out of here right now, but I'm afraid to leave me mother sick unto death. They'll just finish her off if I leave."

She nodded. "You're right. I don't like it, but you're right."

Sitting here with her was the most comforting thing I'd done. I'd missed her more than I realized. I don't think I'd ever missed anyone before. Belle didn't deserve to be treated like this. None of them did.

It was time for me to do more than whine about being confused and unsure of myself and make some changes.

"Well, if we're stuck here for a while, I'm going with you to get the horses. I need some air. Air that doesn't stink of pigs or elves. Did you notice they all smell like flowers? God! It's making me hate flowers."

Jackal's heart leapt. Time spent with Annabelle was always wonderful, filled with longing and feelings he hoped she returned. Dandy's words had given him hope. "Sure, ye can come. Be good fer ye to get out."

They walked back toward the huts to tell the others.

Tiny popped out of the cottage and shook a blanket. "You guys going somewhere?" she asked as if she'd heard their conversation.

Belle grabbed Tina's hands. "Your intuition is uncanny sometimes. Jackal is making a trip on the dragons to get the horses. I'm going." Her voice was filled with the excitement of time away from something onerous.

Tiny tossed the blanket back into the hut and hands on hip declared, "Don't think you're going without me. If you get to ride, I get to ride."

"What about Flossie?" Belle asked. "We can't leave her here by herself."

"Get Granny. She's just in the queen's chamber watching Dandy do her thing. She can watch Flossie."

"I'll get Granny. You two get ready and we'll leave as soon as the dragons show up."

I grabbed Slag. "Run back into the castle and round up Granny. We need a babysitter."

Slag took off at a jog through the orchard toward the stable yard.

I wondered if I should leave Slag here to guard Flossie and Granny. It seemed stupid with an entire cadre of elf warriors doing war exercises in the stable yard mere steps away. Slag would probably complain, too.

Gusts of warm summer air almost blew me off my feet. When I looked to the sky, dragons dropped from high in the clouds, diving like bullets, wings folded. They pulled up at the last minute and settled on the rock wall behind the huts in a storm of dust and dead leaves.

Belle appeared dressed in leathers. She wore strange goggles that fit over a leather helmet. When I laughed, she put her hands on her hips. "What? I'll be able to see clearly no matter how fast Oranth flies. You should get the saddle maker to fashion you a pair."

Slag jogged up, breathing hard. "Granny be on her way."

"Give her a minute," Belle said. "She is old. It takes her a while to get up and down the stairs. Do you think we should leave Flossie here by herself to wait? The dragons are impatient to take off."

"I imagine she'll be fine, won't you, poppet?" I tickled Flossie's chin.

"No, I won't be fine. Take me with you." The little girl's chin jutted out.

Belle wagged her finger. "You run next door to Mrs. Wingate's cottage. She'll take care of you until Granny gets here. She's on her way. It won't be long."

Flossie's face darkened. "I'm scared to be alone. The dark man will come get me."

Belle laughed and pushed her toward the adjacent cottage. "No, he wouldn't dare come here. There're too many elf warriors protecting you. Now go."

I felt a twinge of unease as I watched Flossie and her little dragon trudge to the neighboring cottage. When an older woman came out and put her arm around Flossie's slumped shoulders, I felt better. She'd be fine. We waved to her as we climbed aboard the waiting dragons. Flossie tossed her hair, spun on her heels, and disappeared into the hut.

Chapter Twenty-Five

Belle

Flying on Oranth was the most amazing experience a person could have. With my feet tucked behind the great golden wings, I held tightly to her jutting neck spines. The gigantic golden dragon soared high over the trees and crags of the mountains. With my goggles on I saw everything below clearly. The landscape flew by and in just a few minutes we were circling the clearing where we'd left the horses.

Oranth landed on a dead tree, scaring Thor into headlong flight. Slag's big mare stood her ground and munched the fresh grass growing in the sunny area as though completely unconcerned. The rest of the dragons deposited their riders and took off. It always amazed me at how clumsy they were on land and how graceful in the air.

Jackal stood in the middle of the clearing and whistled. Thor galloped up snorting and blowing, followed by Chub's mule and the wolfhound. The rest of the horses galloped up behind them. It took a few minutes to gather all of our belongings, load the pack animals and saddle the horses. I just started pulling the cinch tight on my saddle when I got a terrible mental call.

It was so loud and so painful, I doubled over, clutching my leather helmet. "Jackal!" I screamed.

He was beside me in a heartbeat, pulling me close to his huge body. I clung to him. "What is it, love?" he asked.

"Flossie, Slygon attacked and took Flossie. I can hear her crying inside my head. Dammit, she said this would happen. Why didn't we listen?"

Jackal patted my back as though I was a child, and suddenly I realized I was pressed against his huge body. The confusing thought that I'd found his embrace comforting was chased away by fear for Flossie. "I have to go after her immediately. This is all my fault."

"Nay, lass, what can you do against the forces of Slygon?"

"We can chase him to his lair and get her back." Mental images of the little girl laughing and playing in the yard hurt like a knife in her belly. She had laughed, actually laughed at Flossie's fears. Her words of, *I'm scared to be alone, the dark man will….. I'm scared!*

I'm scared!

I'm scared!

I shoved my fist against my mouth to still the scream of guilt and rage threatening to escape. My pain and guilt threatened to overwhelm me. I'd let Flossie down. I'd abandoned that innocent little girl and left her at Slygon's mercy when the child had begged me . . . even pleaded to be taken along with us.

"Don't you think we should go back to the castle and see what happened first?"

"No, I don't. We'd be wasting time." I called Oranth again, cried out in desperation. The dragon answered she was far away hunting for fish. My connection to the golden dragon was strong. I urged Oranth to come to me, let her see the terror and panic in my heart. Oranth assured me that she was already on her way and sent me comforting thoughts.

"The dragons are coming," I told Jackal, hands clenched, realizing every second we waited was an opportunity for Slygon to harm her. "The dragons have already flown far away so it will take some time for them to get here. I pray it's not too much time."

"Slag," Jackal called. "Send Chub back to the castle with the stock. "We're going after Slygon. He's taken Flossie."

"Tiny," I said. "Can you go with Chub to help him with all the livestock while we get Flossie back?"

"You need me more than he does. I'm as good a fighter as you and I can blow things up."

"We don't know what's going on at the castle. I'm getting weird messages about other children being stolen, babies. Everyone there is panicking. I'd call Dandy if I could, but Flossie is the one who does that." I rubbed my eyes. Tears steadily dripped down my face. I couldn't stop crying. Damn, I never cried unless I was really pissed off. "We need you to find Dandy and send her to Flossie." Tiny burst into tears and I hugged her. "I feel so helpless," I sobbed. "What if he drains her or turns her into a vampire? I have to go now. Now, before it's too late. Where are those damn dragons?"

"If you really want me to go with Slag, I will," Tiny said. "Don't worry. We'll keep Granny safe and I'll find Dandy. You concentrate on getting to Flossie before that bastard hurts her."

"Thank you." I gave her a quick squeeze. "I knew I could count on you."

Tiny nodded and ran off with Slag to help Chub get the stock ready to ride the long distance through the mountains.

When the dragons landed, Chub and Tiny were already on their way and Jackal was pacing. "Damn this is taking forever. We're gonna have to chase 'em all the way to their lair."

I rubbed my stiff neck, ready to explode with anger, fear, and restrained energy. "Let's ride," I called out as I raced toward Oranth, and launched myself onto her back.

The three of us flew west along with many more from the pride of dragons. Sensing my panic, Oranth decided to take extra able-bodied fighting dragons. They'd left a few to help the juveniles guard the eggs. I counted twenty-two dragons and our three riders. We were a formidable fighting force and depending upon how many riders Slygon had with him, we stood a good chance of getting Flossie back if we could catch him before he got to his lair.

We flew for hours before we reached the Rocky Mountains, my hope by that time hanging on by a thread.

I can smell them, Oranth said to me. *They have yet to reach his castle. There are only five black dragons, and each is carrying two vampires and the children they have stolen, including your Flossie. They are flying slower than us. I tried to speak to our brothers. They are not totally controlled by the dark, but they can only squeeze out short answers to my questions. I ordered them, as their queen, to fly slower which I believe they will do.*

I passed the information to Jackal.

"Be the only piece of good news I've had this day," he yelled across the noise of rushing wind.

We flew on and, in another hour, I spotted them, five black specks moving northwest. Clouds billowed toward Slygon and his dragons. Thick, ugly black clouds pregnant with rain, arrows of lightening shooting throughout. The black specks were only moments from disappearing into the clouds.

"Go faster!" I waved my arm at Jackal. "Tell your dragon to fly as fast as it can."

Our pride of dragons sped up and shot toward the five black specks. In minutes, I spotted Flossie's bright hair. The little girl slumped forward as though straining away from the evil behind her, fighting against the straps binding her in front of Slygon. He would be the one holding her. He knew she was mine.

A dark aura surrounded him. It was thick and black and melded with his dragon to form a swirling inky cloud like the ones they approached. If he reached those clouds, we would never find him. I shot a thought at Flossie and the little girl looked back. I knew when Flossie spotted us. I felt it.

I dropped back on Oranth while Slag and Jackal moved in front of me on their faster male dragons. Oranth was bigger and heavier, a queen meant for laying eggs. Jackal's bronze, Remoth, was faster than Slag's brown, Lionth. Jackal bent low over his dragon's neck, drew his crossbow and fired one of the silver-tipped arrows we'd brought away from Craggy Town. It hit the last dragon rider. Though gravely injured, the vampire turned, saw them and gestured to Slygon. Slygon grabbed Flossie off the back of his saddle and hung her over the side as though he was going to let go. The dying vampire fell across the back of its black dragon and held on.

A tiny green speck attacked Slygon. I saw it and held my breath. Slygon dropped Flossie. The girl cartwheeled through the air, falling fast. I swear my heart stopped, fear for the little girl screaming through me. I urged Oranth to fly faster, but we both knew we'd never catch her in time. *Flossie!* My thoughts shot out to the little girl.

Jackal dove for the ground in an effort to come up beneath her. I raced forward, closing the gap between us, my focus glued to the falling child and Jackal's dragon diving toward her. That was when something amazing happened. Dandy appeared. Flossie was snatched out of the air by Dandy and they both disappeared.

I let out my breath and sobbed tears of relief. I must be mad as hell. I refocused on Slygon and my anger justified my damp cheeks.

Jackal's dragon, Remoth, instantly course corrected, shooting up and under the five black dragons. Slag shot three silver-tipped bolts one after another and hit the biggest black dragon. Pain lanced through my heart as Oranth's grief for a dragon she'd known before he was taken over by Slygon sliced into her. The dragon changed into a bronze as it died, crashing to the tops of the mountain. The vampire riding it fell too, but survived, crawling into a pile of rocks to escape Slag's arrows.

The vampire rider Slag shot lost its tenuous grip and toppled off its dragon. Jackal caught up with the free dragon and cut it away from the other four. Oranth flew up and I was stunned when the big dragon breathed not blazing-hot fire, but an icy-blue flame over the black. Its color instantly changed to green and it slowed. Oranth sped up and caught another black. I nocked a silver-tipped arrow in my crossbow and shot the vampire hugging the black dragon's neck. It erupted in black flames and turned to dust that drifted behind the dragon. Oranth breathed her blue fire over the dragon and it became a brown.

Jackal was flying fast after Slygon. With huge wing flaps Remoth went high over Slygon, then dropped like an arrow toward the evil vampire and his black dragon. Jackal pulled a wooden spear off pockets hanging off the side of his dragon, and held it aloft, ready to throw it when he got close enough. The two remaining dragons were close to the storm. Rain began pelting them and lightening flashed around the two fleeing dragons. Jackal ignored the rain and the lightening and pushed Remoth to fly into the storm after Slygon.

My heart pounded with fear for Jackal as he pursued Slygon. When he drew close enough, he threw the spear with all his immense strength. His aim held. The wooden spear flew toward Slygon, but just before it hit him, Slygon morphed into the huge cobra and dropped to the ground where it disappeared in the driving rain and rocks.

"Fuck!" I screamed.

Oranth caught up with the loose black dragon. Two saddle pockets bulged on the dragon's side. I swallowed hard because I knew the contents. But they'd be safe there, warmer and dryer than if I tried to juggle them atop the gold queen in the wet, fierce winds, until they reached home.

Oranth breathed her blue fire across the black amidst the driving rain and wind. A bolt of lightning lit the dragon as it changed into another golden. Slygon had been riding a perverted queen. *My daughter.* Oranth's thoughts reached me. The golden dragon flew toward them and the two dragons flew side by side.

The one remaining dragon and its demonic rider escaped into a coal-black cloud. Safe. For now. The storm raged around them. Jackal waved his hand and they all turned to go back the way they'd come. I didn't know where Flossie was, but we'd saved three dragons and the precious cargo they carried in their saddle bags. I prayed Dandy and Flossie were safe. As we flew back across the mountains, Flossie's tiny green dragon landed on my shoulder and clung there shaking with terror and the cold. Poor Squeaker. He had a cut on his head and a tear in one of his wings. It was he who attacked Slygon, causing him to drop Flossie.

I stroked his head. "What a good boy you are."

Oranth crooned her pleasure and Squeaker huddled under my arm and dozed as we slowly flew the many miles back to Greenwood and the castle.

Chapter Twenty-Six

Belle

When we arrived at the village surrounding the castle, the dragons landed on the rock wall behind Belle's cottage with a rush of many wings, stirring dust and debris into a cloud that settled slowly. Peasants ran out of their huts and surrounded them. It was dusk, and the setting sun glinted off Oranth's bright scales and those of her daughter whose name was Damoth. When I hopped off, my legs felt boneless. I wobble-walked to the new queen and pulled off the saddle pockets. Inside, two infants wailed for their mothers, one human and one elf.

Melwin Tanithlong, Ivansar Ravenwing's mother, ran out of the castle followed by Phanasia Ravenwing and several other elf maidens. Hovering like an evil shadow behind them, the Grand Vizier, Uriel Silverheart, scowled as he stalked through the orchard. When Oranth saw him, she raised her wings and hissed.

I know, he's evil, I agreed in a silent message to Oranth.

Yes, he's filled with the venom of hate. I feel it. He has lived too long and the darkness in his soul has taken him over.

One of the peasants ran forward when she heard the babies cry. "Did you save my Donny? Is he in there?"

I lifted one of the babies. A boy of about ten months. The child was wet. "Is this him?"

The woman snatched the baby and clutched him to her chest, sobbing like her heart would break. "Thank you, thank you. I thought never to see him again."

Melwin pushed through the growing crowd. "I too lost a babe." I held the elf child out and the woman cried, "That is not my Aframeil."

Her wrenching sobs broke my heart. "There may be other babes. We haven't searched all the satchels yet."

Tears flooded Melwin's cheeks and her face contorted as she sobbed. "I have been unable to conceive for so long. He's the child of my heart. He was here in this village with his wet nurse." She looked around. "I hadn't realized how poor these cottages are. It's dreadful." She covered her face with a scarf. "The smell."

The elf baby was quickly claimed by a Morthian elf maiden as Jackal landed his bronze. Jackal leapt off Remoth and rushed to the two other dragons they'd saved. He found babes in three more saddle pockets. One was Melwin's son. She clutched the child to her breast, sobbing into the baby's curly red hair. None of the other babies were elves and none were children of the peasants living in Greenwood. I held a two-year old girl in my arms. "Jackal, these children must belong to people in Wildwhisper or some other village close by."

"Don't worry, my love," he said. "I'll search for their parents tomorrow. It's getting late."

"Did you just call me your love?"

Jackal's bronze skin turned purple. "It slipped out. You see, I'm in the habit of calling all me women friends and relatives love. Sorry. Won't happen again."

He looked so embarrassed, I laughed. I knew he was telling a fib, but I didn't mind. The thought of being his love was oddly exciting. "Well see that it doesn't."

I took a step back, my heart racing. The moment was awkward and wrong for what he wanted to say, and I knew it. So did he.

He turned away abruptly to talk to Slag who bounced a chubby boy of about three on his knee.

Two of the peasant women stepped forward to take the children. I handed the little girl I was holding to one of the women. The plump serving woman snuggled the child in her arms. "Have no fear, my lady, we'll take good care of them until you find their parents."

"I know you will, but I'm no lady. My name's Annabelle. Please call me that or even Belle. Doesn't matter, I'll always answer."

The woman curtsied, then hurried off to one of the cottages further down the row.

Jackal was on his way to the castle. I ran after him. "Where's Dandy and Flossie?"

"Don't know, Belle," he said, over his shoulder. "That damned fairy coulda popped in anywhere." He turned his head and pointed. "Look, here comes Granny."

The old woman actually ran through the orchard toward them. "I have her," Granny shouted. "I have Flossie."

Granny held her long skirt in one hand and towed the little girl behind her with the other. Flossie made it halfway through the orchard before a tiny green dragon flew toward the little girl squeaking and chirping up a storm. Flossie pulled Squeaker close and sobbed over the little dragon. "Squeaker saved me, Belle. He attacked that black man and bit his nose."

I hugged her as tight as I could, probably squeezing too hard, but I was so glad to see her, then I whirled around with her laughing until we were both dizzy. The tiny dragon fluttered around her head. "Squeaker has a booboo," I said, setting Flossie on her feet and kissing each of her cheeks. "I think Granny should look at him."

"We'll get him fixed up right away," Granny said and then scowled at me. "I can't stand the thought of that devil straight from hell touching Flossie and hurting Squeaker. I'm so dang mad I'm ready to shit meself."

Melwin was still standing in the clearing around our small cottage. She held her baby close as she turned in a circle to examine the cottages. "This is unacceptable," she said. "The conditions here are reprehensible." She rounded on the Grand Vizier. "This is your fault. The queen is ill, and you took charge. You've allowed this to happen because you don't care. These women take care of our babies. Slygon knew he could steal them with ease because they're not guarded." She poked Uriel Silverheart in his purple-velvet covered chest. "Fix it. Clean this mess up and build these people decent homes. Make sure you surround this compound with the same protective shields you put around us."

Silverheart backed away from the onslaught of Melwin's poking finger. "It isn't my fault. The serfs have always lived like pigs. They like it that way."

Jackal fronted Silverheart. "Do what the lady says and get this fixed. I be Crown Prince and that's an order."

"You have yet to be named Regent. I'll take this matter up with the queen when I'm good and ready."

Jackal growled. "You'll take care of it now or answer to me and them." He waved his arms at the dragons and they rose on their hindlegs and roared.

Silverheart's pale face turned ashy. He clutched a fold of his robe and backed away. "We'll just see about this."

Remoth rose into the air and dropped his huge head toward Silverheart. The Grand Vizier turned on his heels and ran toward the castle as though hell hounds were on his tail.

"Happen we will," Jackal murmured.

Melwin watched Silverheart run away. When he was out of sight, she grabbed me in a warm embrace. "You and the Crown Prince saved my child. I will be forever in your debt."

I smiled with embarrassment, relieved when her attention moved back to her child and she scurried off toward the castle to care for him. Then I took Jackal's hand. "We need to talk."

His eyes lit and I punched him. "Your thoughts are," I paused, "Off the mark."

"Damn," he said but he said it with a smile in his eyes. "What do you need to speak to me about?"

"Slygon. He's at his weakest right now. We took most of his dragons. We should take this opportunity to hit him while he's down."

"Happen that's a good plan. I agree, he'll be weak and nursing his grievances. And he only has one or two dragons left. We should nail him before he gets more."

I grabbed his hand and pressed it to my cheek. His face turned a strange plum color. "Belle," he whispered and took her in his arms. They felt good around me, strong like him, and comforting, and exciting in the oddest way. I was suddenly hot and breathless. When he bent down to kiss me, I met his kiss eagerly. It was my first-ever kiss. When his lips touched mine, heat raced through my body. I felt so alive. Our minds came together, and I experienced what he felt, and it overwhelmed me. For moments, I don't know how many, I was lost in the kiss.

"Ahem," a rough voice broke through our strange physical and mental joining. Jackal had picked me up and held me tightly against him. I didn't even remember him doing that. He gently put me back on the ground. I could barely stand. He wrapped one huge arm around me. I was so grateful for the support.

"Got a bit of work to do in the castle," Slag said with a grin. "Hated to interrupt such a lovely moment, but yer mum be calling for you. She has something for you to sign."

"We're going after Slygon, right?" I said from the circle of Jackal's arm.

"We'll plan a raid tonight and leave at first light," Jackal said.

"You promise?"

"Cross me heart."

Chapter Twenty-Seven

Jackal

I found Ashera propped up in bed nibbling on a biscuit and drinking tea. Dandy was in attendance. The fairy glared at me. "Your mother is continuing to improve but not out of the woods yet. So, don't be bothering her or getting her excited."

"I won't," I mumbled, suddenly feeling like an ox in a glass house. "Thank you for saving Flossie. I'm not sure I would have reached her in time."

Dandy nodded, then backed away. His mother's thin hand shot out from under the covers. "I have something you need to sign."

She pointed at a scroll sitting on the bedside table. Her voice was a little stronger, but still weak and raspy. I grabbed the scroll and let it unroll so I could read it, glad for the hundredth time for the small school in Wildwhisper where I'd learned to read English and Elvish.

His mother pointed to a quilled pen and a bottle of ink. "Sign it," she commanded, like the queen she was.

"In a minute," I said, refusing to let her push me too far too fast. "Happen I be reading what I sign afore I sign it, think on."

She surprised me by keeping quiet. I glanced at her before returning to the document. His mother actually smiled as he read. "This makes me Regent, Crown Prince and ruler in your name. Happen Uriel Silverheart will not be happy 'bout this at all."

"I expect you to deal with Silverheart when the time is ripe. You're strong enough to stand up to him in the meantime, and if you would but talk to and be seen in the company of Rain Fairfeather, it would help your cause, get you some powerful support in making changes and taking charge. She's a strange girl but well-liked. It's a good match."

"I ain't gonna do it, Ashera. I won't marry no elf. I got me own plans."

Ashera fell back against the pillows. "Sign. Please, I grow tired."

I placed the scroll flat on the table and started to sign it Jackal. Laughing, I sighed. "What's me damned name again? I keep forgetting."

"Erindriel Glynfire."

"I thought me father was Tanlas Silverheart. So why ain't I a Silverheart? Did you not marry him?"

Ashera waved her hand, a weak gesture displaying the depth of her illness and the toll it had taken on her. "That's a story for another time. Sign. It will give you a place here and power to do as you please. I won't have that toad Grand Vizier ruling my people anymore."

"Spell me name."

She did, and I signed the edict making me Regent, a title I didn't want, dumping a ton of responsibility on me, responsibility I also didn't want or need. All I wanted was to take Belle and go after Slygon to rescue her sister. I'd promised we would, and I intended to keep that promise. After dusting my signature with sand and blowing on the ink, I rolled up the scroll and handed it to her. "There, you have what you wish."

"And Rain?"

"I ain't gonna marry her, Ashera. I have work to do."

She grabbed the front of my leather vest. "If you don't, this kingdom will dissolve into shit."

I was surprised to hear her use that word, but I supposed it was to shock me. I refused to be moved by her attempt to manipulate me. "I be Regent, that's all you get from me. If I have to, I'll hurl Uriel Silverheart out the front gate along with all of his followers. I got no problem doing it. I got dragons backing me and plenty of men who support you and me, but I won't marry Rain what-ever-her-name-is."

"There's a formal dinner in the state dining room tonight. Attend. For me."

I groaned. "I need to make plans to go after Slygon. Now is the time. He's weak. He lost almost all of his dragons."

"You can't leave. Silverheart will kill me and take over."

"Oh, fer fuck's sake." He grabbed his hair. "You throw spikes in me road every time I try to do anything I want or need to do. Can't yer guards keep you safe?"

She lifted her thin hand. "Does it look like they can keep me safe?"

"Dandy, can't you keep her safe?"

"If you're going after Slygon, I'm going with you, so no. We'll have to deal with Silverheart first."

"I promised Belle we'd leave for Slygon's lair at first light." I bent down and whispered, "She kissed me, Dandy. I can't disappoint her."

Dandy sighed. "If she kissed you once, she'll do it again. Stop being so self-conscious."

"But I'm half orc, Dandy, an ugly big lummox and she be, she be gorgeous."

"You worry too much," the fairy said with a smile. "Trust me. Belle likes you. A lot."

The fairy's words acted like a tonic on my soul. I stood up and preened. "She does?"

"Oh, for God's sake. Go do something about Silverheart."

I stepped outside the queen's chamber and ran smack into the tall elf maid with the long blond braid. I recognized her because of the hunter's garb she wore. "You're Rain."

She nodded. "The queen called me here."

She can call you here, and thrust you in my way all she likes, but truth be, I won't marry you. I'm sorry to be so blunt, but that's me way. I have my own plans and marrying to suit the elves is certainly not in them."

She shocked me by bursting into tears. I closed my eyes. I'd never seen an elf show this much emotion. I touched her shoulder, sure she'd repel my gesture. She didn't. She cast herself into my arms sobbing her eyes out. "I didn't mean to cause you pain. I love another," I blurted.

"My father will kill me. He's counting on this to give him a place among the great families and to give him power."

I tried to get her off me, looked up and saw Belle staring at us. I realized how awful this must look to her. There I was holding my supposed fiancé in my arms. "Belle," I called as I peeled the distraught elf off my body. Whoever woulda thought an elf maid, one who was supposed to be a lover of females, would cling like a damn leech to me, a gigantic male?

Belle

Tiny and I huddled in our hut, talking. It was the only place in this den of ugliness we felt like we could speak to each other without someone poking their nose, ears, or minds into our personal business. I wanted to see Jackal and I was too embarrassed to say so to anyone. I wanted to feel his presence. I missed him terribly and he'd only gone to see his mother a few hours ago.

"I'm going to find Jackal," I said. "He promised we would go after Slygon tomorrow morning. Where do you think he'll be?"

"With his mother, I imagine," Tiny said.

"Think I can get in to see him?"

Tiny laughed. "You? You could get into see god if that was what you wanted to do. There's no getting between you and your destination, my dear."

"Well, wish me luck. I'm going to look for him."

"You care about him, don't you?" She grabbed my arm and forced me to look at her.

I pushed her away. "I don't know how I feel. It's weird. When he's around, I feel so much better, safer, more comfortable, even happier. When he's gone, it feels like the world is going to shit. I need to find him."

"Get to it then. I'm staying right here. The elves hate us and running around among them makes me queasy. I've never felt inferior since I met you. Now we're here, all those feelings from when I was alone in school and the older, bigger girls laughed at me are back. It's almost the same."

"I feel that way, too. They hate us." We hugged and I set off down the path through the orchard. My mind was made up. If Jackal wasn't coming back to talk to me, I would find him."

I went in through the kitchen and climbed the back stairs to the big hallway leading to the queen's chamber. It was how food was delivered to her and all those housed near her royal ass. I opened the big doors at the top of the stairs and stepped into the hallway. I turned and looked toward the queen's chamber and stopped. There stood Jackal and a beautiful elf maiden in a close embrace.

My face burned. My heart felt like it would explode. He was playing me for a fool. I screamed and shattered a chandelier right over their heads. It rained glass on them, and as I turned to run back to the hut, I heard Jackal call my name and ignored it.

I felt him chasing me. He was calling me inside my head. I put up a wall to block him and he broke through. *Belle, stop running.*

Get out of my head, you lying beast. You kiss me and then climb all over that elf?

Belle, she was climbing all over me. I didn't ask for it.

I hit the kitchens and slowed to make my way through human serfs slaving over pots of food, baking bread, tables, hot stoves and ovens. I slid by them and headed for the back door. Jackal caught me. He put his hand on my arm and I tried to pull away. He was so strong, his hands huge. He pulled me close, hugged me to his body, and dragged me into the courtyard.

"That elf was Rain Fairfeather," he said as though that should explain everything.

I refused to look into his face. He lifted my chin. "I told her I was in love with someone else and she threw herself on me. She's the one me mother chose for me to marry. Seems her father will be right pissed with her if there's no royal wedding."

I froze. "So, that was your affianced bride?"

"I refused her to me mother. Made her right angry, but I stuck to me guns. I told both of them I ain't looking fer a wife cause I'm already spoken for . . . in a way."

I rolled my eyes. "Presumptuous oaf."

"I know," he said digging into the dirt with his gigantic big toe. "It was the only thing I could think of that would get them off me back. And you know how I feel."

I love you, Belle. I'll never love any other woman.

I allowed him to pull me through the stable yard, where it seemed elf warriors were always practicing, and into the orchard. He sat on a bench under an apple tree and dumped me into his lap. My face flamed. "This is so inappropriate."

He grinned. "But very cozy."

"You're incorrigible."

He nodded. "I know. I have no manners and no idea how to go about courting ye."

He lifted my hair and kissed my neck. I shivered and tried to push him away. "What about going after Noemi? When are we leaving?"

"I'd leave right this minute, but I have to make sure me mother is safe. She's afraid if I leave Silverheart will finish what he started."

"She's just using that as an excuse to keep you here so she can marry you to that hussy."

"Partly, probably," Jackal stopped. "I don't know what to do. Can we put off going after your sister for a day or two while I try to work this out? I don't love me mother, but I have a responsibility to do the right thing. What is the right thing, Belle?"

Tears filled my eyes and dripped onto my cheeks. Jackal saw this and kissed them away. He pulled me tighter against his chest. "I would go right now if I could. You know that."

"She's using tyranny of the weak on you, Jackal. She's using her illness to get you to do her bidding. But I understand you can't walk away from this even though it's driving me crazy sitting here while Slygon is raiding the country and stealing babies."

"How could one so young as you are, be so smart? Yes, she be manipulating me. I get it. I just don't know how to get around the fact she really is sick and Silverheart really is after her throne. I feel like it's me duty to make sure he don't kill her out of hand and just take the kingdom back into the Pit like he wants to."

"Do you want to be king here?"

He shook his head. "Not in the least, but happen it might be my duty, my lot in life, a destiny I can't fight. I be Ashera's son like it or not."

I thought about what he'd said. It was all true. Not what I wanted, but true. He was Ashera's son, now Prince Regent, in charge of all this, the castle, the elves, everything. "I don't see an end," I said. "I don't see you ever able to escape and be yourself and help me. They'll keep you here one way or another. You'll end up marrying that blond elf, and Slygon will go unpunished."

"No," he said. "Have some faith in me, Belle. I'm me own man, think on. I can make my own decisions. It seems to me, getting Ashera on her feet be my first job, then finding enough elves loyal to me to guard her. When that's done, I'll be able to do as I wish."

"And Rain?"

"I ain't marrying her. Period." He tilted my chin, so I had to look right into his eyes. "You know what's in me heart."

I felt my face flame, jerked my chin free and tried to jump up. He held me tightly. I wasn't ready for this. I needed his help to save Noemi and kill Slygon, I didn't need to be sidetracked by emotions I wasn't ready to handle. And did I love him? Did I care for him in the same way he cared for me? I truly didn't know. I dropped my head and stared at my lap. "I'm not ready for this," I mumbled. "I have to save my sister. I can't make plans for my life until I know she's safe. Everything in my mind is on hold until that's done and Slygon is dead. It's all I can think about right now."

He laughed and set me on my feet. "I'm glad you can talk to me and tell me what's in yer heart." He took my hand. "Look into me heart, Belle. See it, not this ugly face and body."

"You're not ugly," I said. "You're....you're you. You look like Jackal. I wouldn't want you to be any different. I like you fine the way you are. Don't say you're ugly. I stopped seeing you as a beast a long time ago. I just don't have time right now to think about myself or what I want. I have to save Noemi and kill Slygon. Odafarus told me it was my destiny just like your destiny is to be king of the stupid elves. I do like you." I paused, unable to put my feelings into words.

He hugged me and I let him. I loved the feel of him against me. His strength was a gift he passed to me when he held me. He made me feel stronger and whole when he held me like this. He made me feel special, powerful, able to accomplish anything.

"I'm heading back to do me duty then," he said.

I nodded and grinned. "Yeah, go kiss some elf ass, make sure your mother is safe and all that crap, but keep your hands off that damn blond hussy or I'll fix her for good."

"Belle," he said. "Mind yer manners. I got no interest in Rain Fairfeather and don't plan to have anything to do with her."

"Then why was she climbing all over you?"

"Her family is right set on her marrying the future king. She's afraid they'll punish her or even kill her if I don't."

"Bah! She's just putting more elf BS on you and you're buying it. This whole place is a seething morass of plots, self-serving under-games, and politics."

Chapter Twenty-Eight

Belle

"Tiny," I said. "It was uncanny the way Dandy knew Flossie was in trouble, popped in, and saved the day. It's almost like the two of them are connected in some way. Did Jackal ever tell you how he found her?"

We were sitting inside our hovel, for there was no other way to describe the stinking ex-pigsty hut we lived in. We had one tiny table and three chairs, a pile of pallets we set out at night and a fireplace to cook on.

"Nope," Tiny said as she examined her fingernails. "I'll never complain about getting a manicure again. Just look at these."

"I know, broken nails, but seriously, how did Dandy know Flossie was in danger? I'm going to ask her."

"I doubt she gives you a straight answer," Tiny said. "She has a way of diverting your thoughts to anything else but whatever she doesn't want you to know."

I looked outside. There were signs the castle might fix some of the problems the villagers struggled to deal with. A surveyor and his helper stood in the middle of the huts writing on a tablet. So far, the surveyor was the only sign anything would get done. And as though she knew they were talking about her, Dandy suddenly appeared in the hut. I slapped my hands on my hips and stared at her. "We were just talking about you."

Dandy wore her pink outfit today. She laughed and shook a finger. "You two are naughty girls."

"Were you snooping?"

Dandy lifted one reddish, finely-sculpted eyebrow, but didn't answer.

"Do you snoop? I mean, not just on us, on the elves and everybody? You have this way of popping in whenever you're most needed. How do you do that?"

Dandy ignored my question. "Things will be better for us now that Queen Ashera signed the edict naming Jackal as Regent. The elves should treat the humans here with more respect. Jackal will demand it."

"Oh yeah," I said. "They'll bow and smile and say all the right things to our faces, but behind our backs, they'll snicker and laugh and point their well-manicured fingers."

"You're right, that probably won't change," Dandy said. "Elves don't think humans are their equals and likely never will."

"They're making a big mistake by kissing up to Jackal," Tiny said. "A lot he cares about what they think. And boot licking isn't the way to make him like you."

Dandy nodded. "I know. The elf court has quickly discovered Prince Erindriel is far from stupid, and he won't play their game."

"Have you noticed the population of elves in the castle has doubled in the last day and a half?" Tiny said. "I mean it's like standing room only in the lower dining room."

"Slygon's scaring the shit out of them," Granny said as she entered the hut, dragging Flossie. "It be yer bedtime, young lady." Granny wagged a finger at Flossie. "I done told you no playing outdoors after dark. Want Slygon to run off with you again?"

"Slygon is growing stronger and making more raids out in the countryside," Dandy said, giving Flossie a hug as she sidled up beside her. "All these elf nobles are afraid if they don't kiss Jackal's ass, he'll send them packing. Returning to the outskirts of the kingdom might be a death sentence."

"I never thought I'd be glad to live in squalor here in the peasant zone, but since the elves avoid it like we're plague infested, I can escape the crowds, and everyone here is actually genuine. The common folk don't look down their noses at us and find the occasional visits of the dragons reassuring. We're all still awaiting the improvements Jackal forced the Grand Vizier to promise."

I was going to lose Jackal to his crown. I could feel it. He'd never get away from this place. His mother would make sure he married that blond elf so she could tie him here for the rest of his life. The thought made me crazy upset. I couldn't understand it. It must be because I couldn't go after Slygon without his help. I had to have him and his two buddies. They were the best warriors I'd ever seen. Without them, any plans I could make would be doomed.

The sudden realization had me seething so I decided to go looking for Jackal. He hadn't been to see me in over twenty-four hours. That seemed pretty odd for a man who said he was in love with me. "Where's Jackal?" I asked Dandy.

"Last I saw, he was sitting with Ashera."

"Is she any better?" I was almost to the point I hoped the queen would just die so Jackal would be free. It would make things a lot easier if she wasn't lying in that bed looking like ten miles of hard road. He felt sorry for her. One thing I knew about Jackal, he had a soft heart. He tried to cover it with his gruff manners, but under that huge chest was a squishy soul and a soft heart that felt the pain of others.

"She was sitting up in bed last time I saw her. The poison is gone, and elves heal quickly. She should be back to her old self in two or three days."

"That's good news. I was afraid she'd languish in bed forever just to keep Jackal glued to her side."

Dandy laughed. "If she thought it would work, she might."

Chapter Twenty-Nine

Jackal

Ashera lay propped against a mountain of pillows on her massive bed. Her voice was growing stronger each day as her body rid itself of the caterpillar poison. "You have a lot of untapped power, Erindriel. You need to learn how to use it or you'll never rid me of Silverheart."

"Yeah, the power, whatever that is." I had no idea how much magic I had or what to do with it and even doubted its existence. Ashera kept telling me it was grand and huge. But to believe that, I had to believe her. "Before I take on Uriel Silverheart, I'm going after Slygon. I promised Annabelle I'd help her rescue her sister and I intend to keep me promise. Not one more babe dies for his unnatural needs. Not one."

"Yes, of course," Ashera said as she stroked her long silver hair. "But before you do that, you really need to go into seclusion with the Oracle. Now that your magic is manifesting, you must meditate and drink of the sacred waters so that your full potential can be realized. I sense you will be the most powerful elf to ever exist."

I laughed. "Sure, whatever you say." I kept trying to humor her. She had this bizarre notion I was the second coming of god. "As long as it's quick, because I'm leaving to go after Slygon as soon as you're on your feet."

Ashera fell back against the pillows with her hand on her forehead. In a much weaker voice she said, "send in my maids and find Granny. I'm feeling so very sick all of a sudden."

"You can't keep me here by pretending to be ill. Granny be way smarter than that. She'll know."

Ashera pouted. "You know the Grand Vizier wants you to marry his daughter, Wendislas. He's been plotting for years to take my place. You have to marry Rain. If you marry Rain, you'll essentially unite the three most powerful royal families, the Fairfeathers, the Ravenwings and the Glynfires. The Silverhearts will be left out. The Grand Vizier would do anything to prevent that from happening. Don't fool yourself into believing the Grand Vizier's not smart or that he doesn't have many nobles on his side. Your brother was engaged to the Fairfeather girl and now he's dead. Uriel tried to kill Rain, but he got to Fulven first."

"If ye know all this, why is Silverheart Grand Vizier? I don't get it. Can't you get rid of him? I sure as hell can."

"Think I haven't tried? I tried poison. I tried assassins. He's too heavily guarded by magic shields and wards, and guards. Once you're married to Rain, the truth can come out and he can be exposed. His followers will turn against him. It's the only way."

I laughed. "The way you elves think is right stupid. I have me sword and dragons. If I want Silverheart dead, he's dead. Your sneaky back-handed ways are not mine and never will be. Wards and guards," I scoffed. "Stupid shit is what I say. One blast of dragon fire take care of all of that. And, as I already said, I ain't marrying to suit yer conniving plan. I'm me own man with me own plans, dreams and desires and you don't get to tell me what to do."

"Marrying Rain is the only way to save our kingdom, Erindriel. Please reconsider."

"On that, I will never change me mind. And call me Jackal. When you call me Erindriel, I feel dirty."

"Fine," Ashera said with more strength than I'd thought she had. No doubt, she was feigning weakness. I wouldn't put it past her. She manipulated everyone around her. All the elves did it. They were so caught up in their petty intrigues and ridiculous squabbles, they wouldn't know a straight answer if their lives depended on it. "At least go to the Oracle and drink the water," she said. "The Oracle will show you who you truly are and help you find the key to using your power."

I stared at her. Everything about her was fake. She wasn't as sick as she appeared. It was all for show, but the Oracle intrigued me. What if I did have untapped power? What if this Oracle could help me? Maybe I should give it some of my time. "So, where do I find yer Oracle?"

"Get the guards to bring Rain here. She'll take you."

"Really, Ashera, you'll stop at nothing to get me hitched to your chosen."

"It won't hurt for you to be seen with her and she knows where the Oracle is. So why not?"

When Rain showed up, Ashera forced me to take her hand to show respect or she said I would be considered rude beyond redemption.

"Come with me, Prince Erindriel." Rain's voice was so cold, I felt my face freezing, but that worked just fine for me. I wanted nothing to do with this icy elf maiden. I especially didn't want her throwing herself on me again. If Belle saw me with her, I could be in serious trouble as it was.

"Yes, miss," I said with what I hoped was enough reserve to keep her from throwing herself on me, yet not piss her off.

"Don't call me miss. My name is Rain."

"Uh, where we going anyway, Rain?"

"Queen Ashera says you must meet the Oracle, so to the Oracle you go, though why is beyond me."

"Yeah, I'm not stupid. I know we be going to the Oracle. The Queen says I have great power and the Oracle will show me how much and how to use it if I drink some water. I was just wondering where this Oracle be hiding since I never came upon him afore."

Rain stopped our steady progression up a steep circular stairway. "Seriously, she thinks you can survive drinking the Blood of the Harvest?"

"She said it were water I be drinking."

Rain laughed. "And you agreed to this?"

I nodded, "She said it was water not blood."

"Well, I didn't want to marry you anyway."

"Think I be wanting to marry you?"

She stopped again. We were halfway up the stairs in the tallest tower in Greenwood. It was made of sparkling green crystal. I'd never seen it before. This castle was a rabbit warren with passages and towers popping up all over the place. "If ye keep stopping like this, we'll never get where we're going. Wherever that may be."

"You really don't want to marry me?"

"It's possible, you know, that I might love someone else."

Her eyes flew open along with her mouth. "Then why have you agreed to be betrothed to me?"

"I didn't and I haven't and if the Queen said I did, she were lying, something all you elf folks seem to do with great regularity."

Rain headed up another set of steep stairs. When I looked up, I saw we had quite a way to go. "My dearest, my beloved Helera, is dead. The Grand Vizier had her killed. I have nothing to live for."

"Well that's news to me. When'd that happen?"

"Last night. An assassin killed her in the gardens. I know it was Uriel Silverheart."

"Why do you know this?"

"He hates me. He did it to make me angry so I would commit a crime and be put to death. Then his daughter could marry you."

"That's the stupidest idea I ever heard of. Was your Helera the blond elf who looked just like you?"

Rain stopped and stared at me. "Yes, we often dressed alike. We are both hunters and warriors. Or we were."

"Happen Silverheart mighta thought he was killing you. Or whatever assassin he sent coulda made that mistake."

I was getting anxious. I shouldn't be jawing with this elf on some staircase in the middle of the castle. I should be with Belle planning our attack on Slygon. All this elf shit was taking up too much of my time.

Rain stopped again and I pushed by her. "I swear, we need to get up this endless frigging staircase and get on with whatever is at the top."

When I looked down at her, I hung my head and sighed. Tears ran down Rain's face in a regular flood. "You're right. Helera did look like me. It could have been a case of mistaken identity." She put the back of her hand on her forehead, a dramatic gesture I'd seen Ashera do. "It's all my fault. I'm unable to live with this pain." She looked over the fragile railing. "I should just end it all, cast myself off the stairs and die."

"That's a right sorry attitude if ye ask me." Jackal shook his head. What drama. Seemed elves were overly fond of high emotion along with over-the-top exhibitions of it. "How does it honor her for ye to talk such nonsense? I can think of many ways ye can get revenge and none of them include dying. Wouldn't ye rather avenge her death?"

"Yes," she said. "I would." She began running up the stairs. When we reached the top of the long circular steps she stopped. "I will wait to kill myself until I have avenged Helera."

"Jeezus God!" I snarled. I was sick and tired of elves. First Ashera with her die-away airs and now this drama queen. "Where do I go now?"

"I can't go with you. If you're really going to drink the Blood of the Harvest, I'll be back in a couple of hours with help to drag your gigantic corpse down these frigging stairs."

More drama. "Is it really that deadly?"

"If you're not strong enough in your power to survive the poison it contains, you will die."

"What about this Oracle. Who's that?"

"The oldest elf among us becomes the Oracle. The oldest elf is Alewing Bluegrove. His entire family is dead. He's outlived all of them and never had children. He was a Priest of the All Spirit in the underworld so took vows of celibacy. There are no more Bluegroves. Just him and he's very powerful. He's devoted his entire life to gaining power and worshipping the forest spirits. He processes and blesses the Blood of the Harvest. Very few survive the test. I can't believe your mother is sending you to Alewing. A half-blood has never been near this tower much less drank the blood."

"Well thanks for the encouragement. You should be right glad she did send me. Now there will be no question of me marrying you. Solution be handed right to ye."

She sighed gustily and did the back-of-the-hand to the forehead thing. Apparently, young elf maidens were as young human girls, overly filled with attitude and fond of high drama.

"Just go through that door. I'm sure Alewing is waiting."

"Uh, what do I call him?"

"You call him Master Alewing for he is the Oracle."

She ran lightly down the stairs, blond braid swinging over her narrow hips. "Good luck," she called back, surprising me. I watched until she was too far down the staircase to see, took a deep breath and reached for the handle of the polished ebony door. Crazy white runes swirled and churned across its black surface. I discovered I could stop their gyrations if I concentrated, though I couldn't read the writing.

When my fingers touched the gold handle, the door opened. An elf, ancient, bent with age, his remaining strands of hair gray, his humped back covered in a white-silk shawl, turned his head and stared at me out of eyes set so deep under crazed brows, they were hard to see. "You're not an elf," Master Alewing said in a voice barely above a whisper. "You'll never survive the water."

"Queen Ashera be me mother. She seems to think otherwise."

"Come here," Alewing whispered.

I hesitated, then moved closer. The ancient elf grabbed my face and drew it down to his level. The elf's eyes were black, no whites, no pupils, just shining black pits inside deep sockets. Alewing penetrated my mind with a tentative probe. It was silly really. A thin whisper in my brain that swirled through my thoughts. It took me a second to push Alewing out of my mind. It was ridiculously easy. The elf cried out. "Your queen is correct. You do have power." Alewing cackled. "But we shall see if it's enough to survive the Blood of the Harvest. Sit over there." He pointed to a cushioned seat with a view out a crystal window.

I eyed the seat with disfavor. "Think it'll hold me?"

"It should. It's solid under the green velvet."

I sat down carefully and looked out of the window into a forest. Tall towers edged both sides of a narrow view right into the thick woods edging the castle. The wall was there below me and then trees, tall trees with the leafy-green tops of summer.

Alewing bustled about the octagonal chamber. "Why does this chamber have eight sides?" I asked as I watched Alewing work.

"Five, eight and twenty-four are the most magical numbers," Alewing said as he poured ruby-red liquid out of a silver pitcher into a gold chalice.

"Why do you keep this blood stuff in silver and not glass or pewter?"

"The blood is mine. It's a living entity and magical. It's also poisonous to most Earth creatures. The silver contains its properties and keeps it from losing any of its power."

"Huh. You'd think the silver would destroy it."

"The interior of the vessel is lined with hematite which protects it from the silver while also containing its properties."

"And why is your blood poisonous?"

"I'm the last of my line. All of the power of the Bluegroves is inside of me. I'm also so old, I can't remember the years of my life. Well over a thousand revolutions of your sun. Elf blood has certain properties that strengthen with age and those properties are poisonous. Drinking the blood is a test of magical ability. The queen had to pass, or she would never have been crowned. If you wish to be king, you must first pass the test. There is also knowledge and magic in the water. If you survive drinking it, you will know more about our race than any other elf but Ashera, and your power will be ten times what it is now."

I took the chalice and stared into its dark red depths. "Would this stuff poison an elf?"

Alewing cackled again. "It will kill anything or anyone who drinks it. You must be able to change the poison inside of you, change its molecules, change its nature and render it benign. If you don't, you die."

"Well ain't that great?" I lifted the cup to my lips. Could I do this weird elf thing and change the old elf's blood? I had no idea how to change it or what that even meant. Would I live? Ashera seemed to think I would, but I didn't trust her or anyone else in this haven of intrigue.

Alewing pulled a dagger with a blade tipped an ominous red out of his white robes. He touched my throat with its red tip. "I don't know why the queen sent you. I can sense the orc warrior within you. I doubt if you'll survive the testing, but drink or I'll prick you with this knife which is also tipped with my blood. One way or another, young orc, you're going to die."

Chapter Thirty

Belle

"My name's Annabelle," I said to the elf girl I knew was affianced to Jackal. I had no idea why she wanted to talk to me, but maybe it would be interesting. I hadn't seen Jackal in a day. Life in this hovel was getting pretty old.

"I heard you ride dragons," Rain said. "Is it fun?"

"I ride the queen dragon. Her name is Oranth. They're not like horses. You don't take them out for a pleasure ride in the woods. They're for fighting evil and that's what we'll use them for."

"Well, when you go, I want to come with you. There's nothing left for me here. My love is dead, I will never marry the prince. I would love to die fighting Slygon. It would give my existence meaning."

I put my arm around her. "Fighting is all there is when you think about it."

"You're a warrior?" She seemed surprised.

"I am."

"Want to spar with me?"

I nodded. "I'd love to." I indicated the hut. "There's nothing here to do, that's for sure."

We walked through the orchard and into the stable yard. In a room filled with amazing weapons, she indicated several shields and swords. "Pick one."

We donned leather armor and went out into the yard. There, among other elves practicing their fighting skills, we went at each other. Once, I lit my sword with fire, but I quickly put it out. This was practice, the fire was for killing. When we were done, she took me aside. "You're good," she said. "No, you're better than good. It's no wonder our prince loves you."

I turned away to hide my embarrassment and Rain grabbed my shoulder. "Don't be embarrassed. He may be half orc, but he's a true warrior and he's facing the Oracle right now. I wouldn't do that for any amount of money. If it brought Helera back, I would, but nothing will do that."

"Jackal is facing the Oracle? What's that?"

"He's to drink the Blood of the Harvest and will likely die of it. Few pass that test."

Pain lanced though my heart. I put my hand over that erratic organ. Did I really care that much about Jackal? "You really think he might die?"

"There hasn't been a successful test in many years. You have to have enough magic to transform the poison in the blood, otherwise, it kills you very painfully."

I felt weak with fear. I needed Dandy. Flossie was in the hut napping. I'd go find her and have her call the fairy. I had to get some answers. I needed to understand what this mysterious test of the blood really was. "I'm going back to the hut. Thanks for this very enlightening information and, oh, for the sparring. You're a terrific fighter. If you want to come with us to fight Slygon, we'll find space on one of the dragons for you."

She nodded and bowed to me. "And you, Rider of Dragons, are a great warrior. I will go with you and fight by your side."

Jackal

I stared into the swirling red liquid inside the golden cup. It seemed alive. It moved and slimy tendrils climbed the side of the chalice as though seeking a way out. When I sniffed, I gagged. "This shit smells like a corpse rotting in midday heat."

"Well it's my blood and I'm no spring chicken," Alewing cackled.

I watched the swirling liquid churn. Fumes blew into my face and I held my breath to escape the smell.

"Quit staring into the cup and drink it or I'll stick you. You've no choice and you're wasting my time. Drink up, dying time is here."

With no other viable options, I closed my eyes, took a sip and gagged. The chalice fell out of my hands as I lost feeling in my arms and legs. My knees buckled. Alewing danced out of my way, suddenly agile and not looking nearly as old as he claimed to be. I felt the swig of the water or blood or whatever it was burn across my tongue and all the way down my throat as I slowly toppled over. I landed on the green tile floor on my side and lay paralyzed. I couldn't move so much as a finger. It hurt to draw breath. Alewing hovered above my face. "I know you can hear me. Change the poison, Prince Regent, or you're dead."

Alewing grunted as he rolled me onto my back with one cloth-shoe-covered foot. *Green, his foot is green.* It was so hard to focus my thoughts. They swirled like the red liquid in the chalice. I went blind and visions floated through my mind. I saw everything Alewing had ever seen, but the visions were a trap. I instinctively knew if I continued to look at them, I would die.

I concentrated on the hot blood still moving into my stomach, and remembered I was supposed to change it. Change it to what? I'd laugh if I could. How about if I changed it into honey? I focused on my first taste of honey. My nurse mother, Eliza, had held me to her breast and dripped honey into my mouth. It was so sweet and delicious. I remembered it more clearly right now than I remembered my name. Erin something or other. Stupid elf name.

I concentrated on the taste of the honey and tried to make the flavor of Alewing's gross blood taste like the sweet golden essence. No matter how hard I tried, it didn't turn to honey, it still tasted like rotten eggs and death and it still burned.

Alewing grabbed my leather vest and pulled my face close to his own. "You're dying orc. Make the change."

He was right. I was dying. I felt myself fading, my thoughts dimming. How did you change poison? What was it? I thought about it, pulled it apart in my mind and viewed its components. Alewing's blood was complex. It was made of memories, a little water, cellular components, tiny little creatures swimming around and shitting. I stared as an idea blazed through my head so brightly, I was stunned by its clarity. It was the creatures. Their feces were killing me. How could I kill them?

I felt for the power my mother told me I possessed in a huge amount. I thought about Belle and how much I loved her. A sudden white fire burned through me, fueled by my love for Belle which was pure and innocent. I let the purity of my love for her fill me with its power, immense power, then I balled it up and blasted the creatures in the poisonous blood with it. They died. When the taste in my mouth changed to sweet nectar, I laughed. I'd done it, changed the hideous old elf's blood to honey, killed the parasites or whatever those creatures in the blood were, and changed it to something I liked.

I opened my eyes to see Alewing's old wrinkled face hovering inches from my own. Disappointment washed across it. Alewing's lips curled. "You did it," he muttered. "Big dumb orc changed my blood. Damned if you didn't."

I sat up. "Happen I should kill ye now. I know why you're so damn old. You've got weird little beasties living in your blood keeping yer heart ticking. I know how to kill them."

Alewing backed away with both his hands out in front of him. "No, no, don't. I truly do provide a service. Drinking the Blood of the Harvest is the true test of power. You know I'm telling the truth."

I jumped to my feet, suddenly feeling like I could tear the crystal walls of this tower down with my bare hands. "Happen ye be right. It made me find something inside meself I never knew existed. Ashera told me I possessed power, but she's a liar like all you elves." I flexed my fingers, pointed at a book, and it caught on fire."

Alewing jumped. "No! don't destroy anything up here. This is my stuff, my possessions. Everything in this tower is valuable to me."

"I could so easily end yer miserable life but happen ye be right. Ye do provide a service. I'd love to see the Grand Vizier drink some of that nasty stuff."

"I know Uriel Silverheart." Alewing's lip curled. "His heart is as black as his soul. My blood would kill him in seconds."

"Ye could be right. Those little beasties are right afraid of purity and light which has me thinking mayhap ye be not so pure or clean or even good of heart."

"I'm old," Alewing snapped. "You live as long as I have and keep your sanity. Good luck." He put his hand on my chest. "For some reason, even though you've the dark strength of an orc warrior, you have a pure heart. Your purity saved you. Your power might come from your ancestry, but it's fed by your dedication to doing what's right. You'll make a great ruler, Erindriel Glynfire, a great king. Go now and tell your mother you live. She's probably worried sick, especially since she also took the test and knows how hard it is to survive."

"If you don't mind me asking, how'd you get them creatures in your blood?"

"I don't mind at all. I was old, my family was all gone, and the Oracle was still alive. He was older than I am now. He invited me to his tower. I had an inkling of what he planned and at that moment, it seemed like something I could do with my life. Losing your entire family is the worst thing that can happen to an elf. It might not seem like it, but we are very family oriented."

"Yeah, no shit, so how did you get the beasties?"

"It's an ancient ritual. I won't go into the details, but he cut his hand, I cut mine and we mingled our blood. I had no idea what would happen. When the Sylashian mites entered my body, I fell to the floor and almost died. I was in intense pain for days. When my body was finally able to coexist with them, Xalimaris lay dead. When the mites left his body and entered mine, he could no longer survive. As you discovered, killing them, would also kill me. I now need them to survive."

"Seems like you're right to hide up here in your tower. Me mum, uh, Ashera, said you were some kind of oracle. Doesn't that mean you see into the future or some such rubbish?'

"Indeed, I am said to have the vision."

"Well look then. I be in a hurry. Places to go, things to do, but since she sent me here, I'm thinking she wants to get some visions or predictions or some such thing. But then, as I already said, elves lie, a lot. Her story is probably trash. No one can see the future."

Alewing slid across the green floor to a corner where a dish of liquid sat on a pedestal. Two seats, one on each side, had been placed for the seer and the supplicant. Alewing waved his hand to indicate I should sit. I eyed the fragile stool with disfavor. "Think it'll hold me? I already broke enough chairs in this place. They ain't built for the likes of me. When I be king, happen I might fix that."

"It's held many. I think it's strong enough for your bulk."

I gingerly lowered myself onto the stool. It had no back so I had to squat on it like sitting atop a barrel. I waited for a few seconds. When I heard no groaning and the stool didn't collapse under me, I sighed with relief. Breaking chairs was annoying and an embarrassment.

"Look into the water," Alewing said, his voice soft and silky. "Look into the water and tell me what you see."

I peered into the moving fluid in the round, flat bowl. It was silvery, not like water at all, more like oil, glistening as it swirled. Suddenly it showed a castle on top of a mountain. The castle was black and black dragons flew above it and perched on the battlements and the towers. "I think I be seeing Slygon's castle."

"Keep looking. Tell me what happens."

I watched as a group of colorful dragons appeared above the mountains in the distance. There was Belle riding her golden dragon. When I stared hard, the golden dragon was not Oranth, but another. Flying beside her on a green I recognized as Bazit was an elf maid with a long blond braid. She looked like Rain. Other dragons crested the mountain, but no bronzes, and I wasn't there.

I told Alewing of the vision. The old man stared into my eyes. "You love one of them. Which?"

"The human woman with the dark hair on the gold dragon."

"The elf maid is your fiancé."

"Not my choice and for the life of me, I can't imagine why she should be there. And I'm nowhere in sight. Is that because this is my vision?"

"Keep looking."

As I watched, a dark cloud emerged from the castle and climbed aboard one of the dragons. The cloud formed into Slygon, then a snake, then Slygon. Then he saw Ashera come out of the castle, only now she wore all black. Then it wasn't Ashera, it was Noemi, Belle's lost sister. She climbed on Slygon's dragon and rode behind him. Suddenly, the water in the bowl erupted into a boiling mass. I cried out as fingers rose from the bowl, reaching for me. Alewing bent low over the bowl and stared deeply into the water. He waved a hand across the bowl and the color of the water changed. I leaned closer to see.

Slygon's keep came into view, this time without dragons, just the black walls and high towers. Alewing touched the water with one long fingernail. Concentric rings formed and moved to the outside. "I sense someone watching us," Alewing whispered. "A being so old and so evil, the water is disturbed."

The water was now white with red drops flowing into streaks. Alewing waved his hand over it and a face appeared. The face seemed to be doing what they were doing, looking deeply into something. This face was terrible. It was the face of an ancient man with a black strip of cloth wrapped around his head covering his eyes. His skin was paper-white and his mouth red as blood with fangs. He moved a long, painted fingernail toward them and said, "Come to my heart, the visions of truth, sent by the spirits of those who've gone before."

As soon as the words were out of his mouth Alewing screamed. "Kokusan." The face disappeared as the water turned an opaque blue. Alewing panted and wiped his eyes with the back of one hand.

"Do you know that man?" I asked.

"He's older than even I, and blind. He's a seer. I thought he stayed in the Pit. I couldn't imagine him coming into the land of sun and blue skies. He can't see and he's vampire."

"Why didn't his eyes just fix themselves?" I asked. "I mean if he's a vampire."

"They were removed by a witch, the lids sewn over the empty sockets, and a spell put on them."

"Who be he scrying for? Himself? It looked like he were in Slygon's castle."

"Yes, he is obviously Slygon's seer and that is very bad news, very bad. It means he can see us as well as we see him, and it means Slygon knows all that we know."

"Well that be a right shot in the gut," I said. "I wonder what he wants with us."

"He wants your Annabelle," Alewing said as he sat back and scratched the stringy beard on his rough chin.

"Annabelle? What's he want with her?"

"He wants her, orc, as you want her."

Anger blew through me. Fierce fury swelled in my chest. "Oh, he does, does he? Well happen he'll have to go through me first."

Alewing grabbed my arm. "Erindriel, you're our prince and will be our king. Have a care for your person. It's very valuable to us. What did you see in the water?"

I leapt off his stool. "I don't know, but nothing that could possibly be true, old man. Yer bowl of water be wrong!"

I stormed out of the tower room and ran down the staircase fuming. What I had seen could not happen, not ever. Why would Ashera ever be in Slygon's castle or with the vampire? Was it Ashera, or Noemi he'd seen? Why would Ashera and Noemi be the same in his vision? It was impossible. And why would Rain be riding

Bazit? And where the hell was he in that picture? Why wasn't he there taking care of Belle? And Slygon . . . if that disgusting creature laid one finger on Annabelle, he'd rue the day he was born.

Chapter Thirty-One

Jackal

The vision in the water was wrong. It had to be. One thing for sure, I wasn't telling anyone what I'd seen. Be a stupid thing to do. Speaking of it could make it happen. I should never have asked Alewing to prophecy for me. Nothing good ever came of poking around in visions of the future. When you snoop, you discover things you don't want to know and shouldn't know. Somehow, this peek into the future was just like snooping.

I found Ashera up and dressed. She still looked wobbly, but she was sitting in one of her fancy chairs, the kind I could never sit in even if I wanted to which I didn't.

When she saw me, she rose, holding tightly to the arms of the chair. "Erindriel, you survived the Blood of the Harvests."

"Ye told me it be water. Nasty old man with his vile old blood. He made me drink it and yes, I live, no thanks to you or anyone, I survived and here I be. Where you going?"

"I want you to take me to the serfs' village. I am queen. I must know if Uriel is following my orders and making the necessary improvements."

"No need to worry yourself. I can go and handle that business. In fact, it be my pleasure."

"No, I must see the conditions my people live under. They serve me. Their safety and happiness is the least I can provide for people who give up their lives in my service."

I rolled my neck and heard it crack, then rubbed the base where my neck met my head digging into the flesh. This entire day was giving me a headache.

"Ye sure ye be strong enough to walk that far?"

"I have a chair being made ready to carry me," she said. "With four strong bearers."

I offered my arm. "Let me support you down the stairs."

Together, followed by what had to be half the court, Ashera and I walked down the hall and the staircase to the kitchens. Ashera examined the kitchens like she might have actually been in them before, finally finished speaking to the cooks and maids, and walked out through the scullery to the alley between the castle and the walls. A chair waited there. She climbed in, the bearers hoisted her aloft and off we went toward the stables.

I didn't like the idea of her going to the village from the beginning and now liked it even less. A terrible feeling filled my gut and spread through my body. That bad feeling you get when something awful is about to happen.

In the stable yard, I spotted Rain working out with the warriors, sparring with swords and hand-to-hand combat. When she saw our train, she walked away from her opponent to talk to me, something I could live without. I glanced toward the human's small village, praying Belle wouldn't see me because even an accidental meeting with this elf, would be problematic.

"You're alive." A statement, and not said as if she were disappointed. Then, "Why is she out here? Doesn't she realize the danger?"

"Happen ye might be able to reason with her. I couldn't."

Rain touched the side of Ashera's chair while I glared at the accompanying crowd of court toadies. How on Earth was I supposed to govern these over-dressed, self-centered, back-stabbing, elves?

"Your Majesty," Rain said to Ashera. "You shouldn't be out here. We've had black dragons flying over almost every day."

"I'm here to see the improvements Uriel Silverheart, my Grand Vizier, promised to make on my behalf."

Rain's expression reflected confusion. "What improvements?"

Ashera beckoned to the bearers. "Take me to the village immediately."

The bearers picked up a trot and headed through the stable yard. They exited into the orchard with me and Rain jogging along behind. The court had trouble keeping up, dressed in formal clothes, heels, long skirts. Even the male elves wore a type of wrapped skirt, along with close-fitting jackets of silk and brocade in bright colors, and wooden shoes with lifts. I hoped if we were attacked, the loudly-colored clothes of the court would draw most of the fire away from the humans and children.

Halfway through the orchard, the smell hit the elves. Ashera held up a hand and the bearers stopped and laid her chair on the ground. "What is that stench?" Ashera asked me.

"Animal waste and the open sewers behind the cottages."

"Why isn't that being dealt with?"

"Uriel Silverheart be your Grand Vizier, Queen Ashera. He would no more answer to me than he would kiss me orc ass."

"Go on," Ashera waved to the bearers who hoisted her chair on their shoulders and continued through the orchard.

Ashera took a scented handkerchief out of her pocket and held it over her nose as they entered the village. Flossie was the first one to meet them. She ran out of Belle's cottage with Granny chasing behind. When Granny saw Ashera, she grabbed Flossie and held her close. Belle came out of the hut followed by Tina. They stood in front of their poor cottage and stared at Ashera.

Every time I saw Belle, she stunned me with her beauty and presence. Just the sight of her beautiful face made my soul cry out with need. I took a deep breath and waited for the feeling to pass. I loved her so much. When she spotted me, she left Tina and walked to the queen's chair where, gob struck, I stared at her like a huge dolt.

"Why is she here?" Belle asked, her voice low and soft.

"Who? The queen or Rain?" I asked.

Ashera answered. "I came to see if the Grand Vizier has kept his promise to upgrade this village. I can see from here, he has not. Do you have protection from my warriors at night?"

"No, your majesty," Belle said. "He has not implemented any improvements I know of. An architect came through, made some notes on a tablet and then left. No one has come here since."

Ashera's hands gripped the arms of her chair so hard her knuckles were white. "We'll see about this. My people will be properly cared for."

Then I felt them and so did Belle. She looked up and screamed. "Oranth! To me."

"Slygon!" I yelled and dove for Ashera. Huge claws grabbed my jerkin and pulled me away from the queen, carrying me aloft. I ripped off my jerkin, dropped to the ground, rolled onto my back and shot a mental bolt of energy at the black dragon above us. It screamed and caught on fire. Black dragons were landing everywhere in the village. The roof of Belle's cottage collapsed under the weight of one. Belle threw Flossie at Granny who grabbed the girl and dragged her into the orchard at a dead run.

Flames from a dragon set the cottage on fire. Tina had her crossbow out. She fired into one of the black dragons and hit it with a silver-tipped bolt. I drew my sword and ran to protect the queen. Her bearers had pulled her under them and Rain, sword drawn, stood over them protecting the queen as best she could. The crowd of court toadies was under attack by two black dragons. Vampires dropped off their backs and went after the unprotected elves. As far as I was concerned, the vampires could have them. I didn't have the time or the patience to worry about them. Annabelle was fighting a dragon and a vampire by herself and she was all I cared about. I raced to support her, sword out, saw her sword flame as she fought off a vampire. I shot a mental bolt into the dragon, but nothing happened. Damn. My gift was too new. I had no idea how to properly use it.

I shoved Belle aside and attacked the male vampire in front of her. My sword skills had greatly improved. I found I could use my mind to make each stroke stronger and more accurate. I suddenly heard a familiar cry and saw Slag and Chub charging into the fray from the other end of the village. A silver-tipped bolt hit the dragon over their heads, it screeched and then flew off slowly.

"Our dragons are almost here," Belle yelled over the commotion.

"Is Slygon here?" I glanced toward the orchard and the spot where I'd last seen the queen and saw dead bearers laying drained of blood beside her empty chair. Rain was nowhere in sight. "The queen. Where is she?"

Belle, Tiny, Slag and Chub followed me into the orchard at a dead run. We hacked into the horde of vampires feeding off the court member who had failed to escape. Rage filled me. Slygon must have Ashera because she'd just disappeared. Belle's big gold dragon attacked a black dragon hanging onto one of the apple trees. Her arrival was followed by Remoth and the remaining pride of dragons. The black dragons flew off screaming in fear, leaving the vampires behind.

I spotted one slipping off into the village and raced after it. The vampire was a woman. Blood stained her lips and her chest. Elf blood. There was no way for her to escape. Her dragons were gone. She stopped with her back to a cottage. I pulled a broken board off the side of the crushed cottage. It made a fine stake. I waved it at her.

"Kill me, orc, it matters not," the vampire said. "Death is not my enemy."

"Don't," Belle said from beside him. Above them, Oranth, her golden dragon, hovered on gigantic wings. "We need her."

"For what?"

"To tell us where Queen Ashera is. No one can find her."

"I've looked everywhere," Rain said as she ran up. "One minute, the queen was there under the bearers, I got in a fight with a vampire, looked back and all the bearers were dead, the queen gone."

I approached the vampire holding my improvised stake. "Talk, bitch. Where is the queen?"

The vampire laughed and laughed. "You mortals are so stupid. Where do you think she is?"

I pressed the pointed edge of the stake into the vampire's throat. "Does Slygon have her?" My vision suddenly filled my head. The vision I'd seen in the Oracle's chamber of Ashera riding a black dragon with Slygon.

"Your queen will be a vampire before the moon is once again full," the vampire said.

Of course. I'd had the vision. I should have known.

"If you're not going to kill this thing, I will." Slag said, took a silver-tipped bolt and shoved it into the vampire's forehead. It exploded, and vampire guts and blood showered us, then the thing burst into flame and became ash.

"This be all my fault," I said. "I should have protected her."

"You couldn't know," Belle said. "I didn't see it happen." She turned to Slag. "Did you see Slygon?" She pointed at Rain. "Did you?"

Slag shook his head. "I never even saw the queen. All I saw was vampires and black dragons and I went to war."

"It be my fault," I said. "I had a vision. I shoulda paid attention to it. We have to go after her before he makes her a vampire."

Chapter Thirty-Two

Jackal

Belle's cottage was flattened, the queen missing, and the court in absolute disarray. The Grand Vizier appeared in the stable yard as our small group headed for the castle. He shoved himself in my face which was a very poor move on his part. "Where's the queen?"

I grabbed him by the throat. It was skinny and white and made my hand look enormous. "She was taken by Slygon. Where were you?"

"I was attending to court business," he squeaked.

"Oh, I'm guessing that means you were taking a shit." I was so furious, I didn't care what Uriel Silverheart thought or did.

Silverheart tried to suck in a deep breath. I squeezed harder. His arms flailed and two of his guards stepped up and moved close to me and drew theirs. "Looks like we got us a standoff," I said. "Yer men better sheath those swords. I be king here now." I shoved Silverheart hard. The older elf fell backward and landed on his brocade-covered ass. "I be king now. Queen Ashera be missing, presumed dead, which makes me yer king."

"Over my dead body."

"That can be arranged, think on." Rain and Belle moved up, stood beside Slag and Chub, and drew their bloody swords. I bent over so I could poke my finger in Silverheart's chest. "You've got plenty to answer for anyway. I think it was you who poisoned the queen and you who killed Helera, or at least had her killed cause you be too big of a coward to do yer dirty work yerself."

Silverheart's face turned the color of an over-ripe tomato. "You have no proof."

"Happen I can get it, think on. I drank the Blood."

Uriel's mouth fell open, his eyes wide in his wrinkled face. "There's no way you passed that test."

"Why don't you climb the green tower and ask old Alewing yerself. From now on, I rule here. Queen Ashera made me Regent, and she's gone. That leaves me in charge and you out of the running. I'd go on home to yer estates if I were you because yer no longer needed here and we sure as hell don't want a slimy, backstabbing murderer creeping around the castle stirring up trouble. I got enough on me plate."

Belle set her sword flaming and Silverheart backed away rapidly. "I'll see you dead for this insult."

"Oh, please, ye couldn't fight yerself out of a box. Ye be right helpless now, Silverheart. I rescind yer title. You're no longer Grand Vizier, just a pompous, self-righteous, murdering bastard."

Chub shoved his bulk in front of me. "Got yerself a new king, old man, a real king."

"You have until tomorrow to get yer shit packed and get out of me castle," I said.

Belle waved her flaming sword and two dragons landed on the top of the barns sending the horses into a frightened frenzy. Oranth roared which didn't help. Silverheart took one look at the two dragons, and his dark face turned paper-white. He pointed at Belle. "Filthy human. You think you can take on the elves because you ride dragons? You've a comeuppance and I plan to deliver it. You'll never marry him." Silverheart pointed at me. "I know you think he loves you, but you're nothing, just slime that crawled out of a human cesspool and he's half elf. And you," he pointed at Rain. "You're disgusting. A lover of women who refuses to recognize her duty. You don't deserve to be queen."

Chub prodded Silverheart with the tip of his sword. "Take yerself off."

Silverheart's guards helped him to his feet. He shot each one of them a look filled with loathing, whirled in a swish of blue velvet robes and stormed toward the castle. Chub turned and grinned at Jackal. "Well that's one piece of vermin removed."

"Don't count on it. Scum like him have a way of reappearing when you least wish it. He's been my enemy from the beginning. At least now he be out in the open, stripped of his power and title so we can move him out of the castle."

The elf warriors gathered in the stable yard and closed in around me and our little group. The head warrior was Gormar Fairfeather. He was followed closely by the other two elves who had traveled with us from New Memphis, Torros Glynfire and Ivansar Ravenwing. They bent their knee to me which made me very uncomfortable. "My King," Gormar said. "Tell us what we should do."

"Gormar, from now on, you be Captain of the Guards. Send five warriors to escort Uriel Silverheart out of the castle and off to his personal estates. Give them the power to use force if necessary. I be thinking he won't go willingly."

Gormar nodded. "You're right and consider it done."

"Then round up a group of warriors and craftsmen to make repairs in the village. I want guards in there at all times."

Flossie nudged my hand and I put it around the little girl's shoulders. "As soon as we can, we need to go after Slygon. I know there's work to be done here to get ready. I hate leaving Greenwood without proper leadership while I go after him, so send me yer father, Felis. I be thinking of making him me Grand Vizier. He's loyal to the crown and I be the crown now."

Belle

I was so stunned by the Grand Vizier's attack and Jackal's response I could hardly think. What did Silverheart mean when he said she, Annabelle, who was not an elf but a disgusting human, wanted to marry Jackal. Is that what the court thought? No wonder they hated her.

When Jackal finished speaking to the elf warriors, he turned to the rest of us. "We be living in the castle. No more hovels in a stinking sewer. I'm King here now and things are about to change."

Jackal stomped off toward the castle with me, Tina, Rain, Granny, Flossie and his two men, Chub and Slag, following. Flossie's little dragon flew around their heads squeaking happily as they headed into the scullery, through it, and up the stairs into the main part of the castle. For some reason it seemed perfectly natural for Rain to become part of their little group. As far as the elves were concerned, she was different, an outsider just as me and Tiny had been at the Academy. When I thought about my time there, it seemed like it had happened in a dream or a long time ago. I was a completely different person now.

Rooms were found for all of us, close to the queen's room. Jackal had that chamber shuttered and barred. "We may be able to save Ashera," he said to me as we walked down the hall toward the smaller dining room. "I'd never violate the sanctity of her rooms. Be unthinkable, you know what I'm saying?"

I shuddered. "Who could live there? She's neither dead nor alive, just missing. And if she's with Slygon, then she's with Noemi. We can go after both of them now."

The big table in the smaller dining room was already crowded with people I knew and loved. Huge platters of food sat in the middle and Chub was arguing with Slag over a haunch of venison. "Be mine, cause I have the biggest appetite," Chub said laughing.

"But I had me eyes on it first," Slag said, refusing to let go of the bony end.

"I'll solve this for ye." Jackal snatched the haunch away from them and plopped it on his massive platter. "Feel free to scavenge amongst my leavings."

Goblets of ale were poured and consumed. Talk turned to their projected attack on Slygon and the planning of it. "I'll be taking Flossie up to bed," Granny said. "I'll leave deciding the details of this undertaking to the king." She raised her goblet. "To King Jackal!"

Everyone lifted their goblets and toasted as one. "To King Jackal, long live King Jackal."

There were five elves at the table, Torros, Ivansar, Gormar and his father, Felis and Rain. They toasted Jackal righteously, but I read confusion in their minds. Elves didn't like change and didn't change easily. Uriel Silverheart had been sent back to his estates, but the rest of the court was talking about Jackal as though he was a usurper. The four elf warriors sitting at table with us were undecided. They knew Jackal, knew he was a great warrior and Ashera's son, Prince Regent, and heir to the throne. But he was no elf. He might have elf blood, but he didn't look like them. He wasn't beautiful, or graceful, he was a giant with massive muscles. To them it didn't seem right. He never spoke the elf tongue and hadn't been raised to have manners or to understand how royalty acted.

When I tried to listen to Rain's thoughts, I realized she hated all elves and blamed them for her lover's death. Her chief emotion was grief. It was easy to read, and I felt truly sorry for her. She was committed to Jackal and his mission, not because she planned to marry him, but because she wanted to fight. I couldn't help but like her. Rain was honest, pure of heart, and totally committed to life as an elf warrior. Any female, elf or human, who wanted to fight beside the men had my respect.

The four elf warriors might have doubts, but they weren't stupid. I read their appreciation of their circumstances. They liked being special, being close to the new king. Felis was proud of being named Grand Vizier, had donned the blue robes happily and wore the king's insignia on them. In his heart though, he thought Queen Ashera might return and it would all go to dust, so he was cautious.

The rest of the court was less than courteous. When Jackal stalked through the hallways and corridors of the castle, some of them eyed him with disdain. I saw it and thought Jackal did too, but I didn't know if he cared. I felt the emotions of the elf population and worried they would rise up and confront him.

After the table had been cleared, Jackal gathered us close. He looked at the doors for servants and hangers-on. When he saw we were alone, he leaned on the table. We all did the same, drawing close to each other. Jackal stared at the four elves. "Can I trust ye?"

Felis nodded. "We're your men."

"Then this is what we're going to do. Ashera be no doubt in Slygon's keep. Our dragons know how to get there. It be a right long flight fer the dragons to make, so we fly close, then rest them, attack in the morning when the sun be up and most vampires asleep. We can't count on Slygon being dead to the world like the rest of them night-crawlers. He be a shifter as well. We'll have to approach with care. He has a lot of black dragons who will be on watch. Belle's dragon might be able to change them, make them normal again. And then there's Dandy. That blasted fairy be never where you need her, but she can change black dragons as well. If Oranth or the fairy can't fix 'em, then they'll have to die. Once the black dragons are dealt with, we'll storm the keep and kill that baby-eating bastard, Slygon, and get Belle's sister and Ashera back. Ye three," he pointed at the three elves who had been with them, "have dragons to fly so ye come with us. Felis, ye be Grand Vizier and in charge in me absence. I have no heirs. If I die, ye'll be king."

Felis bowed his head. It was easy for me to read how honored he was. "Yes, Your Highness," Felis said. "I'm deeply honored by your trust."

"Yes, whatever, you keep the renovations on the human village going. I want those cottages protected and the improvements completed as soon as may be. Get Xalimaris, the Head Wizard, to set up the magical protections for those people. Slygon cannot be allowed to steal any more of our babies. I don't know how this mission be going to end, so Slygon could continue to be a problem."

Felis bowed his head again. "It will all be done as you say, Your Majesty."

Jackal growled. "Call me Jackal. Save that yer majesty shit for the court toadies."

Chub punched him. "Be that haunch you scarfed up turning you bilious."

Slag guffawed. "Still pissed about that, Chub?"

"It looked downright delicious. We ain't had victuals that prime in quite a while."

Jackal rose to his feet and the rest of the table rose with him. Jackal rolled his eyes. "If yer all gonna jump up and down every time I get up, it's gonna give me the willies." He grabbed my hand and pulled me after him. "Happen I have something important to say to ye."

Chapter Thirty-Three

Ashera

Ashera stood in the middle of the tower room staring at Slygon as Noemi glared at the elf queen. She was old. She looked terrible. Worst looking vampire Noemi had ever seen. She must have been sick.

"If you want to be well, you must partake of the infant's blood," Slygon said. "It is the only way to get back your health and your good looks."

Ashera backed against the rock wall and raised a shaking hand to cover her mouth. "No, you're crazy, I could never do that."

"I thought you wanted to live forever."

"Is that truly how you maintain your life?" Ashera asked with horror splashed across her porcelain face. "I-I want to be young again." Ashera shoved her hair out of her face. "But there must be another way. What about one of your servants, or even a human? I could do that."

Slygon offered her the baby in his arms. The squirming bundle cried out, and Ashera gasped. Her knees buckled. She struggled to remain upright, lost the fight and fell to the floor.

"You're dying," Slygon sneered. "Look at you. Your body can't sustain the force of my blood coursing through it without a powerful infusion to elevate and sustain you. The blood of this infant will regenerate your body."

Ashera pointed to Noemi. "Who's she and why is she here? She looks familiar, like someone I've met before, but I can't place her."

Slygon put his arm around Noemi's shoulders and drew her close. "Don't you recognize her?" he said to Ashera.

"Why are you doing this?" Noemi asked Slygon. "I'm not enough for you?"

"Ashera has no conscience. She'll help me get your sister and you will not. I'm giving her a chance to take your place." He pulled Ashera to her feet. "Meet the lovely Noemi. Her sister is someone you know. Annabelle, the luscious half-human your son covets."

Ashera gasped. "Annabelle is this woman's sister?"

"Yes," Slygon said. "She drinks the blood of infants as will you if you wish to survive, be young again. Don't you want that, Ashera? Your youth and beauty will be fully restored. The blood of babies is the only thing that can smooth your skin, shine your hair, and energize you like a young girl. Think about it, Ashera. Would you rather be beautiful again, or ash?" He ran his hand across the infant's face and thrust the now-quiet babe into Ashera's shaking hands. When she turned her face away, he reached down to drag a sharp nail across the baby's tender skin.

"Don't do it, Ashera," Noemi said. "Death is so much better an option." Noemi grabbed the infant away from Ashera and Slygon turned and growled.

"You have the temerity to get in the way of my plans? You're nothing. Just a nothing girl I made vampire. You won't even stand by me and aid me in my desire to obtain your sister, a plan meant as much for you as for me. I know you miss her. We could all be together."

"What you plan is disgusting," Noemi said.

Ashera grabbed Slygon's arm. "What are you planning?"

"He wants my sister," Noemi snarled revealing long fangs.

"You said you wanted me," Ashera said. "Which is it? Do you want me or Annabelle?"

Slygon tossed his long black hair. "I want all of you. Why shouldn't I have a harem of my choosing, all the women I desire?"

"He wants my sister to breed," Noemi said. "He thinks he can get an heir on her because she's pure."

Ashera poked her finger into Slygon's chest. "You're dead. You can't breed anything."

"I can if I drink the blood of a newborn. For one month, I am a man. I am human again. It's my shifter blood. It gives me the strength to overcome death and live as a real man."

Slygon held the babe to Ashera's face and squeezed some blood out of the cut he'd made. Ashera's nostrils flared at the scent of the infant's fresh blood. "No. No," she muttered, but what she really meant was yes. Noemi could see the blood lust in Ashera's glinting eyes. Noemi read her intentions and her fascination with the luscious smell and knocked her away. "Don't let him ruin you." She paused. "Like he has me."

Ashera growled and lunged for the child. Noemi snatched the infant out of Slygon's hands and sank her teeth through the translucent skin into the baby's flesh, severing an artery. Noemi's eyes glowed red as she sucked the child's life into her mouth.

"No," Slygon screamed. "That babe was for Ashera. Fucking little bitch." He slapped Noemi and knocked her into the wall where she sat with blood dripping down her chin. Slygon took the forgotten infant and tossed it into the eager waiting hands of an orc. "Here Gholug, it's of no use to me anymore. Enjoy."

Ashera fell to the stones, obviously horrified. Noemi sat with her back against the wall feeling the blood of the infant coursing through her veins. She heard the wet crunch as Gholug devoured the remains of the infant and sighed. She was damned for all eternity. It was a sound she'd heard many times before.

Slygon scooped Noemi into his arms and backed out the door. "You're doomed, Ashera. You'll live as a corpse until the sun comes up, then you'll die." He pointed to the roof. It was night, the roof was glass, stars twinkled in the black sky. He saw her looking up and laughed. "Yes, the morning sun will shine right into this room and kill you. You've ruined my plans for you, so die, bitch."

"Come, we must go to my seer," Slygon said to Noemi. He put her down, grabbed her hand and led her through a dark passage. "He will show us what our enemies are up to so that we can more easily defeat them."

Noemi knew right where they were going. She'd been to visit Kokusan before. Slygon had no idea the ancient seer loathed Slygon for his disgusting practice of killing infants. The ancient vampire had been a priest before he was made and actually still possessed some of the morality.

They climbed high into a tower resembling a temple. Kokusan sat in the lotus position, thumbs touching the rest of his curled fingers. He didn't look up when they entered. He seemed to be in a trance.

Slygon hovered above Kokusan who wore a white silk robe and strange slippers on his feet with a separation between his big toe and the remaining toes. A pair of odd shoes sat next to him, sandals set on high wooden platforms. The floor of the room was covered with finely woven mats that gave off the scents of the harvest. "What have you seen, Kokusan?" Slygon's voice demanded an answer.

The Asian monk rose slowly, and Noemi noticed his eyes were covered with a black slash of silk. He walked to a well in the center of the room without hesitating. His eyes might be covered, but he could obviously still see.

The seer's skin, pale and thin, nearly as white as his robes, declared him a former human, but now a vampire. He spoke in a foreign language she assumed was Japanese. Noemi easily understood this language. Vampires knew all languages. "Why are you here?" The seer asked.

"I need her sister. Where is she? The human female named Annabelle?"

"Don't do as he said," Noemi cried. "Leave my sister alone."

"Be quiet," Slygon hushed her. "You can't stop me. You know that. Let Kokusan speak. I must know where she is."

Kokusan stabbed the swirling water with one of his long nails. "I see trouble in Greenwood. I see dragons." He pointed the long nail at Noemi. "Your sister is with a half orc. He's in love with her."

The old vampire cackled, his red mouth turned up in the smile of a lunatic. He tilted his head and sneered at Slygon. "There is a secret I can't reveal."

"You can keep no secrets from me," Slygon snarled. "I am master here. Tell me what you see, or I'll kill you."

"No, you won't. You need me. You might be master of this castle, but you're not my master. Kill me if you like. I no longer care. The true death would be welcomed after a life so long I cannot remember the number of years I've lived."

Slygon growled. "Yes, yes, so I'm not your master and you'd welcome the true death. How about I just let you stay in this castle and slowly starve? You say there're dragons in Greenwood. I already know this which makes your observation essentially useless to me. I want to know where the woman, the female named Annabelle is."

"She's in love with a half orc who also loves her. He is the king of the elves now that you have the queen locked up in your castle. The entire elf kingdom is in disarray. The grand vizier has been expelled and is in hiding while the new king. . ." He stopped speaking.

"What about the new king?" Slygon leaned forward expectantly.

"The new king is the halfling orc. He has odd plans."

"What are they?"

"He plans to wed the woman you seek, this Annabelle."

Slygon's head snapped. "The halfling wants Annabelle? He will not have her. She is to be mine."

"No," Noemi screamed. "Leave my sister alone."

"Shut up," Slygon snarled and slapped her hard. She fell onto the rock floor with her head spinning. "Or you'll join Ashera and meet the sun."

"Look into the water," Kokusan said, "and you will see her." Noemi pulled herself to her knees and crawled to look into the well. Slygon and Noemi leaned over the swirling water in the well. There, standing in the doorway of her miserable hut, the perfect place for her, stood Annabelle. The sight of her sister gladdened Noemi's heart. She was still safe, still whole. Nothing else mattered.

"She looks like Selvia," Slygon muttered.

"Selvia is, or was, my mother," Noemi said.

"Impossible," Slygon snapped.

"Say what you like, Selvia was Annabelle's and my mother. Why should you care anyway?"

"Selvia was nothing but a human serf with magical powers who was banished from Greenwood and never seen again. We were very briefly lovers. She must have found succor somewhere and born a child." He turned to stare at Noemi. "That child could be you." He laughed and laughed. "Then I would be your father."

"Well, you're not," Noemi said. "My father was Ruuvaen. He and our mother were lost in a terrible storm that swept our cottage away."

"If Selvia married Ruuvaen who was a Shalandale, you and Annabelle are related to the queen. If Annabelle was Selvia's child, it would explain why she possesses such powerful magic. Selvia crossed with Ruuvaen would make a child with great gifts." He stared at Noemi. "You cannot be my child. You have no power, though you do resemble Selvia. She was freckled and blond. Perhaps Ruuvaen isn't your father. Perhaps Selvia was pregnant when she was banished. She was a slut who finally slept with the wrong elf which was why she was sent away." He scratched his chin. "I wonder who your true father is?"

"Stop this," Noemi said. "My parents are dead. Speak of this no more."

"I must have Annabelle," Slygon moaned. "I must. Ever since I first saw her, I desired to own her to breed her. She's the only pure woman, elf or human, I have ever seen. Her purity glows from deep inside her. I have chosen her to be the mother of my children. I need a son."

Kokusan laughed but said nothing.

"You're vampire and dead," Noemi said. "You can't breed children on any woman so why do you persist in this fantasy?"

"The blood of a newborn makes me human. It doesn't last long, but for a time, I can breed as a normal man would and I have chosen your sister as the mother of my son and heir."

"What need have you of an heir if you will live forever?" Noemi turned to Kokusan. "What kind of seer are you if you can't see how stupid this is?"

Slygon grabbed her black gown and tore it off. When she stood naked before him, he pointed to her white body. "You're barren. You're dead. No amount of infant blood will make you able to have a child. You're beginning to bore me with all this nonsense about your sister. If I want Annabelle, I shall have her. You can do nothing to stop me."

Noemi pulled the rags of her torn dress over her. Her heart was aching. The only thing she cared about any more was saving her sister, keeping Annabelle from becoming the thing of this monster. The thought of her sister having to bear the child of Slygon's loins was nauseating. She would do anything to keep it from happening.

Suddenly, Kokusan cackled, his white face and red mouth clownish as he laughed. "The plans of men and monsters often go awry."

Slygon grabbed the seer's white kimono and jerked Kokusan to his feet. The seer kept laughing his awful cackle. "What do you see?"

"I see you with the object of your desire, of course," Kokusan said.

"No," Noemi cried. "It can't be so."

Slygon grabbed her by the arm and dragged her out of the tower. "Since you love your sister so much, and refuse to help me obtain her, you may join Ashera and meet the sun together."

Chapter Thirty-Four

Belle

Jackal led me out of the dining hall, through the kitchens and into the stable yard. The night was crystal clear. He stopped long enough to ask me if I was warm. I nodded and he pulled me close.

"Where are we going?"

"For a ride."

"A ride?"

"Then I felt the dragons. Oranth's thoughts entered my head like soft fingers filled with love. *Jackal wants to go for a night ride. He thinks you'll like it. I'm warning you, though, I'm in season.*

What? I had no idea what she was talking about. Mares came into season and wished to be bred. Was that what she meant? A quiver ran through me and I filled with strange longing.

Yes, it's the same.

What the hell?

Remoth landed on the wall and dropped into the stable yard. The horses went crazy in their stalls and I heard the stable hands cursing. Oranth landed beside him. Jackal pulled me close and the strange longing I'd felt before grew stronger. When he kissed me, I felt Oranth stir. We were connected in more ways than I understood.

The kiss was deep and long. Remoth trumpeted and Jackal pushed me away. "Get on yer dragon," he said in a raspy voice. I looked into his eyes and saw desire in them. They peered into my soul. "Yes, I want you, but you know I'll never do anything you don't want me to."

"You're in my head again."

"Ever since the damn drinking of that cursed blood, I can read the thoughts of a lot of people and most of 'em I'd as soon do without."

We climbed aboard the dragons and I held on tightly as Oranth launched herself into the air. The exhilaration of her strength beneath me and the wind rushing past filled me with happiness. I loved flying. Jackal and Remoth flew beside us. I glanced at him and he grinned at me. Inside my head I heard and felt his love for me. It was such a familiar warmth, it comforted me, and that strange feeling of longing washed over me once again making me squirm.

It's lust. Oranth's voice in my head said. *You're feeling the lust of my breeding cycle. It's time for my eggs to be fertilized. Time for me to lay another clutch.*

What the hell? How can I be involved in that?

Jackal is feeling lust as well. From Remoth. Remoth is my mate. The joining will take place soon. A rush of heat filled my lower region and my face flamed. *Jackal is feeling this, too?*

Oh yes, he wants to breed you. The dragon's chuckle infuriated me.

I have no desire to breed with Jackal.

Look into your heart, Annabelle. Your body and mind might be connected to me, but if you did not desire Jackal, you would not feel the breeding lust.

But we're not married. I was horrified right down to my soul. Women did not do sex if they weren't married. At least not in my society. I remembered New Memphis and my face burned again. I was not a loose woman. But the longing and the lustful sensations did not go away however horrified I might be.

The dragons landed in a beautiful meadow high in the mountains. Jackal jumped off as I slid to the ground. When he pulled me close, I didn't resist. He kissed me as the dragons launched into the air above us and began circling each other, diving, and flying close in an ancient dance begun long ago when dragons first came into being.

"Feel them, Belle?" Jackal whispered into my ear. "They love each other just as I love you."

I tried to hold him at arm's length. Above us, the dragons were mating. It was a siren song zinging through my blood. I was on fire.

He scooped me into his arms, and we fell onto the grass. Suddenly I was flying and inside Oranth. The mating of the two dragons wasn't over our heads, we were involved. I was Oranth welcoming Remoth not Annabelle lying on the grass naked with Jackal over me. I burned with need. Jackal's strength turned me on, or was it me in Oranth's body with Remoth flying me, covering me? It was all a swirling sexual tornado and I was caught in the middle, reveling in it, loving it, loving Jackal, mating with Jackal.

When it was over, I woke from the mesmerizing dream of the joining, naked in Jackal's arms. We lay in tall grass, the bent stalks supporting us and enveloping us in a sweet-smelling embrace. Above, the night sky was like a velvet cover with sparkling stars sewn into it.

Then I really woke up. Oh my god. What had I done?

I leapt to my feet, grabbed my shirt to cover myself. Jackal rolled onto his back and I just stood there for a moment staring at his naked body. The tattoos, his thing. Oh God, his body was strong and beautiful, and we'd made love. I felt the sticky residue on the inside of my thighs. *Oranth, come get me.*

I'm tired. I need to sleep.

Please, I can't be here. I have to leave.

The dragon's mental sigh was clear. *I will come, but I'm heavy with eggs that are now fully fertilized.*

The golden dragon landed on the grass. Jackal saw me running for her and jumped up. "Belle, don't go. I love you."

I turned for one last look. "You're king now. Go back to the elves. They hate me. They hate all humans. Do your duty and marry Rain. I'll save Noemi by myself." I climbed aboard Oranth with tears streaming down my face, pulling my clothes on at the same time. I knew running was stupid, but I couldn't stop myself. I would never be queen of the elves and Jackal was their king.

"We're all going after Slygon on the morrow. Ride with us, Belle. Don't run off like a silly wench."

Oranth, fly.

Grumbling into my mind, the big dragon launched herself into the air. I hung on for dear life. Oranth was irritable and feeling heavy. Her usual warmth was gone and all I felt from her was how annoyed she was not to be sleeping in her nest while she gestated. Her launch into the sky was harsher than usual. She leaped straight up, her enormous wings shooting us into the air at the fastest pace I'd ever flown. I had to hold on for my life.

So, where am I supposed to take you? Oranth's mental question was snarky. I felt bad for forcing her to fly me anywhere. My plan was to go after Noemi on her. I thought I could sneak into Slygon's castle, blow up everything in my path and kill anything I didn't blow up. I hadn't brought any weapons except the knives I always had with me. If Jackal was going after Slygon tomorrow, I would miss out on the raid.

I don't know where to go. I'm so upset.

Your place is here in Greenwood with Jackal. You just mated with him. I felt it. We were joined. He is now your true mate. As long as Remoth and I are joined, you will be joined with Jackal.

Oh, my, God. Could this be any worse? *He's supposed to marry Rain, the elf maiden his mother chose for him.*

His mother is with Slygon now. One of Slygon's black dragons carried her there. Jackal will mount a raid tomorrow. He's already planned it. Don't you wish to be part of the raid? Don't you want to be there when he rescues your sister?

Of course, I do.

We were flying over thick forest. I had no idea where Oranth had taken me. She was flying so fast we could be anywhere.

I have a craving for fish. I always do when I'm pregnant.

The moon was waning, a mere sliver in the sky. Its light revealed the glistening water of an enormous lake. *Is that Lake Pontchartrain?*

Yes, it's filled with the most delicious catfish. I know right where to catch me a big one.

The dragon flew low above the water with her claws distended. She scooped up a monstrous fish, flipped it high and caught it in her mouth, crunching away with relish.

Oranth's sudden burst of fear washed over the satisfaction of eating the fish I was actually sharing with her. Her terror stabbed into my mind. *Black dragons!*

It was too dark for me to see them, but I sensed them. And then, evil, filthy, ugliness swirled through my thoughts, screaming souls fought inside my head. Slygon.

You are mine. Slygon's thoughts were so different from Oranth's. His dripped with oozing pus, green and scabrous, while Oranth's were like her, golden and pure.

Fly faster.

No kidding.

The big golden dragon was afraid, which terrified me. I hunched low over Oranth's neck as a dark shadow flew over our heads. It was faster than Oranth, who was heavy with her eggs. I should never have called Oranth out into the dangerous night for something as juvenile as my fear of facing Jackal after mating with him. I'd left him alone in that meadow wearing his love for me and nothing else. My heart ached with shame for my stupid selfish act. Now Oranth and I were in terrible trouble. I deserved whatever punishment I received, but not Oranth and her precious eggs.

The huge dragon above them flew lower and Slygon dropped onto Oranth's back. The golden dragon squealed with anger and flipped sideways. I clung to the dragon terrified I'd fall. I screamed and shot a mental bolt at Slygon. I tried to blow him up and he just laughed in my face, grabbed me around the waist and pulled me against his body.

"No!" I screamed and launched myself over the side. I would so much rather die.

But Slygon had anticipated my move and another dragon flew beneath Oranth. Slygon landed on the black dragon's back and forced me face down in front of him. The black dragon above the golden breathed green fire over Oranth. I felt the mighty queen dragon's pain as her screams echoed across the night sky. I struggled wildly, pulled a knife and stabbed it into Slygon's thigh. He smacked me so hard I couldn't think. Fog filled my brain and a mind-numbing noise like a thousand bees humming. I saw Oranth plummet toward the earth trailing green smoke. I reached for my dragon's mind but found only darkness.

Tears filled my eyes and dripped down my face. My stupid selfishness killed the golden queen and the eggs in her belly. I slumped across the black dragon's neck, spines and scales digging into my flesh. I didn't care. All the fight left me. Whatever happened now, I truly deserved.

I'd killed a dragon.

Chapter Thirty-Five

Jackal

With a heavy heart, I flew back to Greenwood Castle alone. Remoth was tired. After we made love, Belle, in a typical snit, had flown off somewhere on her dragon. When I asked Remoth where Oranth had taken Belle, the dragon had been uncharacteristically silent. We were halfway to the castle when Remoth suddenly dropped out of the sky to the ground. *Oranth. I can't hear her.*

What's going on?

She was taking Belle on a ride, wanted some fish so she went to the big lake where she catches fish and the black-heart attacked.

Slygon? I couldn't believe this. My heart felt like it was going to explode. *What are you telling me? Where's Belle?*

I don't know. I can't read her, only Oranth can and Oranth is gone.

How can she be just gone?

Death is the only answer.

Fly to the castle immediately. Call all the dragons. We have to go after them.

We landed in the stable yard where I saw Felis, my newly-appointed Grand Vizier, waving and running toward me. Panting, Felis gasped, "Silverheart is attacking us. He's got warriors from many houses and he's inside the castle. He thinks he can take over and be king."

"I can't fight him right now. Slygon has Belle."

"You don't understand, Prince Erindriel. Silverheart is trying to take the castle."

I grabbed my head. Slygon had Belle, Oranth was dead, and there was open revolution in the elf world. God how I hated all elves right at this moment. All I wanted to do was go after Belle.

"Silverheart came in through the front gates," Felis said. "He has at least fifty warriors with him."

"Gather all our loyal warriors in the keep and meet me here," I told Felis. "These be yer people. Ye best know who will side with us and who will side with Silverheart." I thought maybe I could pawn off this battle on Felis and fly after Slygon with my own men.

Rain ran up to me puffing. "Slag and Chub are on their way here."

I grabbed her arm. "Are ye with me, lass? Slygon has Belle and ye be one of me best fighters."

"I'll fight with you. I'm loyal. So are Torros, Ivansar, Gormar, the Glynfires, the Ravenwings and most of the Fairfeathers. Uriel's wife is a Glynfire, but she's hated her husband for years. Be sure she will side with her family. Silverheart has some of the Morthians, all the Silverhearts, the Faehorns, the Greencloaks and the Sylleths on his side. They hate humans and orcs and have come from their estates all across Greenwood to take the crown for Uriel."

"I can't believe this is happening right now when I need to go after Belle. The dragons should be here any minute."

Slag and Chub ran out of the orchard and into the stable yard. "It's looking right bad," Slag said. "These people don't want ye here, Jackal. They be determined to oust you."

"We be outnumbered," Chub said. "No help coming for us."

"I honestly don't care. Slygon has Belle and that's me only concern," I said to Slag. "Where's Flossie and Granny?"

"Hiding in the remains of the village. We were afraid Silverheart would find them inside the castle and kill them." Slag pushed his arm. "Hey, pull yerself together. Silverheart's in the main hall of the castle. We need to do something."

"Then do it. Ye don't need me. I have to go after Belle." I sent the plea to Remoth. *The Grand Vizier is revolting against me and we need to go after Oranth and Belle. I need ye and all your kin right bad.*

Remoth's thoughts were brief. *I had gathered a few. Now I will send the call for all of us. If Oranth is truly gone, and her eggs with her, we need to kill the devil.*

Slag had the warriors forming up. He ran to them. "I have dragons coming to support us. They can't enter most of the castle. They're just too big. But they can perch on the ramparts and the walls, breath fire into the windows and keep Silverheart from leaving alive." He ran fingers over his head and pulled his hair out of the knot on top of its head. "I have to go after Belle."

The three elves he'd promoted to his personal guard stepped forward. Gormar, Captain of his guards snapped a salute. "Your Majesty, my men will fight the Silverheart intruders with every ounce of their skill and determination. Ivansar will lead and I will accompany you wherever it is you plan to go."

"I'm counting on ye. Ivansar, Torros, you follow Slag and Chub, they've fought more battles than anyone else here and know their business." Jackal grabbed Slag by the shoulders. "I can't be here, but ye know how to fight and how to lead men into battle. Ye don't need me and I trust ye to save my ass."

Slag pretended to look around Jackal in an effort to spot Jackal's butt. "Happen it's a right big ass to cover."

"I know I can depend on ye." The sound of wings, many wings was followed by Remoth's roar. Jackal gave Slag one last pat on the back and ran to his dragon perched on the castle walls.

Noemi and Ashera sat on the floor of the tower room. Above them, the night sky slowly turned a lighter purple. Dawn was on its way. It would take a while for the sun to rise high enough to light the room they'd been left in. The ashes of their predecessors had drifted into corners. This room was used for only one thing, obviously, vampires who had displeased Slygon in some way, were given the true death in this room.

"We're going to die in here, aren't we?" Ashera said.

Noemi could see the elf woman was older and also weak. "Have you been sick?"

Ashera brushed damp gray hair out of her face. "Is it that obvious?"

"I'm sorry if I offended you, but you look ill."

"I was poisoned. My Grand Vizier wishes to be king. I brought my son to the castle. He's half orc. None of the nobles wish to be ruled by a halfling. I know it was Sliverheart who poisoned me, but, truthfully, it could have been any of them. I planned for my son to marry a noblewoman which would have made the bitter pill of his birth easier for them to swallow, but he brought his own woman with him, some trollop Magic from New Orleans. He doesn't want to do my bidding, my subjects will no longer do my bidding, I might as well die. No one gives a shit about me anyway."

"Great attitude. And you're a queen?"

Ashera leaned her head against the stone wall. "I was a great queen."

Noemi laughed. "Well great queen, figure a way out of this mess because I don't want to die."

Belle

"Bathe her and dress her as befits a female," I heard Slygon say. "Get those warrior clothes off her. I find them offensive. And provide her with a lavish feast of . . . of the sort you humans enjoy."

I lifted my head and saw he was speaking to one of his minions, a female of course. "Get her meat. Chickens, deer, whatever kind of meat humans like. Get her plenty of that, too, not just vegetables and grains, mind you, and some tasty desserts, whatever she likes. Bring her wine at once, to rejuvenate her energy. Red wine."

I lay on a sumptuous bed in a dark room. Slygon hovered above me. "You'll get over your melancholy soon enough," he said to me. "After all, it was just a dead dragon. There are plenty more where that gold one came from."

Finally, able to think clearly, I lay as one in a swoon, and assessed my situation. I didn't want to appear too alert, or even send any mental probes. He'd know I was awake and faking.

He bent closer and for a moment I considered trying to kill him, but he was too strong, and I was still too weak. "You're magnificent," he muttered. "You make your sister look a hag in comparison and I thought her beauty beyond compare. Even your scent entices me." He pressed his nose, a finely-sculpted elf nose, against the skin of my throat and inhaled. I fought shudders and remained inert, calm, unmoving.

"You will make a fine mother to my son, maybe even more than one child. Yes, I could breed an entire family on you. Beautiful and powerful as well. In time, you will come to love me. All women do." He preened, standing tall beside me, he puffed out his chest and all I could think was how puny his body looked next to Jackal's.

He placed his hand over my face. I felt him try to glamor me. I pretended to sleep and breathed deeply. I wanted to look badly to see if he'd bought my ruse. If only he knew of all the times I'd played dead for the nuns. That seemed like eons ago.

"The sooner I bed you, the sooner you'll birth my son."

I had to struggle to stifle a gag.

"It doesn't matter if you resist, at least in the beginning. It will make conquering you all the sweeter. I've waited forever to have something pure, a virgin without the stench of another man on her. I must ready myself for this breeding. I need a baby, a newborn infant." I assumed he was talking to himself. I wanted to scan the room for other mind signatures but didn't dare. "One of the maidservants delivered recently which is perfect. The blood of the child will give me the potency I need to get you with child."

When I heard the door shut, I risked a mind probe. I scanned my immediate surroundings for living creatures and found only a rat living inside the walls. I opened my eyes on lush, rich furnishings, heavy drapes covered a barred window set in a casement. There was carpet on the stone floor and a velvet-covered bench. All I could think of was how glad I was Jackal and I had made love, or whatever it was, because I wasn't a virgin anymore. Boy was Slygon in for a surprise. I doubt if I would survive the revelation.

I crept off the big bed. I still wore my leathers. I dreaded the return of the minion with more suitable clothing like lingerie or maybe a slinky dress. I had to get out of here right now. Noemi was in this castle somewhere. I wanted to search for her with my mind. Was he alert enough to detect it? I could make it subtle and soft. She had to be somewhere in this pile of rocks.

I concentrated and disguised my own thought signature to resemble an oafish servant. It didn't take me long to tap into Noemi. She was above me in a tower room. *Noemi*, my call was a mere whisper.

Now that she was vampire, she had more power and she heard me. *Annabelle? Where are you?*

In a bedroom of some kind waiting to be ravished by Slygon.

You must run immediately.

No kidding. I will find you.

Noemi's next thought was a wail of anguish. *The sun is in this room. I'm going to die.*

Where are you? I leapt out of the bed, steadied myself as the room spun crazily.

Tower room meeting the sun with Ashera.

I opened the door, peered out and spotted a stone spiral staircase leading up. *I'm coming.*

I ran up the staircase. It led to the top of a tower. There was a circular room. The wooden door was locked. I blew the lock open and gasped. Ashera had covered Noemi with her body in an attempt to save her. Ashera's body smoked and sizzled. Above, the sun blazed in through windows meant to magnify the strength of its rays. Ashera's arm was almost burned through to the bone. I grabbed it and yanked her into the stone corridor. Noemi leaped to her feet and launched herself out of the scorching rays.

We stood staring at each other for a second, then hugged. "No time for this," she whispered. "Have to save her. She sacrificed herself for me." She bent over Ashera. "She must have decided she could save me. When she shoved me under her body at the last minute, I was so surprised I let her."

Ashera moaned. "She might not make it," Noemi said. "She's newly made and sick besides."

"She was poisoned."

"I'll give her some of my blood." Noemi shoved her sharp fangs deep into her own wrist and let the blood drip into Ashera's mouth. Ashera moaned and lapped up every drop. Right in front of my horrified eyes, Ashera's body began to heal. "Give her some of yours as well."

"Mine? That's gross."

"You're strong and young. Your blood will revive her quickly."

I groaned. "If I have to."

"Sister," Noemi said as she smiled into my face and took my hand. She bent and pricked two holes in my wrist and pressed them to Ashera's greedy sucking lips. Noemi only allowed Ashera a small amount, then snatched my wrist away. She put her own lips on my wrist and tasted my blood. "Yes, sisters." She used her saliva to seal the wound.

As we helped Ashera sit up, I felt Slygon's thoughts. "He's heading for the room I just vacated. We need to get the fuck out of here."

I touched Ashera's shoulder. "Can you walk? We really need you to get up and run with us."

Ashera heaved herself to her feet. She smiled when she looked at Noemi. "We made it."

"Thanks to my sister. Have you met Annabelle?"

Ashera shook her head. "No, but I've heard a lot about her."

The three of us joined hands. "We can beat him together," I said. "And Jackal will come to save us. I know it."

Chapter Thirty-Six

Jackal

"We be near to where I found Belle," I said. "The city walls ain't too far away."

I think I sense Oranth, Remoth said into my head, a way of communicating I still found disconcerting. *In the lake just ahead.*

I felt Remoth's excitement mounting.

Yes, I'm sure of it. I can finally hear Oranth, but her thoughts are jumbled, as though she's waking from a long sleep.

We dipped low as we approached the lake, and there, suddenly to his right I saw the water ripple in an ever-widening circle. Remoth banked right. A sudden explosion of water erupted from the center of the ripples followed by Oranth as she erupted into the sky. She circled toward the beach and landed, her sides heaving with the effort.

Remoth landed beside her. I jumped off the dragon and ran to the golden queen. I wanted to ask her about Belle, but I couldn't communicate with her. My concern for Belle was the only thing I could think of.

Oranth lay on the lee side of a jagged rock. "What happened?" I asked. "Where's my Belle? I can't find her and Remoth told me she was last seen with you. We were worried about you and her."

Oranth says she was attacked by black dragons and Slygon has taken Annabelle, unharmed, but captured. Remoth's thoughts horrified me. *Oranth was blasted by green dragon fire. She nearly died and doesn't know if she has the strength left to birth the eggs she carries, and her injuries have pushed forward her time.*

Oranth lowered her head and I saw black scorch marks dulled the usual golden glimmer of her scales. Open wounds seeped blood where the flames failed to cauterize. "What can I do to help?"

I beat my brains about trying to think of a way to help Oranth and still get to Belle before Slygon had time to . . . I couldn't bring himself to even think of the evil bastard's intentions.

"I've got this," Dandy said, popping in next to me.

"Jeezus frigging Christ," I swore. "Wear a bell or something. You liked to scared me out of an extra life or two."

Dandy raised her arms and blue rays of light shot from her hands as she moved them over Oranth until the entire dragon was bathed in a blue-white glow. The mammoth creature sighed and settled against the ground as though asleep. The fairy chanted in a language I'd never heard before, and the light faded. Oranth sucked in a deep breath as she inhaled deeply, rose onto her hind legs, and spread her wings.

"You're welcome," Dandy said in response to an apparent message from Oranth I couldn't hear. "And I have delayed the birthing a bit as well. We've important matters back at the palace. Dandy moved her arm in a clockwise direction, then chanted as she reversed the circular movements. A swirling vortex appeared, and she said, "Step through the portal. We've no time to return the conventional way."

"Portal? What crazy hex be this?" I stared at the swirling black hole Dandy called a portal.

"It's quite safe," Dandy assured me, and with a wave of her arm, I flew into the portal, everything went all black, and then I was covered with a kaleidoscope of colors. I landed on my feet, wobbled, and then sprawled onto my face. I rolled out of the way as the dragons and then Dandy landed where I'd lain only moments before. They jumped right up as though traveling in such a way was totally normal. Apparently, I was the only one who found whirling through space unsettling.

"Jackal!" Chub cried, ran to me, and clapped me on the shoulder so hard I almost face-planted again. "You've missed all the action, but we've saved a bit of fun for ye. Silverheart's in a nice damp cell awaiting your attention. He's a might scorched by dragon fire and mad as a nest of hornets, but betwixt the dragons and our elf army, he's defeated and admitting to anyone who'll listen he's ready to bow to yer majesty."

Slag and Tiny ran up to us. Tiny patted Oranth and said, "Where's Belle?"

"Slygon has her and Ashera. Happen we need to go get them. Now."

Dragons trumpeted and landed on the walls flinging dust and dirt everywhere.

Tiny's eyes were accusing and angry. Without a word to me, she ran to her dragon, mounted and took to the sky.

"Tiny, wait. We be all coming!" I called, but she just circled overhead.

"That bad man has my Belle," Flossie said, burying her face against my thigh. "Promise me you'll bring her back," she muttered between sobs. "Promise." The little girl suddenly tilted her head. "I can hear her. She's far away and scared. No wait, she's really mad."

If that bastard had dared touch her, death would be too easy a fate for such as him. There are things much worse than death.

"How could this have happened?" Granny drew Flossie away from me and hugged her. "Don't worry, poppet, Jackal will save her."

"Belle ran away from me," I said. "Twere all me fault. I, uh, I asked her to marry me. I misread the signs." I didn't wish to tell Granny about the strange and powerful dragon mating. What would she think? What would anyone think?

Granny punched my shoulder. "You big dummy. She wasn't ready. You should have waited."

"I know. I been told."

Granny sighed and stroked Flossie's red curls. "Well, you shouldn't take all the blame. Annabelle is an impulsive girl with a quick temper. If Slygon has her, he might discover he's bitten off more than he can chew."

"I hope ye have the right of it," I said. "Happen the bastard attacked Oranth with Belle on her back. Oranth almost died and she's full of eggs. Dandy saved the dragon, but Slygon got Belle. Now he has Ashera, Belle and Belle's sister. It's past time for us to mount up and ride for his keep."

The elves and my friends crowded around waiting for me to tell them what to do. For a moment, I was overwhelmed with the responsibility. Then I noticed my men and the loyal elves seemed to have formed a much better relationship. I saw the slapped shoulders and nods that passed among them. Apparently, battling the kingdom's enemies was a bonding experience. "How many died?" I asked Slag quietly.

"Dozens, 'fraid to say, but not one child or unprotected female or elder. We battled a while, fierce and angry, and for a time thought to lose until we got the swing of covering each other's backs and the dragons figured out how to blast the enemy through the windows. Uh, you might have to replace a few. We had to break them, so the dragons could help. Yer loyal elves be good warriors, bro. You've a need to be proud of 'em."

"I'm proud of all of ye." I raised my hands for quiet. "I owe ye all a debt I don't know how to pay. Ye saved the kingdom and many lives. Brave, loyal and fierce each one. I be humble, grateful, truth as right, but happen I need more, with no right to it. We have a greater enemy, Slygon. He has the queen and he has Annabelle. I owe her my life. We need to kill Slygon to make the kingdom truly safe and save Ashera and Annabelle from a fate worse than dying. Who's with me?"

A great roar from the crowd was made more deafening by the dragons perched above them. The sound of approval reverberated around me and I realized I'd been holding my breath. Their trust and respect brought tears to my eyes, but we didn't have the time to indulge in emotion.

Are they here and ready, Remoth?

Aye, already evaluating those in the crowd, Remoth replied.

"Happen we need faster transportation, which means not all can come." I said to the assembled warriors. "See you there," I said as I waved my arm in the direction of the dozens of additional dragons who now tested the construction of the palace walls and began to settle around the courtyard. "These are the new crop of dragons. They're young, but strong enough for battle and the journey ahead, and willing to fight."

The dragons will communicate mentally with their chosen riders. If the riders are too afraid or don't wish to ride, they have but to admit it and the dragons will choose another rider. Be sure to explain that it's a lifetime relationship they should take seriously, Remoth told me.

I explained the bond between dragon and chosen rider to a silent and serious crowd. They would have little time to learn to fly a dragon before they would be riding into battle, first ride for many, last ride for some.

Chapter Thirty-Seven

Belle

Noemi, Ashera and I huddled in a dark corner of an abandoned tower. "He never comes up here," Noemi said. "There's nothing up here and he has plenty of other spaces he likes to haunt."

"Haunt is an apt word," Ashera said shivering. "I'm so hungry and sleepy." She turned and stared at me. I felt her trying to glamour me. She wanted to feed on me. I put up a strong wall and shoved her out of my head. "You're too weak to fight me and there's no way I'm volunteering to be your dinner."

"There're peasants in the scullery and the village outside the walls," Noemi said. "They're used to being food. Ashera and I both need a place to sleep soon. The sun is up, and we don't day walk like Slygon."

"So, do I just stash you two somewhere and come back for you later?"

Noemi's smile was grim. "It's the reality of being vampire. We sleep during the daylight hours."

Ashera spoke up. "I couldn't. Feed off humans, I mean. They're so disgusting."

"Seriously?" I grabbed Noemi's hand. "Let's just leave the princess here and save ourselves."

"She covered me when the sun rose and protected me," Noemi said. "I can't abandon her."

I sighed. "We have to find you two somewhere to sleep and when you rise, something or someone to eat," I said. "Where do you usually sleep?"

Noemi dropped her head. "In Slygon's room."

"Well that's out. Got any other ideas?"

"We can sleep in the seer's chamber. He'll hide us. He secretly hates Slygon."

"Then let's go there now before Ashera completely collapses."

Noemi led us down dark passage after dark passage. We saw no people, humans or vampires. "Where does the army of the undead sleep during the day?" I asked Noemi as we began climbing steep stairs up a tall tower.

"There are dungeons and catacombs beneath the castle."

I sighed. "Of course, there are."

We were halfway up the tall staircase when Oranth's voice entered my mind. *Annabelle. It is I, Oranth.*

I stopped suddenly. Noemi put her hand on my arm. "What is it?"

"Please be very quiet for a moment. I think my dragon is alive. *I thought you died. You're dead and it's all my fault. I'm so sorry! I'm so sorry!*

I'm alive. I can survive under water for some time and when I came out of the water, Remoth and Jackal were there. I thought I was too exhausted to continue carrying my eggs, but Dandy showed up and saved me. We're coming to bring you home.

"We?"

Jackal, Tiny, all your friends, along with an entire army of the king's elves.

"The King? Elves?"

"What is it?" Noemi asked.

"Oranth, my dragon, is alive, and Jackal." I thought for a moment. "Jackal, my love and the new elf king, is on his way here with an army to rescue us."

"Erindriel is coming here?" Ashera's voice was weak. She really did need to sleep and then feed.

"Yes, and he's bringing an army of elves with him. I can't bear the thought of them all being in danger, but we were planning to go after Slygon anyway. I guess it's going to be now."

We climbed into a tower that resembled an oriental temple. The floors were covered with fragrant mats of woven grass. Noemi called out. "Kokusan? It is I, Noemi."

A bent and ancient man wearing a white silk robe hobbled out of a back room. "You shouldn't be here. Slygon could come up here at any moment."

"I know, my friend," Noemi said. "But I have others with me, and I desperately need to sleep."

Ashera suddenly crumpled. I shook her. She was out cold. "Well, Ashera's asleep."

"Come," Kokusan said. "I have a small space where the vampires can hide. When they sleep, Slygon can't feel them."

Noemi and I carried Ashera into a tiny closet in the back of Kokusan's small living space. She shoved Ashera deep into the recess and lay down next to her. "Go to the kitchens and get out of the castle. We'll find you later."

"I don't want to leave you. I just found you." We hugged and bloody tears stained Noemi's face. "Need to sleep," she mumbled.

"The sun is fully up," Kokusan said. "She must sleep." He shut the door on them and pulled me out of his rooms. "Do as she told you. Find the kitchens and get out of the castle before Slygon finds you."

Jackal

I had learned a lot about riding dragons. It was cold high in the mountain. All of my warriors wore heavy furs. Slag and Chub flanked me as we winged our way north toward Slygon's castle and my Belle. She was truly mine now. We'd been together. She couldn't turn away from me now. Thinking about Slygon touching her made me want to kill something, anything. It was better to not think about it at all. Anger clouded the mind. I needed to be focused on the task ahead which was saving Belle, killing Slygon, freeing the ensorcelled dragons and if it was possible, bringing Ashera and Noemi home.

Noemi was vampire. I had no idea what we could do with her. Maybe Dandy, if the bloody fairy ever showed up, could fix her. Was fix the right word? Make her human again? I'd never heard of it being done, but then I'm no expert on vampires.

Remoth's voice popped into his head. *We will save all the dragons. While the riders, humans and elves rest before the attack, I will lead a phalanx of my strongest dragons including the young queen, Damoth. The fairy will go with us and we will try to remove the evil one's spell from all of them. Without dragons, the dark master will be trapped in his keep with no way to leave.*

Sounds like a plan. If you can do it.

We may lose one or two of our brethren, but I doubt it. The black dragons are under a deep and deadly spell, but they are our brothers in their hearts. Though we have never met them, all dragons have some kind of familial link. They don't want to kill us. Bazit said he knew killing dragons was wrong even when he was ensorcelled.

That's great, but remember, all the dragons have riders. We need every one of them to get us all home safely.

We flew across the high mountains, through falling snow and temperatures that grew colder the further north we traveled. At dusk, a very bad time to fight vampires, we landed on a peak overlooking Slygon's castle. The stone keep was made of granite and looked like it was carved out of the solid rock of a mountain peak. It had few windows and the ones in the towers were barred.

There was a large cleared area at the base of the crag the castle had been built upon. I used a new pair of binoculars to view the base of the castle and the area around it and spotted several small villages. That made sense. There had to be a population of support serfs. I saw grazing land and herd beasts. Paths led to the steep cliffs supporting the castle. Steps had been carved into the rock, stairs to the keep with gates of iron at the top. The gates were open. It seemed Slygon feared no attack at that level. Well he was making a mistake because when dawn arrived, that would be how half the elves would enter. Killing all of the vampires, not just Slygon, was definitely on the agenda. Slygon would probably be in the towers. No one knew whether he slept during the day or not. He was shifter and vampire and had more power than a mere vampire. He could no doubt day walk.

The dragons found a crevasse for the humans and elves out of the blowing snow and wind. There were twenty-three dragons and forty warriors, mostly elves, all ready to die for me and to kill Slygon.

Dandy popped in. This time she wore black leather. I hardly recognized her. "That be a change," I said when she sat on a rock next to me.

"I don't need to be seen. There are sixteen black dragons. Slygon has been very busy and it will take all my energy and most of Damoth's to transform them, to break the black spell on each of them. I need to eat."

"We brought some rations, just battle rations for the men. We've no fairy food," I said. "I don't think I've ever seen you eat."

Dandy waved her arm at him. "Don't worry. I brought food."

She whipped out the silvery wand, waved it in a flat space under an overhang, and poof! An entire table filled with roasted chickens, haunches of venison and boar along with pastries and savory vegetable dishes appeared. She pointed the wand at the elves. "Eat now. You'll need to fuel your magic and be strong for the battle. I sense over a hundred vampires in that castle and at least ten orcs."

"Is Belle in there?"

Dandy laid her hand on my forearm and squeezed. "She's there, Jackal, and we'll save her. Don't worry."

"Can't help but worry. I love her, ye know."

"She loves you, too," Dandy said softly.

"No, she hates me. She ran away after . . . after we made love." I stared into the night sky. "I shoulda waited. I woulda waited but for the dragon lust." I looked into her eyes. "Did you know about that?"

"I may have," she said.

"Woulda been nice to have a heads up."

"I didn't know Oranth's eggs were so close to needing fertilization or I would have. Damn dragons and their weird breeding cycles." She patted my arm. "Belle sees who you really are, and she loves you."

My heart did a flipflop. If only it were the truth. "What about Ashera. Is she in there?"

"Ashera is vampire. It's almost dark so she and Noemi should be waking. They were with Belle, but they had to sleep during the day."

"Where did Belle go?"

Dandy shrugged. "I honestly don't know."

"Fuck me, where's my Belle?"

"Don't worry. She's there somewhere and we'll find her. She's very good at hiding her thoughts and her mind. I'm sure she's safe."

"I have to find her, Dandy. I'm worried sick."

"Oranth made contact early this morning. She's alive in that place somewhere."

Dandy got busy, conjured a chair and plates, sat down and began stuffing herself. I'd never seen anything like it and stared at her eating as I took a plate and filled it. Dandy was eating her way through the biggest meal I'd ever seen.

Dandy pointed at the elves. "Eat meat. You don't want to be too pure. The vampires will be drawn to you if you are. The taste of pure elf blood drives them insane."

When it was close to midnight, Dandy climbed aboard Remoth and gathered the dragons around her. They perched on the rocks above and close by so they could listen. "We will try not to kill the black dragons," she said. "They are your kin, dragons kidnapped and put into the service of a dark master. However, they breathe green fire and it can burn through your scales right into your organs. There is a lake close by. If you get burned, dive into its depths. The fire will go out. Remoth will lead. I have to be able to perform a spell and run my wand over them to bring them out of the dark, so our plan is to cut single dragons out of the group and take them to the ground where I can perform my magic. Remoth will put me down in a good spot and you dragons will bring them to me."

I was afraid for Remoth and for the rest of the dragons. The big bronze was the only one of that color in the pride. I was connected to him in more ways than the telepathy. We'd formed a strong bond. Remoth led a group of six.

When they'd flown off, I lay down on a blanket with my head on my folded hands. Chub sat next to me. "I think that meat be under a spell," Chub said. "Did you see how much the fairy ate? Damn me if I could keep up with her. I tried me best, but she was like a starved hound dog. And it's percolating in me guts. I feel like power be coursing through me veins."

"Happen you're right," I said. "I think I can feel it, too."

I closed my eyes and reached for Remoth. The thought of losing even one dragon was terrible. It wasn't just that we needed them. I'd grown to admire and love the beasts. They were amazing. Their power, their strength was all given freely to us to use to defeat Slygon and rescue Belle. It would be an impossible task without them. And to think, not too long ago, I'd been against contacting them.

"Think Belle be okay?" Chub asked. "Think she's actually inside the castle?"

"Oh, she be in there alright. Dandy told me she was. Ashera's there, too, but she's not quite the same person."

"Vampire?"

I nodded. "Yeah, Dandy says she's been turned."

Two dragons landed on the ledge, a green and a brown. The young queen, Damoth, lumbered forward and began licking their wounds. We surrounded the dragons. I couldn't talk to them or ask them what was going on and it was horrible.

Two strange dragons fell out of the sky and landed hard. "Dandy be doing her work," Slag said.

"It's killing me not knowing what's going on. I should have flown with Remoth."

"You'd just be in the way. They know what's at stake."

So far, we have changed ten and five are dead. Remoth's voice echoed inside his head. *We are chasing the remaining three, but I think they are hiding somewhere we can't find them.*

Relief at hearing from the front lines made me giddy. *Come back and let's get going with this attack of ours. It be almost dawn and the vamps will all be sleeping soon.*

I stared at the dawn sky searching for dragons. They'd succeeded and hadn't lost any of their pride. That was great news. Remoth appeared and landed heavily. I ran to my dragon and examined him for wounds. *I'm fine.* The dragons' mental voice was sad. *We had to kill dragons. I'm sick over their loss, but they were trapped inside a living hell forced to do terrible deeds.*

Can you still fly? You must be exhausted.

We found a flock of fat sheep two valleys over and dined well. Nourishment after all our exertions was all we needed. We will sleep for days when this is over. Until then, we have all the energy we need and a vast supply of stomach gas to breath flames. Sheep fat. Yum.

Chapter Thirty-Eight

Belle

I had hidden in the scullery. During the day, serfs entered and left at odd times. Vampires don't eat and apparently neither did Slygon because there was little food and no cooking going on. The serfs seemed only interested in keeping the kitchens spotless, taking the occasional pot or pan, and returning others. I was currently stuffed inside a cupboard containing dishes I doubt were ever used. A layer of dust lay on top of all of them. I felt so helpless and inactivity of any kind made me want to scream. I was building up a reserve of frustration. God help the first person I crossed.

About halfway through the day, the serfs started running around like crazed rabbits. Then Slygon entered the kitchen and I knew why. "Where is she?" he yelled at them.

I concentrated on blanking my mind, putting up an invisible wall. If it was too strong, he'd notice and if it was too weak, he'd find me. Slygon stormed through the scullery and I cowered, waiting for my cupboard doors to be snatched open and my hiding place revealed. I heard the outer doors slam. Terror filled me and the fear he would catch me made me commit a grave error. I threw open the doors of the cupboard and ran. He was waiting for me.

Slygon chuckled gleefully as he grabbed me and pulled me hard against him. I turned my head away as he tried to kiss me. "My beautiful virgin," he crooned. "Soon, you will be mine."

I couldn't contain myself anymore. I screamed and shattered all the windows in the kitchen. The lighting system blew. Lanterns, glassware, dishes, all exploded. Slygon released me and I ran. I raced out of the castle and into the courtyard. It was dusk. In Kokusan's tower, Ashera and Noemi would be stirring.

Freaking, I scanned the courtyard for a hiding place, any place, but I was too slow. Though I knew escape was impossible, I had to try.

Slygon tackled me, carrying me to the ground beneath him. I wished I had my wand, but I'd left my precious dragon-spine wand laying in the grass where Jackal and I had made crazy dragon love. I imagined myself inside a cocoon of blue. Slygon laughed, turned into a snake and wrapped steely coils around my body. "You have no chance, but I love your fight."

He was once again human, elf, vampire, or whatever he called normal. He pressed wet kisses on the back of my neck, and I shuddered with disgust. He jumped up and tucked me under one arm like I was a recalcitrant three-year old. Then he passed his hand over my head. I felt pressure. When I tried to blow up more windows, the pressure increased, and I grabbed my head in pain.

"No more magic, little girl. You've been very bad."

He toted me up staircases and into his personal wing. I recognized it. He opened the door to a room with barred windows and a view of the sun setting, plopped me on a bed, and kissed me. I turned my head away, but not in time. His full mouth touched mine and I tasted blood.

He read my mind. "Yes, I have just dined on the precious blood of an infant. I am fully a man."

I knew what he meant and shivered with horror. "Where have you hidden your sister and Ashera?"

"I have no idea what you're talking about."

He grabbed my chin and forced me to stare into his eyes. "Yes, you do. Where are they?"

The only thing I could think of to change the way things were headed was to blurt out the truth. He thought I was pure. Time for the truth to come out. "I'm not a virgin."

Slygon's eyes literally snapped in his head. He'd been staring out the window, now he was focused on me and I felt his mind probe like a hot poker in my head. "The halfling!" He screamed. "You gave yourself to that damn half-orc monster, the new king of the elves?"

I shrugged. "It was a dragon thing. You had to be there."

He shrieked with fury, grabbed me and threw me on the bed. "Then there's no need to have a care for your precious virginity, is there?"

A timid knock on the door saved me. Slygon crawled off my frozen body and threw open the door. "What?" he screamed.

An ugly, deformed orc stood on the other side. "Master," he mumbled. "The dragons are all gone cepting for three that're hiding. There's been a terrible dragon fight just beyond the valley. Clean dragons are killing your black dragons."

Slygon shot me a look filled with so much hate, I knew when he came back, he'd not only ravish me, but probably kill me."

"I'll return when I've dealt with this small matter."

He slammed the door shut and I heard the bolt slide. I was locked in.

The second I heard the bolt slam shut, I leapt out of the bed. My clothes were a mess. Slygon had torn my shirt. I clutched it over my shoulders. Beneath it I wore bindings to keep my breasts flat and out of the way while fighting. Women have so much to deal with. I searched the closet and found filmy gowns and robes. Not my thing at all and not practical.

It was almost dark. When I stared out the windows, I saw mountains, purple in dusk, and a red sky. Below me, I imagined vampires waking, stretching and climbing out of their crypts starving for blood. Not a great mental vision. I hoped Ashera and Noemi were waking. I sent Noemi a mental message, where I was, where Slygon was. I got a sleepy but comforting feeling in return. Noemi was awake, but only just. Noemi was my only hope. She and Ashera had to come for me. I started pacing back and forth across the chamber.

I was making my twentieth turn on the fluffy-blue carpet when a bright light blazed in front of me and poof! I figured it was Dandy, but it wasn't Dandy who popped in. It was Flossie. The child saw my surprise and laughed her high-pitched giggle. She held out her hand and there was Squeaker sitting on it.

"You're a fairy," Annabelle gasped. "Why didn't you tell us?"

Flossie jumped up on the bed and sat down. She was wearing a miniature of one of Dandy's gowns, a frightening pink frock with white flowers sprinkled across the fabric. A bright-pink sash was tied around her waist.

"You need to get out of here," Flossie said.

"I know, but until you arrived, I had no hope. Have you always known you're a fairy? Were your parents fairies?"

"We really don't have time for this discussion," Flossie said in a very adult voice. "But, no, I was given to my parents as a child. They had no idea what I was. They were kind people and when Slygon attacked them, I was too young to help. It will sadden me for the rest of my life which is a long, long time."

I shook my head. "No wonder you could change your thoughts. I always did think that was the weirdest part of your story."

Flossie drew a silver wand out of the pocket of her gown. "Dandy gave me this. It's pretty powerful." She pointed the wand at the door, and it turned purple. "Rats," the girl said. She pointed it again and closed her eyes concentrating so hard her face squinched. Silver dust floated out of the end of the wand. I'd seen that happen with Dandy's wand. It coated the door.

"Go through it fast," Flossie said.

I stuck my hand through what looked like a solid purple door. Satisfied I wouldn't smash into it, I stepped through. Once on the other side I turned around and stared at the door. It seemed solid and it wasn't purple. When I touched it, I touched wood, my hand no longer passed through it. Flossie popped in and beckoned to me. "We need to get you out of this tower."

"I can't leave without my sister and Ashera."

Flossie shrugged. At that moment, she looked like a miniature of Dandy. It was a typical Dandy gesture. "Where are they?

"Up." I pointed. "In the seer's tower."

"Then I guess that's where we go." Flossie grabbed my hand and we climbed the tower stairs, reaching the next landing quickly. "Slygon won't know you've escaped until he actually goes into the room," Flossie whispered. "I coulda blown up the door, but, you know, noisy and then no door."

"He's pretty mad at me," I hissed.

"What'd you do?"

I shrugged. "Nothing a little girl should hear about."

She giggled. "The dragon mating?"

My face flamed. "Oh crap, how'd you know about that?"

"I'm a fairy, duh!"

"He was expecting a virgin." I made a face. "I disappointed him."

We hit the small landing facing the front of an ancient oriental temple and stopped. "Where are they hiding?" Flossie asked.

"Kokusan, the Japanese seer, stuffed them into a closet so they could sleep the day away. They should be up by now."

Huge timbers supported an elaborate pergola and a roof constructed of ebony. The door was bright red and strange writing traveled up the sides of the panels framing the door. "Japanese writing," Flossie said. "It says, Life has no end or beginning when you're already dead."

"Not the most encouraging message, is it?"

The huge door creaked open and Noemi and Ashera stepped out. Kokusan was behind them. Noemi hugged me. "You survived."

"Barely."

"Kokusan put some kind of spell on us so we could rise early. The sun won't set for another hour, but we are awake now."

Slygon's discovered I was no longer in the room. We knew because his roar of anger was probably heard all across the castle. Flossie lifted one childish eyebrow and pointed at the door.

"Back inside," I said.

In the center of the mat-covered room was a well. I didn't remember seeing it before. "Was this always here?" I asked Kokusan.

"What?"

"The well."

"It is there when I wish it to be."

I gazed into brilliant blue water.

Flossie grabbed me by my torn blouse. "Don't look. It's not really a well as you should be able to figure out for yourself. It's magic water, and endlessly deep. If you fall into it, you'll never come out."

Her warning was too late. I'd already looked. As I stared into the strange green-blue swirling water, I saw Jackal flying toward me on Remoth, accompanied by an entire pride of dragons all with elves riding them. Beside Jackal, Slag and Chub rode their dragons.

"Jackal and an army of dragons are on the way," I said to Noemi and Flossie.

"They will not catch Slygon," Kokusan said. "I have seen his escape in the well."

"But Slygon is after me," I said.

"I know his plans for you, but he won't search for you here," Kokusan said. "I may look into the future for him, but he is no friend to me. He brought me out of the Pit, gave me a place to live and meditate, so I owed him some allegiance. I've fulfilled that debt many times over."

The water in the well churned. When I gazed into it, a face appeared. The face was of a young elf with black hair and beautiful features. I glanced at Kokusan who's red lips were clenched tightly. "Ruuvaen," he said.

"That's my father." I grabbed Noemi. "Look, father's face is in the well."

"Your father is alive," the seer said. "You must go now. There are warriors approaching the keep and Slygon has gone to fight them."

I grabbed the long sleeve of Kokusan's kimono. "Where is my father? If he's alive, why hasn't he come for us?"

"That is a mystery you must solve for yourself."

I glanced one more time into the water and saw Jackal staring back at me as though he could see me. My heart overflowed with love for him, this loyal warrior with his honest ways and enduring affection. He risked his life and everything he knew and loved to rescue me. I knew he'd give up his elf kingdom for me if I asked him to.

Flossie took my hand. "Come on."

I shook her off and grabbed Noemi's shoulders. "Father is alive. We have to find him."

Flossie rolled her eyes, a childish and adult gesture she seemed pretty addicted to. "We don't have time for this crap now. Hurry."

"Thank you," I said to Kokusan. "You risked everything to help my sister and Ashera." Ashera was propped against the wall, her already white face completely bleached of all color. Kokusan pointed to her. "She needs to feed or she's not going to make it. The spell works best for vamps who are well-fed, not starving. So, she may fall asleep at any moment if she doesn't get blood."

I looked at Flossie. "Can you help her?"

The child did her eye-rolling thing again. "Why? She's a freaking vampire. What's she going to do if we save her? Return to Greenwood and resume her throne? I don't think so."

"For fuck's sake, Flossie. If you can help her, do it. We'll worry about what to do with her later."

Flossie waved her wand and a plump rabbit appeared in Ashera's hands. "Eat it."

"It's an animal," Ashera said in a voice filled with loathing.

"So," Flossie's voice was filled with sarcasm. "It's got blood. Drink it."

Jackal

If Remoth was right, there were three remaining black dragons. I wished we could have killed or changed all of them, but three seemed like a manageable number. Three were plenty for Slygon to escape on, but not enough to mount a counterattack or battle us from the air. That meant Slygon was probably fortifying his castle in every way possible, no doubt using all kinds of spells and magical tricks. I might have power, but I had no inkling of how to use it yet. We did have Dandy with us, and she or maybe even the elves, could counter those tricks. That was as long as Dandy popped back in when we needed her.

We were ready to leave when the fairy dragged back into camp completely out of energy, a husk of the vibrant creature that left to do battle. She wrapped a robe around herself and crawled deep into the crevasse to sleep after assuring him she just needed a few winks.

I didn't want to leave her. We needed her support. But the sun was well up, and it was time to attack. We should have left hours ago. I waited for Dandy. My plan was contingent on all the vampires sleeping. What I hadn't counted on was this valley. It ran north to south and the mountains on both sides were so high, the sun rose late and set early making the daylight hours few.

Remoth spoke to me. *The three black dragons are inside the keep. Slygon prepares by placing them on the towers and by putting a shield around the castle. The shield will be filled with snakes. He has an affinity for them and will use them at every opportunity.*

Remembering Craggy Town, I asked. "Will they be real snakes, or only visions?"

There will be some real ones multiplied with visions. It will be hard for you to tell the difference, but the dragons and the elves will know.

"How nice for them. Tell Chub to watch for snakes. If you think they're not real, ask your dragon. He'll know."

Slag shot me a very uncomplimentary gesture using only one finger.

Our plan was still to drop Slag and six elves into the village supporting the castle. Maybe the people would want to help, but they might not. It was so hard to say. The serfs could be humans, half humans or even halfling orcs, dwarves or goblins, and many might not wish to help us destroy their way of life.

"We need to leave now," I said to Slag. "It's already later than I planned. I'm gonna check on the fairy."

I found her unconscious, wrapped in her cloak, deeply asleep. I tried to wake her with no results. I guess she was done in. I had no idea how long fairies slept or needed to sleep.

We climbed aboard our dragons. The beasts were bellowing with battle fervor. They wanted to attack the castle and kill Slygon. All of the saved dragons were ready to help. The noise of the dragons roaring, the warriors chanting elf-war songs and the rush of air as we took off was amazing.

I was privileged to watch as Slag, whose orc face was as green as a meadow in summer, power hurl over the side of his dragon. I would have laughed, but Slag's flying sickness could debilitate him so much he wouldn't be able to fight. Slag shook his head to clear it and the big three-quarters orc on his brown female dragon dove for the village, wings streamlined. Slag was followed by Ivansar and Tanathlil on a green male dragon and Torros Glynfire with three elves behind him on a bigger brown female. Seven warriors to take the keep from the ground and kill sleeping vampires. It didn't seem like enough, but Ivansar's smaller green male could easily get into the keep and breath fire. As a weapon, there was nothing like a dragon with their sharp talons and flaming breath.

With Slag and his crew headed for the ground, I led the rest of them higher. We flew above the castle until I could see the tops of the towers and two of the remaining black dragons. Where was the third one?

We found out soon enough. The remaining black was a huge bronze like Remoth, only now completely black with bronze shimmering under the darkness. The black dragon dove straight at us. I glanced behind. Bazit and Damoth bore no riders so were free to maneuver in ways the others were not.

I waved to Chub. The plan was for Chub and the dragons to take on the blacks guarding the keep while I went in hunting for Belle and Ashera. Chub and the rider less dragons banked hard to go after the attacking black while the rest of us went for the two guarding the keep from the tops of the towers. Remoth folded his wings and I clung to the spikes on his back, glad for the goggles Belle provided. Wind whistled as the dragons' speed in the dive increased.

We dove so fast I could barely make out the black dragons. The four dragons blasted a massive stream of flames at the tower setting the dragon guarding it on fire. The dragon screeched, took off and flew straight at us. The black dragon breathed poisonous green fire. It smelled like rotting flesh. One of the dragons took a hit, squealed and dropped. His rider, equipped with a magic spell provided by Dandy that extinguished the flames, swooped low over the village sending the occupants running for their lives.

Three of our dragons bathed the black in blasts of flames, setting it blazing. It folded its scorched wings and plummeted to Earth. Remoth's sad cry filled my head, but the tower was cleared. The dragon who had been guarding the other tower was gone. Orc archers on the ramparts fired on us. Choosing the daylight hours to attack proved smart. No vampires manned the walls anywhere.

The orcs fired a weapon armed with a long spear. The spear's tip glinted with silver. The dragons saw it coming and easily avoided it. I waved to Chub, the signal for them to take on the orcs while I landed Remoth on the tower and scrambled through a broken window, the bars bent into tortured shapes by the heat of dragon fire. My mission was to find Belle, Ashera, and Noemi if I could, and kill Slygon, a mission I would complete or die.

Chapter Thirty-Nine

Belle

Flossie, who I still couldn't believe was a freaking fairy, Noemi and Ashera, who looked ready to die, and I, stood on the landing, looking down. "Where's Slygon?" I whispered.

"Jackal is attacking. The sun is behind the mountains. He should have come earlier. Slygon had a plan for this attack but only has three dragons left. He might try to leave. I think he took off on one of the black dragons. At least I'm pretty sure he was the one riding it. I can't read him very well. He's so good at hiding his thoughts and his mental signature and I don't want him to know I'm snooping so I have to be really careful."

"Why is he running? Is it that bad for him?"

"Jackal had a great plan. I believe he and the dragons have killed all but the one black dragon. Slygon would be stuck here in this castle with no dragons. He will do anything to prevent that including abandoning his minions to Jackal's forces.

"Should we go down there? Ashera needs to feed or she's going to die on us."

"Vampires that starve don't die," Flossie said with a sneer on her child features. "They just wither and become inert. As soon as blood is available, they're back on their feet so stop worrying about her."

"There're at least a hundred vamps waking up right now in the tombs under this creepy pile of rock," Noemi said. "They're all ruthless and they've all followed Slygon for many years."

I raised an eyebrow. "Well, we must take care not to run into them."

"You got that right," Noemi said. "I mean, I'll fight beside you, but it would be better if we didn't have to fight them as well."

"Can any day walk besides you?"

"I can barely do it. Some are old enough, but none like to. The sun is deadly."

I grabbed Flossie by her narrow shoulders. "Flossie, you're still a child, how can you help us? I mean, you're so freaking little and there's hundreds of vamps."

The little fairy shook off my hands. "I may be a child or in a child's body, but I have almost all my fairy powers. Dandy helped me learn and I can get you out of here. I know I can."

"But Jackal is on his way. Should we wait for him?"

"He has Slygon to deal with. We should stay out of his way. He's going to be very busy." Flossie grabbed my hand and pulled me down a few steps. I was so unsure of what to do. Should I follow this child? Put my sister's and my lives in her tiny hands? I stopped and took a deep breath. It was one thing to be scared, not just for myself and Noemi, but for Flossie who in spite of everything she said was still a child, and I was terrified for Jackal fighting that monster.

"I have an idea where we can hide," Flossie said.

"Where?" I whispered and shivered.

Flossie must have noticed, because she looked me up and down, noticed her flimsy torn shirt and said, "For goodness sake. Where is your vest and why is your shirt torn?"

"Slygon tore off all my armor and was in the process of ravishing me when I told him I wasn't a virgin. He kind of lost it and ripped my shirt. When I checked the closet for something more suitable, like my leathers and a coat, all I found was filmy gowns and silk dresses."

"Must have been a pretty awkward moment."

"You have no idea."

"We have to find you something warm or you're gonna freeze to death and it won't matter if Slygon catches you or not."

"Gee, thanks."

Flossie giggled. We crept down another landing, Noemi supporting Ashera who seemed to be barely conscious of her surroundings. When we reached a landing two stories down, Flossie led us along a dark hallway with doors spaced every twenty feet. The end of the hallway led to another staircase and a big mullioned window. "Are there vamps sleeping in these rooms?"

"Shhhh, yes," Flossie whispered. "One of Slygon's favorite concubines is sleeping in there. Dorna is old and a terrible vampire."

Noemi nodded. "Please don't wake her. She hates my guts."

"Jealous," Flossie whispered.

"And just plain evil," Noemi hissed back. "So old, every shred of humanity is gone. If she ever possessed any which I doubt. She's half elf."

Flossie pointed at a closed door. It was made of ebony, black and shiny. "She's in there," Flossie whispered.

I tore my hand out of Flossie's grip. "We shouldn't be here. Are you nuts?"

"Dorna's dead to the world. I can't feel her at all, and you need something warm to wear."

Flossie slowly opened the ebony door. I was so scared I stopped shivering. Flossie slid into the room and pulled me behind her. Noemi hesitated and then followed us. The bed hangings were closed but sheer enough for us to see Dorna laid out stiff as a board on top of a red and gold brocade coverlet. "Holy shit," Ashera squeaked. "I know her. That's Dorna. I always wondered where that bitch went. She disappeared five hundred years ago. Half-elf related to Uriel Silverheart. Her mother was a witch."

"She sounds charming," I whispered. "Can we get out of here please?"

"Clothes," Flossie said. "You need a coat."

Flossie went into a dressing room and emerged buried beneath a mound of sable fur. She handed me the coat, then headed for the door. Ashera couldn't get over the fact she'd found Dorna. She leaned close to the sleeping vampire and fingered a ruby necklace laying on Dorna's opulent chest. "This is mine," Ashera hissed. "The bitch stole it. I always knew that's where it went."

"Don't," Flossie jumped for Ashera. She was too late. Dorna woke, grabbed Ashera and sank her fangs in Ashera's neck.

"Shit!" Flossie cursed and I was shocked but only for a moment. I mean, an ancient vampire was draining Ashera.

Flossie waved her wand and both vampires froze. Noemi stepped in and disengaged Dorna's fangs from Ashera's neck. The drops of blood on the tips of her fangs were frozen.

"This seems like a good opportunity for Ashera to get some nourishment," I said to Flossie. "Can you wake just her and allow her to dine on Dorna?"

Flossie did her eye-rolling thing. "We're kind of in a hurry."

"I know, but if Ashera doesn't eat, she's not gonna make it."

Flossie waved the wand and Ashera sprang to life. "Eat Dorna, please," I said. "You need the nourishment and if you don't, you might not make it."

Ashera had lost a lot of blood to Dorna. Noemi helped her. "Drinking Dorna's blood will make you strong. She's very old. I'm afraid you should really drain her. If we leave her alive, she may warn Slygon."

Ashera took Dorna's arm and sank her fangs in the white wrist. I had to turn away. The slurping noises were disturbing.

Ashera lifted her head from Dorna's wrist. "I've had as much as I can hold."

"Is she dead, truly dead?" I asked Noemi.

Noemi put her head next to Dorna's face as though listening. "I can't feel her, but she could still be alive."

I looked at the vampire. "She's dead enough for now. There's no food source nearby, so let's hope she stays down long enough for us to get out of here."

Ashera strutted out of the room. "I feel great," she said to Noemi. "Like I could lift a dragon."

Noemi sighed. "We've created a monster."

I slipped the coat on and closed my eyes for a moment to savor the warmth, but Flossie wasn't having any shillyshallying. She grabbed my hand and dragged me to the staircase. "We need to get out of here."

"Right," I said.

We went down four more flights to the bottom floor. This was a side stairway leading to servants' quarters, kitchens, and service areas. Flossie ran down a long corridor. At the end was a door leading to a courtyard surrounded by pig sties, chicken coops, small vegetable gardens and stacks of firewood. A stout peasant chopped wood. Two women fed chickens and slopped the hogs. All wore rags, cloth coats patched in many places, gloves with no fingers, woolen caps pulled low over their ears. When the four of us popped out of the castle, they turned and stared.

Flossie ignored them and led us at a run through the yard and out a gate. None of the peasants said anything. They seemed dull and listless as they went about their business. "What's wrong with them?" I asked Flossie when we were on a narrow trail leading along the edge of the cliffs supporting Slygon's castle.

"The vampires feed off them. They keep them alive so they have a continuous food source, but so weak, they can barely go about their daily chores."

"Why don't they run away?"

Flossie waved her hand to indicate the tall mountains surrounding them. "There's no way out. All they have is this small river valley. They could follow it to the end where it goes underground and still be stuck in this valley. By then, Slygon or his vampires would catch them."

I felt bad for them. When this was over, I would save all of them. I couldn't think about them stuck here being used as cattle for vampires. That was no existence. That was a living death. When I looked back, I saw one of the women look at me. The woman's eyes were dull, her hair limp and her face a pasty white. "If it were me living here, I'd risk running," I said. "Anything but living like this. They're more dead than alive."

"They've been in this valley for a hundred years, two generations," Noemi said. "They're lucky they survived childhood. Slygon loves to shop in the village for the newborn."

"That's disgusting," Ashera said.

Noemi hung her head. I saw the gesture and I knew it was because Noemi had participated in the awful ritual of drinking the blood of infants. She was tainted forever. It was hard for me to realize my only sister was a demon and a baby killer.

When we reached the bottom of the cliffs, we followed a narrow trail emerging in the serf's village. Small children played on the beaten earth in front of sturdy huts. Two women spun wool while they watched the children. "This is the other reason they stay," Noemi said. "If they run, they can't take the children. Slygon allows them to have their babies, only taking one of five to feed on."

"That's horrible. We must free these poor people."

Suddenly, overhead, dragons appeared. I felt for the familiar thoughts of Oranth and reached her daughter, Damoth. I felt all of the dragons' joy at finding me alive. Some of the dragons broke away and headed for the village, the rest attacked the two black dragons on the towers. "We're saved," I screamed. "We're saved."

When I was abruptly grabbed from behind, I ducked, stomped on a booted foot with my boot and struggled wildly. I heard a familiar laugh, sinister, without humor, right in my ear. "I think not."

"Jackal!" I screamed. A hand clamped over my mouth and then fell away. Slygon dropped me as my sister attacked him. Ashera grabbed me and pulled me away. "Come on," she urged. "Run."

"Noemi," I cried. "I can't leave her."

"You have to," Ashera snarled.

I snatched my hand out of Ashera's strong grip and turned to help Noemi. I screamed and Slygon caught on fire. It immediately went out. There was nothing I could explode. All the serfs had run for cover, hiding in their huts. I couldn't destroy them. Noemi hung onto Slygon's back. She'd sunk her fangs in his shoulder, her claws dug into his neck. He turned into a snake and she lost her grip. The huge cobra sank its fangs into Noemi. I screamed, but the snake didn't explode. Without thinking a thing about my own safety, concerned only for my sister. I'd just found her. I couldn't let her die now. I threw myself on Slygon.

"Ashera," I called. "Help us."

The elf queen shook her head.; "No, no, no," she said. "He'll kill me."

The snake bit Noemi over and over then wrapped its coils around us both. I felt the snake's strength. I tried to send a mental arrow into Slygon's brain, and he laughed. I searched for some sign of life in my sister and found only a black emptiness. I shrieked with rage. "You've killed my sister."

Slygon covered my mouth with his hand. "Shut up. She's been dead for years. Now she may or may not survive, but she's out of my way." He pointed a finger at Ashera. "You," he said. "Help me."

Ashera walked toward us like a zombie. "I made her," he said. "She has to obey me."

I frantically searched for Flossie, suddenly terrified for her, but the little fairy was gone. I bit Slygon's hand and he removed it. "Jackal!" I screamed.

We're on our way. Damoth spoke to her.

Slygon's in the village. He has me.

I received no answer. Slygon scooped me up and carried me back the way we'd come, holding me under one arm like a parcel, a biting, kicking, and screaming parcel. Ashera followed, her face blank.

"The dragons and elves will come, and I will kill them. They have no chance against me. Look." He jerked my head up by the hair. Hanging in a silvery cage shimmering with strange magic was Dandy. "I have the fairy. They'll never kill her."

He pointed his long, white finger and the cage rose to hang high above the village. It slowly moved toward the castle as though pulled by a string. My heart froze and I struggled harder against Slygon's grip, grabbed his arm and sank my teeth into it, drawing blood. It tasted foul. When I spit it out Slygon cuffed me, the slap so hard my ears rang, and my head buzzed.

The peasants ran crazy, screaming as they grabbed their children when they saw the dragons. Some ducked into their huts, some ran past us for the imagined safety of the castle. Slygon ignored the dragons and raced up a narrow trail through the rocks and into the castle by way of a small door hidden beneath an outcropping of rock and twisting vines. Dandy's cage entered the castle behind them, followed by Ashera.

Once inside, I stopped struggling. There seemed no point and it wasted energy. Slygon strode down a narrow corridor. It went on forever as though edging the castle wall. We went down, toward the sleeping coven of vampires. Down, into the bowels beneath the castle where daylight never ventured, and the dragons couldn't follow.

It was the last place on earth I wanted to go. I beat against Slygon with my fists, against his legs, his back, to no avail. I used my elbow to dig into his side and tried to squirm away from him. We started down another long rock-lined corridor edged with windows. When I looked out, I saw they were sunk into wells. When we passed a window, I grabbed the sill, clutched it with all my might. Anything to prevent him from taking me into the tombs.

Jackal

I didn't hear Belle scream my name but Remoth did. *Annabelle is afraid for herself, her sister, and for Dandy. Slygon has captured the fairy.*

Flossie suddenly popped in, smaller than Squeaker who popped in with her. The little girl's red hair framed her face in a crazed halo. "Dandy is in Slygon's hands," I said. "How'd that happen?"

Flossie's voice was high and squeaky. "I don't know. She was so very tired after fighting the black dragons and using up all her magic to clean them. He must have put some kind of spell on her when she was weak. If I'd known, I woulda asked the seer. He seemed nice."

"What seer?"

"Slygon has an old blind seer in that tower." Flossie pointed.

"Think he'll help us?"

"He might."

"Follow the plan, Slag," I yelled. "I'm going after Belle."

Slag lifted his hand and waved me on.

The elves spread out across the ramparts. Charred orc bodies, burned by dragon fire, smoldered and stank. "How can we get up to the seer's tower?" I asked Flossie. Her being a fairy was very strange, but I'd always known Flossie was special, just never expected this.

"There's a way. We have to go down to a lower level and cross over to the staircase leading to the seer's tower." She pointed across the castle to the tall tower with the strange windows and the open balcony. "The only problem is we have to pass Dorna's room. Ashera drained her and she might be dead. Or she could sprout to life. You never know. She's really old. She's half elf and half witch so she might sense you and wake. She'll be really hungry."

"If you think the seer can help, we'll have to pass that test when we greet it."

I cast one longing look over the edge of the ramparts into a courtyard. Belle was down there somewhere. Slygon had her. I wanted to go to her badly, but I knew in my heart it would turn into a trap. "Where's Slygon taking Belle?"

"The tombs," Flossie whispered. "He's taken her and Dandy below where the vampires sleep during the day. It's far too dangerous for us. I don't have enough power. He killed Noemi, or at least she's dead for now. Vampires can survive almost anything, and he has Ashera with him. He can control her because he made her."

"Then let's hope your seer knows a way cause it be getting dark out and the vampires awake."

Chapter Forty

Belle

I struggled wildly, kicking and biting at anything I could reach. I stabbed Slygon's brain with a powerful thought arrow. It hit a shield as hard as rock. Slygon laughed. "Never get me that way, girl. Think I'm weaker than you?"

Suddenly, I was no longer afraid, but I was very pissed off. This horrible monster was destroying everything, killing my friends, enslaving Dandy, devouring infants. There had to be a way to kill him. He couldn't be invincible. Nobody was invincible. Everyone and everything had a weak spot.

We passed a row of windows on a long hallway. Each window was set into the rock and in a deep hole. Little light seeped in, and I could see the walls of the keep on each side. Slygon headed for another staircase that went down even deeper. Down was bad, awfully bad. I screamed, and all the windows blew out at once. Slygon waved an arm, deflected the glass, then laughed in my face. "You have no power that can hurt me, child. I am older than you can imagine, and I possess the power of elves, shifters and vampires. I am a god."

I hung under his arm like a limp dish rag as he headed down steep steps into a dark dungeon. There were no lights. Slygon was from the Pit. He didn't need lights. We went down another four steep flights of stairs ending at the bottom in a cavern carved out of solid rock. I saw the chisel and pick marks made by human tools as serfs slaved for this monster to carve a dungeon for his minions to sleep in during the day.

Coffin after coffin lined the floor. There had to be a hundred.

"How did you catch Dandy? She's a powerful fairy." I couldn't believe Dandy was in a cage. It was beyond horrible. I loved Dandy. She'd done so much for me and all of us.

"She was sleeping on a plateau of rock in a crevasse. She used all her power to save the black dragons, meddling witch. She was recuperating. One of the black dragons, Morpheus, told me of her weakened state and flew me there. Catching her proved to be the easiest thing I've done this day. She's wrapped in a magic cocoon inside a silver cage. There's no way she can escape." Slygon preened, proud of himself for capturing poor Dandy.

"Now, you my dear are going to be bait. I fear there is no time for me to make you mine, though it is the dearest wish of my heart. You might not be the virgin I wanted, but you're still pure of heart and a great beauty. I also owe your sister, meddling bitch, for all the trouble she's caused by helping you and Ashera. That beast of a half orc is coming for you. I don't know where he gets his powers. I don't know what he is, but somehow his bloodline must be stronger than I knew. And he has such a pure heart and good intentions," he jeered. "Big dummy. He might have had you first, but Kyran will make you his forever. Eating your precious Jackal's heart will be delicious revenge." He looked into my eyes. "I had such wonderful plans for us. I would have fathered a child on you, but that lummox and the dragons have ruined everything."

He wove his way through the coffins to a huge black one in the center. "In here lies Kyran, my most powerful vampire. It won't be long until he can day walk. He was once an elf." Slygon grew thoughtful as though remembering some beautiful event from long ago. "Such a beautiful boy, but evil through and through. He relished being turned and will be the one to enjoy your body because I will be gone. You are my gift to him. When he wakes, you will be here. He will thrive off your blood and perhaps enjoy your body as well. The dark comes early in this valley. The tall mountains to the west eat the sun, creating darkness much earlier than flat land and lasts much longer. One of the reasons I chose this valley. That and its inaccessibility to anything but dragons."

Slygon tossed me onto the top of the huge ebony casket and strapped me down with thick rope. He waved his hands over the rope adding additional magic. When I was secure enough to satisfy him, he kissed me. His lips were soft and tasted like dead flowers and rotting meat. He nipped me with a fang and drew blood which he licked up. I couldn't fight him, but spit when he lifted his head. "Yes, get rid of my taste." He laughed. "Kyran will make you his and you may enjoy it. He can glamour you first and then you will give yourself to him gladly."

"I don't glamour."

"Well, then you won't enjoy it, but take you he will."

I fought the ropes holding me, squirming and straining against them. "I'll fight him with every last ounce of strength I possess. I'll never submit to him."

"Never say never, my dear. The truth is, quite often we do things we swore we never would."

He took one final look at me, a seeking look as though imprinting my image on his brain. "I detect a familial resemblance. Who was your father?"

"His name was Ruuvaen and he's dead."

"Ruuvaen? Seriously?" Then he laughed and laughed as though that was the funniest thing he'd ever heard. "It's amazing how strange and complicated life can be. Your father's not dead," he said sneering. "It's possible I might know him."

I strained against the bonds even harder. Memories of the years with the nuns, always being restrained, in shackles, trapped in a room, filled me. I screamed with frustration. "You could never know my father. He was a good and kind man."

"Not man at all," Slygon said. "Elf. I thought your power might be from a hereditary source and I was so right. We Morthians are the strongest elves with the greatest powers. How strange we are related, and it would have made no difference to me when I took you, because I am what I am." He licked his lips with a pointed tongue. "Your taste, so sweet and definitely familiar, but I must go." He pointed at Ashera who was slumped against a coffin with her eyes closed. "You, make sure she stays put."

Ashera's eyes opened slightly. "Mmmm," she mumbled.

Slygon grabbed her by the hair and sniffed her. "You smell like Dorna. Did you drink her blood?"

"We killed your vamp lover," I said.

Slygon grabbed Ashera's arm. "Then you will assume her place. You disgust me. Make sure Annabelle does not leave. I command you. I put this on you, and you cannot avoid my command."

Slygon whirled in a flash of black and left me strapped to the coffin. Above my head Dandy floated in the silver cage. A huge cobra coiled around the bars. It dropped its head, flared its hood and hissed at me. I didn't flinch, though it was a real snake, not an imaginary one. Animals have always liked me. Slygon had left it to guard the cage holding Dandy and to watch me. The snake followed my every move and wiggle. If I managed to free myself from the rope, it might try to bite me, but I doubted if it would.

Did he really say I was of his bloodline? Related to that monster? Everything Slygon had said only made things harder to understand. He'd cleared up nothing, just hinted my father was somehow related to him and even still alive.

When Slygon was truly gone and I no longer sensed his presence, I whispered. "Dandy, wake up. Dandy." I sent a mental jab into the fairy's brain, and as usual, there was nothing there. "Dandy!" I screamed in an effort to wake her.

Dandy moaned but didn't answer.

"Ashera," I whispered. "Untie me."

The queen was deeply asleep. "He told me to guard you," she muttered. "Have to obey."

Jackal

Flossie and I descended to the only floor that crossed to the isolated staircase leading to the seer's tower. Flossie put her fingers to her lips and pointed at a black door with a piece of glass over it. The vampire Dorna must be sleeping in there. The sun was setting early behind the mountains to the west. The tall western peaks cut off a good portion of the day. This was not part of my plan. I'd wanted to attack the keep in full shining daylight and now it was getting dark and the hordes of vamps sleeping in this keep were no doubt waking and would attack soon. I needed to get Belle and get out of here.

We crept past Dorna's door without incident, made it to the staircase and started up. The stairs were steep and circular, winding around a small column of rocks that led to the tower. At the top was a large landing with an open door to a temple. Just inside, an ancient oriental vampire with a black silk strip over his eyes stood waiting.

"I am Kokusan and I knew you would come. Erindriel, prince of the elves now king. Your mother is a vampire and might kill you and return to Greenwood to take her place as queen for all eternity." He spoke in English with a thick accent.

"She'd kill me? I'm her only living son."

"When one becomes a member of the undead, priorities change, the heart grows cold and those we leave behind become unimportant, for we are immortal."

I bowed to the ancient vampire. "I need yer help revered seer. I seek to kill Slygon and rescue my woman."

"I will look into the water for you and help if I can, for Slygon has held me a slave to him for many centuries. I owed him a debt for bringing me out of the Pit and I have paid it."

Flossie took my hand. "Come on. He won't bite you. He said he only drinks rat blood now."

We entered the temple and followed the seer to a well set in the center of the tower. Ice-blue water swirled within the pool. It seemed endlessly deep as though its source was far below the castle. Magic.

Kokusan sat opposite us, his legs crossed. He seemed to be listening to something only he could hear. When he bent over and put a long, painted fingernail into the water and stirred, he stared into the blue depths, though I wondered how he saw anything with that strip of silk covering his eyes.

"Your woman is in the dungeon," Kokusan said. "With many vampires surrounding her. They wake."

I leapt to my feet. "Thanks, I be thinking I better hurry."

Kokusan grabbed my hand. "Slygon is coming for you. He mounts the stairs to my keep as I speak."

Suddenly, Kokusan disappeared. One minute he was there, the next minute gone. Flossie grabbed the edge of my tunic. "Be ready. This is the hardest battle you will ever fight against the toughest opponent."

Chapter Forty-One

Jackal

I hung over the rail of the circular staircase and tried to see Slygon. I heard him moving up the stairs and I felt him. "Where is he?" I asked Flossie.

She shrugged. "I think he's above us."

He's on the ramparts. Remoth's voice entered my head. *He's calling the last dark dragon to him. I think he has an escape planned. We'll get him.*

I rushed back into the Japanese temple, ran through the room with the well and into the seer's private quarters. The same mats were on the floor as in the outer chamber. A small stove sat on the floor heated with coals. A teapot hissed on top of the stove. There was an exit. I knew it. When the seer disappeared, I'd seen him out of the corner of my eye run into his quarters at lightning speed and then vanish. Vampires are fast.

I opened the exit door. There was a set of stairs curved up around the top of the tower toward the ramparts and down to the ground. I knew it. The wily old vampire had an escape route. I crept up the stairs, sword drawn, reached inside myself for the power the seer told me I possessed, and I'd been learning to use. The power burned like a fire in my belly, a ball of energy just waiting to be tapped.

I spotted Slygon. The monster was standing on the edge of the walls with his arms outstretched. His eyes were closed. I knew what he was doing. He was calling the last dark dragon. The one Remoth spoke of, the one that had escaped. Slygon might be calling for his dragon but what he got was Remoth and a pride of our dragons with elf warriors riding them. When Remoth appeared, Slygon shot hundreds of snakes at the dragons. Some were real and landed on the dragons with mouths wide ready to bite. It was only a gesture, their fangs couldn't pierce dragon hide, and the elves quickly dispensed with any snakes that attacked them. When Remoth opened his huge maw and inhaled, ready to blast Slygon to ash with dragon fire. Slygon wasn't there. He'd disappeared. I looked around, afraid of what new scheme the bastard had up his sleeve.

Slygon could glamour humans, control snakes and use conventional weapons, but he couldn't belch fire or control energy.

"Where'd he go?" I asked the fairy.

Flossie looked thoughtful. "I'm not sure, but he needs his last black dragon if he plans to escape. He can't just walk out of this valley. He picked it because it's inaccessible. The serfs are trapped, and no one can get in here without dragons. That was his plan; now it's trapped him in here as well. As long as he can't summon his last dragon, he's stuck here. And a dog, no matter how weak, when backed into a corner is a dangerous dog."

Remoth spoke to me. *The last black dragon has gone into hiding as it waits for its master to summon it. We can't allow Slygon to unite with this last dragon. If he does, he will be gone and we might never find him. In his rage at being interrupted, he's put Annabelle where he believes she will be devoured by vampires or turned rather than let her escape him unharmed.*

"There's no hole deep enough for him to hide from me. I will follow him to the ends of New Earth, even back into the Pit itself if that's where he goes to escape and regroup."

Remoth and three dragons landed on the ramparts. The others headed for the village. We were in control of Slygon's keep now. Slag climbed off his brown. Gormar and Ivansar leapt off their dragons. "We're wrapping up the village," Slag said. "Chub will have it under control before a cat can lick its ear."

"I have to find Slygon," I said. "He had Belle, though Remoth thinks he's abandoned her to his minions in the dungeon. He could be down there, too. Seems he'd be right at home in a dreary crypt"

Slag clapped me on the shoulder. "You ain't breasting that evil scum alone. I be accompanying you, think on."

"No, old friend. I can't allow ye to go against the horde of blood drinkers sleeping in the dungeons. Belle is down there."

"Are ye calling me a coward?"

"Hell no. Ye be the bravest warrior I know. I'm just telling ye it will require magic not strength to defeat Slygon in the dungeon. I have magic enough for it and I have Flossie here. The evil bastard has Dandy as well. It's me what has to fight him, and I'll be doing it without having ye to worry me."

"Since when am I someone you gotta worry about?" Slag demanded, his face purple with rage. "I can hold me own anywhere."

I wrapped my arm around Slag's shoulders and led him away from the elves. "Mayhap you can, but Belle is not yer worry. She's mine. I came here to destroy Slygon and that job belongs to me and me alone."

Slag shook his head. "I never thought I'd see the day when ye'd refuse me help."

"Slag take the elves and hunt for that last black dragon. It's Slygon's only way out of here. If we can turn it or kill it, he will be stuck in this keep by his own machinations. He doesn't have enough magic to get out of here without the dragon and there's only one left. It's more important for you to kill or disable that dragon than for you to risk your life entering that dungeon with me."

Slag shook his head. "I be doing this agin me will. You need me at yer back in this fight. I know it in me gut."

I shoved him in the direction of his brown dragon. "Find the missing black dragon and take care of it." I turned to Ivansar and Gormar. "Go with Slag. Take yer warriors and find that black dragon."

They nodded, leapt aboard their dragons and took off. "I had to send them away," I said to Flossie. "This be too dangerous for them. They'd be helpless down there in the dark surrounded by vampires."

Flossie nodded. "Slygon's only hope of escape is to use Annabelle or Dandy as a shield. I know he's gone to the dungeons. Once he has Annabelle or Dandy, he can call his dragon while he's on the ground and get away."

"The dungeons." I stared at the western mountain. A purple glow on the horizon was all that was left of this long day. "We better hurry."

We went back the way we came through the Japanese seer's temple. Once again, he sat in lotus position beside his magic well. "You won't make it in time to save them both," the seer said.

"You be less than helpful," I snarled as we raced through the temple and down the circular stairs. At the bottom there was a choice. Out the postern door or down a long corridor lined with broken windows. Glass shards littered the stone floor.

"Belle's been here, or I don't know nothing," I mumbled to Flossie who nodded.

Flossie poufed into a tiny fairy and rode my shoulder as I jogged down the hallway. When we reached a door in the granite wall of the castle, I stopped. I could feel the evil emanating from below. "This be the way Slygon went," I said. "I can feel him and a shit ton of vampires."

"They're waking up and they're hungry," Flossie said.

The door was locked so I ripped it off its hinges and flung it aside as I raced down the steep stone steps leading straight into the bowels of the castle with Flossie clinging to my shoulder. Slygon was down there. I could sense him. The vampire felt like a huge snake slithering around below in the dark. There was no light in the dungeon. No light at all.

Flossie pointed at the wall and a torch flared. I grabbed it and leaped down the narrow steps two at a time. We went down four levels. There were three levels of dungeons. Apparently, Slygon had built this with prisoners in mind or maybe to hold humans for the vampires to feed on. "Are any of those cells occupied?" I asked Flossie.

"Not with the living," she said. A sudden flare and her tiny dragon appeared beside her squeaking loudly. "Squeaker says Slygon has released a huge snake from a pit below. It's hunting us."

"Perfect." I shivered. "I hate snakes."

When I spotted the ground floor, I slowed. No sense in running into trouble at a high speed. "Go take a look," I whispered to tiny Flossie.

She flew off, was gone only a few seconds, and returned in a rush. With her tiny lips against my ear, she whispered, "Slygon has Belle tied to a coffin and is holding Dandy in his hands." A sob shook her, and she sniffed. "She looks . . . she looks dead. Your mother is down there as well. Slygon told her to guard Belle."

I sucked in a deep breath, closed my eyes and felt for my power. There it was slumbering deep in my gut. I drew it upward, letting it grow and expand until it exploded into a cloud of light that encompassed me and Flossie. Sword in hand, I descended to the dungeon floor, turned the corner and faced Slygon.

"Let her go," I growled.

Slygon pressed his hand against Belle's chest. "The vamps are waking." She spoke softly as though even her warning might alert the vampires rising out of the rows of coffins. "Run."

"Not bloody likely."

"Good luck with trying to get away, you fucking oaf," Slygon said, then he pointed a finger at Dandy still stuffed inside the cage. The cage floated toward the rock ceiling and hung suspended in midair.

And then I heard the lumbering gait of Slag on the stone steps behind me. His footfalls unmistakable. A big hand fell on my shoulder. "I know I was supposed to go, and truly, I did think about it for about one second." Slag's low bray of laughter drifted across the dungeon. "Let's kill us some blood suckers."

Chapter Forty-Two

Jackal

Slag handed me an armful of silver tipped arrows and yanked open the first coffin. Inside, a male vampire lay with its eyes open. It wore armor and fighting garb, seemed like a young man. Its lips were stained red with blood. Slag stabbed it with the wooden arrow tipped in silver and moved on without watching the vamp seize and explode in a spray of blood and gore. "Next," the giant three-quarters orc snarled.

We ran through twenty coffins as fast as possible, then went back to collect the used arrows. "The last one were wide awake," I said. "I be going fer Belle." I glanced at Dandy and saw Flossie trying to get past a massive cobra guarding the fairy. "Don't, Flossie," I yelled.

She turned tiny and flew behind the cage as the cobra followed her with its head.

"I'll keep moving through this field of ugliness like a scythe through wheat," Slag said. "You go for Belle and Dandy."

In the far side of the deep cavern, Dandy floated in the silvery cage above Belle, guarded by the biggest cobra I'd ever seen. The thing must be twenty-feet long. Thin silver cord bound the fairy who drooped, her head on her chest, her knees under her chin. She didn't look up when Slag whooped as he killed another vamp. She didn't open her eyes. I felt no life in her. She looked as Flossie feared, already dead. I saw Ashera slumped against another coffin and felt for her thoughts and got a black buzzing noise. She must be alive, just gone, not home, sleeping the sleep of the undead.

Belle was tied to a massive, ebony casket by a rope that glowed with magic. I knew whatever was in that coffin would be the most dangerous thing in the dungeon, a deadly beast, probably already rising. "Belle, wake up!" I shouted. "Belle."

Belle lifted her head. "The snake," she called. "Watch out. It's real."

"I see it."

The snake uncoiled and dropped on Belle's chest. It spread its hood and hissed, whirled and prepared to strike Belle in the face.

"Got this," Slag yelled. "Duck!"

I dodged left, throwing myself across an ancient oak coffin. A silver-tipped bolt whizzed by, just missing the fast-moving cobra. The snake dropped to the ground and raced straight for me. I threw my handful of silver arrows on the rock floor of the cavern and whipped my sword out of its sheath. The snake struck at me from ten feet away, launching its huge black body at me, mouth open, glistening fangs clearly visible. I took a two-handed grip on my sword, prayed it was as sharp as always, waited until the last moment, focused, and slashed. The snake's head was cleanly removed. The head shot forward, hit Ashera in the chest and latched onto her, dumping its load of venom into her even though it had no body. As if on cue, coffin lids opened.

The undead emerged.

There was no time for the niceties. I slashed and hacked my way toward Belle. The lid of the coffin under her slowly opened. "Get Belle," Slag yelled. "I can take care of this."

I left a path of dying vampires behind. The male in the coffin under Belle threw open the lid, knocking Belle to the ground. It was a young elf, beautiful to look at, but radiating an evil so powerful I felt it. The vampire ignored Belle, grabbed the cage with Dandy and reached inside.

The fairy woke and screamed, the sound weak and followed by gulping breaths. She couldn't save herself. I felt for my power, gathered it and launched a ball of energy at the vampire.

The vampire sank its fangs in Dandy and glanced over her quivering body at me. He saw the ball of energy heading for him and moved so fast I barely saw him. The vamp pulled Dandy in front of his body, so my blast of energy struck the mortally wounded fairy. When my energy blast hit Dandy, the vampire dropped her smoking husk and lunged for Belle. She was out of her ropes. When the vamp hit her, she struggled to throw him off, but he nicked her hand with a fang and licked the blood.

When Dandy was hit, Flossie's shriek of grief and horror filled the chamber. The little fairy flitted to Dandy and clung to her. "Dandy, don't die," she wailed. "Please don't die."

Flossie's sadness and heartbreak filled me with so much anger, I felt like I'd explode. Because of that vampire, I'd just killed Dandy and I'd been helpless to do more than watch, but I'd be damned if that creature was going to kill my Belle. I rushed forward.

Belle was pissed. She screamed, "Stop!" The force of her rage exploded caskets around the room. I ducked and darted around burning vampires who fell out whether they were ready to rise or not. Belle squirmed out of the shocked vampire's slackened grasp and pointed her finger. More of the wooden caskets burst into flames.

The surprised vampire released Belle and lunged for me. "What's yer name, blood sucker? Be wanting to know who I be killing," I said with a smile.

The young vampire was dressed in black armor and carried a sword in a sheath down his back like Belle carried hers. The vamp reached behind his head and drew it. "If it's a fight you want, I shall be glad to provide one," he said. "My name is Kyran. I'm elf, but I'm much stronger than you because I'm vampire as well."

Slag fired a bolt at Kyran. The vampire deflected it with a flick of his wrist. He yelled to Slag. "Orc! Your arrows cannot harm me. You'll never hit me. Before I was made, I was a seer, strong in magic, full of the purity of light."

He slowly approached me with his sword held in both hands above his right shoulder.

I saw the way the vamp held his sword and switched into a left-handed grip, sword on the same side as the vamp's. Kyran saw the move and switched up, so I followed his example. Now he was holding his sword against his right shoulder. I was a much better fighter using my right-hand grip. The vamp wouldn't know that.

We circled each other, dodging coffins, sliding between the rows, switching our swords from one hand to the other. Some of the coffins were open, the vamps emerging and queuing up behind Kyran, still groggy. Suddenly Belle struck. She'd filched a sword from a dead vamp and slashed off heads. Slag came up behind me, killing vamps as fast as he could swing his huge broadsword.

"Come on, Kyran," I taunted him. "Odds looking bad to you? Afraid?"

Kyran lunged and I parried his strike. He staggered from the force of the blow and backed a step. I pulled on my power, reached deep to draw its flow through my body, into my muscles and my sword strikes.

Breathing hard, sweat beading on my brow, I sucked in a huge breath and focused. I focused upon Kyran and his movements, focused on making them slow, making them those of a mortal. *Breath fire on him.* It was Remoth's voice in my head. *Do it. You have the power just like dragons.*

Remoth was right. I'd felt the fire in my gut. I opened my mouth wide and blew a blast of flames at Kyran. His clothes caught and blazed. He had to drop his sword to deal with the flames. I took another deep breath and got ready to blast him. Another vampire attacked me from behind and I expelled the flames across him.

Belle had worked her way forward, behind Kyran's back. Slag had two more vamps waking up behind him to kill. I dug deeper and felt my power growing. I knew I could torch him. I had one more good blast of flames in me. Kyran felt it too. I sensed the vampire's fear and struck not with flames but with my sword. I sliced through Kyran's sword. God bless the forges of Wildwhisper. My blade was stronger.

With his sword broken, the vampire flew to the ceiling of the cavern and Belle rushed into my arms. I pushed her away so I could look at her. "Are you okay? Are you really okay?" Before she could answer, I pulled her close and buried my head in her hair, in the scent and feel of her. Alive. Safe. Nothing else mattered.

"I can't breathe!" Belle muttered, pushing against my tight grip.

"Sorry, I was downright petrified for a few minutes." I glanced at Slag who was staring at the vampire named Kyran as he hovered against the ceiling. "This isn't over, orc," Kyran shouted.

"Happen it looks over to me. If ye want more, come on down and get it."

"You're too strong here, now. When the moment is right, I'll come after you. I'll take your woman too. She looks to be a very tasty morsel."

Belle screamed, "The hell you will!" and the ceiling above the vampire shattered, showering them with shards of granite and shale. Kyran flew toward the exit. "I might be gone for now, but I will return."

"Find yer master and tell him he's next," I yelled after him. "Tell Slygon I'm hunting him."

The vampire whisked up the stairs and was gone. Belle threw herself into my arms, shaking with relief. I held her close, kissed her hair and her forehead with my heart pounding with joy. She gazed up into my face, her eyes filled with something I never thought to see there, love. "Uh," she started. "That thing we did with the dragons in the meadow, it saved me. Slygon wanted a virgin and I'm not one anymore."

I felt my face flame. Why'd she remind me of that? "You know if we got married, we could do that any time we wanted."

She punched me. "That is no way to propose to a woman."

"Sorry, I was thinkin' of meself. Bad habit."

"I love you," she said. "I can't believe it took me so long to realize it." She touched my cheek. "You're the bravest, most loyal, strongest man in this world of ours and you are mine."

I kissed her. It was too good. Her lips were soft, her mouth slightly open, inviting, and my heart pounded like a hammer in my ears. She grabbed my hair and pulled me deeper into the kiss.

"Ahem...." Slag cleared his throat. "That be real sweet and all. Hate to interrupt this romantic scene, but we got a bit of work left to do."

Belle's face flushed, and she dropped her head. "Oh my god, how could I?"

"No, me darling, it's me who's the lummox. I be so wrapped in my joy at your safety, I . . . poor Dandy."

Flossie and Squeaker hovered over Dandy's smoking body. The tiny fairy wept.

I felt terrible. It was me who killed Dandy. And Dandy had helped all of us so much. She'd saved dragons and been there through everything, leading us on a straight path, guiding us through so many obstacles, and now she was gone. "It's all my fault. I shoulda seen the bolt of energy would hit her. I should never had pushed it at Kyran. I just was so afraid he'd get Belle. It were selfish of me."

Belle put her arm around my waist and squeezed. "You did save me, and you couldn't have known that bastard would hide like a coward behind Dandy," Belle said. "She would have avoided the blow if Slygon hadn't drained so much of her energy and left her weak. She could never have survived the vampire biting her, and if she did, what would she have become? What if Kyran had changed Dandy? She would never hold her death against you. She would not have wanted to be turned by him. You were only trying to save us, save us both, and she knew that."

Belle touched Dandy's dead body. "She gave her life for us and the dragons. She loved us all, and especially you, Flossie." Belle caressed Flossie's cheek with one finger.

Flossie poufed into a regular size child. "She was my mother," Flossie said. "Fairies don't raise their own children. They have too much work to do so they give them to families who will take good care of them. She did love me. She told me so when she blessed me with her power. I think she knew she was going to die. I think she even knew how and when."

Belle tilted her head and stared at Flossie. "She was your mother? You knew that and never told us?"

"Fairies keep lots of secrets," Flossie said. "More than you can imagine."

I gently gathered Dandy's body into my arms. "Let's take her out of this dungeon of death and bury her where there will always be light."

Flossie shook her head. "No, the dragons will burn her body. It is traditional for fairies and prevents their bodies from being used for evil. Even a dead fairy has power and that power can be perverted."

"I'll carry her," I said "You summon the dragons. I'm not sure where Slygon has gone off to, but wherever he went, we're going after him."

Chapter Forty-Three

Slygon

Slygon slammed his fist into the wall, taking satisfaction from the cracks that fanned out in the stone. He'd wanted Annabelle badly, but he'd risked far too much. With Kokusan perverted to the use of that bastard orc, Dorna was his only remaining asset. Noemi had been poisoned by one of his snakes. He'd felt her life force dwindle to almost nothing. She might never regenerate. Cobra venom was powerful. Ashera was still too new to being a vampire. She had no power. The half-orc, Erindriel, Ashera's bastard child, was in the dungeons. Hopefully, the vampires sleeping down there would wake in time to destroy him.

He still wished he didn't have to leave Annabelle to Kyran. Why did he feel so drawn to her? He'd been entranced by her purity and the thought of her bearing his children. Then he'd discovered she'd been sullied by the bastard half-orc.

He eased into Dorna's room. The evil bitch would help him escape and then she could die too. There was no need to take her where he planned to go. She was just waking and looked like she'd been sucked dry.

When she saw him creeping quietly around the four-poster bed, she threw open the bed curtains. "What do you want?" Her voice was gravely and rough.

"What happened to you?"

"Ashera and that bitch Noemi came to my room and attacked me. I had to play dead to avoid being completely drained. As it is, I have little energy and I'm starving. I need to feed."

"Can you stand?"

"Maybe." She put her legs over the edge of the bed. "It's a good thing I'm as old as I am, or I'd have gone to the true death. When I catch Ashera, I'm going to enjoy killing her very slowly."

"She's already dead. I left her in the dungeons with a hundred dying vampires. I feel sure one of them finished her off."

"What about Noemi? That little whore helped Ashera."

"She received a few cobra bites. A few too many. She is definitely dead."

Dorna shuddered. "I hate snakes."

"Well the worst has happened, my dear. We must leave and regroup, create reinforcements."

"Leave to where? This is the end of the freaking earth. There is no more isolated place. No deeper hole to hide in."

"Hole is the operative word. We must return to the Pit."

"I won't go back there!" Dorna screamed. "I hate that place. Centuries we barely existed, starved, lived like animals underground. You'll have to kill me first."

"Easy enough, and don't tempt me. I was merely coming here to make sure you went with me to gather an army, enlist more dragons. We won't stay there forever."

Dorna shuddered. "Even a short time away from the clean air and the beauty of above ground would be too much."

"How does death sound to you? Permanent death? The death of a vampire is a terrible thing, Dorna. We lost our souls when we became vampire. There is a special place reserved for us in Hell and it's no fun, I assure you."

"Yesterday, everything was fine. You were on top of the world. Then you had to bring in that bitch Noemi to replace me, then the uppity elf queen, Ashera. What happened? Did you lose the battle with her son? He's very powerful." She laughed. "Ashera told me about him."

Slygon growled as he advanced on her. "He has dragons and two damned fairies. I killed one, I'm certain, but the other one is still alive and helping the bastard. We have one chance to escape and we'll be taking it. Or I will. If you'd prefer to stay here and enjoy the vengeance of that orc bastard, you may."

She took his arm. "I'll go with you. As long as it's only temporary, the Pit can't be that bad. You still have a castle there, don't you?"

He opened his mouth and a cobra emerged, slipping down his body and wrapping its entire length around his torso. Dorna backed away when the snake flared its hood and hissed at her.

"I need to feed badly. Ashera practically drained me."

"Learn to control your needssss," the cobra hissed. "Handy humansssss aren't always available. But never fear. I have alwaysssss had a plan." He slithered to the curtained windows, the heavy red-velvet drapes flew aside, the mullioned windows sprang open and the cobra slid over the sill. On the other side of the windows was a landing. "Here, my dear, sssstep out here with me."

"I don't like you in this form," she said. "I hate snakes."

He shifted into his human form easily. The change back and forth could be done in seconds. He'd made it so many times.

"Thank you," she said stiffly, lifted her skirts and stepped over the raised sill. The landing was big and ran the length of her bedroom. There was no railing, just an epic drop straight down to the rocks below. Slygon swayed back and forth and closed his eyes. *Come to me now. It's safe. The invaders are all busy killing vampires and rounding up stray serfs in the village. Your brothers will not harm you.*

And the fairy?

I have killed one. The other is a mere child.

Nothing happened and Slygon cursed. "Damn those bastard orcs and their cursed dragons. All I have left is this one black dragon and he's frightened of the clean dragons and that damned baby fairy."

"Try to call it again," Dorna said. "It must come, or we'll be stuck here and slaughtered." She'd plastered herself against the rock wall of the keep.

"Is the drop scaring you?" Slygon sneered.

"Yes, it is," she snarled. "There's no railing."

"The dragons couldn't land if there was." He closed his eyes and called the dragon again. This time he felt the flutter of a response in his head and looked to the east. From behind a tall crag, one that kept the valley in the dark well past dawn anywhere else, a black shape winged toward them.

It flew close to the mountains, coming out of the dark and the shadows cast by the rising moon. It landed on the ledge with a rush of air. Slygon grabbed Dorna. "Come, my dear. It's time to go."

Fool that she was, believing because she'd survived so many other of his women, he actually loved her, she allowed him to push her forward. *A meal for you before our trip.*

She stumbled toward the huge beast waiting with his swirling golden eyes half open. She cast one look back at Slygon who smiled. "Bon appetite," he said.

The dragon reached for Dorna and snapped her up in its huge jaws so quickly his movements were a blur. When Dorna realized Slygon's deception, she shrieked. "You bastard!"

"No, I believe my parents were married." He laughed and laughed. Anything else she had to say to him was cut off when the dragon flipped her, screaming, into the air, opened his jaws wide and swallowed her in one gulp. Slygon looked back into the castle. The woman he wanted was down in the dungeons, a gift to Kyran that could easily be taken back at any time. Her virginity was the only thing of value she'd possessed. Once that was gone, he really didn't care who else had her. Dorna would have been a cozy bedmate in the Pit, but she complained a lot and he needed freedom to act. Dragging her along with him would have been an encumbrance he didn't need.

"Well, Dorna, vain and spiteful as you were, you were useful to the last." He climbed onto the black dragon's back and urged the beast to fly.

To the Pit, he ordered the beast. *We'll be safe there.* He felt the dragon's loathing to go into the Pit.

Dragons can't go down there. The air in the Pit rots our brains. It's poisonous to all my brethren. That's the reason so few of us escaped to live under the sun and stars.

But the air is not poisonous for you. As a black dragon you're protected from the malaise that will kill normal dragons. It's all part of the plan. Part of my plan. If Jackal and his men want to follow, it will be on foot or mounted on jackasses. We will be safely ensconced in my old castle. And you, my faithful mount, will have plenty of human sheep to feed on until we return and eradicate our enemies once and for all.

Jackal

I carried Dandy's body up the steps to the surface, holding her like the precious package she was. We exited the castle through the postern gate and walked down the path to the village. Tina ran out to greet us and Chub lumbered along behind. The elves were gathered in the center of the village talking in small groups. When they spotted me carrying Dandy, they rushed to us.

The villagers were a quiet bunch. Still weakened from being used as blood bags for the population of vampires, they huddled in a mass next to the largest hut in a common area. The children were gone, snatched up and hidden, no doubt.

Tina saw Dandy's limp body and burst into tears. She stopped me and bent over to kiss Dandy's forehead. "How could this happen? Fairies are so powerful. I thought they were immortal."

Flossie, acting like a much older person, patted Tiny's back. "Dandy sacrificed herself to save all of us, especially the dragons. She always loved them. Slygon snatched her when she was sleeping and weak from transforming the black dragons back to their original state."

The dragons were perched everywhere; on walls, crags overhanging the village and some on the ground. When they realized Dandy died for them, they bellowed a salute to her. Tears dripped down Belle's face. We were all grief-stricken. Dandy had helped each one of us at some time and we mourned her.

Tina sobbed on Belle's shoulder. "Belle, Belle, I thought I'd never see you again." She held Belle at arm's length. "You look terrible." She fingered the fur coat. "Though I do love this coat. What'd that bastard do to you?"

"Thanks for the compliment. "Slygon tried to kill me, then hand me off to one of his vampires, but thanks to Jackal, he failed."

"Where is that devil now?"

"We don't know."

A sudden scream from the castle ramparts startled us. We looked up in time to see the last black dragon take off in the light of the rising moon. Slygon was astride the beast as it circled the village. "Follow him!" I yelled to the dragons.

The entire pride rose and took off after the black dragon. When they were out of sight, I carried Dandy to the center of the village. "We have to burn her," I said. "Flossie says her body is powerful. Even dead, she carries magic, powerful magic that can be used against us. We must destroy her body with dragon fire."

The elves and the villagers, who seemed to be losing some of their fear, gathered a huge pile of wood and stacked it in the commons. I laid Dandy on the pyre and backed away.

"I can't bear to see her go," Belle said with tears flowing down her cheeks. She took a knife out of her pocket and cut a lock of Dandy's bright hair. "I'll keep this always in remembrance of her."

"Dead like this," I said, "she seems so gray and hollow. How could a creature so filled with life turn into this empty husk?"

"We need dragon fire to burn her," Flossie said. "Dragon fire will remove all the magic in her body, cleanse it, and leave it purified ash. The way it is now, she can be used as a weapon. We need dragon fire."

"Well they be chasing Slygon right now."

Then Remoth spoke to me. *We followed the black dragon to the edge of the Pit, and he disappeared carrying Slygon with him. We can't go down there. The air is poisonous to us. Slygon must have made it so his black dragons don't suffer as we do from breathing the air.*

"Slygon went into the pit," I said to Belle. "Our dragons can't follow. The air is poisonous to them."

"What entrance did he go into?" Slag asked. "There be entrances all over the place. Some be mere cracks, some holes big enough to swallow a city."

"They went into the main hole," I said. "The one that opened in the national park where the super volcano blew."

"That's not too far away," Slag said. "Happen we can follow him down there."

"We will because we must kill the bastard. You know he ain't done with us. He'll hide down there where he thinks he's safe and plot to come back and cause us more trouble."

"That's truth," Slag muttered. "All he loves is causing trouble. And he's capable of creating another vampire army as big as this one in a short period of time."

"Do the dragons know where Ashera and Noemi are?" Belle asked.

"I'm here," Noemi said.

"Jeezus," I swore.

Noemi was supported by two of the serfs. She looked awful. Her face was the color of a ripe plum, purple, bruised. Her arms were the same color. Her body was swollen like a rotting fruit filled with putrid gas. Belle ran to her. "You lived. I thought the snake had killed you."

"Yeah," Noemi said through clenched teeth. "I'm alive, but the pain of the cobra bites is beyond anything."

"I can fix her," Flossie said.

Noemi closed her eyes. "When I'm fixed, I'll still be a vampire. I've come to ask you, Jackal, to give me the true death. I can't go on like this, knowing what I've done, feeding off people, and even committing the ultimate sin, drinking the blood of infants. It's an existence I wouldn't wish on my worst enemy."

"No, I mean fix you, fix you," Flossie said. "You'll be rid of the poison and no longer be vampire. The poison is actually a gift. It removed the bugs in your blood that made you vampire. That's why you're suffering so much. Vampirism is actually a disease. Once you drink the blood, you're changed by the tiny creatures living inside of you. The older you get as a vampire, the more of the creatures you have. You become less human and more vampire. I can cure you because the cobra poison kills the vampire organisms. Weird, but true. The reason you feel so weak right now and are having such a hard time recovering is there are few of the vampire bugs in your blood. You're barely even a vampire right now. You could probably eat food."

Noemi's eyes brightened. "You know, the blood lust is gone. I haven't felt the need for blood since I was bitten."

"You can really cure her?" Belle asked.

Flossie shrugged and her hair flew around her head like a crazy red halo. "I said I could, didn't I?"

"Then do it so we can get this funeral over with and go after Slygon, I said. "Time is wastin'."

The dragons will be back soon," Belle said.

"They need to get back here. We be tired to the bone." It was true. They'd been fighting and running and flying for over forty-eight hours. Most of them were walking around asleep. "Sit down and we'll wait. Try to catch a few winks." I pushed her toward the huts. The serfs brought out chairs and blankets and everyone settled in. It wasn't long before half of them were snoring.

I heard the rush of dragon wings and stood up expecting Damoth and Remoth and the rest of her dragons.

Only it wasn't our dragons.

A black dragon, easily as big as Oranth, swooped low over the village. Its huge mouth open, it breathed green fire on the huts, setting them ablaze with erupting flames that exuded poisonous fumes. The serfs screamed and ran for cover in the common house.

I drew my crossbow and knocked a silver-tipped arrow. Slag grabbed my arm. "What we need is spears."

We ran to a burning hut. One of the serfs stood just inside the doorway with a handkerchief tied over his face. He tossed weapons out of the conflagration; two spears, a crossbow and an armful of bolts. Slag grabbed one of the spears and I grabbed the other. I tossed my crossbow at Chub. "Guard the women." Then we turned to face the huge beast.

The dragon had a rider and the beast wasn't here to fight them. It swooped low. Slygon crept out on a broad wing, dangled off it with his arms outstretched as the black dragon flew over the funeral pyre.

Belle screamed when she realized what Slygon was doing. "No! Jackal, he's after Dandy's body."

I saw she was right and ran for the pyre, holding my spear. Chub fired his crossbow and hit the dragon's outstretched wing. It wasn't enough. Slygon was in position. Suddenly, Ashera, thin to the point of emaciation, raced out of the darkness and threw herself across Dandy's body. Unable to stop his momentum, Slygon grabbed Dandy's corpse and Ashera with it. The dragon immediately changed course and flew straight up as Slag and I launched our spears. My spear pierced the dragon's chest, but the creature didn't slow. Slygon crawled back to his dragon's neck clutching his prize as Ashera fell off the dragon and landed on the empty funeral pyre where a piece of wood pierced her.

Chapter Forty-Four

Jackal

Ashera was three parts dead. We pulled the stake out of her chest and lifted her off the funeral pyre. Noemi supported her head. "She covered me when Slygon tried to send us to meet the sun," Noemi said. She's a good person, just an elf."

Ashera coughed. "Erindriel," she whispered. "I tried to keep him away from the fairy." Bloody tears dripped down her cheeks. "I know how powerful even a fairy's body can be."

"Don't try to talk," I said to her. "Concentrate on living."

"Not in this form." Her voice was a rasp. "I'm old. I've seen enough. I'd need to feed off a human to regenerate, and I will not do it. Let me die now with you. Hold me close and call me mother, not Ashera."

It was true, I'd never called her mother, always Ashera. I gently drew her into my arms. She reached up and touched my face. "Son," she whispered. Her voice so low I could barely hear it. "You'll make a fine ruler, good and just. Take care of my people. I know they're elves and full of prejudice and vanity but try to love them."

"I will, Mother," I said.

She smiled and her eyes closed. Vampires don't breathe so there was no death rattle. Flossie pointed her wand at Ashera's body, and a silver cloud floated out of it. "Her soul," Flossie said. "I gave it back to her. Vampires lose their soul the first time they feed off a human. She died trying to right a wrong and keep Dandy's body from Slygon. I gift her soul back to her so she can pass into the second world and live in the light."

I stood up and brushed the ashes of my mother off me. What a strange twenty-four hours we'd had. Belle wrapped one arm around my waist. "We have to go after him," she said. "He has Dandy's poor body. I can't think how much power that might give him."

"He's gone into the Pit, Jackal," Slag said. "You know I be following you to the ends of the earth, but I never thought it would be into that hell hole." Slag took a deep pull on his horn of ale.

"You think I wanna go down there? Does anyone know what awaits us? I sure as hell don't. But if Slygon has poor Dandy, who I killed, then we have to go after him and take back her body so the dragons can cleanse it. It be me duty to her and to the world, because you know the evil bastard will be back. Mayhap going after him and killing him in his lair below ground before he can rebuild his army will rid us of him fer good."

"I'll go with you," Chub said with his mouth full. He looked up from the huge goose leg he was devouring, and guzzled ale. "Think there'll be grub down there? If not, then we better pack plenty for the trip."

Slag clubbed Chub in the side of the head. "You know, if you'd cease worrying about yer damn belly fer one minute, we might get a bit of work done." Slag dug a hole in the ground with the gnarly nail of his thick big toe. "I'm with ye, Jackal, but we need to leave the women folk behind. I see how it is betwixt you and Belle, and I'm right happy fer ya, but think on, ye'll be so worried about her, ye'll be about useless."

"I can take care of myself," Belle said. "And I loved Dandy as much as any of you and I have twice as many reasons to kill Slygon. So, don't feed me that little woman crap. I'm going after him, like it or not."

"I'm going, too," Flossie said.

"Darlin'," I said. "Every day you look more like yer mother and yer growing faster than a weed. Why yer almost as tall as Tiny and I'm betting taller than her soon."

"I don't think that's a good idea," Belle said. "I know you think you have to because of Dandy, but you don't. You're still a child even if you're a fairy. We can't risk losing you, too."

Flossie stared at me, her eyes a vivid green in her rapidly maturing face. "Try and stop me," she said. "If you can." Squeaker, sitting on the fairy's shoulder, hissed and belched fire to support his mistress.

"You know I can't stop you from coming, but I still think you should stay here, and, uh, you know, guard Granny."

Granny was stirring something in a big pot over the fire in the common area between the burned huts. "I'm making a potion. It's a strong one and when it's done, all of you going into the Pit must drink it. There are bad things down there, evil things you've never seen or heard of, jinn, harpies, goblins, centaurs, even minotaur's. Some be so strong, you'll never overcome them. This potion will give all of you the strength of Jackal for a week, and it will make Jackal almost invincible. When it wears off, you'll be very tired, so drink it, go into the Pit and do what you have to inside of a week."

"We're coming with you," Ivansar said. He waved his hands to indicate the elf warriors. "All of us. We can't allow our king to be without his guard."

"Oh, fer pity's sake," I moaned. "You'd all love to swaddle me like an infant."

Rain stepped forward and knelt before me. "I owe you for ridding the castle of the Grand Vizier," she said. "He killed my beloved and I must repay the debt I owe. You are our king. We will follow you anywhere, even back into the Pit."

"You need us," Gormar said. "We've been there. All of us lived there before the Pit opened. We know the path to Slygon's keep."

"I'll be right glad to have you," I said. "All of ye are brave fighters and worthy to fight beside the best. And we, all of us, we be the best." He lifted his horn of ale. His men, Tina, the elves and all the serfs did the same. "To a safe journey and the death of Slygon."

"Hear, hear!" they all answered and guzzled their cups.

We decided to set out the next morning. Before we left, the elves and I swept Slygon's keep for surviving vampires and any useful weapons. We ended up in Kokusan's tower.

The ancient seer was meditating. I approached him cautiously and bowed low. "Revered master, we're heading into the Pit after Slygon. Do you have any advice, or any words of guidance to give us?"

The old vampire lifted the corner of black silk covering his eyes and I gasped. Kokusan had two perfectly good eyes, or at least they seemed normal.

"Yes, I can see as well as you. I prefer not to which is why I wear the blindfold. When you take away vision, your other senses sharpen. I can smell and hear as good as the best hound dog. There is too much evil in this world. Beneath it, in the underworld I left, there is even more."

"I was born a century after my ancestors escaped the Pit," I told him. "I've been many places, but never there. The stories passed down to us are hard to believe, but from what I hear, I fear there is truth within the legends."

"There is another reason I wore the blindfold," Kokusan said. "It's dark down there, darker than the inside of the deepest cave. I wanted to learn to see without my eyes. To succeed on this journey, you must learn to see without your eyes. In a land without light, truly the blind man is king."

"Do you want me to wear a blindfold? Sounds right stupid to me, but I do appreciate your knowledge."

"I don't want you to wear a blindfold. I want you to learn to see without light."

"How am I to do that, think on?"

"You must try, of course. I will also grant you my eyes when you have need of them for you freed me from Slygon and I will always owe you for that."

"Give me yer eyes? How can you do that?"

Kokusan reached into the folds of his white-silk robe and pulled out an orb. It was white, shot through with blue and had a black pupil. It was a stone eyeball. He handed it to me. "Use this when you need it. I will be truly blind when you're using it, so have a care and use it only when necessary. You will see in the dark, your hearing will be better and your sense of smell triple what it normally is."

I took the orb with two fingers and held it like it was a snake. I wanted its power, but for crying out loud, it was an eyeball. It looked like one and it was shiny as though covered with a film of mucus. But when I touched it, the orb was hard and smooth like a polished stone. I wrapped my hand around it. "I don't know how to thank you. This is a great gift."

"You don't need to thank me. Just kill Slygon and make sure he never sees the light of day again. That will be payment enough." He gracefully rose from his sitting position. "There is one more thing."

Of course, wasn't there always?

"I need a tiny sip of your blood and I will feed you some of mine. In that way we will be connected. The eye will always work for you, but only for you." Kokusan took my wrist in his hand. "You're a very powerful being, Erindriel, part orc which gives you your strength and part elf which gives you intelligence and magic."

I said nothing, my gaze glued to Kokusan's fangs. They were long, sparkling white and very sharp. The ancient vampire raised one plucked eyebrow. "Do it," I said. "And hurry before I change me mind."

Kokusan sank his fangs in my wrist and lifted his head. Two tiny drops of blood appeared in the neat little holes Kokusan had poked with his fangs. The vampire licked the blood, sighed, closed his eyes and stood silently like that for a moment as though savoring the most delicious bite of food every cooked. Then he bit his own thin wrist. A stream of blood flowed down into his hand. "Drink it."

I prayed this wasn't going to be like drinking the oracle's blood, licked up all of Kokusan's blood and swallowed. I felt it burn across my tongue, all the way down my throat and into my stomach where it churned. I burped and hoped flames didn't shoot out of my mouth like the dragon fire I could summon.

For a moment, I felt nothing different, saw nothing strange. Then it happened. I sucked in a huge breath. I *felt* Kokusan. The ancient seer smiled. "Yes, now we are bound together. I will always be able to find you and you will always know where I am. It is an arrangement that can be good if it's used properly."

"Right weird," I mumbled.

"Go now. Find Slygon and kill him. Bury his body in the depths of the Pit where it will never see the light of day again. And be careful. He is more powerful down there. He is in his home, the place where he can draw upon his power. And he has the fairy's body. Never doubt his strength or question what he can do."

"I thank ye fer yer gifts, and I'll take heed of yer warnings."

Chapter Forty-Five

Jackal

We ended up leaving late in the day. It seemed since we were descending into the Pit, time of day wasn't that important. It was dark down there all the time. We were rested and every damn one of us, including Granny, had decided to come along. It was ridiculous and it was insanely foolish, but I couldn't stop them. The dragons knew where the closest opening to the Pit was and headed for it.

Chub flew his dragon close to Remoth and yelled across the gap between dragons. "How far? I'm starving."

I couldn't laugh. I was filled with unease. It was one thing to do such a foolish thing by myself, but to have dragged my friends and the faithful elves into his dangerous mission weighed heavily on my heart. "Soon. Remoth says we're almost there."

Chub grinned, satisfied that he'd soon be fed, and unconcerned about whatever new adventure he was getting into. Slag was another matter. I watched him lean over the side of his dragon and barf everything left in his stomach, careful not to get any on his dragon's wings. The dose of whatever cure Granny gave all of them had vacated his stomach within fifteen minutes of flight.

I wish we could come with you into the Pit, but at least you've got Flossie and the elves. The link between you and the seer disturbs us. Dragons naturally loathe vampires. But the old one's intentions seem pure and the gift of his eye not to be despised.

Wish you dragons could come, too. We could sure use ye. But yer better resting up and helping to carry us home once we return. Don't need Slygon turning any of you black and riding you into battle against us.

We've arrived, Remoth's voice in my head announced. The dragons circled a small village before landing in a nearby field. The other dragons landed, and the small party of warriors grabbed their weapons, bade the dragons farewell, and set off toward the trading village the dragons had told them about. Though a full day's ride from the rim of the Pit, it was on the side of the opening with no pathway down, and few of the Pit's inhabitants, even those who occasionally came above ground to trade their minerals or gemstones for grain or other staples, visited. Hellgate was a trading post that catered to humans and elves.

Once within sight of the village, I signaled the elves. "You go on to the town. Take Noemi with you. She's stronger and while she ain't a vampire anymore, she's got powers and you might need them."

Ivansar nodded and the small group continued while Chub, Slag and I headed into the forest to keep out of sight. The women went with us to wait, while the elves, Noemi and Flossie, poufed into her smallest size, went into town to do business. The villagers had a ten-foot wall around their tiny hamlet for a reason, and they wouldn't look kindly on orcs, even halflings. And any town on the outskirts of civilization was dangerous for women.

"Hope they hurry and get us some real food," Chub grumbled. "I ain't ate a proper meal in so long, me stomach thinks my throat's been cut."

"Happens they know yer tastes, and if they forgets, Flossie will remind 'em," Slag said, slugging Chub in the arm. "One half steer with a side of deer haunch coming right up."

"Never shoulda let them take Flossie. She be but a babe," I said. "After what happened to Dandy, I couldn't bear to lose her." The weight of their faith and loyalty was a heavy burden. "Seeing Dandy there, hollow and empty, a smoking ruin because of my power." I rubbed my hand across a two-day growth of beard. "Worst thing I've ever done."

"It wasn't your fault," Belle said. "Kyran shoved her into the line of fire on purpose."

"I wonder where he went," I said. "He wasn't in the keep when we searched it."

"He was filled with Dandy's power," Belle said. "With Slygon gone into the Pit and no more vampires to support him, I think he either went out into the world on his own or into the Pit with Slygon."

Slag shuddered. "I can't imagine him and Slygon teamed up together."

"Hard to believe Dandy is gone," I said. "Even when she wasn't with us, we knew she could pop in at any moment and we counted on her doing it when we really needed her. Poor Flossie."

Slag tossed his bedroll on the ground, flopped on it, and rubbed his eyes. "I haven't puked that much since I was a babe."

Chub burst out laughing. "Every time you hurled, I swear a bird got it right in the face."

"Dandy gave much of her power to Flossie," Belle said. "She's young but still a very powerful fairy now." Belle tucked her hand under my arm and rested her head against my shoulder. "Believe it or not, Flossie can handle herself."

I nodded and smothered her hand beneath mine, her touch a comfort. "I know. I just be worrying cause she's so young. Keep an eye out," I said to Slag to counter the warmth of Belle's skin touching me. "I'll take a nap now and then I'll stand watch later." I tugged on Belle's hand. "Come, rest a bit with me. Ye quiet me nerves."

She spread her blankets next to mine and the spill of her hair hid her expression. Belle moved with matter-of-fact precision as though lying next to him were a common occurrence. With her this close, especially after the dragon episode, I doubted I'd be able sleep. She didn't look at me as she lay down, just tucked her hand in mine and in minutes, I was out like a light.

The sound of horses approaching roused us at dusk. Belle sat up, her black hair a tumbled mass. She pushed it out of her face and smiled shyly at me before quickly looking away. My heart skipped a beat and I swallowed to enable breathing. And speech. "I hope it's them elves," I said. "Take cover."

I scrambled to my feet and flattened myself behind a tree with my sword free of its scabbard. She did the same. She was a warrior as well as the woman I loved.

Chub crouched behind a shrub and separated a couple branches to peer toward the arriving riders. Suddenly Chub jumped up laughing. "Dinner!" He grabbed Flossie and tossed her into the air.

"Be careful or I'll drop these." She held up four fat hens tied by their necks in twos, one pair clutched in each small hand.

"Ye got me favorite."

"Everything is your favorite," she said, giggling.

"Is it safe to build a fire here?" I asked.

"The town was pretty empty," Ivansar said. "They haven't had much trade lately and were happy enough for their fair share of the fat purse you gave us. We bought mules. They're better for traveling into the Pit. Flossie managed to sweet talk an old man into telling her everything he ever knew and probably some stuff he didn't know he knew. He'd been a trader in his younger days and gabbed on and on. I thought he'd never stop. He told her there's another way in, and though the descent is dangerous, there's no guards around the entrance. He said there's no need. No one ever goes down there unless they have to. Only traders. They seem to have a way of getting in and out without dying. I think it's by a trade arrangement. It has to be. The old man says we shouldn't go at all. He wishes he'd never gone. It's not worth it, he told Flossie, and after listening to his horror stories, I'm pretty sure we shouldn't go either."

"Why only the traders?" I asked. "Do raiding parties ever come out of the Pit?"

"He didn't mention any. I think the creatures from the Pit have all they need. When they do come up, it's at night and they pass right by Hellgate. I think that's part of their arrangement. What they come up for isn't anything good. Mostly vamps and demons come up looking for blood and human flesh. Centaurs have been sighted so we need to keep an eye on the stock. Occasionally bands of orcs come out of the Pit. They pass by Hellgate as well. We better stand watch tonight and leave at first light. The creatures of the Pit live in darkness. They can't abide sunlight so it's safer to travel then."

"There's no light down there at all?" I asked. "I have Kokusan's eye, but that will only work for me."

"I can help with that," Flossie said. She clicked her fingers and the tips of all ten lit up.

"That's fine for you, poppet, but the rest of us need to see as well."

"Give me your hand," she said to me. I placed my big hand in her tiny one. She touched it and all my fingers lit. "Holy shit!" I snatched my hand out of her grasp and wiggled my fingers. "It doesn't burn."

Chub looked over at me and guffawed. "Yer hands be afire."

"How do I turn them off?" I asked the fairy.

"Just think off. I'll give everyone the finger lights. If it's as dark as I fear, we'll need more than that. Maybe there will be something we can use when we get down there. The old man said humans live there, servants to Slygon. They must have a way of lighting their world."

The fairy touched Slag's fingers. He wiggled them. "I'm not sure this be a good thing."

"Forget about yer fingers, Slag. Ivansar, how far be the secret entrance?"

"The old man said there's a way down on the side of that mountain right here." The fair-haired elf turned to point behind them. "Another, smaller quake a few years ago opened some crevices that lead under the mountain. And this one is actually closer to where Flossie thinks Slygon went, the city of the dark elves, Necrosis."

"What a wonderful name," Tiny said. "It means maze."

Ivansar added, "The old man wouldn't even speak the real name of the city aloud. He said it was bad luck and thought it would bring the evil eye on his family and they'd be killed in the night. He just called it the city of Extinction. If Flossie hadn't read his thoughts, we wouldn't have known he meant Necrosis. Not that knowing the name of the city does us a bit of good."

Flossie blushed, and stroked Squeaker. "We won't let you down. You can stop worrying so much, Jackal. Dandy gave me all her powers. She knew she was going to die. I know things too. Somehow, she made me know how to do stuff, too. Lots of stuff."

"But I do worry. Happens it be me job, poppet. So, you and Squeaker gets some dinner because you might be a big bad fairy, but you need sleep like all of us, so you be going to bed right directly." I touched her fiery hair. It was soft and fine under my hand.

"Chub's already got the hens broiling," Slag said. "The elves are roasting up some potatoes and veggies, too. Looks like good eatin' tonight. We all better stuff it, cuz it be dry rations after tonight, think on."

"Happen you be right," I said. "They bring any ale?" I squatted on the ground a short distance from the fire with Flossie settled between me and Belle. Noemi sat on Belle's other side. When the food was served, I watched her carefully. It was hard to trust she was no longer a vampire. It worried me. I wanted to see her eat real food.

She took an orange root from Ivansar and nibbled on it. "Eat," Belle said to her. "You need to regain your strength."

She ate the orange root and Belle handed her a chicken leg. "If you can stomach this, you're fine."

Noemi took a bite of the chicken, made a horrible face, and ran for the bushes. I heard her harsh gagging and retching. "Is she cured or not?" I asked Flossie.

"Remains to be seen," Flossie said in her child-like voice. "I did the best I could. The venom of the cobra should have killed all the infection in her blood."

"Should have ain't very reassuring."

"We all need to watch her," Flossie whispered. "Belle won't believe she's anything but perfect, which is dangerous."

I nodded and took a huge bite out of a piece of chicken.

"Better dress warm in the morning," I said to everyone gathered around the fire. "It be colder than winter in the Pit."

Chapter Forty-Six

Jackal

We waited until the sun crested the mountains to the east and there was enough light to pick our way safely along the rocky, switch-back mountain path. It was barely wide enough for the mounts to climb single file. I followed Slag who led the way, with Flossie up in front of me on a heavy draft mule.

"Wish I'd me own mule," Chub whispered from behind me. "I'd trust her anywhere."

"These be more fit to this rough terrain, think on. They be used to traveling the mountain trails," I said over my shoulder. "We were lucky the town's been breeding draft mules because so many have to ride double for lack of mounts."

Chub's grunt said everything.

"It be damned difficult to see once we reach that rise," Slag said. "The sun isn't high enough to light the other side."

I looked to the east. "Should be light enough once we reach it."

Slag glanced at the rising sun and nodded. Though Flossie promised she'd cast a shield around them that prevented any prying eyes from seeing them, I didn't like using her magic. I hadn't grown up with magic and my own abilities still amazed me. I'd learned to harness some of my power, to call it up on demand without the need of rage or emotional desperation. Still, I felt more comfortable trusting in the things I'd always counted on, my strength, my wits, and my friends.

When we reached the top of the rise, the path switch-backed again. Deep shadow lowered the temperature as well as visibility. Even at high noon the area would be a shelter for predators on two or four feet.

Slag cursed.

Flossie grumped from her spot in front of me and pointed to the ground ahead. "No," I said.

"Don't worry so much," Flossie said.

The hooves of Slag's mule began to glow and cast a light ahead of him, illuminating even the darkest gloom in the direct vicinity. As my mule reached the spot, my view was also brightened.

"There, you see? It doesn't rise more than a little off the ground and even if we weren't shielded as I promised, the light would be masked by the mountain itself."

The outcropping of rocks above them hid the sky. They were in a canyon of rocks, surrounded tunnel-like on all sides, by stone walls. Flossie was right. "Happen ye did well, Flossie. I thank ye."

"The opening is just up ahead, on the left. Past a sharp rock there is a narrow opening in the wall. If the old man hadn't told me it was there, we'd never have found it. It's just wide enough for us to pass through. There's a narrow pathway just inside that leads off to the right. It's very steep. The mules need this light to prevent them from falling over the side."

"You got all this from that old man?" Slag asked.

"Yes, and so many details he would never have remembered without my help," Flossie said proudly.

She waved her hand and was instantly bundled into the fur cloak I had last seen on Belle. I turned around to see Belle who was riding double with her sister. Noemi seemed to be sleeping, leaning against Belle's back while Belle talked to Tiny who rode double with Granny. She still had on a fur coat, so Flossie had just duplicated it. What a bunch we were. Too many to keep safe, though leaving them behind either in Hellgate or camped out close to the town was out of the question. And when I'd suggested they take the dragons and go back to Greenwood, they'd flatly refused.

I followed Slag's mule around the jagged rock Flossie had described. "Have a care," Slag called from inside the black hole ahead.

I slowed my mule as we entered the cleft in the rock and sucked in a breath. This was the Pit, the place all the evil and strange creatures that populated the upper world had come from. It was where my orc ancestor had originated, and it was never going away. All across the planet, holes like this had opened, allowing the creatures of the dark to emerge into the light of day. I'd hoped never to enter it. No one wanted to. Flossie touched my hand. "We'll find and kill Slygon," she whispered. "We have to."

"Happen we will," I said. "Happen we will." I knew to keep my mule to the right, but even without the ability to see past the faint light on the path ahead, I sensed the enormity of the underground world we entered. When I chanced a quick glance to my left, I saw far below, too far below, a light. The stones themselves seemed lit from within.

I pulled Kokusan's eye out of my pocket. The old seer hadn't given me operating instructions, so I held it to my own eye. What I saw shocked me so much I almost fell off my mule. The entire cavern, deep and wide, was illuminated like the sun was out. Far ahead, I saw rocks and walls of shiny material, far below narrow trails and creatures moved about. Slimy, disgusting creatures like worms. And there were rats everywhere.

I briefly considered sharing my view of the Pit with Slag and decided all of my companions would be better not knowing what crawled, slithered and ran in the darkness surrounding us. Ignorance could be bliss.

"There's glowing minerals in the stones that allow limited vision once we reach the lower levels," Flossie announced. She saw me holding the eye. "Did you use it?"

"Aye."

"What did you see?"

"Nothing worth sharing," I said in a flat voice. "Nothing I should share."

She nodded. "It's best only you and I know."

I turned my attention back to the trail, but the fact that those below, whoever or whatever they might be, could see the light projected by the mule's lit hooves added to my growing unease. The temperature dropped as we descended, and the air grew damp. It smelled dank and loamy, an earthy scent that reminded me of a cave I'd once slept in. But there were other scents too. I could swear I smelled the darkness, and the rank odor of those who dwelled in it, organic and foul, like the rot and decay of souls.

The only sounds heard were the clomp of hooves, an occasionally loosened stone clattering down into the abyss below, and the constant drip of water running down the rock walls and off stalactites above onto stalagmites below. None of us made a sound. Fear was contagious, and we could all sense the evil permeating this hell hole.

One of the mounts stumbled, followed by a cry for help. I braced myself. Then loosened stones ricocheting off other rock surfaces below crashed as they fell. I heard a hideous thud, and the combined cries of one of the mules and its rider. I knew without turning to look one of the elves had plummeted into the pit. Our entire caravan stopped, and I eased off my mule handing the reins to Flossie. I slid past each animal until I reached Ivansar. "Who was it?" I dreaded knowing. What if it was one of the three I'd been traveling with for so long?

"Gormar's cousin, Saelihn," Ivansar said. "He and his mule are gone. He was a good warrior."

I walked along the line of mules and riders, putting my hand on each leg, consoling, offering my strength. No one spoke. I stopped next to Belle and touched her leg. She wore her leather britches and carried more weapons than me. I stared up at her. I couldn't see her, I didn't need to see her, to know how sad she was. She stroked my face with tender understanding. "It's not your fault," she said softly. Her reassurance was unnecessary but endearing. She still loved me even though I'd just lost a man. "They all knew where we're going and the risk."

"I know, but it don't help." My love for her grew every day. Sometimes I felt like it would burst in my chest.

"You feel responsible for all of us." She paused and I knew her smile pushed back at the darkness around us. "It's one of the things I love about you."

"I, uh, I love you, too," I mumbled so low only she could hear, still embarrassed to be speaking my feelings aloud. I examined Noemi sitting behind Belle on the mule. Was she glowing? I stared hard and decided it was just her white skin. She had a dusting of freckles across her nose and they stood out. I wanted to trust her, but I couldn't stop thinking she was trouble. It was a gnawing doubt that I couldn't let go.

Knowing there was nothing else I could do, I walked back down the line, touching each leg, the neck or sides of each mule until I reached mine and climbed back on. We continued the descent.

"I-I should have done something," Flossie said.

"Like what? You couldn't know." Below us growls and other, more disturbing sounds were followed by the unmistakable flapping of wings. "Naught you could do, poppet. Mind your head."

Bats. Thousands of them. Displaced, no doubt from the eruption of brutal activity around the fresh carcass of the fallen mule and rider.

"Gargoyles," Flossie told me.

"Ye jest. Gargoyles?"

"They live down here mostly. Sometimes they fly out of the caves and eat animals and, uh, people."

"Well that be lovely."

"We're nearly at the bottom," she said.

"Flat ground ahead," Slag passed back along the line, confirming her prediction.

I urged the mule into a faster walk as the path widened onto flat ground, then quickly trotted to the other side of the open area to make way for the rest of the warriors. I dismounted and handed the reins to Flossie, drawing my sword. The elf and his mount had landed on a rocky shelf of the cliff above us, but from here we could hear growling and slurping noises as whatever was up there ate and fought over the choicest morsels. Scattered stones plummeted toward us. I quickly covered Flossie with my body. She giggled as the stones bounced off the invisible shield she'd erected. "Told you I put up a shield."

Her smug expression changed and in the dim light of the hooves and glowing minerals I saw fear in her eyes. "What is it?"

"There's too many of us. I need to save my energy for when we reach Necrosis and Slygon."

Jackal looked up.

"Gargoyles," yelled one of the elves.

The warriors were already armed, but though the mineral lit rocks that surrounded us made it possible to see the dozens of gargoyles, the beasts couldn't see us hidden inside Flossie's shield. The gargoyles circled, searching. The creatures knew we were here. One flew close enough to hit the shield. It sparked, illuminating us cowering under it. The ugly beasts battered against the shield determined to unearth the pile of food below.

Flossie cried out and pressed her hands against the sides of her head.

"Get ready! They be coming in!" I yelled. "Let the vile things in, poppet. We need some exercise to relieve our tension. Here." I shoved her under the mule. "You and Squeaker stay hidden there so I've naught to worry about."

"Circle the mules," I shouted. The elves were already doing it. I urged Belle, Noemi, Tiny and Granny into the center. "Stay together," I said and gave Belle the evil eye. I knew her. Obeying orders was not her forte.

"Tina and I can fight," Belle snarled. "Stop treating us like we're made of glass. We're both trained fighters."

She pulled her bow off her back and I nodded. "Sorry. Didn't mean to. Try to stay close to the mules. They be the biggest targets and the gargoyles will want them. Lot of food in one of the mules."

Flossie released the barrier and spread her hands to create a dim light. It was enough. We could now see the creatures flying toward us. The gargoyles dove. Prepared to crash against Flossie's barrier, they descended with explosive velocity. The gargoyles were momentarily surprised when there was no shield, so we were able to hack away at a few before the entire swarm of vile creatures were on us.

They had a wingspan of nearly four feet and at the end of each bat-like fold was a jagged claw. If those claws weren't enough of a weapon, they also had another claw at the end of each short arm and the beasts' legs were able to shred or grab their prey, pulling it into their razor-sharp teeth and fangs. Gargoyle eyes glowed yellow which provided archers with a target. Several were struck with arrows and fell to the cavern floor.

Belle, Tina and the elves kept a barrage of arrows flying. The hideous creatures fell on the dead ones, eating them swiftly. I severed the wing of a brute whose wing claw left a nasty gash on my mule's hindquarter. "Die, ye filthy bastard," I snarled as I plunged my sword into the beast's heart through its tough gray hide.

The elves knelt and loosed volley after volley of arrows, killing surge upon surge. The heavy corpses fell and splattered on the rocks.

Another nasty beast dived at me, reached out to gash my face, and raked three wicked nails against my left cheek. One of Tiny's crossbow bolts pierced its heart and it crashed to the ground at my feet. She raced to retrieve the arrow for further use. They had to be running low.

I ignored the pain of the slashes, spun and split a gargoyle open from neck to slashing tail with my sharp blade. I leaped back, swung to my left and felled a beast about to attack an elf from behind.

We fought on for twenty minutes. It seemed like hours before the last remaining creatures screeched a retreat and flew off to lick wounds. The beasts hauled the dead ones with them, probably to stock their larder. I leaned against the warm side of my mule panting from the exertion. Belle handed me a flask of water which I accepted with true gratitude. "That was right awful," I said, then took a long drink.

"I've never even seen one of those creatures before," Chub said, reaching for the flask.

"Aye, nasty beasties," Slag agreed, waiting his turn with the water.

"How many of ye be hurt?" I asked, walking toward the elves.

"Minor cuts and scratches, thankfully," Ivansar said. "The gargoyles don't have scales like dragons, and though their hides are tough, our arrows were able to pierce them. We were also able to reserve our silver supplies for later by retrieving as many arrows from the fallen as possible before their friends carried them off for lunch."

"Aye, as much as I'd like to rest, we need to move on afore they regroup and return."

"Not before anyone who was scratched or clawed uses this to cleanse their wound, no matter how small," Granny said. She handed Ivansar an earthenware crock filled with unguent. Ivansar sniffed. "Ugh, this smells worse than the gargoyles."

Granny cackled. "It might smell like shit, but those beasts have a kind of saliva that causes wounds to suppurate. There's bacteria in their mouths what causes infection. They lick them claws and you can get the infection from those wounds, too." Granny spread some of the reeking goop on my cheek. "Without this, the wound will fester and spread poison throughout your body."

"Ye jest?" Slag glanced down at a gash across his forearm and swore.

"Let me see that," I said as Granny moved on to treat the next elf. Slag's wound was already turning green and seeped yellow pus. "She's right," I said loud enough for all to hear. "Come and get your wounds cleaned and healed, no matter how small. Their claws and teeth spread poison."

The warriors began examining themselves for even the most insignificant scrape and lined up to receive treatment from Granny.

"Happens old Granny has saved our butts more than once," Chub said. "Knows a good meal too. Valuable asset, says me." Smacking his lips, he added, "I can still remember them ribs she cooked fer us back in Craggy Town."

"Craggy Town seems like it was years ago," Tiny said.

Belle nodded. "So much has happened. Sometimes I think it will never stop."

I pulled her close. "It won't until we kill that bastard Slygon and get our Dandy's body back."

"I know we'll get him," she said.

"We will or die trying." I pulled a package out of the saddle pockets on my mule and handed Chub a fistful of salted dried meat. "May as well eat now. I'm feeling a little gut pinched meself, and if I'm hungry I know ye be starving to death."

Chapter Forty-Seven

Belle

I was worried about Noemi. She didn't seem to have any life to her. She sat behind me silent and passive. If I asked her a question, she'd mumble an answer. It was disturbing. And the only thing she'd eaten since she was cured was one lousy carrot which she'd probably vomited along with the chicken.

"You okay?" I asked her as I helped her off the mule and to a seat beside a fire I was building.

"I don't know," she said in a thin voice. "I feel so strange."

"Maybe it's because you're no longer a vampire after being one for so many years. You're mortal now. If you don't eat and take care of yourself, you could die."

"What's her problem?" Granny asked.

"She feels weird," I said.

Granny cackled. "I bet. She's a mortal now. Her heart is beating. She's breathing air just like we are. Her body will have to get used to functioning without the parasites in her blood, cause that's what they were. Bugs living off her. Well more symbiotes, mutually supporting creatures. They helped her be immortal and she provided them blood which they needed to survive."

We lit a small fire out of dry, dead mushrooms, to heat water for coffee. I pointed my finger and set the strange-looking fungus on fire. The smoke was acrid and had an odd, sweet smell.

"I think we better find something else to burn," Flossie said. "This can't be good for us."

She was right. I felt woozy. Suddenly, Slygon appeared before me, smiling and laughing. *You're mine.* His face elongated and twisted, then his mouth opened impossibly wide, exposing his fangs. I batted him away, but my hands passed right through him. And then

Kyran appeared, his handsome face gazing at me with tender care. *Don't worry, I won't let him take you away from me.* I smiled at Kyran, happy to be with him, knowing he would keep me safe, would cherish me. But then he disappeared, and Noemi was there, angry and snarling. I screamed and backed away.

Noemi grabbed me by my shoulders. "Stop, Belle, it's the mushrooms. You're tripping."

I shook my head. "I saw Slygon and Kyran."

"Kyran could be even more evil than Slygon," she said. "I knew him. He was bad through and through. He loved being a vampire, reveled in his power, enjoyed killing." Noemi shuddered. "I'm putting out that fire."

I had to realize the mushroom visions weren't real, not visions like the ones I'd had of true events or warnings.

"Poison," Noemi said as she stomped on the flames and smothered them with dirt. She scrambled out of the way as Jackal stumbled past her, swinging his fists at open air and shouting against an invisible foe.

I grabbed him by his massive shoulders. "Jackal, it isn't real. The burning mushrooms are poison." He coughed, rubbed his eyes, and dropped his head in his hands.

"The mushrooms are giving you weird visions," Noemi said. "It's like a drug."

I flopped on the ground next to her. "You're okay?"

She nodded. "I could tell they weren't right."

Flossie waved her wand and a strong breeze dissipated the last of the smoke.

"Didn't wanna wake up from that dream, so good it be," Granny said, stumbling to her feet.

"Nearly cut me head off," Chub mumbled, shoving Slag away.

"Weren't my fault, think on," Slag declared.

"Everyone okay?" Jackal asked, still rubbing at his eyes and shaking his head.

I leaned on Noemi so I could stand and then counted heads. Someone had to. "Where's Tiny? Part of my vision was real," I said. "I think he's got Tiny."

"Ye were hallucinating, love," Jackal said. "Tiny be right here with us." He glanced at Flossie. "Right?"

Flossie shook her head. "I don't think so."

"He's got her," Noemi said. "Kyran took her. I can feel him." She held her hands out flat and closed her eyes. "He's still close."

"Everyone look for Tiny," Jackal shouted. All of us raced around the perimeters, calling her name. I heard the rising panic in Jackal's voice. Once they got farther away from their camp, darkness so thick she put her hand out expecting to feel it, surrounded her. She lit her fingers, but the small amount of light couldn't penetrate the thick shadows.

Jackal lit his fingers and ran over to her. "What did ye see? In yer real-like vision?"

"Remember that vampire? The one in the coffin I was tied to? I saw him. He's out there." She waved her hand to indicate the blackness surrounding them. "He's after me."

Noemi came up beside me and held me close as a booming voice echoed through the huge cavern. "Annabelle, come to me and I'll send your friend back."

I felt the magnetism of his voice. I stumbled toward it, my hands out, fingers lit. Jackal grabbed my shoulder. "Stop. Ye be staying here. This be a trap." He shoved me into Noemi's arms. "Don't let her follow the voice."

"I won't," Noemi said and held me tightly. I clung to her terribly afraid for myself and for Tiny. The bastard had my Tiny. I felt dizzy and the inky blackness made it worse.

"We can't go on without her," I said to Noemi. "Maybe I should go to him. Tiny would never leave me in the hands of a killer without dying in an attempt to save me and I can do no less."

Jackal heard me. "Belle, yer not even steady on yer feet yet. He'll end with both of ye in his clutches. Let me and me pals get her for you. I'm good. Me brain's got no more fog. Promise. Strong as an ox."

"But he doesn't want you. You heard him. He's going to hurt her if I don't do as he says, and I can take care of myself."

"Over here," Kyron spoke from the edge of the darkness. I strained my eyes staring into the blackness and made out the dim form of the beautiful vampire, his skin glowed. He had Tiny in his arms. She was unconscious.

I shoved Noemi off and ran for them. Noemi followed me. Blood stained Tiny's throat. "He's fed off her," Noemi said. We stopped a few feet away. I was glad for my sister's presence. She exuded confidence and power. When I looked at her, she glowed just like Kyran. "You're still vampire," I gasped.

"I was too far gone, little sister," she said sadly.

"I'll trade her for you," Kyron said to me. "We belong together. You already feel it, sense it. Come to me, Annabelle. Be with me. I'll make you happy, forever. And you know you want to save your friend."

I drifted away into a memory. He did care about me, cherished me. We were so happy together, until Jackal took me away.

Noemi flew across the space between us and knocked Tiny out of Kyran's arms. "You," Kyron snarled. "You're supposed to be dead."

Noemi slowly circled him. "I'm hungry, Kyron," she said. "Starving really. I actually ate a carrot. I thought I was cured. I'm not," she added sadly. "But I am hungry." She launched herself at Kyron. "Run, Belle. Grab Tina and take her away. I got this."

"Oh, Noemi, I can't leave you."

"Save Tiny," Noemi screamed as she attacked Kyron with her fangs out. The two vampires rose a foot off the ground, easy to see because they both glowed. I raced across the open space, grabbed Tiny and pulled her into my arms. I was strong, but I couldn't lift Tiny's ninety pounds. It was too much. Then Jackal was there beside me, pulling Tiny away from me, urging me to my feet. "Run Belle, get back to the others. I have Tina."

Gormar suddenly shot past us and charged forward carrying a silver-tipped arrow lifted high above his head. The elf moved so fast, I barely saw him.

"Come with me, love," Jackal said. "Gormar and Noemi got this."

I blinked and shook my head to clear it. "That bastard glamoured me. The mushroom smoke weakened my barriers."

Gormar reached Kyron and Noemi and raised the arrow above his head. "Go back," Noemi screamed. "I can handle him."

I stopped Jackal. "Wait," I said.

We watched, shocked, as Noemi, blood dripping from her fangs, repeatedly attacked Kyron. The vampire was losing to her. "I'm full of venom," Noemi said. "I can manufacture cobra venom. You're dying Kyron and you don't even know it yet."

Kyron was rapidly weakening. His arms looked too heavy for him to lift, his face even whiter. He fell under Noemi who dropped on top of him, latched onto his throat and tore it out. She gulped down the flood of thick, red vampire blood. When Kyron seemed drained, she held her hand out. "I need the silver bolt."

Gormar handed it to her. Noemi stabbed Kyron but missed his heart as the vampire suddenly disappeared in a puff of purple smoke.

Noemi leapt to her feet. "Thanks, Gormar," she said as she swiped her arm across her face to remove the blood on her lips. "One down," she said to me. "Slygon is next."

"Where did he go?" I asked. "Is he dead?"

"I believe he is," Noemi said. "He must be, though the purple smoke is something I've never seen. Let's pray he is because he's evil and a bitch to fight."

"What are you?" I asked. "I thought Flossie had changed you into a human."

"She's like Slygon now," Flossie said. "She's vampire and shifter. Noemi is part cobra."

"Well that's some fucking weird shit," Granny said. She wore a plaid scarf across half her face. All ye need to cover yer faces. The mushroom spores are poisonous."

Jackal laid Tiny on the ground and Granny knelt beside her. I dropped to the other side with a scarf over my face as Granny lifted Tina's hand and chafed it. "She's been drained of quite a lot of blood by the looks of her. She'll have to ride with someone. We need to haul our asses out of here. The mushrooms are about to explode and spray spores."

Immediately after the words left her mouth, a gigantic puffball blew thousands of spores into the air. Jackal yelled. "Cover yer faces."

"She can ride with me," Gormar said.

"Let's get the hell outta this place," Slag said, his voice muffled behind a thick scarf tied around his enormous head. "Is Tiny gonna be okay?"

"Of course," I said.

Granny took Tina's pulse and felt her throat. "She needs a lot of rest and as much of this tonic as we can get down her, to rebuild her blood, but I think we got her in time."

"It's my fault," I said. "He was after me."

Noemi put her arm around my shoulders. Her arm felt strong. "Are you going to live?" I asked.

Noemi laughed. "I'm as good as I can get, little sister. I'm not getting rid of the vampire bugs. They're too strong for Flossie's magic. And now, Slygon's made me a shifter. But, hey, when I meet him again, his ass is mine."

"No, it's mine," I said smiling.

"We'll share the killing of him," Noemi said.

"Gather our stuff," Jackal called, nodding to Slag. "And get this train moving. This be a bad place."

"Ye got that right," Slag said. "This be the freaking Pit and as far as I be concerned the whole damn place be cursed."

Gormar took Tina up in front of him, and I made sure she could hold onto the saddle horn. "I'm going to be fine, Belle," Tina said. Stop looking so sad. It doesn't suit you. Anger and battle are your thing."

I hurried to mount my own mule and urged it up behind Jackal. Watching his back made me feel safer. He was ridiculously huge, and I was beginning to find that a comfort.

We wove down a path between a forest of enormous glowing fungus. "Keep yer faces covered," Granny scolded from somewhere in the middle of their long line of mules.

"At least they light the trail," I yelled back at her.

"Having a lighted trail won't matter if you be freaking dead," Granny spat.

What seemed like hours later, Flossie told Jackal to stop. "We're almost there," she said.

"There as in where, exactly?" Jackal asked.

"I can see it in my head, like a vision, but more like a sense of knowing where something I'm trying to find is located. It's hard to explain, but we're nearing Necrosis. I can see this tunnel leading to Slygon's castle. We can't ride the mules through it, so we need to find somewhere to leave them. If we want to sneak up on him, we walk and sneaking up on him is the best thing for us."

"Happen that's true," Jackal said. "Though all the Kyran commotion probably already told him we're on the way."

Chapter Forty-Eight

Jackal

"Time to face Slygon," I said.

We formed up in pairs. I walked down the line, patting each warrior on the shoulder, clouting some in a friendly way. With Slag, Chub, Belle, Tiny, Granny, Flossie and the elves, they numbered sixteen. "Strength and honor," he said to each of them. "Strength and honor."

They headed in twos into the tunnel. The mouth looked like the gaping maw of some gigantic creature. It opened in the flat face of a huge wall completely blocking the underground cavern. All I could think was what a great place to get dead. All the enemy would need to do was set up an ambush at the exit. "If this is the only way to Slygon's castle, you'd think as clever as he believes himself to be, he'd realize that and set up guards at least."

"He's clever but has not military experience," Noemi said. "He's lived as a virtual king down here for so long, he expects no resistance."

"We'll still take care and proceed with caution when we come to the end."

Gormar walked beside Tina, holding her arm. Ivansar and Torros paired, Chub and Slag. Granny walked beside Flossie. The tunnel was well lit, the walls glowing with minerals and weird luminescent lichens, the air dank, the floor of the passage tramped flat and smooth by the passing of many feet. When the tunnel forked, Flossie signaled for Slag to move into the right corridor, and they moved out with purpose, eager to get out of the damp, narrow passage running through solid rock. Water dripped off the low ceiling, the walls brushed their elbows and the rock beneath their feet was worn smooth.

"Holy shit," I said and stopped dead when we rounded a bend and saw the end of the tunnel. Ahead, it opened into the largest underground cavern imaginable. "Slag," I called softly. "Go right, I go left."

We crept slowly forward, the remainder of our group waiting. When we left the tunnel, I hugged the rock wall staring. I used my power to feel for any guards, vampires, or other weird creatures, and got nothing. "I think it's clear," I said.

"This goes on fer miles," Slag said in a voice hushed with awe. The ceiling was so far above, we couldn't see it. There was atmosphere inside the cavern. Clouds drifted across the dark ceiling far over their heads, dropping rain. The rain water was warm, almost hot. The walls of the huge cavern were lined with phosphorescent moss creating a greenish glow that provided light.

Ivansar gasped when he emerged from the tunnel. Everyone turned in circles gawking at the wondrous sight. Flossie popped her coat out of existence. "It's going to get hotter," she said and pointed.

"We're close to the volcano," I said. Glowing lava flowed from cracks in the floor of the cavern. It formed one great bubbling river that ran through a crevasse across the floor of the valley.

"Look," Flossie said, pointing to a steaming body of water. "We can take hot baths."

Chub snorted. "Had me one just last week."

Belle slipped her hand in mine. "At least there's water. We won't die of thirst."

"No, not of thirst," I said, pointing to a dark shape circling the city at the opposite end of the valley.

"Black dragon," Noemi said as it landed in a tunnel high in the cavern's wall.

"He be here. That be Slygon's beast," Slag said.

I nodded as I studied the landscape, trying to formulate a plan. There was a small village beyond a pile of large boulders to their right. The lava river flowed closer to the far wall of the cavern and disappeared underground. Mud pots burped evil, sulfurous gas between them and the village, but there was a trail cutting through them. The villagers must travel out this way or traders come in, because the trail was clearly marked and well-worn.

The beings that inhabited the village appeared humanoid. They had corralled hogs and sheep behind stone walls, and seemed able to grow some sort of crops, but all I could tell was they were nothing I'd ever eaten. I knew that because they glowed. The dwellings too were made of stone. The humanoids walked like the peasants living close to Slygon's castle in the outer world, head down, dragging slowly from one spot to another like they had no energy. Slygon must be farming people to feed his vampire flock.

What was even more ominous was the larger walled city that stood between them and the far side of the valley where high towers rose from a castle hanging off the wall of the cavern. That must be Slygon's lair. Who else would build a castle in this underground world, but its king?

"Where did the elves live?" I asked Ivansar. "You and yer people lived down here before the Pit opened. "Where did you live?"

Ivansar pointed to the far wall. "There's another tunnel over there. It's impossible for normal folk to find. We have many spells on it. The tunnel leads to a fair valley we called Uethsari. It's lighted like this cavern but with healthy growth not the disgusting, slimy vegetation you find on the walls here. We have homes there, and some dwarves and other clean creatures lived there. It has a higher ceiling than this cavern, atmosphere, rain, clouds. We rode unicorns and flying horses. It's bigger than this cavern." He glanced around. "I remember it as a beautiful place. This place is dark, disgusting, ugly and frightening."

"Sounds wonderful," I said.

Gormar stepped up with Tiny beside him. "It's a great place to visit, but we'd rather live in the sunlight."

"I'd like to see it," Tiny said. "Will you take me there someday?"

Gormar hugged her and looked down at her fondly. "If we kill Slygon, I'll gladly take you anywhere you wish."

The walled city beyond the serf's village was made of stone held together by a black shiny substance that gleamed. Even from this distance, Jackal thought the city looked alive. It pulsed, as though it had a beating heart, and he sensed evil in its inhabitants. The fact that they could tolerate the heat radiating from the lava flow that snaked past their town meant they must be different. "Who do you think lives in the city?" I asked Ivansar. "The lava flows right close to the far walls before it disappears."

"Evil elves turned by Slygon or born black," Ivansar said. "Elves have bad seeds just like humans. Some younger ones would run away, looking for a new life. Before the Pit opened, this was what they found. There are ways, trails, paths, even roads to other parts of the underground world, but this valley was the closest to our world, the elf world. The young elves would come here curious, knowing the danger, thinking they were bad asses and end up dying or turned."

"I see no guards on the walls," Slag said. "Mayhap they think they're invincible. A course, they wouldn't have much need of them here, in this pit of hell. Who would attack them, think on?"

"We will," I said. "If we have to."

Chapter Forty-Nine

Jackal

"Do you see a way to get to the castle without being butchered?" Slag asked me.

"No. It commands a view of the valley floor and it's backed against the cavern wall. We be sitting ducks no matter where we come from."

"Wonder why the slimy bastard ever left his palace here," Gormar said. "It's protected, it's safe, it's grand enough for any king. It seems it would be enough."

I laughed. "I don't think you get who our Slygon is. He left the underworld because he needs to feed, and he seeks power." I waved my arm to indicate the valley and the castle at its end. "Think this be enough for a power-mad vampire like Slygon?"

Slag shook his head. "For him, there will never be enough. He's an empty vessel with a leaky bottom. All he pours in, runs out through the hole. He'll never be satisfied."

"Well damn," I said. "I never woulda thought Slag could be a philosopher but happen that be exactly right. Slygon will never be satisfied and now us and our nasty dragons have ruined his plans."

Chub rubbed his belly. "Can we just kill him and get this over with? I want me home and me dinner."

"Let me know when ye come up with a plan to attack that." I pointed to the castle. "As soon as ye tell me how to capture that thing up there without all of us dying, we can go home. I thought the sewer the elves mentioned earlier wouldn't work, but right now it seems it may be an idea worth thinking about."

Whether by nature or magic, the castle of Necrosis itself was formed of gleaming black lava that towered over the valley. Its spires and turrets covered an area three times the size of the elf kingdom above ground.

I went on a hunt for Ivansar. The elf was seated on the ground talking to three other elves, so I sat next to them. "Your clan lived down here for centuries upon end with Slygon and his minions. I be thinking I dismissed the sewers too soon. Tell me what you think."

"We were just discussing that," Ivansar said. "Torros and Gormar were once among the crazy young elves who thought venturing into this valley fun and exciting."

"The two friends didn't survive," Gormar said. "But we were able to escape through the sewer system."

Jackal groaned. "Yup, I knew I heard ye right."

"There's a garderobe on every floor of the castle," Gormar said. "The holes lead to the sewer beneath the castle which flows into the lava river. You must exit the sewer as soon as it clears the walls, or you end up in the lava."

"Shit and lava, you're kidding?" I shook my head. I wanted to get into the castle, but this was a little extreme even for Slag. "Ain't there some way to go over the walls? How'd you get inside?"

"We got captured," Torros said, and tossed into the dungeons."

"I think getting captured would be a bad idea. I think jumping into a toilet equally as bad. Are you sure there's no other way into it than the front door?"

"The front door, as you call it, is really a huge gate made of a strange metal Slygon mined from a meteor. It glows and is dangerous to touch. It's opened by a mechanism inside the walls."

"If you can't touch it, how did it get made?"

"By dead men," Torros said. "Or that's what I heard. It was built a long time ago and the stories told about it have been passed down through many tellings. I do know not to touch it."

I leaned back and thought. "We're gonna have to use Flossie. No other way to get inside."

"Flossie?" Gormar said.

"She can turn herself tiny and open the gate. Once it's open, we have to face Slygon's vamps and since it's always night down here, they don't sleep like they do on the surface."

"We might be able to fix that," Ivansar said.

"Fix what?"

"What if we blew a hole in the ceiling of this cavern and let daylight in?"

"Now that be a nice thought, but we have no way to do that. And then it might fall on our heads."

"The elves in the next valley do," Gormar said. "They have dragon fireballs. If Gormar and I can get over the lava river, and we have done it before, we can make it to the elf world and back in two-day's time. And we can shelter from the falling ceiling inside the tunnel we came through to get here."

"Dragon fireballs? What are they made of?"

"Elves have long wished to be able to recreate dragon fire, so they studied it and discovered natural elements that will explode when ignited."

"That sounds a lot like the bombs the people of New Orleans were using against the orc raids," Belle said as I squeezed her knee.

"The dragon fireballs are better for caves, castles, bunkers and enclosed spaces. They ignite the oxygen inside the contained space and, well, it's spectacular," Gormar replied.

"I can't see us sitting here looking down on this valley and Slygon's keep while we wait for you to return," I said. "I vote we send Flossie in, get her to open the gate and just go for broke. It won't be a surprise attack. The bastard has probably already sensed Belle and knows we're coming. He's probably just waiting for us, like a spider, ready to pounce. Look at the walls. No guards, or none that I can see from here. He's so confident we're not a threat that he doesn't feel he needs them. Our only hope is that his arrogance will be his downfall."

"How about this?" Ivansar said. "We go ahead with your plan and attack with Flossie opening the gates, but if needed, these two," he pointed to two young elf warriors, "Jassin and Theodre, go for dragon fire. That way, if we're stuck or caught, they can blow the ceiling and light up the vamps."

I patted Belle's knee. "It puts us down two men, but it will probably make no nevermind anyway. Got any idea how many vamps be in there?"

Gormar nodded. "There used to be over a hundred. Many went to the upper world with Slygon. Many died there as we know, so I'm thinking at least fifty, less if we're lucky."

"I wouldn't be counting on any luck cause so far it's been hiding its head. Send yer two men and tell them to be quick."

"Maybe they could bring some warriors with them," Torros said. "There used to be hundreds of warriors eager for an adventure. Surely some would come support us in our hour of need."

Chapter Fifty

Belle

"What be bothering ye?" Jackal asked right into my ear. His breath on my neck sent shivers through my body.

"Waiting sucks," I said. "I'm terrible at it."

"We decided to give the elves one day and then attack. Counting down the hours was rough, but it's finally over and we're getting ready to go."

We stood above the town watching while we waited. The town was quiet as though all were sleeping. The people below didn't even know we were up here and probably wouldn't care if they did. And who could blame them, trapped in this valley, raised like livestock to feed vampires?

A middle-aged man came out of one of the stone huts and ran his hand through long lanky hair. He picked up a bucket and shuffled down the main street, head down, shoulders slumped. "He looks human," Jackal said. "I wonder how humans are stuck in this god-forsaken valley. Do you think Slygon brought them in to use like fodder for his vampires?"

"That's too horrible to even contemplate," I said. "Imagine living your life like that, just waiting for the moments when the vampires wake and come to get you."

"Makes me wonder if they, ye know, ring a dinner bell," Jackal whispered into my ear.

"It's not a joke. You and your two buddies laugh at everything." I turned to punch him in the shoulder, and he pulled me close. His eyes were golden today. Sometimes they were green. They changed with his mood. I'd even seen them blue.

"I love ye, Belle," he said. "Since the first moment I seen ye." He stroked my braided hair.

"I love you, too," I whispered.

He pulled me hard against his massive chest and lifted me high enough to kiss. His kiss was soft and searching and I closed my eyes to enjoy it.

"Ahem!" A loud throat clearing startled us out of the intimate moment.

Jackal laughed and dropped me.

"Sorry," Chub said. "Didn't mean to uh, to bother you, but we're almost ready to leave.

"No bothering about it. If ye need me, I be always available." Jackal winked at me.

I stared into the valley and spotted an old man, the basket he carried barely above the ground. "Jackal, what's that?"

Chub and Jackal looked up. "Hear it?" I said, clutching Jackal's sleeve. "Wings."

"It's the black dragon," Chub said. "Look."

The beast swooped low over the village. The man carrying the basket didn't even notice it. When he was snatched in the great open maw of the dragon, he dropped his basket. The dragon flew toward them chewing slowly on the man's body. "Hide." Jackal grabbed my hand and jerked me behind a rock. The rock was too small to hide Chub. The giant half-orc stuffed himself into a crevasse in the rock wall and we froze.

A stream of the unfortunate villager's blood splattered across the rocks as the dragon flew over their previous position, caught air under his big wings, flapped, and took off for the castle. "Well, that was disgusting. I thought these people were being farmed for the vampires. I didn't realize they were dragon food as well."

Flossie popped in as a tiny fairy and sat on Jackal's shoulder. "Gross," she said. "Poor man."

"Aye," Chub said. "They must have to capture folks to replenish the population the rate they be feeding off 'em."

Slag walked up, armor on, weapons on his back, sword belt buckled around his narrow waist. "I got everybody ready to go," he said. "Even Tiny be ready. She's a lot better. Granny is going to stay here and keep us a base camp. She can't move fast enough, and I'm worried she'll be hurt. She can wait here in case them two elves return with the dragon firebombs."

"You should let me go in instead of Flossie," Noemi said.

"How?" I asked her. "How can you get in when we can't?"

"Last night, I shifted," Noemi said in a quiet voice. "It came on me out of nowhere. One minute I was in this body, the next I was a snake."

I backed up a step. "You turned into a snake?"

"A cobra. Not as big as the one Slygon turns into, but big enough."

"You don't sound very happy," Jackal said.

"Would you be?" Noemi looked up at him and I saw her pupils narrow, turn gold, and go vertical.

Jackal shook his head. "Nope, don't think it would be at all pleasant."

"Well, I am what I am. Poor little Flossie shouldn't have to go when I am perfectly able to get into Slygon's castle. I could probably knock on the front door and get in."

"Door's poisonous," I said. "Elves told us it was. What other way could you get in? Through the sewers? I hate even thinking about them."

"You're right. If the door is out, I guess Flossie is up. I'd do it, though, even through the sewers. I owe all of you my life, whatever that's worth." She hung her head and I hugged her.

"I don't care what you are. You're my sister and I love you."

Bloody tears raced down Noemi's white cheeks. "And I love you. More than you'll ever know."

Jackal carried Flossie on one shoulder and Squeaker on the other. "Well poppet, think ye can get the gate up fer us?"

"There's other obstacles we have to pass first," she said.

Jackal sighed. "A course there are. Like what?"

"Witches and the black elves."

"Witches?" Chub scoffed. "What trouble be that fer all your magics?"

"They're very powerful and old, able to conjure some really terrible familiars," Flossie explained.

"And why are they here?" Tina asked as she joined their group. "We have a castle with vampires, a town filled with half-dead humans, black elves living in horrible circumstances, and now witches. I don't get it. Why?"

"They live on the other side of the village, between it and the castle," Flossie said. "They get along with the black elves and some of them live in the city. There's a cave in the cavern's wall and the really old ones have lived there for centuries."

"Why don't they leave?" Jackal asked. "Must be a pretty pathetic existence. And what's keeping the elves here? They could easily move to above ground and enjoy life."

Ivansar nodded. "I wondered that myself. The elves have lived in that city for centuries. Some did go above ground when the Pit first opened. Most of us left, though a few resisted change and stayed, but I don't know if any more went up, or if they've all stayed here."

"So, which is it we're supposed to be afraid of?" I asked. "The witches, Slygon or the black elves? Cause at this point, I really just want out of the Pit. I want this entire venture finished. I'll fight anything."

"Maybe we should bring Granny," Flossie said. "If anyone knows how to handle witches, it's her."

"I'm afraid for her," Slag said.

"Why don't we ask her what she wants to do?" I said. "She's a grown woman and can make up her own mind. Besides, if she wants to go and can take care of one of our problems, I'm for taking her. Granny is a powerful healer and can wield a mean wand when she needs to. She deserves a say in her own destiny."

When we got back to camp, we found Granny sitting on her bedroll looking like she'd just lost her last friend. When she saw me, she jumped up. "You need me, right?"

"Of course, we do," I said, pulled Granny to her feet and hugged her hard. "We'll always need you."

Granny grabbed her backpack, dug around in another pack and pulled small packages wrapped in scraps of fabric out. She stuffed all these inside the backpack, tucked her wand inside the belt of her long dress, and stood up. "Let's kick this pig," she said with a crooked grin.

I grabbed her arm and together, we walked back to Jackal.

He saw Granny and grinned. "Didn't wanna stay behind, did you?"

Granny laughed. "If that's where you needed me, I would have done it, but no, I came on this trip to see that bastard Slygon dead and I'd much rather be included in the kill."

Jackal patted her arm. "Happen we got us a witch problem."

"Witches I can handle seeing as how I am one."

"They're very old and horrible," Flossie said.

Granny patted the fairy's arm. "Don't you worry. They live over there don't they?" She pointed at the far side of the elf city.

Flossie nodded.

"It's possible I've been there before. Possible I might know me some of them witches. And if they got the same problem they had when I was there, it's with something worse than the black elves who most of the time, think themselves too good to mess with lowly witches."

"I'm not gonna worrit myself with any of it right now," Jackal said. "Happen, we'll face it when we get there." He turned to Slag. "We ready to move out?"

Slag nodded.

"Then let's do this."

Chapter Fifty-One

Belle

Jackal and I led as we slid down the steep, rocky trail to the valley. I'd never carried this many weapons, and still felt like I could use several more. Throwing knives were stashed all over me. I had my bow slung over my back and my sword in its sheath. I wished with all my heart I hadn't left my wand in that damn meadow, but I had my Gifts.

Noemi walked beside us. She carried no weapons. We'd found her leathers. She wore them and a vest. It was hotter than Hades here. The lava river close by threw off waves of sweltering heat.

We eased to the valley floor on the well-worn trail. Travelers, traders, orcs, and marching humans had worn it into the lava rock over centuries. Once we were down the cliff, I followed Jackal as he headed for the village with Noemi behind me. Slag took up the rear. Tiny was behind Noemi, then Chub, then the elves. Flossie had poufed into her tiny form and gone ahead to do the critical part of this mission, open the castle gate.

The villagers were going about their duties. I wondered how they knew when to sleep and when to work. From the chores they were doing, this must be what they considered morning. I caught Jackal's arm. "Do you think the villagers know it's morning topside?"

"I think they have a way of keeping time, so that be a yes. If they're all just rising now, slopping the hogs, feeding the chickens and such, then it must be morning up there."

None of the folks in the village gave us a second glance as we walked through town. There were three main streets and a dozen side streets. No shops, but one big market filled with food, root vegetables, smoked meat, and grains, a few apples and oranges. Food that could be transported in and kept for a long time.

We tramped through the stone village and out the far side. A glossy black plain stretched out before us, empty of any life, separating the village from the dark elf city and the castle. Any attacking party would have to cross it and be entirely exposed. Of course, it wasn't lit, so the only beings able to see you crossing would be evil, and I knew we would need lights because though the surface looked smooth, it was grooved and had dips and hollows anyone who couldn't see would tumble right into. Unfortunately, the lights would make us walking targets which was, no doubt, what Slygon had planned.

I took a step onto the black surface and saw there were swirls and rolls in it. "This is a special kind of lava flow," Ivansar said. "I've seen it before. It makes these patterns when it's super-heated and flowing like water."

"It's hot under my feet," Jackal said. "Think there's lava still flowing under the surface?"

Ivansar bent low and placed his hand on the smooth black surface. "Yes. I can feel it."

"Think it will hold up under our weight? Chub be right heavy."

"I hope so," Ivansar said.

We stood at the edge of the lava plain and stared at the gate of the castle. It was at least a mile away, over heated lava with a crust of unknown thickness, totally exposed to anything or anyone on the castle walls.

Jackal pulled out his binoculars and examined the castle walls, the cavern walls and the city. I stood beside him dancing from one foot to another. I was filled with crazy energy. "Whatever waits between us and the castle is powerful. I can feel it," I said to Jackal.

"I feel it too, but I don't see shit. There's orcs on the walls, though. I can make them out. They're standing guard up there. Looks like six of them. The elf city looks almost abandoned. Mayhap Ivansar is right and they all went topside."

Ivansar nodded. "It's possible they left or the witches or the vampires got them. Orcs we can handle. It's Slygon and the witches I'm worried about."

Jackal dropped the binoculars into a pouch.

"I smell a jinn somewhere up ahead, too. Ugly creatures, very capricious. You never know what they might do," Ivansar said. "Elves can smell them."

"What? A jinn, like from a lamp for wishes?" Chub asked.

"No, they're real. That's just an old tale. There are few left." He looked Jackal in the eyes. "Elves can feel them. It's why you can sense it. My men and I have been discussing it, and we think this one could be a soul eater. The presence of evil is strong."

"They're not of this world or the world above," said a young elf I recognized as a cousin to Ivansar. His name was Merikoth, and I suspected his strong allegiance to Jackal was due to his hero-worship of Ivansar.

"Where be they from then, Merikoth?" Jackal asked.

"Another dimension. They access our world through time warps, rips in our world's reality. It's not surprising there would be such a location here, in the bowels of Below Earth. Especially this close to the volcano. They travel in the shadows, mostly, and can make themselves appear as shadows."

"My cousin has studied jinn. It's of particular interest to him," Ivansar explained. "One ate his brother."

"Yes. They're fascinating. Some think they're demons, but I know better."

"Let's get across this lava flow," Jackal said. "If we happen to meet up with yer jinn, we'll deal with it."

We walked quickly and as light on our feet as we could across the swirls and dips of the lava crust. Jackal led, followed by Chub. I walked behind Chub, terrified he'd fall through the crust at any moment. The closer we drew to the castle, the more my feelings of unease increased. Suddenly two tornados emerged from a deep crevasse about a hundred yards in front of us and whirled toward them.

"Jinn!" Merikoth screamed.

I dropped to one knee and held my hands out in front of me. Granny knelt beside me with her wand in her hand. "Use your power," a voice came out of the air and a ghostly figure appeared above Jackal. "You have the light inside you. Jinn fear the light."

"Dandy," I whispered.

Chapter Fifty-Two

Jackal

When I saw Dandy's ghost, I freaked out. Was she haunting me because I'd killed her? But then I felt her faith and her trust in me, and I knew I was able to accomplish anything. Until this moment, I'd doubted our success, but if the fairy watched over us from the afterlife, we might make it.

"Set up a shield around the king," Ivansar screamed. The elves knelt next to me and I pushed them away. "You'll get in the way of me fighting arm."

They backed away and chanted words I didn't understand as a bright light grew in strength, shimmering around all of us.

Sparks flew, and a huge black shadow formed into an enormous beast, towering above us. Slavering jaws dripped bloody saliva. The creature had way too many teeth clearly visible in its wide-open mouth. It was completely hairless and had four arms, paws equipped with huge claws, a round head with six white eyes complete with red eyeballs, and the body topped out at least ten-feet. The core looked like burning, flowing, swirling lava.

"Wow," Merikoth said. "It's a true jinni. I never thought to see one. The sparks are from it hitting the shield. It's shapeshifted into what it thinks will be the most terrifying image to us."

The excitement in his voice was irritating. I glared at him. "Glad yer so happy to finally see one of these monsters and it picked a fine freaking shape cause I'm terrified. Now how do we kill it?"

"You know how to do it," Dandy said. "Use your power."

There was an electric charge in the air, like the tingling in my body when I called forth my magic. I reached inside my mind and found the power. It pulsed, ready to spring forth at my call.

"Do it now," Dandy's ghost said. "Use your power."

"Get out of here before I light ya up like fireworks!" I shouted to the hideous monster.

The creature's laugh sent chills crawling up my spine, the hideous sound so loud it echoed throughout the enormous cavern. I thought even the witches must hear it. Even Slygon buried inside his castle. The laugh lacked both mirth and humanity. Suddenly, the monster on the other side of the elves' shield faded, blurred and reshaped itself into a perfect likeness of my Belle.

"What the hell?" muttered Slag.

"You wouldn't hurt me, would you, Jackal? You told me you loved me," the thing said in a slow, sultry travesty of Belle's voice. I wasn't fooled. First of all, Belle would never talk like that, and second, she was pressed against my back. When it pursed its Annabelle lips and blew me a pornographic kiss, my control broke.

"Fuck this." I raised my hands and shot a beam of pure energy at the creature. Then I opened my mouth just like Remoth had taught me and breathed dragon fire at it.

The arrow of light and energy hit the elves' shield and burned back at them. "Duck!" Chub screamed, and we dropped to the lava as my powerful bolt of energy reflected off the shield and shattered the stones around us, raining shards of sharp lava rock everywhere. The dragon fire got through the shield and hit the creature hard. It fell backwards, shocked to be hurt.

"Bring down the shield!" I pushed Ivansar. "I got this."

"Done!" Ivansar said.

The creature must have realized the shield was down. It dropped the Annabelle guise, drew its enormous body up to an even greater height and roared. I noticed its lava core was burning less brightly. My dragon fire must have put some of it out or destroyed it.

I sucked in a huge breath. The air reeked of sulfur and burning gas. I gathered my energy and held my hands out. I felt the power of the earth run through my hands and into my chest. I shot it at the creature and at the same time breathed dragon fire at it. This time the beam of white energy along with the dragon fire hit the monster in its burning core. The core absorbed the energy, pulsed, grew larger and larger, sucking the monster into it until all that remained was an enormous ball of lava.

"Down!" I yelled. "This could be the end of us."

"We be already eating lava," Slag mumbled.

I focused my power, felt Dandy's hand on my shoulder adding to my strength. It was right there, like the best sword I'd ever owned, a weapon of such strength it amazed me. When I was ready to shoot it at the jinn, the monster lurched away from the purity of the white light I produced. The jinn screamed in fear and agony as I shot the clean light into it. The monster burst into flames, then exploded into a shower of ash.

I remembered to breathe and sagged to my knees. I felt drained rather than triumphant. I sensed the shadows ahead swirling with activity. There were more of them, and I didn't know how much strength I had left. Belle put her hand on my shoulder, and I felt her power surge into me. We were joined by our power. It felt like she was feeding me. "You can do this, Jackal," she whispered, her breath brushing my ear. "I know you can."

"I feel you, me darling. We got this."

I lifted my arms and sucked in a breath. "I'm with you," Belle said.

A swirling tornado of ugliness hurtled toward us out of the chasm in front of the empty elf city. I felt for my power and the sweet surge of energy from Belle. Our combined power leapt into my hands. In each palm a swirling ball of energy glowed, ready to use. This was almost better than breathing dragon fire. I faced the jinn with the balls of fire in my hands. "Come on, you bastard. Taste some of this."

Belle hugged me from behind, her head pressing into my back. All of her magnificent power was mine to use. I combined it with my own, braced my feet and sent the balls of energy into the swirling jinn. When the hideous creature blew up, Belle crowed against my back. "I love blowing up shit."

Dandy whispered into my ear. "Together, you can do anything."

"It's true," Belle said. "Together we're unbeatable."

"It ain't over yet," I said. "There's more coming."

A surge of power flowed into me, through me, and I shot it into the screaming mass of black and rust-colored monsters headed straight for us. The enormous flood of energy hit the monsters. They swelled, growing bigger and bigger. "Down!" I screamed, turned and fell across Belle and Tiny to protect them as the swelling mass blew. Chunks of molten lava flew above our heads as the jinn erupted in a fiery, massive explosion. The noise was awful.

The quiet that followed, broken only by the distant drip of water and the bubbling of the lava river, felt like an enormous sigh of relief from the cavern. "Where did all that power come from?" I asked as I looked around at all of them lying flat on the black lava floor. "I thought we were done for. Me and Belle were about drained."

"It came from us," Ivansar said. "You just learned the enormous strength in unity. Elves, and that includes you, your majesty, draw energy from the earth, from living things, plants, trees and vegetation, which is why we're mostly vegetarians. Fairies draw power from the universe. Elves can suck it right out of the ground, which is why our power is not diminished underground. What you felt was our magic flowing through you."

I clapped Ivansar on the back. "You really do have me back. You okay, Belle?" I asked as I slowly rose to my feet.

She sat up and pushed a lock of loose hair off her forehead. "Aside from being squashed by a giant, I'm fine." She took Tiny's hand. "You gonna live?"

Tiny grunted. "I feel like I just got hammered by an elephant's ass. Where's Granny?"

"Here," Granny said. "This nice young man," she pointed to Ivansar's cousin, "I think his name is Melkinthorpe, saved me."

"Merikoth," the young elf said with a grin.

"Right," Granny said. "Melkinthorpe."

Our laugh contained a note of hysteria. Relief at getting by the jinn filling us with craziness.

When we were on our feet, we checked each other for wounds and seemed to have escaped anything more serious than scratches and scrapes from falling on rough lava.

"What a rush," I said as I glanced at Ivansar and nodded to the elf warriors standing ready.

Ivansar, usually a staid and sober elf, laughed with me. Relief had all of us giddy. "We'll always have your back."

"Now that you understand how your magic flows, you need to be able to replenish it, to give yourself strength when you need it most, against Slygon," Dandy said.

"Aye. I be tuckered out now." I closed my eyes and focused on the earth beneath my bare feet. I focused on the pulsating energy I sensed below me. As I focused, I became more acutely aware of the earth. It was a living, breathing entity. I drew the power through the bottom of my feet, up my legs, through my torso, and into my chest. When the last trace of my exhaustion was gone, I felt vibrant and refreshed. "Damned if I don't feel brand freaking new," I said.

"Yes, you did it, you learned to channel the magic of the earth. Now you are truly ready to battle Slygon," Dandy said, smiling. "And I must be going. Trust yourself, Jackal. Everything you need to know is inside you already. You're more powerful than you imagine."

Her body began to fade. "Don't go," I begged, feeling the emptiness she would leave behind. "I still need ye."

"I can't stay now," her voice was fading fast. "I'll always be watching you and Flossie. My love for all of you is strong and will never die."

Chapter Fifty-Three

Jackal

An emptiness filled me. Dandy's strength during the jinn attack had made me feel invincible. Now that she was gone, all my insecurities and fears returned.

"I'm still here." Belle grabbed my arm. "Remember when we joined our power?"

"Ye could see me sliding, couldn't ye, lass?"

She hugged me. "You don't need Dandy to be strong. Together, we have all the power we need." She patted my chest and I grabbed her hand. I held it against my cheek. "You're the strongest man, creature, elf, whatever you are, in this world," she said. "We'll get Slygon. I know it. With you on our side we can't fail."

Granny lifted her skirts and stepped over a lump of lava protruding from the swirling valley floor. "We best be getting ourselves moving," she said. "Time's a wastin'."

It only took us a few minutes to find a bridge across the now-empty jinn chasm. We paused outside the walls of the dark-elf city as I sent out feelers, searching for activity inside and found nothing. "Belle," I said. "Feel anything in there?"

She shook her head. "Not a thing. What the fuck? Did all the elves leave?"

"The jinn could have eaten them, or they left," Ivansar said. "I can't feel any life."

Granny punched me in the arm. "On the other side, in the caves, the witches are moving around. Them, I can sense." She pointed at a crevasse in the cavern wall, on the other side of the small elf city. "You know, I lived there a frigging long time ago. It feels like they're still there, but not nearly as many."

"How many is not as many?" I asked.

Granny tilted her head and closed her eyes. "I can feel three. Let's see, there's Alizon, Hagatha and Isadore. Isadore being the one to watch. She's the oldest and the most powerful and has a nasty temper besides being a royal bitch."

"I don't wanna watch them," I said. "I want them gone, out of my way. I want to disappear them, kill them if I must, and get onto the castle. Flossie be there waitin' for my signal. Slygon or one of his uglies could discover her and kill her. She's in the wind and we need to get to her. We're wasting time right now discussing them. Can't you talk to them? Make them go away?"

Granny shrugged. "They know I'm here."

"And?"

"They seem upset by my presence, as though I'm in the way."

"You'd think they'd be jumping fer joy. I done killed the jinn. They're free to leave and go up into the light if they choose, think on."

"I don't think any of them are sane anymore."

"A course," I grunted. "Nuttier-than-squirrels-witches, just what we need."

We entered the dark-elf city through opened gates. "This is creepy," Belle said.

Empty homes and streets, dark windows, shadowed, silent corners, were all we found. "They're all dead," Ivansar whispered. Scorch marks marred the black-marble walls, gray roads and alleys. The scorching was everywhere along with the sulfur stench the jinn left behind. Small piles of ash lay inside some of the marks. Gormar stepped forward and pointed at one. "An elf died here. A black elf, perhaps evil, but an elf. This is a city of death."

"Slag, ye lead," Jackal said. "I be going to take up the rear for a while."

Slag stepped forward, pulled his sword and headed toward the back of the city and the castle which now loomed above us. It's tall obsidian walls made the inner city even darker. We were forced to light torches to see where we were going.

"We might as well send up flares and scream here we come at the top of our lungs," I said to Belle.

"The torches don't matter," Noemi said. "He knows we're here. He's calling me."

Belle grabbed her sister's arm. "Don't let him."

"He made me. I have to obey."

"Noemi," Belle sobbed. "You can't go."

"I have to," Noemi said and began floating. "I'm so sorry, Belle. I'll do my best for all of you."

"I love you," Belle screamed.

"I love you more," Noemi called and then she was gone.

Belle threw herself against me sobbing. "He'll pervert her to his own use," she said.

I wrapped my arm around her. "It's okay, darlin'," I said. "Noemi is smart. She'll think of some way to help us and get away."

Belle scrubbed her eyes on the back of her arm. "Damn her. Damn him. God, I hate Slygon."

"Put all that hate into moving us forward," I said to her.

She glanced up at me and smiled. "I can do that."

"I know."

"We got more to worry about than Slygon right now," Granny said. "The witches are about."

We entered a dark canyon between the walls of tall, black buildings. Ahead, the gate leading out of the city and up the slope to Slygon's castle was barely visible in the light of our torches.

"What's that?" I yelled.

An elf warrior screamed as he went down under the weight of a growling beast. I spun and slashed it with my sword. The elves dropped to their knees and loosed a volley of arrows into the thing. It was huge, pink, and slimy with short legs and huge feet armed with long claws. It held the elf down beneath its gross weight as it scored the screaming elf with its claws. Tina drew her bow and sent bolts into the thing. The elf kept a death grip on each side of the nightmare creature's head. The elf's grip was all that prevented the thing from sinking its teeth into the elf's face. The enormous, maggot-like entity swung its scale-covered body back and forth, spreading a noxious puss across the legs and body of the helpless elf. "I can't move my legs," the elf screamed. "I'm paralyzed!"

Belle rose up on her toes. Tiny touched her elbow. They screamed and the pink blob blew up sending slimy pink and green glop everywhere.

I leapt out of the way dragging Belle and Tiny with me. "Gross," Belle said.

"But dead. Good job," Granny said as she stared at the gross, green and pink snot-like substance coating the elf and the road. She opened her pack and pulled out her wand. "This is the work of Isadore," she said as she waved her wand and removed the numbing effect of the goo from the poor elf.

"Isadore's familiar," Granny said. "Now that we've killed it, she might leave us alone." Granny sprinkled some powder from one of her mysterious packages on what remained of the stinking corpse and muttered a spell. The hideous pink and green mess disappeared in smelly green smoke. She waved her wand over all of them spreading sparkling dust. "It's a shield. Might help, might not," she mumbled. "You never know what Isadore's up to. I should have known she'd at least test us."

A loud bang was followed by a billowing puff of green smoke. For a moment I was sure another of the slug creatures would appear, but instead an old crone, hunched over, landed in front of Granny and slowly stood up. When she saw Granny, she cackled with glee. "Hilda, you old bag, you came back."

The ancient crone was as brown and wrinkled as a raisin. She had dreadlocks down to her waist and wore what looked like a feed sack with four holes cut in it, sewn at the top. Her skinny legs stuck out below the bottom like brown sticks. She wore clumsy leather brogues on her feet, probably made for a serf or a farmer. She threw herself at Granny and wrapped her match-stick arms around

Granny's neck. Granny held her at arm's length. "Isadore, why'd you send that beast after us?"

"I didn't. Alizon did. She's gone off her rocker, that one has." Isadore glanced around at the elves, me, the rest of us, her runny old eyes yellow and crusted. "Who the hell are these people?"

"We've come to kill Slygon," I said. "And all his evil minions."

Isadore cackled madly. "Aye, he's a bad one. Did you kill the jinn? They wiped out the elves. Jinn happen to like dark elves. Find them right tasty, they does, evil as they are. That soul sucker slurps 'em right up quicker than you can say evil is as evil does. Which reminds me, got any food?"

Tiny dug in a pack one of the elves had laid on the road and emerged with journey bread and an apple. She handed the food to Isadore. The crone took the apple and handed it back. "Got no teeth to eat this, though I'd surely love to." She grinned, showing us a mouth with no teeth, just swollen gums.

Granny rummaged around in the same pack and found an orange. The elves always packed fruit. "Suck the juice out of this. You got scurvy."

Isadore scarfed the journey bread and sucked on the orange. "Need to get your asses out of this town. Alizon knows yer here and she'll come after you."

"What can it matter? Seems everyone and their brother's after us. What's one more witch? Happen we were almost out of this cursed city when you popped in."

"Can I come with ye?" Isadore's old eyes sparked with hope.

Granny put her arm around the withered, hunched shoulders of the witch. "Of course, you can."

I snorted and pointed at Slag. "Why the hell not. We're already a walking invitation for disaster. Slag, get us moving. I'm sending the signal to Flossie right now to open the gates."

We left the city behind and climbed an ancient road. The pavers beneath our feet were hard to see, but were made of stones, shaped into squares and worn smooth by the passage of many feet. We entered a walled section and the hairs on the back of my neck rose. I don't like being boxed in. This was a perfect place for an ambush, but there was no other way up to the castle. I figured it'd been planned that way.

The walled road climbed then became stairs. When I examined the obsidian walls of the castle, I saw they were unclimbable, slick, with sharp, pointed tips. A sudden volley of arrows rained on us. "Shields," Slag called. "You elves get that shield working."

"I got this," Granny said. She waved her wand and black sparkles flew over us, joined together, and formed a solid shield. "It will follow along with us."

A grinding noise ahead told Jackal the gate was rising. Flossie was doing her job.

Then the vampires struck.

They roared down the walled stairway, a vengeful horde, hungry and armed with their strength and their fangs.

Isadore and Granny pushed past Slag and the elves to stand tall in front of them. Isadore was a powerful witch. She created a sun over their heads. It spun and swirled and glowed with powerful light. The vampires screamed and slowed but kept coming. One grabbed an elf and pulled it through the shield. In seconds, the elf was drained. The vampires were all men. When the ones who'd drained the elf were done, they threw the corpse at the shield.

The witch's false sunlight was holding, but Isadore was failing. She dropped to her knobby knees panting. "Can't hold out much longer."

Belle grabbed Isadore's shoulders and fed her energy into the old witch. "You can do this," Belle said.

I felt for my power, concentrated, held my hands out in front of me and sent the power, channeled down the chute-like walls of the staircase, straight at the vampires. I followed it with a blast of dragon fire.

The burst of power mixed with the dragon fire creating an enormous fireball. The vampires burst into flames and Slag and the elves attacked. Belle screamed and the walls enclosing the staircase exploded. The slope leading up to the castle walls was revealed as lava rock. We stood on a bridge. Molten lava flowed beneath our feet. The heat rose now that the walls were down, suffocating us.

"Run!" I shouted.

Slag picked up old Isadore and tucked her under his massive arm as we raced for the gate ahead of us. It was only half open. Where was Flossie?

Chapter Fifty-Four

Belle

The gate wasn't open, and it exuded an ominous vibration. "Don't touch the gate," I screamed at the elves as they dove for it. "Slide under."

Slag was first. He had to duck to get under the massive metal gate. I knew if he cleared it the rest should have no problem. The metal was flat and non-reflective. The dull pitted surface looked like it had been beaten into shape by a million small hammers.

I followed behind Melikoth. His bow drawn, he ran under the gate and immediately loosed his arrow. I felt the gate when I went under it. It was hot. Touching it would be deadly.

On the other side, a small group of orcs waited. Slag roared his battle cry and went after them with his axe, hacking parts of the huge green creatures and slinging them and green blood back at us.

The elves drew their swords and the fight was on. I fired my crossbow, directing the bolt into one of the orcs's eyes. An elf dropped to the stone floor, cleaved in two by an orc sword. We lost another before Slag, Jackal and the rest of their party cleared the small courtyard of orcs.

"Silver arrows," Ivansar cried.

The vamps were more careful, and there were so many of them, I knew we would run out of arrows, even though we retrieved them for reuse.

"Look," Granny yelled, pointing. When I glanced up, I saw two flying white horses cross above the castle, each bearing an elf and sacks of round objects behind their saddles.

There was no time to be happy or excited about the arrival of the two elves with the firebombs. We were struggling to stay alive beneath the slaughtering attack of the vampires. When I saw the shadow of the hated black dragon fly over and go after the elves on the flying horses, I almost cried.

"To the battlements," Jackal called. "We gotta kill that dragon."

Slag hacked his way through the vampires to the gatehouse. I followed in the huge halfling's wake.

Chub took on three vamps at a time. He protected us while the elves followed me and Slag into the gatehouse, up the stairs to the walls. The battlements circled the walls of the castle and were protected by huge slabs of jagged obsidian. I kissed my last silver bolt, nocked it into my crossbow and fired. Once it was away, I closed my eyes and focused, sending it farther than any normal bolt could go with my mind, guiding it, praying for a hit. The bolt struck the dragon in its throat. I heard a silly giggle beside me. "Good shot," Flossie whispered. When I turned to look for her, she wasn't there.

Slag hit the dragon's wing with his arrow. The huge segmented wing collapsed, poisoned by the silver, and the dragon slowly tumbled toward them. The two elves riding the white flying horses hovered close to the ceiling sticking round objects to the rock. "They're going to blow the ceiling," Torros said to me. "Pray it's day out there."

Jackal pulled me toward a covered part of the battlement. "Seek shelter," he shouted.

Granny and Isadore had finally made it to the walls. Most of the elves and Chub were up here with us. Chub was backing through the doorway, fighting vamps the entire way, blocking them from swarming the battlements with his bulk. When he got to the landing, he turned and ran. Two tall male vampires, white as ghosts, lips red with someone's blood followed Chub, while the rest headed for me and the elves. We were trapped in the covered battlements, no way out, vamps swarming us.

"Here," Jackal screamed. "There's a door."

I grabbed Tiny and shot fire at the vampire trying to get to us. "Out. The door." I drew my sword and fought the vampire. It was six inches taller than me with long arms. I hacked at one of them and threw a bolt of fire at it. Its clothes ignited, and it shrieked and tore at the flaming cloth. His attention on his burning rags, I followed Gormar into the keep. "We have to find Slygon," Jackal shouted.

Suddenly, Flossie popped in. "I know where he's hiding," she said. "Follow me."

Flossie was in her small form wearing one of Dandy's pink dresses. She flew straight down a long, arched hallway toward a tower at the end. A circular staircase headed to the top of the tower. Flossie flew up it and we followed.

Jackal pointed at the bottom of the staircase. "Guard the stairs," he said to Chub and Slag. "Keep any vamps from coming up."

We flowed up the stairs as a group. Granny and Isadore planted themselves in front of the two half-orcs and began chanting. Granny spread green powder on the stone floor around them. A shimmering silver shield formed over the half-orcs and the witches.

At the top of the stairs, seven vampires guarded an arched double-doorway. The center of the arch was shiny with stained glass depicting black dragons spitting green fire. Jackal screamed his war cry and stabbed the biggest vampire, an enormous female wearing next to nothing. A gaping robe of red silk partially covered her breasts and body, but it was plain she was naked under it. She was armed with a broadsword she swung like it was a piece of straw. Jackal's sword pierced her, but she batted it away and the wound healed immediately. Chub's back appeared at the top of the stairs. Granny and Isadore between Chub and Slag, who was fighting off more vamps.

How many were there? The supply of undead seemed endless. Exhausted and sweating in the sweltering lava-heated castle, I struggled to keep my sword arm working. I sucked in a deep breath and pulled enough remaining magic to get a second wind and downed three more vampires.

Suddenly, an enormous explosion echoed through the cavern outside. More explosions followed. The castle floor shook, and the walls trembled. "Take cover!" Jackal shouted.

There was nowhere to go.

The floor dropped a foot and stopped, knocking us to our knees. The vampires looked up as something huge crashed into the roof. Jackal threw himself over me. Slag and Chub covered Tina and the two witches. The elves flattened themselves against the walls.

The ceiling abruptly collapsed.

Huge chunks of rock and slate shingles hit Jackal's back. He grunted but didn't move. All around us, the roof of the castle was collapsing. When I peeked around Jackal's thick arm, I saw light, blue sky, and the sun shining into the castle.

Daylight!

I swallowed the lump of relief in my throat and rubbed my eyes against the back of my sleeve. They stung from the smoke as the vampires screamed and caught fire, because, of course, I never cried.

The big vampire woman in red threw open the double doors and dove inside. I followed the evil bitch, looking for my sister. Where was Noemi? She'd been drawn here by Slygon. He'd forced her to leave me. I would find her or die in the effort.

The roof in the room had collapsed leaving it open to the light. The female vamp's skin smoldered, but she had just enough time to dive under the massive bed in the middle of the room before she ignited.

I froze.

Slygon stood at the foot of the bed holding my sister. Noemi was limp, draped over his arm, the back of her bare neck visible. It looked frail and white. Even though the sun blazed through the open roof, her skin didn't smolder. Slygon had been hit by a piece of falling roof and a cut on his forehead dripped dark-red blood onto Noemi's white neck. He smiled at me and I screamed. "Noemi! Wake up."

She didn't respond. I thrust a bolt into my sister's brain. It was blank. There was nothing clicking inside her mind. But she couldn't be dead. Vampires turned to ash when they died. And then I remembered she was part snake. Maybe her shifter nature, even though it was new, was keeping her alive and from burning up in the sunlight.

"What have you done to her?" I demanded as I circled Slygon, my sword out. He kept his back to the bed where the female vampire lurked out of the burning rays of the sun.

Jackal pushed me aside. "I got this."

"No, Jackal, Noemi."

"I see her," he said.

Slygon faced Jackal. Hampered by Noemi, he tossed her aside and raised his sword in two hands while I rushed to Noemi. I fell over her, lifted her head, and touched her throat feeling for a pulse. It was there, a tiny beating thread whispered under my searching fingers. She was weak. I saw bite marks all over her body. She'd been drained almost to death. She needed blood. I took one of my knives out of a sheath inside my vest and cut my wrist. I pressed the open wound to Noemi's lips. She latched on without opening her eyes and sucked. I let her feed until she showed signs of life then pulled my wrist away. Behind me Jackal, light on his feet in a fight, switched his sword rapidly from right-hand grip to left. Slygon sliced at him. Their swords clashed.

Noemi moaned in my arms and her eyes opened. "Belle," she whispered. "You came for me."

"Always," I said.

She struggled to sit. "You fed me."

Jackal slashed at Slygon scoring a deep hit. Slygon screeched. Suddenly Kyran flew into the room. His skin smoked from the sunlight, but he didn't catch fire.

Chub and Slag stepped in to support Jackal.

Kyran drew his sword.

Three half orcs and a human against two day-walking vampires.

But they didn't count on Noemi. She flew at Slygon with her claws outstretched. I added my power to aid her, our connection by birth and now through the blood I'd fed her strong. She changed into a cobra and latched onto Slygon's neck just as Jackal sliced across

Slygon's body with a huge slash of his katana. The slice opened the vampire from shoulder to his opposite hip. Blood and strange guts gushed out as Noemi hung on to his throat.

Slygon stumbled and fell to his knees and Noemi wrapped her snake body around his neck still pumping her enormous reservoir of venom into him.

Slag and Chub fought Kyran who's skin smoked and sizzled when the sun hit it. He was weakened and the two orcs moved in, one from each side.

Jackal

Slygon was dying. To save himself, he morphed into a snake. Noemi's venom could no longer affect him. She fell away and slithered under the bed. I heard the female vamp shriek and figured Noemi had just bitten her. Good riddance.

Recovering quickly, Slygon lunged at me and sank fangs six inches long into the meat of my thigh injecting the terrible venom. But I'd been to the seer in Greenwood and knew all about bad things in blood. When I felt the venom, I searched inside myself for it, found the poison, and changed it just like I changed the poison of the seer's disgusting blood. Instead of dying from the venom as Slygon expected, I reached for my dragon's breath, opened my mouth and scorched the vampire in his slithering snake form. He abandoned his smoldering snake body and morphed back into a vampire.

When I looked up, Kyran had Belle in his grasp and was holding her against him his fangs inches from her throat. "I'll drain her."

"And I'll kill you," I said.

"You'll have to go through me to get him," Slygon said as he quickly regained his power.

"Why won't you fucking die?" I snarled. "Jeezus, you're freaking annoying."

"Don't worry about me," Belle screamed. "I can take care of myself." She screamed and Kyran lost his grip. Belle fell to the floor and scrambled under the bed.

"Slag, back me up. Chub take my left."

Noemi slithered out from under the bed. She looked stronger. I had no time to watch her as Slygon attacked. Slag eased around his right while Chub circled to the left and I faced him head on. "You're dead," I said to him.

Kyran bent over to go after Belle, and Noemi struck him in the throat. Her fangs dug in. Kyran grabbed her body as she sought to wrap the coils around him and tore at the snake, ripping chunks of snake flesh apart with his bare hands. Noemi kept her fangs buried in his throat and ignored the damage he was doing to her snake body. Belle erupted from under the bed and screamed. Kyran caught on fire. The weight of Noemi hanging from his throat drew him into a beam of sunlight and the vampire, already burning from Belle's blast, blazed into an inferno and then exploded spraying them with flaming vampire parts. Noemi dropped away and tried to morph into her human form. I would have gone to Belle, but I had Slygon to face and for some reason, he was edging toward the bed. Belle held her sister, both of them watching as I faced Slygon.

"I got this," I said to Chub and Slag. "But watch him." They eased a few inches away, swords up as the elves rushed into the room and the backs of Slygon's legs hit the bed.

I was afraid he was going to dive under it. "Don't," I said, then I opened my mouth and breathed dragon fire over him. I had no idea why I could do this, it took mountains of energy, but the result was worth it. The dragon fire scorched Slygon to the bone. His flesh melted off his face leaving half a skeleton with melted skin like putty dripping from his eye socket. His clothes flamed and he ripped them away, the bed covers caught and blazed into flames as the dragon fire burned all his clothes away and melted his skin.

A heard a roar above us and felt Remoth. *We came in through the opening. As long as we can see sky, we're good.*

"Oranth," Belle screamed.

Slygon was panicking. He was burned, his flesh melting from a fire that would not go out but fed off his flesh. He tried to morph into a snake but only completed half of the transition. The damage of the dragon fire was too much. He fell to the floor as Oranth's big head appeared in the hole in the ceiling and tried to slither under the bed screaming in pain, his life spilling out of him faster than even he could heal. Oranth opened her huge mouth and prepared to toast him.

"No," Belle yelled. "Not enough room. Jackal's got this, don't you?"

She looked at me with an expression of such love and trust, for a moment, I was unmanned. "Please don't kill me," Slygon begged.

I laughed in his face. "After all you've done, you expect me to spare yer miserable life? Dying time is here." I waved to Chub and Slag to back away. I felt the elves behind me and drew on their energy. I felt Belle and drew energy from her. I inhaled deeply and blasted Slygon with more dragon's breath. It was a huge gush of the intense fire. The blast encompassed him, and as he burned, Belle drew her sword and sliced off his head.

Belle's grin was crooked and rueful as she looked into my eyes. "Had to do it. Odafarus said I was the one."

With Slygon gone, Belle fell to the floor beside Noemi. Her sister was crazy twisted, half snake, half human. The human parts were burned, the snake broken with bones thrusting through places in the skin. Belle looked up at me, tears gushing down her face. "She's dying, Jackal."

"Where's the damn fairy and Granny?"

Flossie popped in and knelt beside Noemi. "This is bad," Flossie said. "She's half in her vampire form and half in her shifter form. There's nothing I can do to fix this."

Suddenly Tina shrieked. "You're dead bitch," as she yanked the shrieking female vampire out from under the bed. The vampire was a ghastly green color with blood dripping from ugly snake bites in her neck, but she managed to stand up. She struggled for a minute with Tiny who stabbed her in the chest with a short fighting knife. As the vampire staggered and fell backwards, Gormar parted her head from her body.

The bed shook and bounced up and down. Burnt cushions and comforters fell to the floor. "What the hell?" I said backing away from the bed. Above me Remoth sent a message. *Flossie knows.*

Knows what?

"It's my mother, Dandy," Flossie said. "She's under that bed."

"What?" Belle peered under the bed.

Slag and I lifted the entire bed, tossed it aside, and we all stared at a shiny black obsidian box.

Flossie waved her wand and the lid lifted to reveal the pitifully dehydrated shell that had once been a vibrant, happy fairy.

Tiny gasped. "Dandy."

"This must be what Slygon was trying to get to," I said. "I couldn't figure out why he was edging fer the damn bed. He meant to steal the last remaining magic from her corpse to use against us. I thought he be looking for a place to hide since he was a giant coward when faced with death."

Tears streamed down Flossie's face as she waved her wand to replace the lid and made the small coffin even smaller, into a tiny box that floated from the floor to Flossie's hand. She gently tucked it away in the folds of her skirt and said, "We can take her home now, and give her a proper memorial, letting the dragons she loved purify her remains with dignity."

Noemi groaned and coughed. I knelt beside Belle. "I'm sorry lass. This is a sad way to end our venture."

Noemi grabbed Belle's vest and pulled her close and whispered. "Slygon said our father is alive. He has a picture of them as boys. Together."

"What?" Belle had tears running down her face. "Please, save your energy. You don't need to talk now."

Noemi waved her hand slowly. "I'm dying. I can feel myself slipping into eternity."

Flossie, in her tiny form hovered over Noemi. "I can tap into Dandy's power and cleanse you. You'll die, but you'll die with a soul. Dandy just told me how to do it."

"Don't go," Belle cried. "Stay with me."

"I can't." Noemi's voice was thread and weak. "You know it's true, Belle. I'm dead. Let me go a clean soul."

Belle sobbed harder.

"Do it," Noemi whispered.

Dandy's ghost appeared above Noemi. "For your bravery, you shall go to god a pure and clean soul."

Flossie touched Noemi's tortured face with her wand. Pure white light flowed into Noemi in a stream of radiance so blinding, I looked away. When I looked back, Noemi lay in Belle's arms, a woman once more, wearing a flowing white dress, her face beautiful and peaceful in death. Her body was covered with sweet lilies of the valley.

"Lay her down," Flossie said, "and back away."

Belle gently put Noemi on the floor and stood up. She turned into me and hugged me with all her strength.

Dandy and Flossie spoke together. "You gave your life to save others. Go to heaven and live as an angel. Be at peace, Noemi Ruuvaen." Noemi's body burst into flames and burned hot and fast. In seconds, it was a small pile of ash. A wind blew out of nowhere, picked up the ashes and they disappeared.

"Goodbye, beloved sister," Belle said. "I'll love you forever."

"And I love you," was heard faintly floating out of the air.

Tiny burst into tears. I took her under my arm and hugged her. We sobered as we recalled why we had risked our lives to come here and defeat Slygon. It made our victory bittersweet, but all the more poignant.

Chapter Fifty-Five

Jackal

With the vamps dead, Slygon dead, and the orcs dead, I felt pretty damn good. Noemi's death left a black stain on our victory, but we'd found Dandy's remains and I'd finally earned the faith Dandy had placed in me. Belle's sad face was the only cloud on my horizon.

"I wish we coulda saved her," I said. "But she went with a clean soul."

"I want to search for that picture. Noemi said Slygon had a picture of him and our father."

"We should be getting out of here, love. The dragons are going to carry us home."

"I know where it is," Flossie said. She waved her wand and a hole in the headboard opened. A shelf slid out. On it was a box inlaid with gold and gems. Belle carefully crawled over the burnt coverlets and grabbed it. Her hands shook. "Should I open it?"

I will never understand women. "You wanted that photo. Open the box. Flossie seem to think it in there."

The box was closed by an ornate clasp. Belle turned it and the lid flew open. Inside lay a small round miniature painting of two young elves. The boys seemed identical. "This can't be my father. He didn't look like Slygon. Father's hair was gray, and he had a few wrinkles. He had smile lines and his eyes twinkled."

"Slygon was a vampire, Belle," Flossie said. "It changed him." Flossie picked up the miniature. It was painted. It wasn't a photo. "If these two boys are Slygon and your father, then Slygon was your uncle. That's why you have so much power."

"Noemi said Father was alive., Flossie. Do you know where he is?"

"No," Flossie said, "but we can search for him later. We must leave now. The dragons grow inpatient and we've been here too long already."

"She's right lass. Time to fly."

"Someone's got to go back and get the stock before they get eaten by gargoyles or some other disgusting creature from this hell," Slag said. "Can't leave them behind."

"I'm guessing that someone would be you," I said. "No stomach for a dragon ride? Ye still be needing a ride home from the village after you return the beasts, you know."

"If it means a shorter dragon ride, so be it."

"Take care of yourself, man," I said.

"I'll go with him," Jassin said. He was one of the young elves who had fetched the flying horses and set the bombs. "I can ride one of the horses and help him."

Two other elves volunteered to help Slag and they left, running down the stairs and out of Slygon's keep as we climbed to the battlements. The two elves had set their bombs exactly right and opened an enormous hole in the roof of the cavern. The sun was starting to set in the real world. We helped Granny and Isadore onto a dragon. Tiny and the elves climbed on dragons and finally I put Belle on Damoth. Oranth had gone to the hatching grounds to lay her eggs. "You going to be okay, lass? I can always take you up with me on Remoth."

"I'll be fine," Belle said as she pulled her goggles on. Hurry and get on Remoth. It's almost dark. There could be more demons coming out of this hideous pit from hell when the sun sets."

I looked deep into her eyes. "Is the time right yet? Annabelle, will you marry me?"

She sucked in a breath, caught off guard by my proposal. "I screwed up again, didn't I? This be a terrible time. I'm sorry. Forget I asked."

"It's okay," she laughed. "Will there ever be a good time? You're the king of the human-hating elves and I'm an orphan with a demon for an uncle."

She bent down and I kissed her. She tasted like honey and flowers. God, I loved her. "Happens they hate orcs, too, and I'm half orc. Belle, me darlin', I don't care if you be a human, a serf or a slave. I love you and I want you to be my queen."

She hugged my neck and touched my face with her hand. "I love you, too. Yes, I will marry you."

I shouted with joy and Damoth bellowed. "Be the biggest wedding Greenwood ever saw."

* * * *

The flight back was long, but for me with all I had on my mind, not long enough. Remoth dropped from the sky, Damoth beside him. It seemed if he and Annabelle were going to be married, Remoth would become king of the dragons. It was their custom. The riders often paired up.

They landed on the walls shadowing the small village near the castle and I was happy to see that the improvements I'd asked Felis to accomplish had been implemented. The villager's huts were now sturdy, clean and larger. Judging from the light showing through the glass windowpanes, they now had power. Smoke issued from the chimneys, proving they were supplied with firewood. My chest swelled with pride when the villagers rushed out of their new homes to greet us. The elves too came pouring from the castle, anxious to hear the news brought by their returning warriors.

Felis was the first to greet us.

I shook his hand. "Where's Uriel Silverheart? Did he cause trouble after we left?"

"We need to discuss this later," Felis said. "Let's celebrate your return first. Business later."

"Happen yer right," I said.

Cheers went up from the assembled crowd as the elf warriors walked through the village to the stable yard where all the elves and villagers crowded around, eager to hear good news. I raised my hand and waited until the crowd grew silent. Then, grinning, I shouted, "Slygon be dead!"

The people, my people, erupted in joyous clapping and shouting, hugging each other and kissing their children. Belle slipped her hand into mine, sharing the joy. I couldn't imagine being happier than I was at this moment. Then I heard it, the chant of, "Long live King Jackal! Long live King Jackal!" Not Erindriel, but Jackal, a compliment from the elves I could scarce believe.

My heart overflowed with joy. Again, I raised my hand. It took a bit longer for the crowd to settle down this time, but when they finally grew quiet, I said, "I know yer happy now, but there still be a few among ye who don't fancy me yer king."

I lifted the hand holding Belle's to dispel the shouts of denial that arose from my words and continued. "Ye be glad that we killed that evil bastard, Slygon, think on. But it weren't me alone. It were us all." I paused to gage their mood, still holding Belle's hand high, and swept my other hand around to indicate the crew who'd accompanied him. "Happen it took all of us to avenge the fairy, Dandy, who gave her life so that we could be free of the evil bastard's reign of terror, and the others those vile vampires slaughtered without mercy. We lost some good men, and Queen Ashera."

The crowd grew solemn at the mention of the queen's death. A few of her handmaidens burst into tears. "We'll have a memorial service fer Dandy and the queen and the rest of our dead, and a monument built in memory of those what died at the hands of that devilish horde, so as not to ever forget. After that," I added, beaming down at Belle. "There will be a royal wedding. We will all come together and appreciate what we have, ending all these disputes and infighting."

I glanced around at the elves, pausing to give a meaningful glance here and there. "We be moving forward after we mourn our dead, celebrating life, life without Slygon."

I didn't miss the head turns or the way some of the elves glanced at Annabelle and then at one another, but once the humans in the village erupted into excited congratulations, they joined in applauding the upcoming wedding. They knew there'd be feasting and a party to beat all parties.

"All be good and everything's wonderful, but can we get something to eat now?" Chub asked. "I can't remember when last I had a decent meal."

Belle looked at me and we burst into laughter. "Surely you can arrange food for your returning heroes?" Belle teased.

"A feast! Happen we're all starved!"

Pandemonium broke out as the villagers and kitchen staff raced toward the castle. "I could use a hot bath," Belle said.

"Reckon I've smelled better before, think on."

She chuckled and reached up on tiptoe, intending to kiss my cheek. I turned my head and captured her lips, loving her more at that moment than ever before.

"Are you sure you love me?" I asked. "I'm ugly and half orc. I'm never going to be handsome."

She stroked my face with a soft touch filled with warmth. "There's no room in my heart for anyone but you, Jackal. And there never will be."

I picked her up and swung her around, my soul soring as high as dragons can fly. "I can't promise we'll always be happy together," I said. "But I can promise I will love you with every breath in my body until the day I die."

www.ingramcontent.com/pod-product-compliance
Lightning Source LLC
Chambersburg PA
CBHW031611180726
48284CB00005B/1505